# THE RIVER BRIDE

*a quebec summer mystery*

## Nadine Doolittle

**Gatineau Hills Publishing**

Gatineau Hills Publishing 2014
261 Lac Bernard Road
Alcove, Quebec
Canada J0X 1A0

www.nadinedoolittlebooks.ca

ISBN 978-0-9937704-6-3

Cover Image by Eleonor Design
Cover Design by GatineauHillsPublishing/Canva
Logo Image by Michelle Lannen

*Dedicated to...*

*Lynn, Lari-ann, Cameron, Sean, Robin and
Christopher.
Hearts of my heart.*

*Evil is like a small fire.*
*First, it burns weeds and thorns.*
*Next, it burns the larger bushes in the forest,*
*And they all go up in a column of smoke.*

ISAIAH 9:18 (NCV)

# PREFACE

THE GATINEAU HILLS can be located on a map of West Quebec where its citizens are served by the very real MRC des Collines Police Department. Happily, this dedicated regional police force is not as busy investigating homicides as they are in the author's imagination. The incidents and characters depicted in this novel are a work of fiction.

# ONE

T HE VILLAGE of Stollerton woke to the smell of a burning forest. Smoke hung over the Gatineau Hills like a milky wraith. Although the fire was northeast, Montreal way, strong winds had pushed the blaze deeper and further into the heart of the wood, and then funneled the smoke over Québec's surrounding towns and villages. The smell of burning timber reminded residents of September, disconnecting them from the summer heat that shimmered off the highway and flattened the vegetation. A thin clear heat that scalded before you even knew you were hot.

Alvina Moon held her breath against the smoke and steered the van north along the highway, following the sketchy instructions of the kid who put her on to the story, a fifteen-year-old, not the most reliable source but Dave was adamant about following it up. A group of local kids were building a raft in defiance of being banned from jumping off the covered bridge. They were planning to float the structure downriver on August 1, the Civic Holiday to honour of the citizens of the Gatineau Hills, and moor it across from the Chateau Diotte. The owner of the hotel was having a fit. It was a good story. The kind of thing the locals loved to read. The raft was being constructed at a secret location south of the Paugan Falls.

The van with *Stollerton Record* emblazoned on its fat sides, clipped along at ninety kilometres an hour. Alvina glanced at the clock. She was making good time, feeling confident of her direction until the highway abruptly bent east away from the river and into farm country. The fields were a mist of purple clover, yellow buttercups and a tall white flower, a weed that chokes out the pasture in times of drought. The kid said the turnoff wasn't clearly marked. She must have passed it somehow. Fragments of the old highway poked through on her right but there was no way to get to it that Alvina could see. If she didn't find it in the next five minutes she'd have to go back to the office empty-handed, Dave's sarcasm sounding in her ears for failing to use her head. *Failing to make the grade, Moon.*

Dewy perspiration filmed her face. She was lost. Or maybe the kid lied to her about the raft. A little rush of panic gripped her. There was an opening up ahead. Alvina signalled and turned off the main highway onto a rough patch of road that miraculously led back down to the river. The old highway just like the kid said! Dave told her it hadn't been used since the fifties. The asphalt was pale grey, almost white with age and pushed up in places by weeds. A faded yellow line ran up the centre. The road led down to an abandoned trailer park. Rusted electrical hook-ups marked each lot, overgrown now. A large stone barbeque was set apart in one lot; its chimney toppled over. Her parents had taken her camping once in Southern Ontario, the year they didn't get hired by any of the summer repertory companies. Alvina remembered sleeping in a tent and eating Rice Krispies in a little box that split open to make a bowl. They were probably camping because they were homeless that year and she was too young to know it.

The river was on the left-hand side of the road, winking in the sun. Milkweed and sweet pea grew along the bank. The municipality had a rule against clearing the natural plantings at the edge of the river. A Manitoba maple leaned heavily over the water. Alvina peered through the windshield. There was a derelict pink and white trailer set off the road to her immediate right, surrounded by a copse of white pines. She pulled onto the pad of gravel in front of it and parked. The sharp clean scent of pine needles lifted on the hot air. Alvina got out and glanced around.

No raft. No raft-building teenagers. A bored kid's stupid idea of a practical joke. She eyed the narrow road. Backing out of here wasn't going to be easy. Frustrated, she swung around, glaring at the thick overgrowth, expecting to find a hidden camera. If someone wasn't filming this, then what was the point? No point, no point at all. Small town asshole kids playing a small town prank. She should quit this lousy job. Her classmates were all working for city newspapers. Her parents had lied when they said she could do anything she set her mind to. Alvina was beginning to understand she could only do what her guts permitted. And that wasn't much. After graduation, the *Record* was the first paper to offer her a job. She was too chicken to turn it down.

A raven cawed overhead. She looked up, following the sound. The sky was high, curved and white like a glass bubble. The bird landed on top of a tall pine tree that loomed above the abandoned trailer. The sun shone on his glossy black wings and his beak was fearsome. She watched him watching her. The sun burned, scalding the tip of her nose. Acrid smoke from the forest fires filmed the air.

Her eyes went to the trailer. The campground was reverting to wilderness. Why did the owners abandon it? Maybe they stopped coming when the new highway went through. Or maybe the current was too fast for swimming. Vacationers generally preferred lakeside cottages to the river. An idea was forming, not a great idea but better than coming back with nothing. She could do a story on forgotten campsites on the river. The old people loved nostalgia pieces. Camping stories made great summer reading. Dave would hate it but Dave hated almost everything she came up with these days. Alvina reached into the van for her camera.

It was a cute trailer, shaped like a canned ham. The pink and white aluminum siding had faded. Alvina wandered to the rear where the old license plate was still attached: *Québec 1962*. Its round red taillights were circled in chrome. The window was open, slats of grimy glass opened with a crank inside. Alvina knew the type from her parents' caravan days. A blinding bit of metal caught her eye, the manufacturer's logo: a highly stylized chrome palm tree that swept out and over the model name of the trailer: *Oasis*.

Alvina lifted the camera and took several shots. The trailer looked even lonelier in the viewfinder. The chrome palm tree had dulled from fifty years of neglect. No one left to shine it up, to take care of the little Oasis. Palm trees in Canada. It was kind of sweet, the innocence people had back then. They were so hopeful, Alvina thought. That's what went wrong. There's always a backlash to optimism.

The raven screamed. A light wind rustled the pines.

She came around the side of the trailer to the entrance and stood on its rusty metal step to peer through the window in the door. There was a dinette table with banquettes on each side, dusty, possibly infested with mice. She jerked on the handle. To her surprise, the door was unlocked. It opened with a sigh and a bloom of heat pressed out, carrying with it the smell of something dead. Alvina clamped her hand over her nose and stepped inside, leaving the door open.

It took several seconds for her eyes to adjust to the dim light. The walls were paneled in birch that had yellowed with age. The banquettes were upholstered in blue and green plaid and the dinette table was pink laminate with gold starbursts. She took a photo, knowing that at least half their readership would be thrilled with this flashback to the sixties.

A sickly sweet smell was coming from somewhere. Alvina glanced behind her at the tiny galley kitchen. The square vent above the stove wasn't in the locked position. Maybe an animal had got in and died in one of the cupboards? There were two drawers, a pantry cupboard, and another long horizontal cupboard above the dinette window. She tried a kitchen drawer. The wood had absorbed humidity over the years and swollen shut; she couldn't get it open even after wrenching on the handle. It was obvious this trailer hadn't been used for years and years. A film of dust coated everything.

Beyond the tiny kitchen was a sitting area built in under the window at the rear of the trailer. Maybe somebody had been here after all, Alvina thought, coming closer. The foam bench was covered in the same nubby blue-and-green plaid as the banquettes. It was opened flat to serve as a bed. A white sheet was draped over it. The pine trees rustled against the roof and a breeze made its way into the trailer through the slatted window.

The sheet billowed up and down.

The hairs on the back of Alvina's neck prickled. She wasn't superstitious. She didn't believe in ghosts, karma, crystals, palm reading, tarot cards, or any of the other supernatural creeds that her parents had stuffed her childhood with. She reached down and snatched the sheet back. A heavy black stain covered the fabric about the size of the human head. Instinct told her it was dried blood. There was so much of it—whoever owned the trailer obviously had no hope of getting it out. It had soaked through into the foam. Alvina dropped the sheet with a shudder.

The smell was stronger here but it wasn't coming from the blood. Alvina yanked on the pantry cupboard door immediately to her left. A stench funneled up to her nose and gagged in her throat. Her eyes blurred. She looked down at a heap of black fur. A nest of decomposing squirrels. Maggots writhed over the bodies.

Alvina lurched to the doorway. The metal stair tripped her going down and she fell headlong to the gravel, skinning her knees and palms. In pain, she crouched on all fours gulping air that was acrid with smoke but at least it wasn't dead squirrel smell. The maggots were disturbing. Alvina tasted bile and struggled to keep her stomach down. Gravel spiked her sunburned calves.

A voice cut across the still hot air. "Hey! You! What're you doing there?"

She looked up into blinding sunshine. The figure of a man stood at the river. His face was in shadow. Sunlight filtered through the smoke, forming a brilliant halo around his head. For a wild moment she thought he was walking on water until she saw the curving shelf of rock he was standing on. Water lapped at his feet.

"I can see you. Don't try to hide."

She jumped to her feet. The horizon tilted, dizzying her. "I'm not hiding. I fell down."

"What were you doing inside the trailer?"

She looked for a vehicle. There was none. He seemed to have arrived out of nowhere. He was young, in his late twenties, and holding a bouquet of daisies. Alvina shielded her eyes. Sunlight sparkled on the river behind him.

"The door was unlocked. I didn't break in. I lost my balance on the step. I didn't go inside." Her heart was hammering. The lie came to her instinctively. Dave would go ballistic if the *Record* was charged with trespassing.

The guy came toward her with a loping easy stride. Just like a wolf, she thought distractedly. He was wearing cargo shorts, heavy work boots and a green tee shirt that was the colour of moss; threadbare, rumpled and soft. A fishing boat with a ten horsepower motor was beached on a shelf of granite; Canadian Shield that was a smooth as a helmet.

"Who are you?" he demanded.

Alvina pointed to the van as though that would explain everything. "I'm Alvina Moon from *The Stollerton Record*. I was looking for the raft some local teens are building. I think someone must have been playing a joke on me because it's not here."

"The raft is docked upriver. Below the twist at Martingale. You turned off too soon."

Heat rose to her face. "It's further up? Oh, right. Stupid me. Sorry. I don't know this area very well; the *Record* doesn't get up here much. Our Lady of Sorrows holds a White Elephant sale once a year but that's about it. I thought this was the place the kid told me to turn. It looked like it could be according to his directions."

He gazed at her, as though uncertain if she was telling the truth. Then using the daisies, he gestured. "Stay on this road, keep going in the same direction and you'll come out to the highway. It's rough but you can get through all right."

"Okay, thanks. Thanks a lot. I'm sorry I disturbed you."

His hair was the colour of pale gold and his skin was burnished bronze. He gleamed like a cold northern sun and though it was July and hot, she imagined she caught a whiff of arctic ice as he moved past her, his eyes on the trailer. He closed the door and leaned against it for a moment as though at a shrine, shutting the dead squirrels inside.

The man turned and stood in front of Alvina with a stillness that was oppressive. Close up, his eyes were almost black.

She found her voice. "I didn't mean to trespass on your property."

"It's not my property. I didn't expect to see anyone, that's all. No one comes here."

"Except you."

"That's right."

Suddenly he turned and took a run at the river, hurling the bouquet of daisies, cellophane and all, like a javelin into the water.

"The river activists would freak out if they saw you doing that," she said, watching the bouquet float downstream.

He turned, an unwilling grin creasing his face. "Are you going to report me?"

There was danger in his maleness in this solitary place, in the arctic light he cast. She followed the slope of his shoulders, the drift of his arms and his long square fingers. His hair gave him unspeakable beauty— wavy and blonde in a land where there were few blonde men.

Alvina looked away, alive with a pleasure that wasn't familiar to her. "I can't report you. I don't know who you are."

The raven cawed. The man looked to the sound but didn't answer her. Alvina's stomach clenched and she felt flushed with heat again. She stared down at her Converse sneakers aware of how asexual she was dressed. The shorts she had on were the worst she owned and she didn't own many so did she have to choose the ugliest pair? Cut off at the knee, formerly a baggy pair of khakis she thought she could salvage. And a boy's sized white tee-shirt emblazoned with I ♥ the Hills. She was skinny; it was hard to find clothes that fit properly.

"I guess I better get going before the raft builders bail on me. Thanks for the directions." She moved to the van.

He gestured to her scraped knees. "Did you hurt yourself?"

Alvina bent to examine her wounds. Pine needles and gravel were stuck in the blood. "I'll live."

"Come here. I'll wash it off. I have some antibiotic in the boat."

She followed him to the shelf of rock and waited while he fetched the tube of ointment.

"Take your shoes off. Stand in the water."

She did as she was told, removing her shoes and wading to where the water was ankle deep. He knelt before her, flushing the grit from her knees using his hands as a scoop. He wouldn't look her in the eye. Alvina had a dog like that once. Refused to make eye contact. A rescued dog that had been abused. She could feel the tension bouncing off his body when he touched her skin. His fingers trembled when he dabbed her knees with the ointment.

"Is this is your boat?" she said to break the silence.

"Yeah, it's old and slow but it gets me around." He placed his hand on her leg and held it there. "I think you're all right now."

"Yes. Thank you. Sorry for bothering you ... is it okay if I ask your name?"

And then, just as suddenly, his hand dropped from her leg and his face closed. The man stood up, looming over her. "Look, I just want to be left alone. The newspapers or the television news or the general public haven't got a right to know anything about me. Do you understand?"

"Sure, no problem," said Alvina with a shrug of nonchalance she didn't feel. What she felt was humiliated and she had no reason to be humiliated—she hadn't done anything wrong. The guy walked her to the van like he was escorting her off the property. He helped her in, closed the door and stepped back.

Alvina drove away, her eyes travelling irresistibly to

the rear view mirror. The northern man stood in the middle of the faded highway, looking like a ghost, as insubstantial as the haze filming the hills.

She tried to draw in a deep breath but choked. This smoke was suffocating the life out of her. The wind was supposed to shift tomorrow, thank god. She didn't think she could stand another day of this. She'd started out liking the smell but after awhile....

Alvina guessed human beings were like animals that way. The smell of smoke drove people to fear.

DEL MUSGRAVE stood in the middle of the road watching until the van was out of sight. He shouldn't have bitten her head off. If she didn't know his name before, he sure as hell made her determined to find out now, and he had to be careful. Del turned stiffly, unwillingly until the trailer was in full view. It looked worse every year. The same and worse.

All around him was silence. Birdsong was smothered by smoke. He'd had a dream this morning that he was on fire. It was only the smoke from the forest fires infiltrating his sleep. That was the trouble with dreams. They set you up to expect something.

Del gazed at the trailer. This anniversary was going to be no different from the last. Seven years of existing in a blank of mind and heart. If this was Teresa's revenge, it was a good one. She wasn't haunting him. This was the opposite of being haunted. His wife had thoroughly vacated his life. Del had nothing and he felt nothing. The pilgrimage to the trailer at least delivered a sense of horror. Daisies were Teresa's favourite flower. He tossed them with the same thin dry prayer each year: *Come back.*

She never came back but she never quite left either. It got worse every year, not better. The more he concentrated and willed her into being, the darker and less material she became. He was cold inside, and dry. Winter dry.

Del stepped into the boat and pushed off from the rock in one smooth movement. The motor sputtered to life. White smoke laced the trees in the hills, the ghosts of an incinerated forest, miles away. He could try to paint that if Gerry could spare him from the Camp. If he had the right tints and the wind didn't change. The smoke and flames were driving deeper into the heart of Québec. Gerry said he'd have to cancel the fishing group coming up this weekend if the fires got any closer.

Del flung his head back. It was no use—whatever else he had going on wouldn't hold. Not today. Even seven years later. Plans and ideas came to nothing. Maybe if he had a memory of his own, a memory that had not been experienced through everyone else's memory of her, he'd be less obsessed. There were days he felt insanity was creeping up on him. The craving to experience her was beginning to drive him mad. Grief, lust, yearning, the smell of her soap, her voice— he'd take anything. Del had pinned a sketch he'd done of Teresa in the nude over their bed. She was sleeping when he sketched her, one arm crooked under her head and the other plumped under her breast. She was hot and furious when she woke up. She didn't like to be spied on. He should've held her down, forced her to pose for him in the stifling heat of the cabin. He should have but he didn't. He was still a decent guy back then.

*I got to clear out. Move away. Flowers and prayers don't give up the dead. Leave her here. Beat her at her own game.*

But even as he thought it, Del knew he wouldn't leave. This land—this inhospitable shield of rock and forest, this ribbon of river—this land was his. A visitor saw nothing but a travel brochure. But survive a few winters, a season of black flies and the spring runoff, and the wilderness gets stuck inside you. If he left, he'd lose his inspiration and if he lost that, he'd have lost everything. There's no escape for the painter or his subject. Teresa knew that much about him, at least. She had him trapped coming and going.

Del twisted the throttle and cast a quick glance back at the trailer.

He paused. Something was different. He saw it with a painter's eye. Pinpricks of sunlight glittered behind a veil of white smoke. A bridal veil ... tantalizing, almost visible ... Del stared, his eyes watering, trying very hard to see the thing he could only sense was different.

That girl came into his mind. Alvina Moon. She had shivered when he touched her leg. Not much, just a vibration. Her skin was warm and his hands were cold from the river. He liked how she smelled of summer wind and sunburn. She wasn't wearing perfume. Most of the women he'd been with were the same. There was nothing outstanding about her. There was nothing to her at all. A plain, skinny girl.

He had to be careful. And as always, he was. But something was pushing on him now; an uncomfortable, half-formed animal that wanted out. A feeling that was restless and disturbing, of being newly wired to something that wasn't Teresa and wasn't himself.

Del peeled off his shirt, kicked off his boots and turned his face to the blinding, brilliant sun. His shoulders bunched as he breathed in the smell of destruction. He wanted something. Something that girl had. Whatever it was, he felt it when he looked at her. It hovered in the bridal veil of smoke and light and he couldn't turn it out of his mind.

As Del Musgrave motored upriver, he had an electrifying thought: He was finished with being careful.

# TWO

**M**ONDAY MORNING, amazed that she was actually going through with it, Alvina pressed the buzzer of the MRC des Collines Police Department in Stollerton. She fiddled nervously with her satchel and her hair while waiting in the foyer to be admitted into the main building. Stick to asking about the blood. Anyone would be curious about that.

But it was the northern man Alvina couldn't get out of her head. His hand on her leg and the smell of pine needles dying in the wind. The flowers he'd thrown in the river. She had puzzled over everything he had said and done in their brief meeting. Why was he there? What did he want? Who was he? There was no one she could ask. Not about him maybe, but about the trailer, she could find out what happened in the trailer. She could ask the police about the blood. It seemed like a great idea at two o'clock this morning. Now, she wasn't so sure.

A constable opened the frosted glass doors. The municipalité régionale de comté des Collines police was relatively new; an eight-year-old regional police force funded by the rural municipalities of West Québec. Alvina identified herself in French to the constable and stated her business. Her French was passable; the constable's English was better. She was ushered down a tiled corridor to a sergeant detective's desk and was asked to wait. The air conditioning was going full blast. She shivered and fumbled her Stenopad out of her satchel.

There were nine sergeant detectives on the MRC des Collines staff investigating suspicious deaths in the region. They had a huge territory to cover. West Québec was over two thousand square miles of rock and wilderness. Homicide was rare but sudden violent death wasn't. People were struck by lightning, lost in the wilderness, crushed by tractors or falling trees, drowned, burned in house fires—the list went on and on. It was the job of the sergeant detectives to rule out foul play in unexpected death.

A well-dressed detective sat down at the desk, a coffee from Café Trémolos in his hand. He greeted her in French. She recognized the accent, the suit and the coffee immediately. Detective Sergeant Rompré. West Québecers used a workingman's French, a patois of Irish, French and American that was forged in the logging camps that had founded the region. Rompré's French was cultured, from Québec City.

"*Bonne matin, mademoiselle.* How may I help you?"

"Detective Sergeant Rompré." Alvina nodded her head. He didn't remember her. She'd covered a suicide Rompré had investigated a year ago but Dave pulled the plug on the story before it could come to anything. That was her first lesson in small town reporting—some toes were too critical to the survival of the paper to be stepped on. The toes in this case belonged to Hester Warnock, the publisher of *Deeper Vibe* and more importantly, the owner of their building.

"I have a couple of questions about an abandoned

trailer I came across near Martingale. There is a dried blood stain inside on the bed, quite large. I thought I should report it just in case the blood was related to a crime. Or maybe you know about it already?"

DS Rompré sat back in his chair. His eyes were on her, dark brown and unreadable.

"What were you doing inside the trailer, *mademoiselle*?"

Alvina reddened. Hester Warnock was a friend of Rompré's. He might tell her Alvina was snooping around private property. "I was on my way to a story and I got lost. I took a wrong turn. When I came across the trailer I didn't think, I just went inside ... and there was blood." *Please don't contact the owners and Dave and make a big deal out of this.* "It's probably nothing but I wondered about it. Maybe there's a story there. I don't know." Her voice trailed off.

Rompré leaned forward and tapped a file number into his computer. He frowned. "It was most definitely something, mademoiselle." Reading the screen, he said: "Detective Sergeant Giroux was the investigating officer on the case. Seven years ago, the body of a young woman was found bludgeoned to death inside a trailer near Martingale. Her killer was caught, tried and convicted, and is currently serving a life sentence in Bordeaux Prison."

Alvina wrote it down. Bordeaux Prison was a men's correctional facility in Montréal. "I assume he wasn't from around here." It was a fact that urbanites caused most of the problems in the region. They sped on the back roads, tossed their garbage out of car windows and trespassed anywhere they felt like. They thought they could get away with anything in the country.

"The girl's assailant was a local businessman."

"Really? And the victim? Was she local too?"

"*Oui*. She was a resident. Teresa Fillion, nineteen years of age, employed as an *au pair*. Her husband, Del Musgrave, is a guide at Martingale Hunt and Fishing Camp."

The mystery was solved. Officially (and unofficially, according to preference) married women in Québec were identified by their maiden names. The northern man emerged from the shadows, sad and a little disappointed that he had been identified. *Del Musgrave*. The flowers, hurled into the river cellophane and all, had given him away. He was mourning his murdered wife. Alvina abruptly and quietly decided not to ask any questions about him or to mention meeting him there.

Rompré cut into her thoughts. "There is little more I can tell you. It is regrettable, but this is no longer a police matter. Once forensics cleared the crime scene, the trailer became the property owner's responsibility. I suggest you alert Marlee Bremer to the issue of the unlocked door."

"Marlee Bremer owns the trailer?" Marlee Bremer was CEO of Bremer Family Motors, the *Record*'s biggest advertiser. She intimidated the hell out of Alvina.

"Bremer Motors is the registered owner of the lot and the trailer. But since her husband's incarceration Mrs. Bremer has had charge of all property in the company name."

Alvina started for a moment, not sure that she'd heard him correctly. "I'm sorry?"

Rompré sat back in his chair, coffee in hand. "Teresa Musgrave was in the employ of the Bremer family for the summer. It was Mr. Trey Bremer who took the girl to the trailer and killed her. If you wish to know more, the *Record* will have to provide us with a formal request to receive a copy of the transcripts from the trial. There is a fee, of course, and accessing the file will take time."

"No, no. There is no need. You've answered my question. *Merci beaucoup.*"


THE *STOLLERTON RECORD* was on the second floor of an historic building in the centre of the village. The main floor was occupied by the alternative weekly, *Deeper Vibe*. Alvina poked her head into their reception area to say hello to the editor-in-chief.

"How's it going, Ray?"

"Dead as a dog in July. You're late this morning."

*Deeper Vibe*'s office was in an old vaudeville theatre with a stage and a carved proscenium arch at the far end. Alvina told her parents they should come and see it sometime. She thought being actors, they'd love it. 'One day,' her mother had said. Everything was 'one day' with them.

"I couldn't sleep last night," she said.

"Out partying?" Ray laughed.

Alvina blushed. It was true that her roommate, Missy and her friends drank beer and played Scrabble until the wee hours of the morning on Saturday, but Alvina wasn't invited. ("You won't know anybody, Vinny." A pet name, slightly loathed.) It was just a matter of time before Missy announced that she'd found a new roommate and Alvina was asked to move out altogether.

She peered up the stairs. "Is Hester in yet?"

The publisher of *Deeper Vibe* had her office upstairs across the hall from the *Record* and was always at her desk first thing in the morning. The *Vibe* was the most widely read alternative weekly in North America; Hester Warnock was a pit bull for the truth.

"She says it's too hot to work," said Ray, "but between you and me, she's lost her edge. She doesn't have the balls to go after a story anymore. It happens. It'll happen to you if you stick around here long enough."

Alvina climbed the stairs to the office thinking at least Hester had an edge to lose. Her top story this week was an interview with a guy who had a giant pickle in a jar. His girlfriend had seized custody of the pickle in the breakup and was threatening to send it to him one slice at a time if he didn't return her laptop. Last Monday's edition of the *Record* was still piled on the counters at *dépanneurs* up and down the line. Nobody was reading newsprint anymore except the old people. They liked stories about stolen giant pickles. Current events bored them. They had lived through it all several times over.

It's pretty fucking sad when you envy eighty-five-year-olds, Alvina thought as she opened the office door. They had death on their side. They didn't have to worry about the world changing on them. Alvina was only twenty-three and she already felt left behind.

"You're late!" Dave bellowed from the front office. "I gave up fishing to get here this morning. Grab a coffee and let's go!"

Today was hotter than yesterday. Their half of the top floor was laid out like a railway car. No cross ventilation. Dave's office looked out over the river but his window didn't open and the window in the back office was painted shut.

Alvina dumped her camera bag on the reception

desk, grabbed her notes and a pencil and hustled into the publisher's office. "Sorry. I slept in."

"Well you're here now. Where are you with the raft story?"

"Not quite there." Alvina flipped her notes open. She hadn't written anything on the raft story. Not a word. "I'm interviewing the Diotte's owner closer to the date. Some of the kids said they might be willing to do half-pikes off the raft. I'll get photos then."

"What's the Diotte owner going to tell you? The kids are building the thing in Martingale. I want you up there before they float the damn thing down the river and dock it at the Diotte. I want pictures and a full story and I want it *before* the Civic Holiday so readers know what's coming, not after when it's already old news! I thought you went up there on Friday. What the hell were you doing all day?"

Her stomach churned. "I tried to find the raft—I turned off where the kid told me to—I was on the right road but it led to an old campsite and an abandoned trailer. The model is called Oasis. I Googled it. Oasis was a line of trailers built in the 1960's by a company in California."

Dave swiveled in his chair and crossed his beefy arms over his chest. His white short-sleeved shirt was pulled tight over his middle. "I know what it is Moon, without the aid of Google. My parents used to have one. What were you doing there?"

"Nothing." Alvina looked away. "I took a wrong turn, that's all. I thought since I was there, the campsite would make a good story."

"It wouldn't. Did you take photos?"

Alvina's throat tightened. She was never a good

liar. "I had my camera. You're always telling me to get photos. I thought it would make a good summer piece."

"I can't run them, Moon. A girl was murdered in that trailer. I'm not saying no to the idea, but not that campsite. Not that trailer. Okay? Delete them from your camera please. What else you got?" He flipped open the story ledger with one finger.

She searched the pages of her Stenopad. "The Arts and Letters Festival starts this week. I could interview one of the organizers. They're holding it on the covered bridge this year. It could be a nice filler piece."

"Good, good. Bremer Family Motors is a major sponsor. Make sure you work their name into the copy. We got to keep Marlee happy, especially now since she's almost *all* we've got."

"I don't know why Mrs. Bremer keeps advertising with us. She's never happy. Her assistant faxed over another revision to this week's ad by the way. It's in the file on my desk ready for Sunday's layout." She had met Marlee Bremer just once at the dealership. She was the sort of woman who declared everyone worthy as long as they conformed to her definition of worth, and it was clear in that brief meeting that Alvina didn't.

Dave leaned back. The chair squeaked in protest. "Marlee Bremer is loyal. She's a survivor; she's what I call a real lady. Raising three little kids alone and running a business. For the longest time, the *Record* was her only friend."

"How do you mean? Did her husband leave her?"

Dave's eyes became glassy. Alvina pretended not to notice.

"You could say that. Her husband has been in prison for the past seven years for murder. He killed their *au pair* in that trailer you stumbled across—the Oasis. Marlee is only now being welcomed back into the community and that's largely due to the *Record*. The press can work wonders if you spin it right," Dave grunted. "People were coming up to her in the street and accusing her of knowing her husband was a sexual deviant right to her face. They want to cast stones? Okay, well, I had no qualms about using this paper to defend her. Trey Bremer was not the upstanding family man he pretended to be."

"You knew him?"

"Yeah, I knew him." The chair squealed as Dave abruptly stood up. He turned away, his whale-sized shoulders hunched, and stared at the view from the window like he'd never seen it before. A sweat stain streaked his shirt. "I heard some things in that man's company that I chose to ignore. I was no saint myself at the time. If I'd been sober, I might have seen the danger but I thought it was just talk."

"What kind of talk?"

He waved his hand dismissively. "The kind of bragging shit men tell other men about women. I didn't mind listening to his bull as long as he was buying the drinks. Trey never believed he'd get caught. That was his whole problem." Dave snorted. "Right to the bitter end he thought he'd get away with raping a girl. He wasn't the brightest bulb. Narcissists rarely are. The trailer and the lot belonged to the Bremer family. Trey used to summer there as a kid. Yet he told police he found her body through dumb bad luck. The investigating officer said it's common for the killer to join the search for the missing person. The cops didn't completely rule out an unknown assailant but it was unlikely. It's not easy to discover that turn off from the highway."

"Unless you get lost."

Dave sat down, shaking his head sorrowfully. "You've always had a lousy sense of direction, Moon."

Alvina tucked her hair behind her ears. "You said she was missing. What was she doing in the trailer?"

"It's a long story. Not a pretty one, I'm afraid." Dave hunched over his desk. "Bear with me, my memory is rough. I got the call Monday morning—I'll be damned—it's exactly seven years ago today. My source said a body had been found in a trailer off the highway. Off I go, hot on the trail and when I get there, I find Trey Bremer giving a statement to the police. He said he'd gone looking for Teresa. She hadn't shown up for work that morning. For all that, it never occurred to me it was her body in the trailer. Never in a million years. She didn't even look human by the time the heat got at her. She had this green dress...." His neck reddened. "The point is you don't leave a body to rot in the wild like nature intended. It's a violent, ugly process."

Dave cleared his throat loudly. "The way it happened was Trey usually drove her home from work. She didn't drive or they didn't have a car—I can't remember which. You've heard of Del Musgrave, the artist? Paints in the style of the Group of Seven, *coureurs de bois*, that sort of thing. I don't see the appeal myself, but the critics say he's the next Tom Thomson. No? Okay, doesn't matter. He was Teresa's husband, that's why I bring him up. My buddy, Gerry, employed him back then as a guide at Martingale Hunt and Fish Camp. Still does, I believe. Del put in odd hours at the Camp so Trey often drove Teresa home, up the highway and across the old bridge at Martingale. But that night Bremer didn't take the bridge. Instead, he took her to the trailer and held her there for several hours. During which he raped her repeatedly and then bludgeoned her to death."

Horror shivered through her. Not for the girl who was dead but for Del Musgrave who had to live with her death for the rest of his life. How do human beings survive pain? How do you get through life with the hate you'd have and not turn into a monster?

Dave was staring at the scarred surface of his desk. "Even the experienced cops were throwing up. The heat in that trailer ... and the blood was everywhere. The coroner said it was one of the worst beatings he'd seen in his thirty-year career. Death was instantaneous. There were no defensive wounds."

"She didn't have time to fight back."

"Or she didn't want to."

Sweat dripped from Dave's forehead. His blue eyes shone bluer than usual.

"It didn't take the investigators long to make the arrest. Trey's prints were all over the trailer. His bodily fluids," he added delicately, "were found on the fold-out bed. The tire marks in front of the trailer matched Trey's vehicle and the cops found pine needles on the soles of the shoes he was wearing that day. His were the only tire treads at the scene."

"What happened to Teresa's husband?" She had to ask.

"Young Musgrave went off the deep end. Refused to go to the trial. He wasn't called as a witness for the prosecution but you'd think he'd want to see justice done. He didn't give a victim impact statement like most of them do. Maybe it was grief. I don't know. They were both too damned young. That was the problem. They were like babes in the woods. They weren't married long before she was killed."

"Did you know her? The victim?"

"Yeah, I knew her. Teresa Musgrave." He folded his hands on the desk. "She interviewed for an internship at the *Record* that summer but she wasn't qualified. I saw Marlee Bremer was advertising for an *au pair* so I put in a good word for her there."

He looked at Alvina as if expecting her to say something. She didn't know how to respond. Older people were always feeling guilty about things they were too late to change.

"You don't have to talk about it if you don't want to."

"No, no, it's fine. It's probably good to tell you the whole story in case you run into Marlee. The whole episode is off-limits—the murder, the trailer, the works. Never mention it. Never ask her about it. Got it?"

"Got it." Her heart bumped. She was supposed to pass along the message that the trailer door was unlocked. "What did she look like? Teresa Musgrave. Was she pretty?"

"Oh, hell yeah. Teresa was beautiful. A real stunner. Long chocolate brown hair and green, green eyes."

Alvina felt swallowed by disappointment and loathed herself for it. She thought she was over being jealous of beautiful girls. Her own looks were serviceable—hair of a pale, indeterminate brown, medium length, and straight. Her brows were nicely shaped, but pale. Her mother told her she had pretty eyes, hazel with thick dark lashes like her father's. But no one had ever called her beautiful.

"Her looks were wasted on Musgrave. They lived in

a cabin I wouldn't house a dog in. Del still does as far as I know. No ambition. He's got a screw loose, that guy. Gerry says he's reclusive, likes to be left alone to paint but he's not normal about it, you know? The road to his property is nothing but a bush road. Old Tommy Dowd's place. You didn't know Tommy Dowd did you?"

"I don't know anybody. I know you and Ray and Hester and that's it."

"That's got to change, Moon. You have to mix more."

"I may not know people but people know me."

"Small town reporters are always well-known. Doesn't make us popular. Going out and mixing makes us popular."

There was no point in arguing about this with Dave. Dave Gomer had lived in Stollerton for thirty or forty years. He didn't have a clue how hard it was to make friends here, or that she had tried and got nowhere. One girl told her she'd met her best friend in the *womb*. Their mothers had taken yoga class together during their pregnancies. Alvina couldn't compete with that kind of history. But Dave would see a gang of young people in the village and assume that Alvina wasn't mixing, like it was a choice. And he was depressing her talking about Del Musgrave like he was abnormal. The one person she wanted to know.

"Does he have any friends?"

"Who—Del? I doubt it. But that's his doing. The only thing you need to know about Musgrave is that he hates the *Record* and we hate him. He doesn't exist—I don't care how famous he gets, his name will not appear in this paper. Is that clear Moon? He wants to be left alone —we leave him alone."

"Why does he hate us?"

"Because he's an asshole. He's cold as hell when anyone from the media tries to talk to him. The city press pestered him when his wife was murdered. Not us—we were very respectful, but Musgrave tarred the *Record* with the same brush, so screw him."

Dave slapped his hands flat on his desk. "Right, back to work. I've got you covering the Arts and Letters Festival and I want that raft story this week. I want it for the next edition. No excuses. And find out if we're still under a burn restriction. Get a quote from the municipal fire department. We got to let the cottagers know brush burning and bonfires are not permitted until it's lifted. That should generate letters. What else you got for me?"

Alvina looked at her notebook. "Um, that's all I could find. Sorry."

"Don't be sorry, be productive. I've got nothing in the story bank from you. What's going on with these forest fires? Either the wind has shifted or the SOPFEU managed to get the blaze under control. Find out which it is. Fifty fires are raging across this province. The Maniwaki base is working flat out to suppress them. That smoke we had on Friday was from here to New York."

SOPFEU was short for Société de protection des forêts contre le feu. Only Dave was allowed to use the organization's acronym in his stories. Alvina was expected to write the whole thing out. Some seven hundred fires destroy hundreds of hectares of forest every year in Québec and seventy percent of them are caused by humans. SOPFEU's objective was to discover a fire before it grew beyond half a hectare and extinguish it before it burned three.

"If the goddamned recreationalists had the vaguest idea the kind of damage their 'footprint' left behind, maybe they'd stay the hell home. What's the *Vibe* working on?"

"Nothing much. Ray said Hester isn't even coming in."

"She can get away with it. The *Vibe* can run a piece on the effect of heat on the chakras and call it a day. We don't have that luxury here in the real world, Moon. When you're finished with the raft, research these fires. Call the SOPFEU, ask if there's a chance it could come this way and don't let them redirect you to the website. I don't want public relations, I want the story. Is your French up to it? You won't find an English speaker that far north."

"I'll tape the conversation on the answering machine and translate what I miss later. Will you be in the office tomorrow morning?"

"Doubtful. You know I go fishing in the summer. Why?"

Dave expected Alvina to manage the office when he was away and he was away a lot these days. She hoped he hadn't started drinking again. Ray told her that Dave's drunks were legendary.

"It's just there'll be no one at the desk if I'm gone to Martingale." Alvina tried to make her voice light.

"I think you and I both know the public will not give a good goddamn. This hundred and fifty-year-old rag is on its last legs. Put a sign on the door and get the story. Bring me back something good. I want photos of that raft looking like an eyesore."

# THREE

S HE DIDN'T see Del Musgrave again until two weeks later at the closing of the Arts and Letters Festival. He was walking toward her.

Alvina had arrived late as usual, barely making it in time for the closing ceremonies and a last chance to get a couple of photos before the paintings were packed away. Dave had been frosty about her output lately. These days just getting to work was taking everything she had. She wasn't being straight with him when she sat down, notepad at the ready, just as if he could count on her. Privately she felt like she could disappear at any moment. Coral and Oliver Moon would tell her she couldn't receive until she was willing to let go of expectation. She would, if she knew what that meant. They probably didn't either. Her parents made their living pretending to be fictional characters.

The day clung to the sky turning it milky blue. The covered bridge was in deep shadow, it took her eyes a few seconds to adjust to the gloom. Paintings were hung the length of the long wooden structure, suspended by wires. The organizers had clamped light sconces over the art work, natural light being scarce. A crowd of mostly beer-drinking young people were gathered in the middle of the bridge in clumps.

That's when she saw him. He was moving through

the crowd toward her, his head ducked down, trying to avoid eye contact by the look of it. Alvina was directly in his path.

"Del! Hey Del!"

A girl at the far end of the bridge was calling and pressing through the crowd to reach him. Alvina recognized her—Dagmar Weibe, one of the artists and organizers of the festival. Her blonde hair was pulled up into a ponytail and she was wearing a black tank top and coveralls. The girl flushed when Del stopped and turned around, waiting for her to catch up. She spoke hurriedly with a demand in her voice that sounded nervous. "Aren't you staying for the closing ceremonies? There's a gang of us heading over to the Diotte later."

"I'm too old to hang out in bars."

"Shut up." She laughed, showing perfect white teeth. Tinkling dangling chains hung from her neck. "Well, what are you doing to celebrate then? You sold every painting. You have to do something."

He smiled, or at least Alvina thought he did, and murmured something to Dagmar. Dagmar laughed loudly. "You're only saying that to make me feel better for not selling a thing. Does it ever get any easier?" Her eyes flashed. The canvases she was carrying depicted red oily vulvas and salmon-coloured breasts.

Del shrugged as he turned away. "No. But don't let that discourage you from trying."

"Wait!" Dagmar protested, still laughing. "Del—no fair! What did you mean by that? Get back here, Musgrave and explain that remark!"

Alvina watched him coming toward her as if from a great distance. Between them was a clump of art lovers.

He deftly rounded them. Another three steps and their meeting would be unavoidable. She raised the camera to her face and aimed the lens at a painting, praying he wouldn't notice her. She pressed the shutter. The flash burned a hole in the gloom.

Del Musgrave stopped.

"The bad penny," he said. A smile almost made it to his mouth. "Alvina Moon. This is twice we've crossed paths in as many weeks."

"Hello." Her heart dropped with sickening speed to her stomach. "I'm covering the closing ceremonies. I didn't know you were going to be here. Your name wasn't listed in the Arts and Letters press release."

"So you do know who I am."

"I just found out. You're Del Musgrave, the artist."

"But that's not all you know about me."

"I didn't know when I saw you last. I'm sorry about that." She squinted, trying not to see him. "I didn't mean to intrude on your grief."

"The grief was over a long time ago. How's the knee?"

She looked down at the scabs. Her hair swung in front of her face. The knees were healing nicely. "Fine. There might be a scar. It's my own fault for being so clumsy. That last step is a killer." Alvina head snapped up, her eyes wide. "I'm so sorry. I am so sorry I said that." Her face would have burned even if the day wasn't hot.

He cut her off. "It's just an expression. You don't have to watch everything you say around me, I won't break. I don't know why I bring those flowers every year. They haven't worked yet to bring her back. When I saw you in front of the trailer, I thought—"

There was an awkward silence.

"You thought I was her?"

"You're nothing like her."

"Del Musgrave!"

One of the festival organizers, Graham Seguin hustled toward them. "As a courtesy, I hope you will provide us with your biographical material the next time you crash the Festival. We were thrilled to have you, of course, but your appearance was extremely frustrating from a promotional point of view." The man cast a cool glance at Alvina. "I see you found Miss Moon. Naturally you are free to give interviews to whomever you choose, but the *Record* isn't the caliber of media we were after. With your name in the press release we could have attracted one of the bigger magazines, or even television, to cover the festival." Graham glared at Alvina. "My blood pressure skyrockets every year I do this and I wonder why the hell I bother."

Graham hustled away to yell at another hapless artist who was struggling to organize a collection of pottery.

Del seemed embarrassed, searching for something to say.

"Did you want me to interview you?" Alvina asked to break it.

"Hell, no. I don't know where Graham got that idea. I don't give interviews. I asked if the *Record* was sending someone. That's all. He must have got the wrong idea."

"He told you the *Record* was sending me?"

"Yes."

Again, the silence was uncomfortable. She wished he'd just excuse himself and keep walking like he did with Dagmar Weibe. She knew how he felt about the

*Record.*

Instead, he asked: "Did you ever find the raft?"

"I guess you don't read my articles. No raft. No story. Tomorrow is my last chance."

His neck burned. "I must have missed that. I went straight to the photos of the forest fires."

Dave's piece on the SOPFEU had taken centre page. The photos were incredible. Some of the fires burning northwest of Montreal were classed as out of control. The initial suppression attempt—an amphibious water bomber attack—did not halt the fire's spread beyond the perimeter. The SOPFEU attacks forest fires aggressively, relentlessly and efficiently. No action is wasted. "It's a war," Dave had written. But several of the fires they were fighting had jumped the control line. Dave called it a campaign fire—a fire of such size, complexity and priority that it would take everything the SOPFEU had just to hold it, and months more of hard work to suppress it.

"I can't imagine it," said Alvina. "Hectares of forest, football fields, going up in smoke. How can a little blaze get so out of control?"

"A fire can twist into back burns with the wind, and then there are ground fires that travel through the root system, popping up in the middle of fields. Crown fires incinerate the canopy and it becomes an umbrella of spark and flame. Nature starts a few fires of her own. Not all of them should be put out. A fire rids the forest of pests and diseases, but there's always the risk it'll become something too big. It's all about knowing when to act."

He took a step and she shifted her position to allow him to pass but instead of leaving, he caught her by the wrist. The contact was electrifying. She met his eyes —hazel eyes like her own, the colour of bottle glass. He was even better looking close up. Strong featured, the shape of his head was good; a broad forehead and largish nose which shouldn't be attractive but on him it was. His eyes were pulled down at the corners making him look older than he was, but his mouth gave his face vulnerability.

Taken individually, his features were nothing special but as a whole, he had something. Alvina tried to settle on a word that described what Del Musgrave had. It wasn't charm; he wasn't charming or confident like most good-looking men were. Del Musgrave had a hot place inside him that fired out from his eyes whether he meant it to or not. It was magnetism. Her mother said the really big actors and actresses have it—irresistible auras that they turn on and once they do, it's impossible to turn away or ignore them.

"I've been thinking about you," he said. "I was rude the last time we met. I made an assumption about why you were at the trailer."

"That's all right." She struggled for calm. "It was a reasonable assumption under the circumstances."

The crowd surged past, pushing him into her. He caught her to keep her from stumbling. They were pressed into a dim corner out of the path of the crowd. Closing ceremonies were beginning. The mayor had taken the makeshift stage at the far end of the bridge and was clearing his throat into the microphone.

"Do you really have to stay for this? Let's get out of here," he said suddenly. "I'll take you to the raft myself. You'll get better photos from the river."

"I don't know ... it's getting late. Will the kids still be

there? Dave expects pictures of the action." The rapids rushed far below them.

He glanced at the sky that was streaked orange with the setting sun. "It won't be dark for another hour or more. They'll still be there. You won't make it in on your own in that van you're driving. It's only an access road. Even the kids travel in by boat or on bikes."

He smelled of oil paint and cold water. She thought he'd smell of wood smoke for some reason, and then remembered there was a forest fire raging the day she first saw him. The sense memory must have stayed with her.

"All right," Alvina said. "Let's go."

It was too late to say anything else. It was probably too late the moment she met him, a white arctic light blasting into her consciousness. It was definitely too late the moment he touched her wrist.

THE GATINEAU RIVER is narrow and twisted in places, and wide and smooth as glass in others. Villages sprang up where the river allowed and thick mixed forest claimed the rest. The covered bridge spanned the rapids. Downstream, a calm open bay marked the village of Stollerton.

Alvina's camera and notebook were between her feet. It wasn't easy to talk over the grind of the motor. They bounced over choppy current as Del steered upriver. She gripped the edges of the blue and gray aluminum fishing boat, a Harber Craft two-seater that was really uncomfortable. "My boss, Dave Gomer gets around by boat in the summer too," she yelled. "I'm not sure which one is his dock. He takes his boat to and from work as soon as fishing season opens. He's crazy about fishing."

The river was clean though it had been a logging waterway for over a century before the trucks and super highways took over, but it was cold, always cold even in July's high heat, fed by the Paugan Falls in Low that were dammed now. Above the Falls she didn't know what the landscape was like; stone and trees and more trees, she supposed, all the way to Maniwaki.

Del said: "That's Dave's dock there."

Alvina risked a glance, fearing she would see Dave and he would ruin this for her in the way that bosses could. Dave's red and silver Princecraft boat was tied up at the end of the dock, batting lightly and rhythmically against the pylon with the current.

Falling summer light glittered behind the hills. River geography was a revelation to her. The shoreline was rougher, wilder than Alvina had imagined. The occasional dock could be seen, flung out of the wilderness, making a break for the water. The wide smooth rock she'd seen at the trailer was rare.

Del's navigation was flawless, steering to exactly where the current was the least demanding. The river narrowed and then rounded to a cove where the ragged shoreline gave way to a green lawn and pink roses. Civilization carved out of the wilderness. A house clad in cedar shakes stained gunmetal blue sat at the crest of the embankment. Its trim was as fresh and white as a handkerchief. Copper sunlight winked over panes of glass. Stone steps led up from a dock that sagged a little from winter ice damage. A girl sat at the end, her feet dangling in the water. She looked to be eleven or twelve. She watched them but didn't wave.

"Who lives there?" Alvina pointed.

"That's the Bremer home."

She nodded, pretending not to recognize the significance. Maybe they would spend the whole night pretending. Del turned the tiller and the girl on the dock watched their progress as they slid past Marlee Bremer's house.

Alvina faced front. The wind felt good. "Is your place near here? Old Tommy Dowd's."

Del laughed. "How do you know about old Tommy?" His voice carried over the chugging motor. "Tommy was a trapper, the last of the breed. He was in his nineties when he sold up. He had this shitty little cabin and forty acres on the river. Crap bush. No good for logging or farming, just no good. I paid cash for it. Tommy didn't want much—he couldn't have got much. The property is too far away for anyone who works in town and too mean a living for anyone local. No electricity. I dug a well and installed indoor plumbing not long after I moved in."

They passed a short dock perched on a smooth round of granite. "Right through there. The path leads to my place. The motorboat was included in the sale. It gets me around almost four seasons until the ice takes over. Then I snowshoe or ski."

Over millions of years the river's current had eroded the rock to a smooth slope that could have been a whale it was so big. Black forest fringed the shore. A path cut through the woods. "You live back there? You're miles away from everything."

"Hell no," he laughed. "Martingale is only a short walk in that direction through the bush." He pointed across the river. "I get my groceries at the *magasin* and fuel for the boat. Laundry facilities are at the lodge where I work. I don't need anything else."

They travelled on in silence, the motor whine filling the space between their talk. The abandoned campsite and the trailer where his wife was murdered slid past. The swimming rock where Alvina had first seen him was caught by the setting sun and glowed dully.

"I have something to tell you," she said. It was now or never. The murdered wife was sitting between them in the boat. "I went inside the trailer. I lied to you when I said I didn't. I wouldn't have if I'd known what happened to your wife there. Dave says you hate the *Record* and I can understand why when your privacy is constantly being invaded. I am truly very sorry."

Del killed the motor. The boat slowed and then stopped. The sounds of night birds, bullfrogs and insects filled the air. They bobbed in the middle of the river, the current tugging them lazily downstream. He was silent.

"I'm bad at small talk." Her face was hot. "Please say something."

"You saw what was inside."

"Yes." She felt like she couldn't breathe.

"No one's been inside that trailer since it happened. It's been closed up for seven years. I knew something was different—changed. It's been driving me crazy." He touched his forehead. "I don't do public shows. I crashed the Festival hoping I'd see you again."

"Why?" *He doesn't mean it like that. No. Don't even think it.*

"I'm going to tell you something but this stays between you and me, a regular conversation, because you're interested and not pretending to be just to get a story."

"If you want to talk, we can talk. I can't help what I do for a living. I was doing it before I met you, but I'm still a person. I'm interested in—in having a regular conversation with you."

His handsome features were intensely alive. That hot place Alvina had seen in him was alight and burning in her direction.

"My boss, Gerry Dunn, is this little Irish guy. He told me that in Celtic mythology there are thin places on Earth—thresholds where the visible and invisible are in close proximity. They're found where mountain meets river. The Gatineau Hills were once mountains, ancient mountains from Earth's earliest geological age. Mountains and river, see? We're at a threshold. This world and the next are only separated by a veil. I saw —I thought I saw something that day at the trailer. You were inside—"

Alvina heard what he wanted to know before he said it. "She wasn't there, Del."

He nodded slowly, as though he expected this disappointment. His skin darkened. "You must think I'm crazy talking like this."

"If you knew my parents, you'd know this is a normal conversation for me. But I'm not a believer. I think we create spiritual phenomena to help us cope with the finality of death. It's not insanity; it's more like a survival mechanism to make us feel that our time here has a purpose."

"You're saying I need a psychiatrist, not a medium. I'm hallucinating."

"I think you saw something that was real to you, but it wasn't supernatural. And you shouldn't take it seriously."

Del turned and pulled on the starter cord. The motor blared to life, drowning out further conversation. Crestfallen, she pretended not to notice the change in him. An occupational hazard of being a good listener—people would open up to her only to regret it later. Backstage relationships were temporal and flimsy and the kid doing her homework in the Green Room was not a therapist, but that didn't stop actors from spilling their guts out to her. She wasn't resented for seeing them at their weakest, but she certainly wasn't loved for it.

Alvina raised her voice over the motor. "You miss her. It was terrible, unforgivable what happened. It doesn't help when someone tells you what you saw was all in your mind."

Del said with finality as though he'd been waging an inner war: "I needed to hear it. It helps explain some things. The truth is I don't see her in my mind or anywhere else." He looked past Alvina, his attention on steering the boat. "I expect to see her the same way I expect to see a painting before it's started. I paint what's beneath the wilderness, not the material view. It's the same with Teresa. She's there, on the other side of the veil. I can feel her. Or I thought I could. Here, and not here. I expected her to come back to haunt me and she didn't. And then I needed her to."

Alvina's skin prickled. "Why?"

"I don't know. I guess because she wouldn't."

She turned her gaze to the passing shoreline. They were making good progress. It wouldn't be long before they arrived at the raft. "Tell me what you saw," she urged. "It doesn't matter if I believe in the supernatural or not. Tell me anyway."

His voice rose impatiently as though he didn't want to talk about it anymore. "There was a girl's face in the light, behind the veil of smoke. I thought it was Teresa. Maybe it was you. You were wearing a shirt with a red heart on it. A powerful psychological image wouldn't you say?" He grinned at her. "A shrink would say I was projecting when I had the vision. I arrived there as a groom looking for my bride and I found you instead with banged-up knees."

He was being flippant, making fun of his experience. Alvina wished she'd kept her mouth shut about the supernatural and just let him speak. Now he was self-conscious.

"But you saw something you couldn't explain."

"Hell no, I could explain it. Teresa had come back to haunt me."

The dead only haunt the imaginations of the living. Alvina knew this intellectually but the response she had was visceral. Her hair rose on the back of her neck. "Why would Teresa haunt you?"

His hair was wind-blown off his face, clearing his eyes that were narrowed against the wind. "We're almost there."

He wasn't going to answer her. He probably didn't know the answer. Del had no idea why his dead wife would haunt him or why he sought her in a thin place of rock and river. He suffered from an acute and intense knowledge of death. Teresa was gone, but the space she had claimed in his life still hadn't healed over. If Alvina believed in the afterlife—if there was such a thing— she would tell him Teresa would probably come back when he had something to lose, and then he wouldn't want her. The little she knew about love was that it was grittier and more demanding than a Valentine's Day card would have us believe. That's why it was so hard to pull off.

Del twisted the accelerator and the boat shot ahead, skimming over the water. The prow lifted. Alvina clung to her seat, keeping her expression perfectly calm. She wouldn't let him see that she was nervous. Alvina knew how it was with people whose behaviour was chronically misunderstood. She'd grown up with them. Del needed to be trusted.

"The raft is around the next bend. Look up ahead on your left."

She turned, squinting into the wind. The raft loomed into sight, looking worse than Alvina could have hoped for. It was a two-storied nightmare of odd-sized wood, exposed nails and overall shoddiness. The kids had dragged a mouldy pink sofa onto the lower deck and were lounging on it, drinking beer and smoking pot. The headline practically wrote itself.

*Huckleberry Finns on Collision Course with Hill's Honchos!*

Dreamy summertime Stollerton was about to be invaded by a floating dump manned by a half dozen stoned teenagers. Alvina could have laughed, the story was so perfect. Not the big story she always dreamed she'd stumble across, but there was enough conflict in it to excite the public. Dave would be happy.

Fuelled by beer and testosterone, the boys showed off for the camera, obliging her with stunt diving off the upper deck. The girls were quieter but willing to talk when Alvina asked questions. She got some surprisingly insightful responses to the issues the raft would raise for the business community. With kids this age, it was usually a race to keep them focused long enough to get an accurate spelling of their names and some non-libelous quotes before they blanked out. Alvina's source, the fifteen-year-old who had leaked the story in the first place said the raft was more than a place to get away from parents and break the rules. It was a statement—a protest against commercialism and the branding of teenagers' brains to sell products. "A floating Fuck You," the kid said. A great quote but unusable in the *Record* even if she substituted the problem vowel with a star.

Alvina fired off several more shots then slid her camera back in its case. She turned to Del, enthused. "Thank you, thank you, thank you for bringing me tonight! I never would've got this story in the morning." Try getting juvenile delinquents to wake up at nine a.m., never mind talk. "This is exactly what Dave wanted. Whew. Not fired. Moon keeps job."

"Got everything you need then?" His mouth was pulled to one side in a smile and he yanked on the starter cord. "Okay, let's go. There's something I want to show you."

The stars were coming out. Blue sky was melting to indigo. The trip downriver was quick, faster than the trip up had been. Del slowed as he reached his dock. The night was falling heavy and fast. Alvina peered at her watch. Nine-thirty. The air was cool and thin on her face.

He cut the motor and pointed. "Look."

She peered into the black of the forest that lined the shore. Hundreds of tiny eerie green lights blinked on and off, darted and hovered through the trees. Fireflies. More than she'd ever seen before.

"It's so beautiful," she breathed. "I've never seen anything like it." Alvina turned to him, not troubling to hide her awe. "You know something? I'm glad we have a stagnant economy and no one can get cell phone reception and Québec's agricultural laws have a chokehold on development. I hope things never get better because look—we have fireflies!"

"Hippie." He grinned, his teeth flashing white.

"You are lucky, you know that, Musgrave?"

Shadows hollowed his cheeks and eyes. Only his hair remained bright. Del's breath suddenly surfaced in his chest. A change came over his face. She waited, caught in the unforeseen shift that had happened between them.

Alvina turned back to the fireflies, her heart pounding. According to one guy she went out with exactly five times before he stopped calling, she made guys uncomfortable. He said she gave too much away and she thought isn't that what people in love were supposed to do? She was learning though. Give as little as possible.

"I'm glad you came." His voice was behind her.

"I'm glad I did too."

The smell of the river rose up to her nose mingling with the scent of dry hot pine sap. Her belly fluttered. His hands reached for her and covered her eyes. He had broad hands for a painter, she thought distractedly behind the long fingers that were blunted square at their tips.

"Look up."

She tilted her face to the sky. Del removed his hands. "What do you see?"

The night sky filled her vision. A sky of black velvet

studded with millions of glittering stars. Her head bumped against his shoulder. His fingers brushed her neck, supporting her.

"Oh my God," she gasped. It was dizzying. "There are so many."

"You can't see the less luminous ones in town because of the light pollution. But they're there. They're always there."

Her teeth started chattering in spite of the heat.

"Are you cold?"

She wasn't cold. She was terrified with brittle rapture. "A little."

Del started the motor and steered the boat down the silver river under a profusion of stars.

# FOUR

ALVINA PUT on a summer dress of orange floaty fabric that her mother had given her, and slipped her feet into flat sandals. At the last minute she decided to apply makeup and put her hair in a clip to keep it off her face. She walked to work, her eyes on the river, wondering if she would see Del Musgrave again.

The *Record* office was an oven when she came in. Dave was at his desk, his head in his hands. She was surprised to see him in so early. He had even made the coffee—not his usual routine. Alvina eyed the pot. It was bound to be too strong.

He yelled from his office. "Let's get this shit hole of a day started. It's too fucking hot in this building. It's inhumane. It's like a sweat lodge up here."

She dumped two sugar cubes in her coffee, grabbed a sharpened pencil from the cup on her desk and took her regular seat in the battered leather chair across from Dave. His desk was a scarred oak surface littered with papers, pens and notepads. A bank of gray filing cabinets lined the wall to her right but Dave rarely filed anything. Piles of papers and research were stacked on top. His office smelled of ink and dust and failure.

Dave screwed up his face to focus on her.

"What's wrong? Is there a problem?" Alvina's head

began to pound.

"Is there a problem? You tell me. I had a call from Marlee Bremer at nine o'clock this morning."

Alvina tensed. "What did she want?"

"She wanted to know why my reporter was in a boat last night with Del Musgrave. She hoped we weren't planning to run a story on her husband's incarceration without discussing it with her first, which was a polite way of saying she was really pissed off. I had to back-pedal like crazy because I had no idea what she was talking about. I thought you were covering the Arts and Letters Festival."

"Del took me to where the kids are building the raft. It's easier to get there by boat. That's all it was. I didn't ask him anything about Marlee or her husband's incarceration."

Dave heaved his bulk in the chair. "Bullshit. Musgrave hates the *Record*. Why would he help you with a story?"

"I don't know. I ran into him at the Festival. We got to talking about the raft and forest fires and then he said he'd take me in the boat. He said I'd get stuck if I tried to take the van down the access road. I emailed the copy and photos to you last night."

"I haven't checked my email."

Alvina looked away. Whatever she said now, it would be the wrong thing.

Dave set his elbows on the desk and linked his fingers together. His arms were freckled with pale orange dots nested in fine gold hairs. "Okay. Well, the shit has hit the fan. Marlee has asked to meet with us and I have a bad feeling it's to pull her advertising. Goddamn it, I told you Del Musgrave was off-limits!

What's the matter with you?"

It was a rhetorical question. Her boss wasn't interested in knowing what was wrong with her. Heat shimmered in the hills beyond his window.

Dave cleared his throat, a long gurgling sound that didn't sound healthy. "Look, Alvina. I haven't been straight with you about some things lately. As you know, it's been a tough couple of years for the *Record*. Advertising used to carry us for thirty pages; these days I'm lucky if I can drum up enough to pay for six. The Internet is killing us. It's not just the classifieds either —they're just one more thing on top of a string of one more things."

Advertising was the life blood of a newspaper. With the exception of Bremer Family Motors, the *Record* subsisted on the income from the Births and Deaths page, announcements from the government and a shrinking community events listing.

He rubbed his mouth. Dave always rubbed his mouth when he was troubled by something. Her boss made a sound that was a cross between a grunt and a moan and she knew the end was coming. Alvina watched him as if from a great distance, Dave Gomer hacking away through the heat and the silence to get to the point.

"A couple of guys from MetMedia have been sniffing around. I'm not saying it's definite but I don't see that I have a choice. I can't keep her going. I have to get out now while I still have something of value to sell. You see what I'm up against?"

"Sure," she said, although she didn't. "It's a business decision."

His eyes hardened. "If it were that simple, I'd be

sleeping like a baby and do I look like I'm sleeping like a baby? The *Record* was founded in 1854. It's the only newspaper serving this area—one of the few independents left in Canada and we're dying. Smothered out of existence. MetMedia doesn't give a shit about local issues. It's over, Moon. You kids—you bloody kids—you never question or challenge a fucking thing. You think a tweet is news. Who cares about content? Who cares how it's spun? Ah hell, if it's not a fucking app, you aren't paying attention anyway. You don't know what you don't know and when it's gone, there'll be no getting it back."

"Stop yelling at me!" Alvina yelled. Her body shook and her eyes grew hot and teary. "Don't blame this on me—I don't want the *Record* to go under! It was your idea to sell out. I'm just trying to make it easier for you and I'm sick of trying to make things easier for people!"

"What the hell are you on about? Okay, don't freak out. Just keep it together for God's sake. I can't have you losing it on top of everything else." He rubbed his belly. "I had the Big Lad breakfast this morning. Between that and Marlee's phone call, I got a hole burning in my gut the size of Labrador. This business is giving me a fucking ulcer."

"Do you want me to get you an antacid?" Alvina said mechanically. She had stocked a supply in the top drawer of her desk.

"No, no, I'll be fine. Sit down. We need to talk. I need to make some things clear. See, the huge fucking carrot I dangled in front of these guys to get them to bite was the advertising contract we have with Bremer Motors. That's why I'm jumping down your throat over this thing with Musgrave. Marlee is sensitive and I can't let anything mess up at this stage of the game."

"Sure. Whatever." Alvina was too stunned to argue. "When does all this happen?"

"Four weeks but until the deal is finalized, it's business as usual around here. And then we close the doors. Don't look so stricken, Moon. God, you're like a baby fawn in the headlights. I've got connections at the city papers. I'll make a couple of calls and get you some interviews lined up. You'll be okay. You're a talented writer."

Quivering, Dave swiveled to face the window. "It's me who screwed up. I failed this town and they have no clue. It went down on my watch. The others managed to keep it going through wars, the Depression, the Seventies—it folded on my fucking watch."

Traffic noises filtered up to them. The village was coming to life. Outside, the day was already sultry. The air refused to move or offer any relief.

"Ah hell." Dave mopped his face. "This community won't give a damn when we go. They'll probably throw a party." He lurched to his feet. "Okay. Our meeting with Mrs Bremer is in twenty minutes. When we get there let me do the talking. I'll explain about the raft and break the news to her about the sale at the same time. Hopefully she won't put MetMedia through the meat grinder when they talk contracts next week."

Alvina reached for her camera bag although there was no point. There were no more stories to cover. The world had changed. A sharp tilt and a way of life slid off the planet.

"Wait!" Dave shot her a crafty look. He turned back into his office and emerged seconds later, dangling a set of keys. "We'll take the fucking van. If we're going out, we're going out in a blaze of glory. It'll bankrupt us in gas but at least she'll see us coming."


MARLEE BREMER'S kitchen smelled of fresh brewed coffee and home-baking. Alvina knew the Bremers had money but it was a revelation to see that money close up. Five bedrooms upstairs and a den on the main floor. A sunken living room with a stone fireplace; a pale yellow sunroom and country kitchen with granite counters and beamed ceilings.

"It cost far more than we could afford at the time," Marlee was saying as they followed her through the house. Her speech was clipped, emphatic. "Trey and I wanted a home that could accommodate a growing family. The river view is impressive, isn't it? We're very fortunate here. This is the poor man's Muskokas—waterfront, trees and loons for a fraction of the taxes. Alvina, if you will carry the scones, I'll bring the coffee and we'll have our meeting outside. It's a beautiful morning and the season is too short to stay inside, don't you find?"

Dave had portrayed Marlee Bremer as a fragile single mother barely keeping a roof over her head. That wasn't the woman Alvina met. Marlee had greeted them at the door dressed in an expensive linen suit of pale green that set off her green eyes. Her hair was cut in a sleek bob, blonde streaks over darker yellow hair. She was the sort of woman who would get her colours done and pay attention to fashion trends rather than develop a personal style.

Alvina picked up the plate of homemade scones and followed Marlee and Dave through the French doors to a flagstone patio. Stone steps linked the patio to a path that wound through rose bushes and down a green lawn to the river's edge. Twelve-year-old Violet Bremer sat by herself at the end of the dock. Her two little brothers, Harry and Stanley were away at day camp.

"I try to make her wear a life jacket when she's near water but my daughter has a mind of her own," Marlee grimaced.

Violet was the snitch. That was obvious to Alvina. The girl had spied on them from her perch on the dock and then reported back to her mother in high-blown, dramatic fashion. Alvina knew the type. She hated kids. They were so random. You never knew what they were going to say or do, but they would inevitably get you into trouble.

Marlee set the coffee tray down on the patio table—a custom-made wrought iron beauty. Hugely expensive. Alvina tried not to stare at it. Their hostess gestured for them to sit. The worst of the meeting had yet to begin. They'd got through the preliminaries all right. Marlee didn't have too many objections to the newspaper changing hands. She said she hoped MetMedia would be sensitive to her position in the community and Dave assured her that he would see to it. No one seemed overly concerned that Alvina would be out of a job.

"Isn't this nice." Marlee sat down across from them. She reached for a scone and then stopped herself. "No. If I start on these, I won't stop. I only have five pounds left to go. Black coffee for me." She took a sip and made a face. "I'm not used to it without cream. There doesn't seem to be any point if I can't drink it the way I like."

"You must wear yourself ragged in the summer between taking care of the kids and running the dealership."

Dave mopped his brow of sweat. Alvina felt sorry for him. The patio was beautiful but the house was cooler.

"If you're willing to delegate and not waste time in meetings, it's amazing how much work a CEO can get through in a few hours." She peered at Alvina. "I think we've met once."

Alvina shook her head, pretending not to remember.

Marlee lifted the coffee pot and filled Dave's cup. Her fingernails were beautifully manicured. She wore a thick gold band of diamonds on her ring finger. "We're all being very polite here but should I assume Alvina knows the reason why I was so upset this morning?"

Dave cleared his throat. "I had to tell her. She came across the trailer and wanted to do a story on it. I had to explain why that wasn't going to happen."

"I see. I'm surprised anyone knew where to find it after all these years." She cocked an eyebrow in Alvina's direction. "How did that happen? Did someone tell you about it?"

"No. I took a wrong turn and discovered it by accident."

Marlee's mouth compressed just slightly.

"Here is my problem, Alvina. My daughter told me she saw 'that girl reporter'—her words, not mine—with Del Musgrave, and now I find out you just happened to stumble across the scene of the crime. Knowing my history with the media, can you understand why I'm feeling very, very uncomfortable right now? You are starting your career, I realize that, and I know this could be a great opportunity for you. Dave, I know I have no right to object—"

"We're good, Marlee. We're fine with hearing your

concerns. We understand. That's why we're here."
Dave's big shoulders lifted, his hands opening. "It was
all a misunderstanding. Alvina met Del at the Arts and
Letters Festival and he offered to take her to the raft the
kids are building. It's a story she's working on—"

Alvina cut him off with a trace of irritation. "I was
looking for the raft when I came across the trailer.
Meeting Del Musgrave at the Festival was a fluke. Well,
not much of a fluke. He *is* an artist and it was an artists'
festival. We didn't talk about anything in particular. I
think he wanted to get a look at the raft too and taking
me was just an excuse."

"You didn't ask him about his wife's murder?"

"No."

"Why not?"

"It was none of my business.

There was a silence.

Marlee Bremer turned her gaze to the river. "It's a
perfect day isn't it? Summer is such a gift after the long
winter months. Not many bugs this year either which is
a blessing. Help yourself to a scone, Alvina, before they
go cold. Dave, can I pour you another cup of coffee?"

Alvina said: "I'm sorry if I seem insensitive but I
don't understand why you were upset." Her ears were
hot. She could feel Dave's eyes on her. "How would
talking to Del help me in my career? There is no news
value in a crime that was solved seven years ago."

"You think I've overreacted? Del Musgrave is
becoming more and more famous for his art. The press
has become very interested in him. I doubt the public
could care less but the press is no longer concerned with
serving the public. They rely on celebrity, violence and
sex scandals to do their jobs. Del Musgrave's story offers

all three."

"But Del doesn't give interviews."

"I don't either but since when has that stopped a young, ambitious reporter? Stories have been pieced together and posted online with less than what you know at this point."

"I wouldn't take advantage of a person that way." Alvina was trying very hard to control her voice. "I don't 'piece' together stories for personal gain." She risked a look at Dave. He nodded slightly and she knew she was on solid ground. He'd back her up. Dave wasn't bad as far as bosses went. Probably one of the better ones.

"All right." Marlee gave a tiny, swift smile. "Please accept my apology if I've offended you. A private citizen has no idea what it's like to live under media scrutiny until it happens to them. Public humiliation in a small village is more real and damaging than it is in a city. I have children to protect and I've been doing it alone for seven years. Trey's mother is travelling in an RV with her second husband. His brother Toby is still in and out of rehab. My own mother made it clear she's already raised her kids and isn't interested in helping me with mine. They don't make grandmothers like they used to."

"The media might have gone easier on you if you'd divorced him." Alvina flushed. Dave shot her a look. He could argue with her but it was true and he knew it was true.

"Divorce was out of the question," Marlee answered coolly. "There was too much at stake. Trey was named CEO when his father died but his mother is the legal owner of Bremer Family Motors. If Freesia Bremer was allowed to take over, she'd run the place into the ground. I'm the acting CEO until Trey gets out of prison." She shot a look at Alvina. "Keep that yourself if you can. The good people of Stollerton would be up in arms if they knew the company was paying Trey's legal fees. "

"Trey will never get out of prison," Dave grunted. Coffee had dribbled on his shirt.

"I'm not so sure about that." Marlee lowered her voice. "His lawyers want to bring in a sexual behaviours specialist to examine Trey. Trey always denied it was rape right from the beginning; his lawyers are starting to believe him. They say if they can make a case for consensual sex there is no motive for murder and Trey could win on appeal."

"The brass balls of the guy," breathed Dave. "He's tried this once already. The jury didn't buy it the first time. The medical evidence convicted him. It gives me the creeps just thinking about it. His lawyers are trying to rationalize rape and frankly it pisses me off that you don't tell them to go to hell. What if he wins? The community will freeze you out and the kids. The *Record* won't be around anymore to have your back."

Alvina bit into a scone and tried not to look like she was listening. They made an odd pair, she thought. Dave Gomer, the chauvinist newspaperman in his too-tight, short-sleeved shirt coming to the aid of the ice queen in the power suit. A sexual deviant had made them allies.

"The cost of it all terrifies me. The legal bills are staggering. This specialist alone is more than I can manage. Trey seems to think I should sell the *house* if necessary just to get him out of prison. Why is he doing this? Why doesn't he stop—just *stop*. Hasn't he humiliated me enough? What if this drags on for another seven years?"

Dave hunched forward. "You're a mother. You have your kids to think about. How is this affecting them?"

Violet Bremer was standing at the end of the dock, her towel bundled under her arm, staring in their direction. She was tall for a twelve-year-old.

"Harry and Stanley are fine. Violet worries me though." Marlee arched a look at Dave. "She's found religion."

"Oh boy." Dave twisted to examine the girl who stared back at him.

"Yes. The Evangelicals. I have to get up every Sunday morning to drive her to church. I wait at Café Trémolos with a book and a latte so it's hardly an onerous task. She doesn't expect me to be religious. But I find it disturbing. She believes her faith will set her father free. She prays for it every day."

"That's not good," said Dave. "She's in for a hell of a disappointment."

Violet dropped her towel and executed a perfect dive into the river.

"I tried to explain to her that some people are doomed because they choose to be doomed. We can't give our love to those people. They'll drag us down. I was trying to give her some insight into her father. Do you know what she said? She said Jesus Christ chose to be doomed and we give our love to him."

They all looked toward the kid in the water. The river glinted.

"I don't blame her for being loyal. She's just a child. She doesn't know what her father has done, how he's put all of our lives in jeopardy. Violet grew up believing in the myth of her perfect family. I'm responsible for encouraging that delusion, if you want to call it that. Violet calls it Truth. I thought if I gave the children a family history they could be proud of and want to emulate—particularly the boys—it would protect them psychologically. It never occurred to me that Violet would turn her father into a martyr." Marlee sighed. "At least the church is friendly. She used to have a terrible time in school with the other kids. She's very bright. A near photographic memory. Doesn't make her popular though."

A change came over Dave's face. For as long as Alvina had worked for him, the man had two expressions—irritated or ecstatic. Dave Gomer's was not a placid temperament. This was the first time she'd seen him express nothing. His large baggy face was blank.

Violet pulled herself up on the dock and was lying on her back, baking in the sun.

"Sunscreen, honey!" Marlee called. "Are you wearing sunscreen?"

The kid didn't look up.

With Dave and Marlee distracted, Alvina decided this was the best time to deliver her message. "I'm sorry I didn't mention this earlier, but the trailer is unlocked. I discovered it when I was there. Detective Sergeant Rompré said it wasn't a police matter but he advised me to tell you about it so you could secure the property. Also, there's a dead squirrel inside."

"You went inside?"

"I didn't know there was a reason not to. I saw the blood. I had to report it to the police."

Marlee's voice charged across the table, low and bitter. "And they think I should secure it, do they? As though I treasure that disgusting—I'd have it hauled away and crushed tomorrow if I could."

"So do it." Dave's eyes were glassy. "It's company property and you're the CEO of the company. What if someone got in and hurt themselves? Goddamned hippies don't think anything of trespassing on other people's property. They'd sue your ass. It's a liability waiting to happen."

"Violet!" Marlee's voice echoed shrilly across the river. "Didn't you hear me? I said sunscreen!"

Alvina cast a sidelong glance at her boss. Dave had his hand over his mouth.

The wind lifted and rolled over the table. Their coffee had gone cold. Marlee's eyes were on Violet but Alvina guessed it wasn't Violet she was seeing. In news reports of a rapist's arrest there was always a wife or a woman in the man's life. Alvina used to wonder about that woman. What was her marriage like? Were there clues to his deviant behaviour that she forced herself to ignore? If you loved a man—really loved him—could you ever really know him? Wouldn't the love get in the way?

"Where are your parents, Alvina?" Marlee tapped the edge of her coffee cup with her nails.

"Touring. They're actors. We keep in touch on Facebook."

"Oh. How interesting." Her voice lifted. "I don't know if I could that. But I suppose that's the only option now for parents with grown children. Do you want children?"

"Not really. They're a lot of work."

Marlee gazed at her, astonished. "No, they're not. Whoever gave you that idea? Granted, some mothers expect too little of their children. I've heard of six and seven-year-olds who won't settle down to sleep without their mothers in bed with them. In my case, I ran a tight ship. Dinner was at five, then bath, story and bedtime. No negotiation. Violet and Harry were asleep by seven-thirty. Children love routine. Establish a routine and they are no trouble at all."

Alvina tried to imagine her parents passing up an opening night party to establish a routine and failed. They got pregnant with her when they were still at the National Theatre School. She was more of a mascot than a child.

"Trey and I had everything," Marlee said meditatively. "The perfect life. What was so wrong that he had to take Teresa to that trailer? I think he wishes I would divorce him. It would ease his conscience." She fixed her eyes on the hills across the river. "You are absolutely right, Dave. The trailer is a liability. I'll arrange to have it hauled away. Bremer Motors can sell the property and donate the money to a worthy cause. I should have done it years ago. Let the dead bury their dead."

Dave nodded and squinted at the sky. "You know something? I think it's going to rain."


STOLLERTON WILTED in the late afternoon heat. Alvina's eyes flicked over the parched lawns and the dusty driveways she passed on the walk home. Even the foliage lacked energy. Front gardens winked at her. Candy apple blooms. Dove grey lambs foot crowded with deep purple violets. She passed the park, a patch of beaten grass, three picnic tables and some shrubs planted by the business association. A banner announcing the Stollerton Arts and Letters Festival sagged between two jack pines. A hand-made town; a do-it-yourself place. Anyone under the age of thirty had to be part of the arts crowd to fit in here. She should be thrilled to be leaving it.

The road edged away from the riverbank and followed the railroad tracks. A short trestle bridge spanned the creek that dumped into the river. Alvina balanced on its glinting silver rails. The water moved far below, visible between the ties that smelled of hot motor oil and metal.

They didn't have a real train; only a steam train that brought tourists but the business association was proud of it. Today, those tourists weren't roaming the sidewalks or clogging the patio at Café Trémolos. The heat had driven everyone indoors. Last year they complained of having no summer; the complaint this year was too much summer.

In the winter they'll forget the heat, Alvina thought. They'll forget the mirror river and the drone of the backhoes digging up the sidewalk and the glossy green trees. She stepped into the cool of the *dépanneur* to buy a foil-wrapped hamburger and a carton of chocolate milk for dinner. Last Monday's *Record* was piled on the counter.

Coral and Oliver Moon always said they loved her at the end of every phone call. But those calls had become few and far between. Alvina left a message with their service. They weren't easy to locate since they'd given up the apartment in Toronto to save on rent. Her forty-three-year-old parents lived a nomadic life of house-sitting and crashing with friends. She could check their Facebook page to find out where they were.

Missy had finally gone out, slamming the front door on her way. Missy had a habit of slamming the doors and cupboards when she was upset. Or angry. Or hungry. She was always dieting. Or broke. Or just pissed that Alvina was in the apartment taking up space— space that Missy could use if Alvina would only be a bit more sensitive to someone else's needs.

She sat on her bed and opened her hamburger. A vision of Del and never seeing him again landed in the pit of her stomach. Her appetite vanished. She carried her dinner to the fridge to save it for tomorrow's lunch. Dave said it would be a big day, packing up the office. There were a discouraging number of photos to be returned. Twenty days to clear out thirty years of junk.

The sky purpled. Hazy sunset circled the hills like a band of gold dust. Dave wasn't nearly as pleased after the meeting with Marlee Bremer as Alvina thought he would be. In fact, the whole tone of the meeting changed after Marlee decided to get rid of the trailer. It was like she'd been waiting for the right excuse and Alvina had given her one: *Secure the property*.

Consider it secured. Although, crushing it was probably not what DS Rompré had in mind. Marlee went even further by deciding to go public. She granted them an interview for this week's edition of the *Record*. She said she didn't want her motives for removing the trailer to be misconstrued. Dave claimed he was happy with the result when Alvina filed the copy, but he kept rubbing his mouth all afternoon. People were always saying they were one thing and then acting another.

As she wiped the makeup from her face, it seemed to Alvina that her life was peopled with paper dolls.

*The Stollerton Record—July 25, 2014—Stollerton, Quebec*

## SEVEN YEARS LATER: An exclusive
## interview with Marlee Bremer
by Alvina Moon

Marlee Bremer, wife of convicted murderer and rapist, Trey Bremer, wouldn't seem to have much to celebrate. "But I do," insists Mrs. Bremer. "We've turned a corner. It's been a very tough seven years but we've got through it and we're on the other side." Mrs. Bremer credits the love and the resilience of her children for keeping her focused and positive throughout her ordeal.

"The most difficult thing to cope with was the prejudice I encountered. Some individuals believed I knew what Trey had done and protected him. Nothing could be further from the truth. My concern was for my children who were small at the time, and my newborn. They were the ones I was protecting."

Seven years ago, local businessman, Trey Bremer was convicted of the rape and murder of nineteen-year-old Teresa Musgrave (née Fillion). The victim worked in the family home as an *au pair*. The scene of the horrific crime was an abandoned trailer called Oasis, a model manufactured in California in 1962 and owned by Bremer's company, Bremer Family Motors. The former CEO and pillar of the business community, has always maintained he is innocent of both charges. While his lawyers continue to seek an appeal for their client, his wife has plans of her own to make peace with the past. Mrs. Bremer is arranging to have the trailer towed from the lot and crushed. The riverfront property will be sold and profits from the sale will be donated to a local shelter for battered and abused women.

"It has taken me a long time to realize that I still have my life despite what my husband has done. When you have life, you have hope. Yesterday was a bad day. Tomorrow might be a better one. We carry on with the love and support of our community."

Mr. Bremer is currently serving a life sentence for murder in Bordeaux Prison, Montréal.

# FIVE

L AUGHTER SOUNDED from Café Trémolos across the street. Alvina set her satchel down and half-glanced over her shoulder at the crowd of young people gathered on the patio. Missy was there sipping a cappuccino along with Dagmar and a guy named Stu. Alvina had seen them together a few times at public events in the village. Stu was an artist too; tall, narrow and not good-looking although he had his moments. This morning wasn't one of them. His fierce black eyes were red-rimmed and his hair looked scorched. It stood up like spikes on an iron rail fence.

Alvina crouched down to search through her satchel for the key to the building. The front door was locked. Ray was usually in by now. Her tee-shirt was already sticking to her back.

Dagmar shouted. "Hey Alvina! What the hell?" She waved a copy of the *Record*. "Are you the rapist's real estate agent now? How much did Bremer pay you for this propaganda?"

Alvina steeled herself. This was the kind of thing Dave warned her about when he hired her. Small town reporters must never hang out in bars, air their dirty laundry, or rise to the bait. "It's not propaganda," she called back. "Marlee Bremer is selling the property. She's donating the money to a woman's shelter. Didn't you read it?"

Everyone on the patio had turned to listen to the exchange.

"Yes, I *read* it," said Dagmar. "There's an obvious agenda. The Bremers are big advertisers with the *Record*. Marlee Bremer knew more about her husband's criminal tendencies than she admitted and the *Record* is helping her whitewash that fact. She sucked you in and used you, Alvina. This story is a load of crap."

There was a smattering of applause. Alvina groped blindly for her key. "If you feel that strongly about it you should write a letter to the editor. To further the debate."

"What *debate*? This article is pure exploitation. Everyone is saying so. How do you think Del Musgrave is going to react when he reads this?"

Alvina looked up. Her hair was glued to her damp neck. "The story is about a woman getting on with her life. The property belongs to Bremer Motors. Del Musgrave's feelings don't enter into it one way or another."

Dagmar jumped off the patio and she crossed the street toward her.

Alvina's heart hammered in her throat. *Oh crap.* Dagmar's blonde hair was pulled up into a pony tail that bounced as she walked. Alvina thought distractedly of her mother's warnings not to wear her hair like that or it would fall out. Dagmar looked cool in Army surplus shorts and a pink tank top. The chains around her neck tinkled.

"Look," Alvina pleaded, jamming the key in the lock. "Marlee Bremer asked for the interview. Her husband committed a terrible crime, which is almost worse than being the victim if you think about it because she married the guy. She wants to do something to try to make it right. The story wasn't even about Del."

"Don't be dense," Dagmar said when she reached Alvina. "His wife was raped and murdered. It'll always be about him. He's a guy—guys are supposed to protect their women. Trey Bremer basically emasculated Del when he raped Teresa and there's Marlee Bremer claiming she didn't know her husband was a monster. The woman is sick."

A mother and her young daughter walked past them; both tiny and blonde, wearing identical rimless glasses and the same contented face. "I've got to get to work," Alvina said. "I'm not trying to duck this conversation, Dagmar. It's just I can't do anything about the article now. Present your argument in a letter to the editor and we'll publish it."

Dagmar leaned against the building. "Never mind all that. I wanted to talk to you about something else. Someone told me you left with Del after the Arts and Letters Festival. What was that all about?"

Alvina looked up, wary. "He was helping me with a story."

"What story?"

"The raft. He took me upriver to get photos."

"Oh, that story." Her chin lifted. "I only ask because I expected him to come by the Diotte that night. I was worried something might've happened to him. Del is complicated. We're involved but it's a complicated relationship. He's talked to me about what he's gone through. I'm a little protective of him."

Baffled, Alvina fumbled to open the door. The door knob was burning hot. "He doesn't need protecting from me if that's what you're worried about. I'm not trying to ... to *hurt* anybody. The raft was a spontaneous thing. I wouldn't have gone if I'd known you were waiting for him. We didn't talk about anything personal."

Dagmar straightened, already preparing to remove herself. "It's cool. I don't own him. But I wanted to warn you, he's not going to be happy with that article or you. Maybe you didn't mean to hurt him but you have. Don't expect anything more from him after this. Sorry."

She turned and skipped back across the street to the patio, her chains tinkling. Alvina pushed the door open and quickly stepped inside, feeling dizzy and high as if she'd been holding her breath. She climbed the shadowed stairs to the office.

Dave's office was silent. The hills across the river closed in. She opened the window. Cicadas whined in the heat and the birds shrilled; sharp, hot sounds new to her ear. There were no messages.

Alvina sat at her desk, took a breath and burst into tears.

The paper lay open on her desk. The headline swam. It was a good article. She was proud of it—of how she handled the subject—honestly and sensitively. The shelter would receive close to thirty-thousand dollars once the fees and taxes were settled. And as Marlee said, Trey's crime was the elephant in the room. As a businesswoman, she'd earned the community's respect but she hoped the article would bring her and the kids into reconciliation with their neighbours.

It was a good article.

That wasn't the problem. The problem was ... the very thing that was making her cry her eyes out ...

was Dagmar leaning against the building full of pity and good-will, informing Alvina that she and Del Musgrave were involved in a sexual relationship. She wasn't disappointed by the news, just discouraged. And something else she couldn't name. It had to do with how she felt after being with Del on the river. Miserable with her life in a way she couldn't explain.

He would hate her now because of the article. Regret he'd ever laid eyes on her. She wished he'd just sent her away bleeding that first day so she didn't have to know he even existed. Better to have an infected leg than this restless, lost … nothingness.

Alvina sat in the dust motes and silence. People were too painful to be around these days anyway. They brought out the sharp little knives in her brain.

Her eyes roamed over the empty office.

Abruptly, she pushed her chair back, grabbed the keys to the van from Dave's desk, and pounded down the stairs into the blistering heat.

DEL MUSGRAVE'S home was buried in a heavily forested corner south of the Paugan Falls. Alvina caught glimpses of the river on the drive up before crossing the iron-work bridge at Martingale to continue north on a road that was rarely used. A dirt road, originally cut for logging trucks, was now used as an access road to hunting camps in the area.

The day tipped into afternoon, a white hot day. The van was stifling even with the windows down. The trees, sky and earth drained of colour until they were as white as the sun. A symptom of stress, she thought. Her stress increased as she turned onto his drive. He was going to tell her that he couldn't trust her. That he had made a mistake in thinking he could.

The van scraped against the thick bush crowding either side of the narrow lane leading to his home. The road, which was more like a cow track, broke open to a meadow that might have been a field at one time. Alvina squinted through the windshield. A pile of peeled logs were stacked in the meadow's overgrowth. And there was a cabin, a rectangle of water-stained plywood with a mossy shingled roof. It looked as though it was held together with electrical tape.

She put the van in park and turned off the motor. The engine ticked in the silence. Dave had likened Del Musgrave to Tom Thomson, a genius with paint and the wilderness. A guy with a screw loose.

Alvina climbed out of the van. The smell of scorched earth rose to her nose. The sky was a mirror, too hot to move. Her eyes flicked to the cabin's large picture window that faced the meadow and she caught sight of his reflection in the glass. Del was painting at the edge of the forest, half-hidden by the trees, shaded and cool. His tee-shirt hung from his belt. Long muscles in his back bunched and flexed as he moved the brush from palette to canvas. So intense was his concentration that he didn't hear her approach. She walked toward him, wading into the tall grasses. The sun beat the meadow with a numbing heat. It was then that she saw the thin white scars in sharp relief against his tan. Three of them: two were vertical from shoulder to ribcage and one cut horizontally across his lower back. Thin and silvery as fishing line. But fishing line didn't cause those wounds.

"Del?"

Del turned. A series of expressions came through

his posture; tightening in his shoulders, the stiff-necked twisting to look at her, his mouth repressing irritation.

"Alvina." His jaw twitched. He turned back to the easel.

"I'm sorry to interrupt you. It's important."

"When I'm working, nothing is important." Del stabbed at the canvas with sharp angry strokes and then set the brush down, as though restraining himself. "I thought you knew that."

He must have read the article. She felt sick. Seeing him was like being on one of those thrill rides she hated so much when she was a kid. Needing to see him and being scared to death to see him at the same time. A bundle of nerves, Alvina clutched her arms about her waist, acutely aware of how immature she looked. She'd worn her skinny jeans and a long tee-shirt with a picture of Woodward and Bernstein silk-screened on the front, a gift from her dad when she graduated from Ryerson's School of Journalism.

"How did you find out where I lived?" Del pulled the tee-shirt from his belt and yanked it over his head. The long grasses rustled as he came toward her.

"Dave has a map of the river in the van for his fishing trips. The roads aren't marked but I figured out which was yours from where your dock was in relation to the bridge at Martingale."

"I prefer to be alone when I'm painting. Some people don't understand that. They think everyone is like them and need to be at the centre of things. They think they're doing you a big favour by coming around. Are you one of those people?"

Pricks of light burst behind her eyes. "No, I'm not one of those people. I only came to explain about the article in the paper."

He looked puzzled. "I picked up the *Record* to see how your raft photos turned out. I didn't look at anything else." Del crossed his arms over his chest. "What article are you talking about?"

Alvina wiped her face with the back of her hand, trying to come up with the words to explain. "It was an interview with Marlee Bremer. When you took me in your boat, I had no idea that was going to happen. I swear I didn't. We had a meeting with her about the paper and then out of the blue she decides to clear the air about her husband. Your name wasn't mentioned. The main point of the article was Marlee's decision to sell the property. She's having the trailer towed away and crushed."

Del went as still as the summer sky.

"There won't be any more stories after this one, I promise." She might as well be talking to the air. He wouldn't look at her. "The *Record* is being sold. The new owners are MetMedia and their focus isn't local. So that's the end of it." Alvina sucked in a breath. "I am sorry about the trailer. I know what it meant to you."

"It's fine. Thanks for letting me know." Del jerked his thumb toward the easel and the fringe of forest behind him. "Look, if you don't mind, I have to get back to work."

"Yes, of course. I'm sorry I bothered you. I'm just really sorry about the whole thing," she added miserably.

He stared at her, irritated and puzzled, as though he couldn't make her out and wasn't sure he wanted to. And then he was in front of her, standing very close. His eyes and skin were brilliant. "You're always apologizing.

Are you afraid of what I might do?"

Her face burned but she looked him in the eye. "Yes."

"Why?"

"Because I'm a reporter and you don't trust people like me. I didn't trick you or lie to you the other night."

"That's not what I meant. I meant, why are you afraid of me?"

The breeze that curled over them had the weight of a handkerchief. Heat bugs sawed the air. Alvina's voice barely crawled above a whisper. "Because you might decide to sue the paper."

"And that's all you're worried about?"

"Yes." A lie. The paper didn't worry her at all. It was becoming harder and harder to look at him.

"I'm not going to sue the paper."

Alvina nodded, but strangely, there was no relief from the tension between them. "Then I guess that's it. I'm sorry for the trouble. I better get going. It was good talking to you again."

Del walked her to the van. "Thanks for stopping by." As though she had paid him a social call. "I don't mind if you want to come back sometime and talk some more. If you feel like getting away and you don't mind the quiet, I don't mind seeing you again."

The thrill, the deeply satisfying warming thrill of those simple, polite words cheered her and strengthened her like nothing else could. Alvina's guilt and fear evaporated like breath on ice crystals.


HER FIRST task was to bag and dispose of the dead squirrels. To clear out the stench. People don't want to encounter that sort of thing when they come to look a property. Marlee collected Stanley's sand pail from the back of the Blazer, filled it with water from the river and flushed away the decomposed hair and bone.

The boys were splashing in the river. Violet had wanted to go swimming and really it was perfectly safe as long as the children wore their life jackets. Trust Violet to refuse to wear hers. The current was fast further out. Trey would disapprove. But what choice did she have? Violet was stubborn and Marlee couldn't be in two places at once.

She stood in the dim trailer with the dripping bucket in her hand. She didn't know what she would find when she came here. The police tape was gone. The pool of blood was still on the bed. Marlee took a cautious step toward it. Why wouldn't the police have the decency to clean that up? The river was right there —easiest thing in the world to get a bucket and slosh some water over it. As Marlee drew closer she could see that the blood pool was only a stain. The police cleanup crew must have hosed the rest away. Of course they wouldn't leave a deadly pool of blood behind. The smell wouldn't be very nice. Still, they didn't do a very good job of getting rid of it. It was hard to breathe. The air was mouldy and foul.

That stain worried her. It would take some elbow grease to get it out. Marlee eyed it critically. The white noise of the highway was troubling; she didn't like sounds pushing in on her when she needed to think. Cicadas whined outside, high and long, a summer sound she had forgotten. There was a smear of something else on the blue and green fabric, thin and white like watery glue. It had dried and was crumbly to the touch.

Cold rage rose up in her core.

Marlee always believed that if it ever happened to her she'd know what to do, and then it did and she had no idea. Maybe if her mother had been around she could have advised her. And then she thought, no, it was too late to reinvent what her mother was.

She stumbled away from the bed to the doorway, leaned against the frame for support and closed her eyes. She thought about her house, concentrating her mind on each room. Thinking about her house calmed her down, restored her to the woman she knew she was deep inside.

The sun warmed her face. She was wearing her scrubby clothes, the ones she reserved for her cleaning days: a pair of yellow Capri slacks, Ked running shoes, and a green sleeveless blouse that she had tied at her trim waist. Her freshly styled hair was protected by a green scarf. The day was a scorcher, but not with the cloying heat of yesterday. The forest fires were out, or maybe the wind had changed direction. She should watch the news tonight to find out what was going on.

This campsite was where she and Trey first met. She was thirteen, he was fifteen. Her mother hated him. Marlee loved him.

Maybe it was better not to think back to their beginning. If she had it to do over again she'd pick an honest boy over a good-looking one. She'd been with Trey for so many years she forgot the impact his looks had on women. Would a man like that have to force himself on a nineteen-year-old girl? It would be possible to convince a new jury that the sex act was consensual. Trey's lawyers thought so anyway. They were convinced the sexual behaviours specialist could explain what happened that night and render it palatable enough to win her husband an acquittal.

So Marlee fired them. She had her reasons and they were good reasons too—ones she did not feel obligated to explain to M. François Nault. "There is hope, Madame Bremer." Hope wasn't good enough, she told him. "I have three children to provide for. I can't risk their futures gambling on Trey's release. It's up to Trey now. If he wants parole, he'll have to tell them the truth about what happened that night and accept treatment." And by the way, she was having the trailer destroyed.

For seven years Trey had had the attention of his lawyers and the media hanging onto every sanctimonious declaration of innocence he made. He had his righteous indignation and his smug lies, leaving her to cope with the humiliation of being his wife. He had told the court, the police, the judge and the jury that their teenage babysitter liked rough sex. Teresa would do things for him that his wife wouldn't. And their eyes had gone to Marlee sitting in the courtroom. Eight months pregnant. Her legs like sausages; her hair and skin, thin and paper dry. They only had to look at her. Oh, but that's not all. Trey had to take her humiliation one step further—he told them he fell in love with Teresa. He couldn't have hurt her—he was in love with her.

Those words, spoken in open court and repeated in every newspaper and news report covering the trial, *I fell in love with her*; those words were like the tide. Some days they swallowed her whole. Other days they just sounded in her brain like a steady white noise. *I fell in love with her.* And everything that once held her together, her indestructible life with Trey, had crumbled like dried putty.

They were having a baby—a baby he said he wanted. She ran a tight ship—Trey knew that. He had nothing to complain about. Other women forced their husbands to get up in the night with sick toddlers and teething babies but she didn't. A tight ship.

He probably wished she were dead instead of Teresa.

Marlee was having trouble breathing. The yellowed walls of the trailer seemed to pull in close and sinister. She strained to look past the dirt on the floors and the cobwebs hanging from the ceiling. The trailer was disgusting. Filth on the bed and God knows what was growing under the sink. She wasn't going to let her children to grow up in their father's filth. It didn't matter how much she scrubbed, the dirt would always take control.

There was a splash in the distance. Marlee peered into the glare bouncing off the water. The boys seemed very far away. It was like looking through the wrong end of binoculars at tiny bugs with padded orange bodies and stick legs and arms. At this great distance if anything went wrong, it would impossible to reach them in time. If anything should happen. Harry couldn't fight that current.

A child screamed. Marlee gripped the door frame.

It would serve him right. It would. The pain would leave her and enter him. "He'd know too," she muttered. "He'd know why I did it. He'd know he was one hundred percent responsible."

"Marlee! What the hell are you doing?"

Trey stood at the open door of the trailer carrying two small children, dripping water.

"I'm cleaning the trailer. Why, what's the problem?"

He screwed up his face like he did before he yelled

at one of his employees. "The problem is I drive up and the kids are in the river and you are nowhere in sight. If I hadn't arrived when I did, they would've been swept downstream."

Marlee stared. She shook her head still trying to understand. "What are you doing here? You're supposed to be in prison."

"For God's sake, Marlee! Didn't you hear what I just said? The kids could have drowned. What is the matter with you?"

She blinked and looked at the foam mattress he had used as a bed. "Isn't it obvious?" She made a sweeping gesture with her hand. Was he really going to pretend he didn't know?

Trey stood stock still, his anger crumpling to fear. Marlee squinted. The light around him and the children was blinding. They drifted away, fading into the white summer sun. Leaving her behind in a dark earthy hole, all alone, just her and the baby who wasn't born yet.

"Mom, who are you talking to?"

Marlee blinked. Violet was standing in the driveway wrapped in a towel. Wide grey eyes that were the image of Trey's. Her wet bare feet were covered in brown pine needles.

"Clean those off before you come in," she said mechanically.

"I don't want to come in." Violet's shoulders were lightly sunburned. Her hair was kinked and damp. "When's lunch? I'm hungry."

*Lunch.* Her kitchen, and then her house came into her mind room-by-room; the paint colours, the furniture and the white cotton sheets, rescuing her from madness. And then suddenly Marlee's voice cut the air like a gunshot, fired by fear. "Stanley—Harry!"

"What!" Harry called back.

*Oh thank god thank god.* Her sons were playing on the swimming rock, alive, still alive. The boys were not drowned. Not dead. None of it was real, only a dream, a terrible daydream.

Marlee's voice shook with gratitude and shame. "We're going home," she called and then turned to her daughter. "Go help your brothers while I lock up here." She peered over her shoulder into the dim of the trailer, half-expecting to see the hallucination in material form. This place was poisonous.

Violet shouted. "Hey Mom, is this trailer the one with the silver palm tree on it?" She was trotting backwards, lifting her bare feet over broken chunks of tarmac.

Marlee stepped out of the trailer, grasped the chrome handle and slammed the door shut. "Yes, but it's not silver, it's chrome, a chrome palm tree on the back. It's the manufacturer's logo. Now watch where you're going before you trip and fall."

She set her mouth. Violet was just a little girl back then but obviously she still remembered. Marlee didn't care how it might hurt Trey's chances for an appeal—she was going to have this poisonous memory towed out of their lives and destroyed. Marlee fished the keys out of her pocket and locked the door. The pink and white Oasis looked drab and discarded in the late afternoon sun. How glamorous it had looked when she'd first laid eyes on it. Trey's grandparents were crazy about everything Californian.

The carpet of pine needles under her feet smelled dry and dirty hot. She inhaled deeply and experienced a sense of freedom welling up inside her. A bird wheeled overhead and cawed.

"Harry, Violet, Stanley! I have to go to the village to pick up some things for your lunch but if you hurry we'll get ice cream cones from Sur La Lune."

As her children gathered their belongings, Marlee turned to gaze one last time at the trailer and take a moment to remember the girl who had died here. Perhaps Teresa's last thoughts weren't of the man, or of love or regret or anything that she imagined death to contain. Marlee hoped there wasn't pain. She hoped that each thin fraction of life that was left to Teresa that night was filled with remembering the sweet pleasures of living. The smell of clean fresh water on her heated skin and the summer wind in her hair. Marlee hoped as Teresa took her last breath that there was peace.

Seven years ago in this very place, the world kept spinning, business as usual, even as another soul was flung off the planet.

Marlee walked back to the car, smiling victoriously.

# SIX

ALVINA MOON opened to the door to the office, juggling her keys, lunch and camera bag and almost missed seeing the envelope on the floor. She scooped it up and poked her head into the Vibe. "When are you closing up for vacation, Ray?"

"Next week. Hallelujah. What have you got there?" Ray nodded at the envelope.

Alvina flipped it over. Penned in green ink on the front: *Alvina Moon. Private.* "It's for me. A classified, I guess. The old people can't make the stairs in this heat and they haven't got a clue how to send an email. I had a call yesterday from a lady in the senior's home. She said she tried to send me a classified ad but it just wouldn't take. I asked her, what wouldn't take? She says, the computer."

Ray laughed.

Alvina peered up the stairs. "Has Dave come in yet?"

"Nope. You're on your lonesome. Give me a shout if the crowd gets out of control."

They both laughed although it wasn't funny. At the end of August she was out of a job.

The heat in the office was deadly. The morning sun had already cooked the building. There was only one message on the answering machine. She pressed PLAY and Dave Gomer's voice filled the room much as his bulk did when he was there.

"I won't be in, Moon. I'm fishing but I've got my cell phone with me in case there's an emergency. Call Mavis Brant back and tell her we'll cover the fucking Pickerel Supper if she buys a fucking ad. We're not running a charity here. That's all. Stay cool."

An electronic voice followed informing Alvina when the call came in. The machine was so old it still used miniature tape cassettes. Dave claimed it was more convenient than voicemail for screening calls. Alvina tried to upgrade the system once, explaining that all he had to do was look at the display panel on his phone to see who was calling before he picked up. Dave balked. He could hear who was calling with an answering machine couldn't he? What if he was away from the goddamned display panel? What if he couldn't find his glasses? The answering machine could not be improved upon. And that was the end of that.

She set her lunch on the reception desk and turned to the window. The window was as old as the building itself. It took muscle to get it open. The keening of cicadas and redwing black birds floated in on puff of sultry morning air.

Alvina sat at her desk and sliced open the envelope with the letter opener. Nothing inside but a ruled sheet of paper folded in half. The phone rang and she answered it, took down the caller's classified ad and then booted up the computer. She made a pot of coffee. The oscillating fan behind her grunted and wheezed. Hot air moved over her neck. Alvina removed the slip of paper. The author had used green ink. The penmanship looked immature.

*Where did he get the flashlight?*

Alvina flipped the note over. No signature. She picked up the envelope. No name, return address or identifying marks of any kind. Where did *who* get the flashlight? She opened the story file on the computer and typed FLASHLIGHT in the search function. There were three hits: a story on the Stollerton Scouts, another on what to stock in an emergency kit. The third was the murder of Teresa Musgrave. A flashlight was found at the scene.

The hair on the back of Alvina's neck prickled. She clicked on the file icon. Dave had covered the trial but strangely, there wasn't a lot of copy considering the interest there must have been in the story. It didn't take Alvina long to read everything she could find on the hard drive. She picked up the phone and punched in Dave's cell number.

"This had better be an emergency," he said. "I had a pike on the line."

"I found an envelope on the floor this morning. I thought it was a classified but there's a note inside. It says 'Where did he get the flashlight?' I did a search and there are only three stories we've done with the word 'flashlight' in the copy. One was the murder of Teresa Musgrave."

Dave grunted. "Weird. You'd think there'd be more than that considering the number of power failures we get in the hills."

"The clip I'm looking at says a flashlight found at the scene was believed to be the murder weapon."

"That's correct. Trey grabbed it in the heat of the moment to bash Teresa's skull in. The Crime Scene Unit found it in the trailer under the table. It was covered in Teresa's blood and hair and Trey's fingerprints."

"And they were able to prove that the flashlight was his?"

"They didn't have to. The girl was dead and his prints were on the weapon."

Alvina scanned the copy on her computer screen. "And I guess her blood was on his clothing."

"Yes and no. Trey testified he came home and hung the suit he was wearing that day in the laundry room. Marlee said she took it to the drycleaner's but they had no record of it and Marlee couldn't produce the claim chit. So big deal, lots of people lose their claim chits and lots of drycleaners lose suits. That's reasonable doubt. But CSU went back to the crime scene and found the burned remains of a suit in the fire pit. It was a match to the fibers they found in the trailer. Trey was the last one to see the girl alive, he burned the clothes he was wearing that day and his prints and DNA were all over the girl and the trailer."

"But Dave—Trey Bremer wouldn't have had a flashlight with him. It was early July. It doesn't get dark until nine o'clock. If he brought Teresa to the trailer between five and six o'clock he wouldn't have needed a flashlight to see where he was going. It's broad daylight at that hour. So where did the flashlight come from?"

"Maybe it was already there."

"I doubt it. I was in that trailer. It's been empty for two decades. The kitchen drawers were swollen shut in the humidity. I couldn't get them open. Even if the flashlight had been left behind, how did Bremer know that it was? He rapes her and then searches the cupboards to find a weapon to kill her? That makes no sense."

Dave's breathing was noisy. Dave Gomer always

sounded like he was either about to blow a gasket or have a heart attack, Alvina never knew which. "Who sent the note?"

"I don't know. There's just my name on the envelope. No return address. Nothing inside except a slip of paper with the message. No signature. It is written in green ink."

"OK—I get it now. Somebody's trying to make trouble for Marlee. That interview she gave was bound to flush out the crackpots. This is some shit-disturber's idea of a joke."

"I think whoever sent it is trying to clear Trey Bremer. It could be worth checking out."

Dave's voice was sharp. "Trey Bremer is a killer. He had a flashlight. He bashed Teresa's brains in with it. End of story. And what do you mean you couldn't get the kitchen drawers open? It isn't enough you break into Bremer property you had to go snooping through their stuff? Goddamn it, I don't need this aggravation right now, Moon. The deal with MetMedia isn't finalized. You know what I'm up against."

"I think Marlee Bremer would be glad we followed up on this tip if it led to proving her husband's innocence." Alvina's pulse hammered at her neck. Ray was right—she didn't have the balls to go after a story if this is what it took.

"Trey Bremer is not innocent!" She heard Dave suck in a deep raspy breath. "Let me explain something to you. Seven years ago I could've sold this story a hundred times over to the wire services. Okay? I wouldn't do it. I'd put that woman through enough. I'm not doing it to her again. You heard how this has affected Violet Bremer—ask her how she'll enjoy starting school in the fall with her father's crime back in the news. You can take my word for it because I was *there*—this tip of yours is bullshit. You're being played, Alvina. Someone sure has your number. You're not dragging the *Record* into this."

Alvina moistened her lips and pressed her fingers to her eyes. Her head throbbed. "So what do you want me to do about this note? Should I give it to the cops?"

"Hell, no! Put it in the shredder and forget about it!"

"Okay, okay, fine that's all I needed to know."

She looked at the note and the envelope with her name on it. It couldn't be that much of a mystery if Bremer's lawyers didn't question where the flashlight came from at the trial. There must be a reasonable explanation for where it came from. Alvina turned on the shredder and slid the page on the intake shelf. The motor rumbled.

"It's strange that he left it at the scene," she said mutinously. "He kills the girl to cover up the rape and then leaves the weapon for the police to find. It's sort of counter-productive."

"There was a struggle, he popped her one and when she screamed holy hell, he lost control. The CSU guys pieced it together. Trey dropped the flashlight after killing her and it rolled under the table. Maybe he couldn't find it or he panicked and left it behind. The Crown's theory was that he intended to come back the next morning to clean up his mess, but Marlee took off to run errands and he was stuck at home looking after the kids."

"How does a person kill someone with a flashlight? They're not that heavy."

"The old ones were. This one was constructed out of

metal. It had a long black handle like a truncheon, like a cop would carry. There was a wide lamp at one end. They don't make them like that anymore."

"You wouldn't find a flashlight like that in most households. Did they circulate a photo?"

"Alvina," Dave sighed, "the police weren't eager to make an open-and-shut case complicated by asking hypothetical questions of the general population."

"But he denies committing the crime. He's never admitted his guilt."

"And that proves what exactly? Bremer is a classic narcissist. He can't believe he didn't get away with rape and murder. He can't believe we aren't buying every word he says. You have to understand, I knew the guy. To Trey's way of thinking, he *isn't* guilty. Teresa should have put out for him, that's how he sees it. She provoked him. He's an upstanding businessman—we should turn a blind eye. The fact that society doesn't agree with him pisses him off. Do you see what I'm saying? Not everyone is who they claim to be."

"No. Of course not."

"Are you going to shred that note like I asked you?"

"Yes, Dave. I'm doing it now. Can't you hear the shredder going?"

"Good girl."

Dave hung up.

*Good girl.* The summer Alvina turned ten her parents took a job with a theatre troupe touring Europe. They left her in the care of some actor friends of theirs. For eight weeks, Alvina was the best behaved kid those people ever saw. No trouble at all. Good girl her father had said when he heard their praise.

Oliver Moon didn't know what he was talking about.

Alvina wasn't good—she was petrified. Nothing terrible happened to her, if being abandoned didn't count. Her parents' friends weren't thrilled to have a ten-year-old for the summer. They tried not to let it show but they had no children of their own. None of her parents' friends had kids back then. They agreed to take responsibility for her, which wasn't the same as wanting her around. Of course she was a good girl. She has been a good girl for thirteen years.

The envelope had her name on it. Whoever sent it was either messing with her or trying to tell her something. Which was it?

Didn't matter—it was too risky to pursue. Dave made his feelings clear and she couldn't afford to alienate him right now. She needed his connections with editors to get a job at another paper.

But what if it wasn't bullshit? This could be a big story. A very big story.

Impulsively, Alvina snatched the note off the shredder and stuck it back in the envelope. She flipped the switch and the motor died. Her heart was pounding. She tucked the envelope inside her camera case and turned back to the computer screen.

This is crazy, she thought. Where did he get the flashlight? Why ask that question of all questions, and why ask it anonymously? Dave said someone was trying to make trouble for Marlee Bremer. But how could that question make trouble?

There was a fluttering in the pit of her stomach. Nine times out of ten, this is the kind of question a person asks when they already know the answer.

# SEVEN

LVINA FOUND Marlee Bremer at Café Trémolos enjoying coffee and a croissant on Sunday, just as she said she did when Violet was at church. Mrs. Bremer wasn't thrilled to see Alvina—that much was obvious. The expression in her eyes was cold, formal and bored. Alvina suppressed the leap of nerves in her stomach.

"Would this be a convenient time to ask you some questions about the murder of Teresa Musgrave?"

The boys, Harry and Stanley, were outside on the patio watching the teenagers horsing around on the river raft. The owner of the Chateau Diotte had managed to force its removal from his dock. Undaunted, the kids had floated it downriver to Café Trémolos where the owners were more amenable to youth protest. Besides, most of the kids camping out on the raft were their summer staff employees. This was one way to make sure they got to work on time.

"Convenient?" Marlee's laugh was hollow. "I doubt it. Where is this coming from? Does Dave know you're here?"

"Yes." This was a lie. When Dave found out, he'd freak. Alvina's face grew hot. "There are a couple of follow-up questions I wanted to ask you for the retrospective Dave is planning for the final issue. It's a sort of 'where-are-they-now' of the biggest stories the *Record* has covered ... that kind of thing ... I'm really sorry."

"So am I. I was under the impression the interview I gave you people last week was the end of it. Dave never said anything about a follow-up. What does that mean? A follow-up to what?"

"Loosely, the idea we had was to report on Trey's appeal process and some of the issues his lawyers will be raising."

"Such as ...?"

Alvina pretended to consult her notepad. "Where did he get the flashlight?"

The silence that followed stretched on too long to be anything but deliberate.

"It's a question that has surfaced," Alvina said. Her lips were dry. "I wondered if you knew the answer."

Marlee sat back, her brows raised. "Everyone knows the answer, Alvina. Trey found the flashlight he used to murder that girl in the trailer. I'm sorry to be short with you, but did you seriously track me down on a Sunday to ask me *that*?"

"You saw the flashlight in the trailer before the murder? It's just I'm trying to get confirmation the flashlight was definitely in the trailer when your husband brought Teresa there and I can't find it in any of the news clippings."

"To be perfectly honest, I haven't been inside that trailer since I was a teenager. I'd almost forgotten the company was the registered owner. The property taxes on it are paid out of the dealership's account but our financial officer takes care of that. I don't know if there was a flashlight in the trailer at the time of the murder. I assume the police have already answered that question as part of their investigation. I'm sorry, I can't help you."

Stonewalled. "I understand. Thanks anyway. I'm sorry I bothered you."

Alvina's eyes strayed to the teenagers drinking beer on the raft. The beer bottles were stupid, she thought. The complaints will pour in to the *Record* tomorrow: *Local youth show blatant disregard for the sanctity of the Gatineau River!*

Scratch that. In another three weeks, *The Stollerton Record* would be defunct. It didn't matter how hard they'd worked or the good they had done in the community or whose toes they didn't step on—the paper was ignored to death. Alvina had nothing to lose. What could Marlee do—fire her? Run her out of town? She wasn't aware of it at the time; Alvina only became conscious of it weeks later, but this was the moment she became dangerous.

"What was Teresa like?" Heat prickled the back of her neck. "I'm sorry if that's an offensive question. I don't mean it to be. I'm not trying to upset you."

"And yet you ask offensive questions." Marlee wiped a dot of milk foam from the table with her napkin. "I'm ashamed to say that I don't remember. There was a time when I was sure I'd never think about anything else but life is pretty relentless. I forgot Teresa Musgrave by inches. Certain sights or smells used to trigger a memory. Now even those have faded."

"Dave said she was very beautiful."

"Did he? I wasn't aware that he gave her looks any notice."

"He was the one who recommended Teresa wasn't he?"

"Yes, he was. Bremer Motors was undergoing corporate restructuring that summer. Trey had meetings at the head office in Toronto; I was alone a lot with the children. Dave suggested we hire Teresa. He gave her a glowing reference."

Marlee's eyes flicked to her boys outside on the patio.

"I keep wondering about the flashlight," Alvina said, awkwardly bringing the conversation back around. "It's just that if it wasn't in the trailer, how did investigators connect your husband to the murder weapon? Did Trey own a flashlight like that?"

"Not to my knowledge, but it could have come from the service bay at the dealership. He could have put it in the glove compartment of his car at some point and forgot about it. I'm not suggesting his murdering Teresa was premeditated. But once the damage was done, he must have believed he had no choice but to kill her. Either that or he suffered a psychotic break."

Horror tickled Alvina's spine. "Was that a possibility?"

"Not according to the Crown. Trey was examined by a court-appointed psychiatrist and found to be in his right mind and able to stand trial. Meaning he could distinguish the difference between right and wrong, which I doubt. I don't think any human being can tell right from wrong. I'm not talking about the law—Trey broke the law—but when he broke it did he know he was committing a moral crime as well? He was an immoral man who believed himself moral. How can the law control a person like that? Right and wrong meant nothing to him that night."

"He burned the suit he was wearing. I don't know ... that sounds pretty calculated."

Marlee methodically wiped croissant crumbs from her fingers with the napkin. "You wouldn't think so if you'd seen his reaction when the police asked him about it. Nothing could have been less calculated. It was a light grey suit, summer weight, very expensive—he was stunned they were able to identify it from the fibers in the trailer. Did he own such a suit? Of course he did. He was wearing it the day he drove Teresa home. I remembered telling him he should change first but Teresa seemed to be in a hurry to get going so off they went. Trey told the police he'd left it in the laundry room to be dry-cleaned. I distinctly remember being in the laundry room on Saturday morning and there was no grey suit. The homicide investigator I spoke to was Detective Sergeant Giroux. I told him I remembered taking it to the dry-cleaners."

Alvina cleared her throat. "You lied because you believed your husband was innocent? Please, don't answer if you think it will get you into trouble."

"It won't. Not anymore." Marlee's voice was flat. "Yes, I believed Trey was innocent. He told me he had taken Teresa to the trailer because she wanted to rent it; she was planning to leave Del. I believed him. I thought he'd been caught in the middle of a domestic situation."

"Teresa was going to leave Del?" The news alarmed Alvina although there was no reason it should. "Did anyone else know about this?"

"I doubt it. Trey probably made it up. Maybe it was true. I don't know. He'd lied about everything else so I have no reason to believe even that part of his story was true." Marlee's mouth tightened. "One lie led to another and another. All I had to do was pretend to believe him. All I had to do was confirm his story about the suit and he'd be home free. It's not as easy as it sounds to keep a fiction like that going. There are dozens of little intimacies to be got through in a marriage." Her head lifted. "I couldn't take it anymore. The police were searching for the suit at the dry-cleaners. I contacted the officer in charge of the investigation and retracted my statement. There was such a look of pity on his face. Detective Sergeant Giroux thought I was too addled by pregnancy to remember my own name much less which suits I had taken in that morning. I let him believe what he wanted to believe."

Alvina tucked her hair behind her ears. She glanced at her notes. "But when you didn't find the suit in the laundry room—but Trey told the police that's where he'd put it—you must have realized then that he was guilty."

"No, sadly, I didn't. When you don't want to see something, you won't. I was asleep in Harry's room the night Teresa was murdered; I didn't hear Trey come home. I assumed he'd hung his suit in the closet in our bedroom. My mind didn't immediately leap to murder when he told police he'd put it in the laundry room. I didn't want my husband to be a rapist and a murderer. I believed there had to be a rational explanation. Unfortunately, I was wrong. They found the charred remnants of Trey's suit in a stone fire pit near the crime scene."

The corners of Marlee's eyes pulled tight. "How's that for a where-are-they-now story? This is where the rich and privileged Bremer family are now, brought down by 'bloody thoughts and violent pace.' That's from *Othello*. However, unlike the Moor, Trey won't admit he did anything wrong, including rape, even after they found his semen in the girl's body and there was only one way that could have happened."

There were actually two ways, Alvina thought.

And then it was clear. She sat very still as though any movement would shake loose what she was thinking and reveal it on her face. Teresa didn't fight back. Dave's exact words were: *Or she didn't want to.* Not that she *couldn't* as in her life was threatened—but she *didn't want* to.

"Did you ever regret hiring her?" Alvina asked abruptly.

Marlee fixed Alvina with a thoughtful stare. "I believe what you are asking me is did I blame her for what happened. No, I didn't. But I did regret hiring her. Teresa had only ever worked in the bar. I assume that's why Dave recommended her so enthusiastically. His ex-wife, Dot was a co-worker of mine at the dental clinic before Violet was born. A certain loyalty was expected. In a nutshell, I hired Teresa to make other people happy. No good deed goes unpunished."

"Maybe she wasn't qualified," Alvina said and reddened, "but people help people get jobs. You advertised for an *au pair* and Dave was only trying to help her out by getting her foot in the door. You'd never have hired her otherwise."

Marlee took a sip of the large latte in front of her. "There is some truth to that. Did you know Dave sobered up after she was murdered? The fact is—no matter what your boss has told you—I did not advertise for an *au pair*. Trey and I discussed it; I said a teenager would only add to my workload and be of no use with the children. It was Dave who sold me on the idea more for Trey's peace of mind than for mine. I had a touch of edema. He said Trey worried about leaving me alone with the kids when he had to travel. I gave in to keep everyone happy."

Alvina blinked. *Never repeat what's said in the office.* How many times did Dave have to tell her that? "I must have mixed you up with someone else," she said. "I do that. My mistake."

She set her notes on the table. There was one more question she wanted to ask but Marlee Bremer wouldn't answer if she thought she'd see it in print. No one would.

"Mrs. Bremer, you were pregnant and the dealership was undergoing changes. Your marriage must have been under a lot of pressure. Stress does crazy things to people. I get that. I'm not suggesting an affair, but was Trey the sort of man who would give into the temptation to cheat if he was under stress? It could explain why he's convinced he's innocent."

Marlee set her coffee cup down with an air of deliberation. The smile on her face was stiff. "These are strange times we're living in. Don't you find? No, of course you don't. You're too young. Maybe Violet's religion is getting to me. Rationalizations don't comfort me like they used to. We do what we want to do and then we're upset when we have to live with the consequences. Did Trey cheat on me with Teresa? If rape can be defined as cheating, the answer is to your question is yes. I am convinced he raped her. Whether he acted under stress, a breakdown, a lapse in judgment, or out of just plain greed and entitlement, I don't know. We all made bad decisions that summer out of fear and selfishness. I include Teresa in that. She was gullible and vain enough for Trey's purpose. The kind of girl who'd let a married man take her to a trailer. But I've been told that it's wrong to blame the victim for getting herself into a scrape." Marlee smiled thinly. "Certain behaviours set certain events in motion. This conversation is setting in motion something else again, something none of us may like. Why did you ask me about the flashlight?"

Alvina pretended to refer to her notes. "It came up in discussion. I wondered where it came from because of the time of the year. It doesn't get dark in the summer months until late. A flashlight isn't what I expected."

"I see." Marlee nodded. "Trey's lawyers asked the same question of the Crown. From what I can recall of the original investigation, the murder weapon likely came from the service bay at the dealership. It was a long time ago, Alvina. Seven years. I doubt if anyone would consider it a valid line of inquiry now." She abruptly rose to her feet. "If you'll excuse me, it's time to round up the boys and pick Violet up at church."

"Oh sure, of course. Thank you for speaking to me." Alvina stood up awkwardly to shake hands as Dave had taught her to do at the end of an interview. "Tell Violet I said hi."

Marlee took Alvina's hand and looked at her closely. "There is something I want to ask you now. It's an awkward question but that only seems fair after I've answered yours. Ever since I met you at my house with Dave, I've been wondering if I should warn you. Are you dating Del Musgrave?" Marlee shook her head. "Never mind, you don't have to answer. I can read it on your face. Only—I'm not your mother, I have no right to give advice—but if I were your mother, I'd say stay well away. I don't expect you to agree. Maybe Del has changed, I don't know. The Del Musgrave I remember was handsome, gifted, and completely unpredictable. That kind of man is very hard for a young woman to resist. I had my own irresistible mystery man when I was your age. I married him."

"It's not like that with Del. I barely know him."

Marlee nodded but Alvina could tell she didn't believe her.

"I hope you do everything you can to keep it that way. This is kindly meant. If you are in any danger of becoming attached to Del Musgrave—that is not something you want."

"Oh no, no—I'm not—please don't think that." Alvina sputtered. "He's involved—he has a girlfriend. Dagmar Weibe. She's an artist. So, no worries, there's no chance of me becoming attached." She grabbed her notepad and shoved it in her bag, avoiding Marlee's gaze.

"Oh! I didn't realize. I don't know Dagmar Weibe. Wait—I recognize the name. She helped organize the Arts and Letters Festival, didn't she? Bremer Motors was a sponsor. I remember seeing her name in the promotional material they sent over. What's she like? Is it serious between them?"

"I guess so. I don't know either of them very well. Dagmar gave me the impression it was serious."

"Well, that's wonderful. That's very good to hear. He's been through so much, I'm glad he's moving on with his life." She turned her piercing green gaze on Alvina. "Though I think you might be a little disappointed."

Alvina opened her mouth. Gulping air, red-faced.

Marlee glanced at her watch. "Oh lord, I'm late.

Harry! Stanley! Let's go!" She began moving toward the patio to collect the boys who hadn't budged from their post. "It's been a pleasure talking to you, Alvina. I'm sorry the *Record* won't let the past stay in the past, but there's not much I can do to prevent it, is there? As a courtesy to me and my children though, I'd rather you didn't print what I've told you. Simply say that Marlee Bremer is unaware of the specifics of her husband's appeal and therefore could not comment."

This time Alvina found her voice. "You said that our conversation was setting other events in motion. What did you mean by that?"

Marlee turned, frowning. "I don't remember. I'm not sure what I meant. Probably just that our problems never seem to go away. No matter how hard we try or what steps we take, a new evil is set in motion. That's all. Sorry, but I've really got to run. Good-bye, Alvina. Try not to work too hard."

Marlee's fine blonde hair didn't move as she firmly herded her boys to the sidewalk, one in each hand, confidently in charge. Coral Moon would disapprove. Coral believed in a child's independence. Alvina reckoned Harry and Stanley never had to forge their mother's signature on their field trip permission slips.

A woman like Marlee Bremer would notice if her husband was having an affair. She ran a tight ship. So if it wasn't an affair, it was an impulsive one-night-stand —consensual, which is why Teresa didn't fight him. Then why did Trey kill her? And he must have killed her—there was no other explanation for the destroyed suit. An innocent man doesn't burn the clothes he was wearing. There was something on his suit he didn't want Marlee to see.

And round and round it goes, Alvina thought, because if he killed her, where did he get the flashlight?

She sat down at the table and considered ordering a coffee. The heat inside the café had driven the rest of the customers outside to the patio. She was alone. Del Musgrave floated across her consciousness, slipping ahead of her through a dark green forest.

It wasn't what Marlee thought it was. Alvina wasn't thinking about him because she wanted to go out with him. She didn't have the confidence to go out with a guy like Del Musgrave. She liked wondering about him, she liked seeing him—it was exciting. But so was riding a motorcycle. She couldn't cope with that on a daily basis either. You'd have to be a girl like Dagmar. Or Teresa. The demon angel. A girl so powerful that two men were broken by her. And one remade. According to Marlee, Dave sobered up after Teresa was murdered.

Her thoughts drifted to the murdered girl. The coroner's report said Teresa had died instantly. Alvina doubted it. She didn't believe in instant anything. There were too many processes to go through to shut the human body down. The will to live would have to be severed. Human beings needed time to accept death. It couldn't happen in an instant. Alvina was sure death was kinder than that.


TERESA MUSGRAVE sat in the shadowed corner of his office in the green chair reserved for guests. She crossed one perfect leg over the other and smiled at him. Her white teeth flashed. Her dark hair was lustrous in the falling light. Dave watched and waited. The day was bleeding from the sky and he still had a paper to get out. She looked just as she did when she sat there seven years ago, asking him for a job. He was a little in love with her back then.

Not now. She was a horror show now.

Deep in his heart Dave knew she wasn't real, only a manifestation of his guilt, a product of his desire to drink. She always showed up when the craving was at its worst. Unlike most recovering alcoholics, Dave Gomer rarely talked about his last drunk, even in the safety of a meeting. It had begun with a bottle of scotch at three in the afternoon and ended eighteen hours later with him coming to on his dock and no recollection of how he came to be there. Ray had struggled for his sobriety. Not Dave. Seven years ago, sobriety hit Dave like an avalanche because on the night of his last drunk, Teresa Musgrave was murdered.

He fixed his eyes on her. Her smile broadened, filled with lasciviousness. He had always suspected that behind that school girl face was one perverted mind. Death had revealed it.

She's playing you, Dave told himself. Making you thirsty.

Teresa flipped a lock of her hair over her shoulder, revealing her full, pale breasts. She was naked. She was always naked when she appeared to him, looking just as he had seen her in death only without the blood and broken bones.

He watched her, warily. If he had any sense he'd get to a meeting but he didn't think he could trust himself to leave the room. The office was safe at least. No booze in the office. Ray had stuck his head in before he left on vacation and asked him if he was all right. Alcoholics have a sixth sense about other alcoholics. He said he was fine, and he was, or he would be. Some days, sobriety was maintained on a minute-by-minute basis. This was one of those days.

Dave rubbed his mouth.

*Where did he get the flashlight?*

Moon was a good reporter. She didn't know she was, she lacked confidence and he was able to play on that, thank god. But she recognized the hot spot of a story when she saw it. Where did Trey get the goddamned flashlight? If it wasn't in the trailer—where'd it come from?

Teresa winked at him.

"You know there was no flashlight in the trailer. Don't you?"

Yes, of course she did. That's why she was here.

Beautiful, beautiful girl. So young. So perfect. Nobody was supposed to get hurt. Nobody was supposed to take it seriously. "I just set the trap," he said softly to the apparition, vaguely aware he was crossing the sanity line. "Trey didn't have to take the bait."

Teresa smiled and tilted her head, her eyes gleaming at him from under lowered lids. Hollows of light that disturbed Dave.

"Trey liked to look. Maybe he thought being married would keep him out of mischief. Men don't get super powers on their wedding day. Most guys haven't got an accurate picture of themselves, of their weaknesses. I took advantage. I admit that."

*Where did he get the flashlight?*

Her arm reached up to shield her face, her eyes widened in fear.

Dave pressed his hands over his face. "Look, it was just business. Leave me alone. I don't know where he got the goddamned flashlight. I don't know anything about what happened that night."

He had come to on the dock with the high hot sun burning his retina like the wrath of God, fire and brimstone in the air, and rolled to his side to release a plume of gas from his tortured gut. The gas foretold of something worse on the way. He barely made it to the shoreline before voiding his bowels. Pickled eggs and scotch really cleaned a man out. That was Saturday.

"No one knew you were dead."

The apparition gave a small soundless laugh. Obviously one person knew she was dead.

Sunday, he'd stayed sober because Dot was in a venomous mood. She had a mean streak Dot did, for all her education. She divorced him not long after. So much for that.

"On Monday, Trey found your body."

Dave never told Ray what had sobered him up. Ray did the twelve steps; Dave learned them for the meetings but never worked them. Ray had a Higher Power; Dave had a murdered nineteen-year-old girl and a phone call.

He'd had blackouts before but never like that one.

Dave opened the bottom drawer of his desk, reached to the very back and withdrew a small cassette tape. He set it on his desk and looked at it. "If you've never had a blackout drunk you can't understand how it's possible to have a whole conversation and not recall a word of it."

He would never get rid of the *Record*'s old answering machine. He didn't dare. The cassette tape was the reason why. He had a spooky superstition that if the tape wasn't played on that machine and that machine alone, it would be blank. Erased from history. The tape and answering machine had become artifacts, the only proof he had that it really happened. He kept them the way some alcoholics keep a bottle of booze in the cupboard. They were his curse and his salvation.

Teresa's mouth opened wide, black and broken, her jaw shattered. She was never going to let him go. Dave's eyes went to the lower drawer of the filing cabinet but that bottle was drained seven years ago. Another artifact. His office was full of them.

"What do you want? I can't change the fucking past! I can't even remember it." He rubbed his mouth. "It's not my fault." The whole night was a blank. He'd been drinking beer all that day but scotch was the main event —his Friday night celebration for being such a damn fine fellow. "I don't even remember leaving the office. I don't know how I got the boat upriver over the rapids. I'm lucky to be alive."

He heard the girl laugh.

Dave hissed across the empty shadowed room. "You aren't real, you cunt. You're only here because of an anonymous note. I told Alvina to shred it. You won't beat me."

The deeper the dark, the more solid Teresa became. She shifted, uncrossing her legs and placed her feet flat on the floor. Dave waited. The desire to drink was worse than he'd ever known. Teresa smiled, evil menace in her eyes, silently reminding him of her death in the trailer, of the phone call, of the heat and the stink and his mercenary use of her. What she wanted—what she always wanted when he found her here—was to break him.

To kill him.

Just one drink. Just one to take the edge off. To help him think. Somebody wrote that note. Somebody knew something. Trey's kid had started going to church. That troubled Dave. Marlee said Violet had a photographic memory but she was only four or five at the time. Even if she remembered, she wouldn't have understood what was going on. Would she?

What would cause a young girl to get religion?

"Suffer the little children." Dave pressed his hands over his eyes. It couldn't be a coincidence. Violet was sitting on the dock during his meeting with Marlee and right after that the *Record* ran the article mentioning the trailer. If her memory was as exceptional as Marlee said it was, Violet would put the two of them together. She was old enough now to understand what was going on that day. The kid had quite a time playing inside the trailer. *Where did he get the flashlight?*

"Let's pray to God that's the only question she has."

Teresa touched her tongue to her pale, dry lips.

His gut burned. Dave tossed the cassette in the bottom drawer and banged it shut. "You wanted it as much as I did. You practically begged me to set it up! The point is Violet has to be set straight. Get therapy or counselling. If it's come down to writing anonymous notes that could hurt her mother, you see what I'm saying. Obviously, I'll do my best to explain and apologize. Make amends to the kid."

Step Nine of the program had always seemed pointless to Dave. Confessions only pissed people off. Sometimes there was pity or fear—contempt was the easiest deal with. Forgiveness was rare. Laughing it off was rarer still. Dave didn't realize how many humourless people he knew until he sobered up.

"But I'll destroy the goddamned recording before I'll turn it over to the police. They'll say I did it. They'll say the flashlight was mine or Violet will say it to get revenge. If that's what you're here for, you can go to hell. Whose evil set this whole thing in motion? *Trey's.* The sins of the father, sweetheart. You're haunting the wrong guy."

Her skin looked shiny and ill. Her eyes were black, dragging him back to that morning, to his roiling gut, to the swaying dock and the stink of flame in the air.

Suddenly, Dave understood. The knowledge was like a curtain parting on a thing to which he had only half-paid attention seven years ago. There had always been something off about that morning, something out of place.

The bound archived issues of the *Record* were on top of his filing cabinets. He pulled out the year he needed and carried the book to his desk. He opened it flat and thumbed through the months to the issue that ran the week Teresa was murdered.

Startled, Dave looked up at the green chair half-hidden in the grey corner.

Teresa was gone.

# EIGHT

EVERYTHING LOOKS better in the morning.

It was raining for one thing. Alvina Moon liked the rain, especially in the summer when the smell of rain on hot dusty pavement was the sweetest smell in the world. And today, she had nothing to do at the office except sort out the files and pack. No copy to write. No deadlines to meet. No messages to return. No story meeting. The papers had been signed on Friday. *The Stollerton Record* was officially defunct. Dave would sell off what he could of the office equipment and furniture. Disposing of the rest of the office clutter fell on Alvina's shoulders. The new owners weren't interested in the *Record*'s legacy. Dave was donating the archived editions and photos to the Historical Society. MetMedia was hiring a skeleton crew of freelancers to cover local events and the entire classified ad system was being streamlined. Paperless, they called it. Contact with the public would be online only.

"That lets out the old people," she said out loud.

The office was shadowed in soft greys. Alvina switched on the lights. The phone rang. She picked it up in Dave's office on the third ring just ahead of the answering machine.

"Good, you're there," said Dave, as though there

were whole days he forgot she worked for him. "I'm not coming in this morning. Take the key if you go out because Ray's on holiday. There's no one around to let you in."

"I put a spare under the flower pot outside about a year ago. You're not fishing in the rain are you?"

"It's the best time." Dave grunted. "Another thing. I want to confirm that you shredded that anonymous note like I asked you."

Her heart pounded. Marlee must have called to complain. "Yes. Why?" Alvina vowed to shred it as soon as she got off the phone.

"No reason. I just couldn't remember if you said you'd done it or not. You did, so we're good. There's a stack of empty cardboard boxes in the back room. Pack up everything that isn't essential to get the next three editions out. Shred or archive everything else. You know the drill."

She glanced over Dave's desk. "One of the archives binders is open on your desk. Were you working on something?"

"Don't worry about it. Just leave it there. I'll take care of packing up my office when I get back. Try not to burn the place down."

He hung up.

Alvina began with her desk, opening the bottom drawer where she kept the files on each advertiser. She culled the defunct list, whittling the mass down to half a dozen files. Maybe she should call each one and encourage them to be the *Record*'s last advertisers.

Dave's cynical voice crowed in her ear. *That's using your head, Moon. Who wouldn't want to be the last business to advertise in a dead newspaper?*

Dave Gomer didn't know everything Alvina thought, picking up the phone. She decided the first advertiser to approach would be Marlee Bremer.

DAVE GOMER ended his call to the office and then turned off the cell phone. The rain had started falling sometime in the early hours of the morning. Rain was good for fishing. His tackle box was stowed under his seat; there'd be time to get a few casts in before heading to the office.

He chugged upriver, the prow of his red and silver Princecraft bobbing gently over the swells. The mallet he used for clubbing fish slid out from under the passenger seat. Dave kicked it back with his foot and wondered with a newspaper man's instinct if the rain was helping the SOPFEU with the fires. He pulled his hat down tighter over his ears. The blue windbreaker he had on was holding up under the drizzle but the wind had lifted; he didn't want to lose his lucky fishing hat.

A dock stretched before him like a weary finger aiming for the opposite shore. A figure stood on it behind the fine grey mist. Dave waved.

"What are you doing out here," he called as he drew alongside. "Only fools and fishermen are out in this weather."

"I was waiting for you. It's about what you told me last night—we need to talk."

FOUR OUT of the six businesses Alvina called agreed to renew their advertising. She dubbed the final issue The Historic Edition and everyone wanted a spot in that one. She had enough to pay for eleven pages at least. No word yet from Bremer Motors. She'd left a message for Marlee at the dealership and on her voicemail at home to be on the safe side. Dave would've shot the idea down before she got the chance.

Alvina poked her head into his office. Papers were piled everywhere. The boss didn't realize how much work there was to do, but then the boss never did. Dave's office wasn't going to pack itself. She could start with the filing cabinets. She opened the top drawer of the bank nearest the window. It bristled with beige files. Anything older than seven years Alvina tossed. Seven years, she thought, being the statute of limitations for audits or general legal issues. The first and second cabinets were emptied and their files sorted into Archive, Recycle, and Shred. So far, the Recycle pile was the highest. Years of living with her nomadic parents had trained her to cull. She was glad Dave wasn't there to see his carefully catalogued notebooks tossed into the recycling bin.

The rain pattered against the large window. The river fretted under the wind. The village, not surprisingly, was moody and quiet. Alvina opened the second drawer from the bottom of the third filing cabinet and an empty bottle of scotch rolled forward. There was a shot glass, half a pack of cigarettes and a stack of yellowed newspapers from the Eastern Townships. Alvina tossed the papers to the Recycle pile without a second glance. The scotch bottle was bone dry. Ditto the shot glass. With a shudder of relief, she tossed both to the blue bin. The cigarettes were lobbed into the garbage can.

She turned to his desk.

THE TALL green pines that shrouded the shoreline looked taller, blacker and more ominous in the rain. They'd travelled far upriver, almost to the Paugan Falls where the fishing was best. The waterfall was dammed in the 1920's for a hydro-electric station. Below the rock face were quiet coves and deep green shallows. Rain pinged all around them.

"There isn't much more to say." Dave pushed his hat back on his head. It had been difficult talking over the whine of a twenty horsepower boat motor. He was glad to turn it off. "I told you everything I could last night. The note was destroyed so there's no way to trace it back to the sender. With everything going on at the office and being out of a job soon, Alvina will forget all about it. I'm sorry it came to that, but at least there was no permanent damage."

"But the damage is permanent. Innocent people suffered for a perverted game. They wouldn't have been in the trailer at all if it weren't for you."

The river sloshed against the sides of the boat.

Dave sighed heavily. "Look, maybe I should make something clear: I didn't come to you last night because I had a guilty conscience. I've owned up to the wrong I did when I was drinking and I've done what I can to put it right. That's as good as you're going to get. I'm not going to get all weepy and remorseful at this late date. Remorse is a slippery slope to taking a drink. Alcoholics learn that the hard way."

Rain seeped through his slacks. Dave checked his watch. He debated reaching for his fishing rod. Might as well get a cast in seeing as they were here.

"Besides, it won't help anything and it won't change

anything," he said. "I appreciate that it's a lot to take in. Learning the truth has upset you. But what I did back then wasn't intentionally hurtful. Alcohol destroys the ability to reason. Maybe if I'd been in my right mind ... but it is what it is and we have to face it. I'm not interested in getting Trey out of jail. As far as I'm concerned, on a moral level, the right guy was convicted."

"On a moral level."

"It wasn't *my* flashlight. Let's just remember that. Let's just keep in mind what we're talking about here before this conversation goes any further. I didn't commit any crime."

"That's not how I see it, Dave."

The rain pattered the leaves of the trees. The boat caught a swell and pitched right. The mallet rolled out from under the passenger seat. Dave's eyes went to it.


ALL FOUR drawers in Dave's desk had been emptied and the files, research, and personal correspondence winnowed down to one boxful. The pen drawer was still left to be emptied but that was easy; mostly dried out pens, gummy paper clips and Post-it Notes. Alvina pushed on the lower left hand drawer to close it. It banged shut and something rattled within. She pulled it open again and peered into the back. The lower drawers of the old desk were deep and long, designed to hold metal file racks. Alvina spied a small cassette tape in the far corner and pulled it out. It was the kind they used in the answering machine. Dave used to swap them out for his interviews when he couldn't be bothered looking for a fresh cassette. She carried it to her desk, stuck it in the answering machine and pressed PLAY.

*"Dave, are you there? Dave, buddy, if you're there, pick up. I've got a problem. Teresa wouldn't get in the fucking car and I couldn't stand there arguing about it. I had to leave her."*

Alvina froze. There followed the sound of the telephone receiver being fumbled and picked up. Dave's voice came on the line. It sounded gluey.

*"Hey Trey. Hey man, what? Where the hell are you?"*

The machine had kept recording. Dave forgot to press STOP. Alvina stared down at the slowly turning tape.

*"Thank Christ. I'm in the phone booth in St. Jude. Marlee expected me home three hours ago. Do me a favour, buddy—get Teresa from the Oasis and bring her home. Talk some fucking sense into her while you're at it."*

*"What are talking about? What's going on?"*

*"I don't have time to go into it. It's late. I've got to get home. You've got the boat, right? Do this one thing for me. It'll take you twenty minutes."*

*"Okay, I'm heading up there now. No problem, no problem buddy. You can thank me in the morning. Just get your ass home."*

The call was disconnected followed by the time-stamp: Message sent at 9:38 p.m. The tape stopped with a hard click.

Alvina sat down. Rain tapped lightly against the window.


DAVE REMEMBERED the obituary for Teresa Musgrave that ran in the *Record*. He didn't write it, the stringer working for him at the time was assigned to it. It was the typical thing: Teresa Musgrave was full of promise, a loving wife, a valued member of the community, a keen employee. Dave wondered why life was only measured by accomplishment. Why didn't obits include the real stuff of living—the disappointments, failures, heartaches, or the long stretches of simply marking time? *For seven years, Dave Gomer marked time. He didn't drink. He didn't fornicate. He caught forty-nine fish.*

"I was a drunk with no alibi. I couldn't tell anyone about that phone call. Who were the police going to believe—the upstanding family man or the booze hound who claims he was so drunk, he couldn't remember navigating the rapids under the covered bridge? Trey was setting me up to find Teresa's body so the police would think I killed her."

"How do you know you didn't? You said you had a blackout."

"Well, that's the thing, I didn't know, see." Dave hunched in his coat. "Maybe I did go to the trailer and try something on. I had a thing for her. We all did. I could have lost it when she turned me down. I was a nasty drunk. Maybe it was my flashlight. I didn't know anything for sure—I had blacked out. Trey was arrested but he had a reasonable explanation for the DNA and the fingerprints. They'd had sex, the trailer was his; it was natural they'd find physical evidence that he'd been there. Even the prints on the murder weapon—Trey said he picked it up when he found Teresa's body on Monday. The only thing he couldn't explain was how the clothes he was wearing that day came to be burned in the campsite's fire pit."

"He can't explain rape."

"He can and he did. Whether or not we believe him is another story. Something got out of control that night." Dave squinted at the sky. "We'd better head back.

Those clouds are going to open up." He turned and bent over the motor. "I've already said I have no interest in liberating Trey. I'm going to tell you something that doesn't change anything at my end, but you have a right to know. What you do with the information is your business. There was a burn restriction on that week. I looked it up in the newspaper's archives. When there's a restriction on, there is no smoke from campfires and so forth. When I came to on my dock, the smell of smoke was in the air. At the time, I didn't give it a second thought. Last night I realized what it meant."

"The suit was being burned."

"Yes. Except the smoke was on the wrong day."

Dave yanked on the starter. The motor flared to life.

It only took a second. With one intake of breath, his hand was on the throttle. With another, the club had come down on his skull. Dave turned with a look of surprise and pain on his face, and finally, comprehension. His arms would not move as swiftly as his brain urged them to. Again the club came up, and then down with greater force. Dave slumped sideways, his mouth sagged open. His eyes fixed. The motor choked. The musical clatter of rain on the metal fishing boat was the only sound.

There was no one around. Stillness and drizzle. And grey water. It was all over in a matter of minutes.

VIOLET BREMER sat at the end of the dock, legs crossed, hunched under her mom's giant yellow umbrella. Rain hit the nylon with little splats.

She turned and peeked around the umbrella to see if anyone was moving in the house. All was quiet. Birds were in the garden, chirruping in the precipitation.

Rose bushes grew where the children's sandbox used to be. Stanley was only four when their mother ripped it out—totally unfair, he loved that sandbox. But her mother was the kind of person who believed the ends justified the means. Violet had learned that phrase from a book she was reading about the bombing of Hiroshima.

Worry balled in her stomach. Sometimes it was necessary to kill people. That was something to think about.

Square panes of window glass winked at her from the house. Her mother could be spying on her. She did that sometimes. The office door was closed when Violet got up this morning, which meant Marlee was in there working and didn't want to be disturbed. But the office window faced the backyard. She could be watching. Violet turned away. She was figuring some things out about her mother. It was like breaking a code. Each year she got closer to the truth.

She lay back on the dock with the umbrella propped over her like a yellow roof. The sound of the rain tapping on the nylon helped calm her down, helped her to remember. She had a freakishly good memory. It wasn't like it was a secret. Her teacher had told Marlee about Violet's gift at last year's parent-teacher meeting. Maybe her mother didn't think it mattered for anything except getting good grades in school. Maybe she thought it was no big deal to give that interview to Alvina Moon right in front of her daughter.

Violet's stomach cramped. Her stomach had been more or less killing her ever since she saw the article in the *Record*. Up to that point, she knew very little about her father's conviction, what actually happened or where. Violet didn't even know it was their babysitter her father was accused of killing. She remembered the night the police came, the crying and yelling, but she was too little to understand what it all meant. It was one thing to remember—it was another thing to understand. The topic was strictly off-limits in their house.

Fine for Marlee, Violet thought. She didn't have to put up with the kids at school and their lame jokes. *Violet Bremer's father used to sell cars for a living. Now he makes the license plates!* Hilarious.

She was bothered she couldn't remember more about their babysitter considering Teresa was in charge of them that summer. Harry had called her Teesah and Violet remembered her shoes—a wedge heel and straps that tied up her calves. And her long brown ponytail. There was a trip to the library to return a stack of picture books, Violet scuffling along the blistering hot sidewalk behind Teresa who was pushing Harry in the buggy. That was the day Mr. Gomer gave Violet the blue jay feather, except she didn't know he was Mr. Gomer back then. She didn't know who the feather-man was until Mr. Gomer came to the house with Alvina Moon and she realized it was the same man. That was the thing with being almost a teenager. She was beginning to see the people she knew in full.

But she couldn't put it all together and she was beginning to have doubts, beginning to wish she couldn't remember a thing. Every corner of that summer was shadowed with menace. When Violet went back to the trailer with her mother, she remembered too much. Not all of it, but enough to worry her. The world wasn't as mysterious or wonderful at twelve as it had been at five. The fun things weren't that fun and the scary things were far worse than Violet imagined.

Rape for example. She refused to believe her father did that to Teresa. Even letting the idea come near her was repulsive. Smashing a person's skull with a flashlight was different. She could imagine someone doing that. Violet had smashed rocks and dishes and toys when she was little. And other things. She'd bashed in the faces of dolls and almost killed a bird once before she stopped herself.

Maybe she should talk to a priest about what she had done. She didn't know any priests though. How did a person get an appointment? Did you have to be Catholic? Violet used to go to the Anglican Church in Stollerton but she switched to the Church of the Evangelist a few months ago. The evangelicals were much more specific about God and sin. She never thought about God's vengeance until now. What if she'd made a huge mistake?

She sat up. Worry cramped her stomach. She was always such a worry-wart but this time she really had something to worry about. If her father was guilty then he belonged in prison. What if she was responsible for getting him out and the next face he smashed in was her mother's?

*Step on a crack, break your mother's back.*

Burning acid shot up her esophagus. She was too young to have an ulcer. Cancer maybe. Stomach cancer and a slow horrible death. God's punishment. The wages of sin is death.

A low buzz cut through the patter of rain. Violet looked up. A motor boat driven by a fisherman in a blue nylon windbreaker and a beige fishing hat was travelling downriver. Mr. Gomer, coming back from fishing. She watched him pass, automatically memorizing the small details she saw; the colour and name of the boat written in black letters on its side. She took in the man's posture and the absence of a fishing rod. She didn't do it on purpose—it wasn't spying. It was like taking a photograph that got filed in her brain. He raised his arm in brief salute as people in boats generally did to people on docks.

Violet frowned.


ALVINA WAITED all day but Dave never returned to the office. She left two messages for him; one on his cell phone and one at his house. He never called back.

She removed the tape from the machine, slipped it in an envelope and tucked it in her camera case along with the anonymous note. The keys to the van were buried in the pile of stuff on Dave's desk. She fished them out, turned out the lights and locked the door. The *Deeper Vibe* office was locked up. If Ray was here she could have talked to him but he'd left on vacation. She knew where Hester Warnock lived but Hester was a friend of Detective Sergeant Rompré's. She'd tell her to go to the police and Alvina wasn't ready to do that without talking to Dave first.

Not knowing what else to do, she drove out to Dave's home.

Her boss lived across the river in a small, neat white house. Alvina knocked. When he didn't come to the door, she followed the short path to his dock. Rain splattered the weathered boards. A raven cawed and wheeled above.

"Dave?"

Alvina drew to the edge of the dock.

The boat was gone.

# NINE

THE MARINE unit recovered Dave's boat four miles upriver of his dock, caught in a tangle of scrub. A navy blue windbreaker and beige hat were found on the seat.

"It is necessary you file a formal missing person's report if you believe there is cause for concern."

Constable Lemen obviously believed there was cause for concern. He was taking Dave's disappearance very seriously, coming to the *Record* to ask *mademoiselle* a few questions. At least his English was good. Alvina could've managed the interview in French but she was glad she didn't have to. She was out of her depth.

"I'm not sure if there's cause for concern. He didn't show up for work again today and I can't reach him on his cell phone. It's been two days. I don't know what to do."

A ball of tension was forming in her stomach.

"Mr. Gomer's vehicle is missing. Is there someone he could be visiting? A friend?"

"His car is still in the shop. It has been for a couple of weeks. He could be visiting a friend. It's possible. I don't know who Dave's friends are—he's just my boss."

"How did he seem to you when you last spoke? Was he despondent?"

"He was bothered about closing the paper but I

didn't think it was serious."

"There is an empty bottle of vodka in his fishing tackle box."

"What? No—he hasn't had a drink in years. He's A.A."

"Who is his sponsor, *s'il vous plaît*?"

Alvina found Ray's number where he was vacationing on Prince Edward Island. "This is his sponsor, and a friend of his." She handed the phone to the constable to make the call. "Maybe Dave went to see him. I hadn't thought of that. If he was depressed, Ray is the one he'd turn to."

But Dave wasn't with Ray or anyone else. Dave Gomer had disappeared. Vanished into thin air.

"Call Dot," Ray advised Alvina when Constable Lemen put her back on the line.

"They want me to file a missing person's report. I don't know what to do, Ray."

"Call Dot," Ray repeated. "She not his wife anymore but she's the closest he's got to a family. If he can be found, she'll know where to find him."

"You think he's gone off on a bender? They found a vodka bottle in the boat. He had a lot on his mind. With the *Record* folding maybe he thought it didn't matter anymore."

"Alcoholism isn't something we put on and take off like a coat. It matters until the day he dies. If he's had a relapse the sooner we get to him, the better." Ray paused. "Vodka is not what I would have expected. Dave was a scotch man. Imagine tossing away seven years of sobriety on a bottle of vodka." Ray grunted. "I'm not buying it. Call Dot. She works at the dental clinic. She'll know if you should file a missing person's report."

DOROTHY GOMER wasn't opposed to discussing her ex-husband, so long as it was made clear that whatever she said in the negative should be taken with a grain of salt. Her therapist said it was perfectly normal to feel anger when a marriage ends, sometimes even for years. "Especially when it ends in betrayal," Dot added archly. "So he's been missing since Monday and suddenly Ray Milligan thinks I'm the one to talk to. Well, this should be a short conversation."

"I don't know if you were aware but Dave sold the *Record* to a media conglomerate and he's retiring. The last time we spoke he said he was going to be late. I assumed he was going fishing but the police found his boat and there's no sign of Dave. His coat and hat were there but we don't know if he was wearing them that day or if they were left behind from before. I'm worried. Was Dave a strong swimmer?"

"The Dave Gomer I knew would've drowned in a puddle." Dot adjusted the cuff of her blouse over her wrist. "Fishing, huh? Must be nice. Must be nice to have nothing to do but sit on your ass all day while the rest of us are out making a living. Maybe I should take it up and he can work my hours at the dental clinic. I'd be retiring too if Dave hadn't poured every penny we had down his throat. Did he tell you how we met?"

Dorothy Gomer's little post-war saltbox home was stifling. It was as if the woman had an objection to outdoor air. Every window was closed up tight.

"No," said Alvina, weakly. People were always going on about how they met.

Dot sat on the edge of a brown flowered armchair like she was spring-coiled. One false move and she'd shoot through the roof. Her hair had been done recently; a pale unnatural red streaked with blonde and cut close to the head. She wore a yellow sleeveless top and with a sheer flowered blouse over that. Her slacks were yellow too. The outfit was one Alvina recognized from the Sears catalogue. Dot liked jewellery; a thick gold bangle dangled from her wrist and several gold chains were around her neck. Her eyeglasses had tiny chips of diamonds in the corners. She was tanned and in pretty good shape for her age.

"My girlfriends had dragged me out to Keefer's in Martingale to hear some country-western band and there was David Gomer, the publisher of *The Stollerton Record*, holding up the bar. His teeth were a mess. I don't think he knew what a vegetable was. I thought here's a guy who will appreciate a good woman. I felt sorry for him. I hope he rots in Hell." Dot's mouth pressed together and her eyes reddened behind her glittery glasses. "Don't write that down. That's the anger talking."

"Dave told me he had a drinking problem once," Alvina offered.

"By *once,* he was referring to the entire fourteen years of our marriage." Dot propped an elbow on the arm of the chair to support her head and stared at Alvina with hard brown eyes. "What I want to know is —where was this concern for Dave Gomer back then? No one went looking for him when he was married to me and would disappear for days at a stretch. The police didn't care. Ray didn't care. I was on my own with the anxiety."

"I don't think it's the same thing this time."

Frosted pink lipstick bled into the down of Dot's

upper lip. Her eyes gleamed. "No, because he's stone cold sober now, isn't he. After drinking for the whole of our married life, Dave Gomer miraculously sobers up."

"Yes, I suppose that's why we're worried." Alvina reddened and looked down at her notepad as if that would help. "I'm sorry, Dot. I'm not sure what to tell you."

"You don't have to tell me a thing. I was married to the man for fourteen years. I know all about him." Dot's neck corded. "Marlee Bremer called me after the divorce, very coy, very clever. She wanted to know what happened between me and Dave." Dot snorted. "Two can play at that game. I said why don't you ask Trey? I'm sure he'll tell you. That shut her up. Who does she think she is rubbing my nose in it?"

"Rubbing your nose in what if you don't mind saying?"

"Oh, I don't mind." Dot waved her hand. Crooked brown fingers tipped with frosted talons. "I'm a very forgiving woman. Even when my friends were telling me I had a right to take him for every penny I could get in the divorce, I said no dice. Forgive and forget. That's my motto. Just as long as we're clear and I can trust you not to repeat what's said here, although I'm not the person in this story with something to hide."

Alvina set aside her notebook, baffled. Who had what to hide? She didn't dare ask in case that set Dot off again in another direction. "I won't repeat it."

"All right then, you want the truth? Marlee Bremer is the reason Dave and I split up. Oh yes. You didn't know that, did you? That's something he doesn't tell everyone who asks. I'll bet even Ray doesn't know the whole story of Dave's last drunk. He got sober because he ruined her life. Never mind ruining my life. Fourteen years of tearing my hair out, did he listen to me when I pleaded with him to quit? No. He stopped drinking because of what he had done to her." Dot flushed scarlet and touched her hair, composing herself. "Emotions run high in these cases. Marlee used to work with me at the dental clinic before her kids were born. It's personal."

"What had Dave done to her?"

Dot released a pained sigh. "You've only known Dave sober. When he was drinking he didn't have a moral bone in his body. The trouble began when Trey inherited the dealership and decided the *Record* wasn't hip enough to run their advertising anymore. Dave came up with a scheme to change his mind. It's hard to believe this is how it works in business until you know what men are like—especially when it comes to sex. They'll do anything to get it, even if they're already getting it, if you know what I mean." Dot's brows lifted.

"Not really," said Alvina.

"Let's just say Trey was restless that summer. His wife was pregnant with their third child. To make a long story short, Teresa Musgrave had caught his eye. The mistake Trey made was in confiding in Dave because Dave used the information to leverage a deal. That's as polite as I can put it. The plan was all very hush-hush. Dave swore me to secrecy." Dot made a noise of disgust. "As if I'd spread a thing like that around like a common fishwife. I said didn't think his wife would thank him for it. Some people think fidelity is a joke. Well, it isn't a joke as Dave discovered. It came as quite a shock to him when Teresa was murdered."

Alvina couldn't take her eyes off Dot. "Trey was charged with rape."

"Oh that wasn't rape. Oh no. Dave was well in on it. He knew Teresa was no saint when he got her that job. Oh yes, he *got* her that job. Dave put the cuckoo in the nest and let nature take its course."

"I don't understand what that means."

"No, I suppose you don't. You're a good girl. It's hard to imagine girls your age who are more worldly, let's say. But they are out there and Teresa was one. I wouldn't call what my husband did blackmail—Trey knew full well what he was getting into—but once he took the bait, Dave had him right where he wanted him."

"He was trying to help her out." Alvina's head felt light and fragile. "Dave didn't know what Trey was like."

"So he claimed. I didn't believe him—I'm no fool." The glance she gave Alvina was quick, tight and furtive. "Your sainted boss knew enough of what was going on in that trailer to get a lucrative advertising contract out of Bremer. Dave Gomer had to be the big man and look what happened. After Trey was arrested, I warned him to keep his mouth shut. I said you don't know how Del and Marlee are going to react. Amends are only to be made if no one is going to get hurt. I said for once in your life do what I tell you and stay out of it."

Alvina's mouth felt like cloth. "Did Dave listen to you?"

"If he did it would've been a first." Dot wiped a bead of lipstick from the corner of her mouth with the tip of her finger. "He sure as hell danced to Marlee's tune. I guess ruining Del Musgrave's marriage didn't count. But Marlee? He couldn't do enough for her. When your husband tells you, after everything he's put you through, that another woman is keeping him sober— that's called an emotional affair! Dave acted like he'd never heard the expression before. He couldn't see the situation from my point of view at all."

"The police asked me for a photo in case they have to organize a search. Do you have one I can give them? I can't find anything in the office. The files are packed up."

"If they think it's necessary. With the paper sold, my guess is Marlee or no Marlee, the temptation proved too much and he's gone back to his old tricks. They should check the bars."

Alvina followed her to a small desk that held the telephone, some notepaper and a flowered canister filled with pens. Dot opened its narrow drawer and withdrew a snapshot of a robust, handsome man with a thick head of hair and the beginnings of a beer belly.

"What about his boat? You don't think he could have had an accident?"

"There was a rainstorm on Monday; it must have come loose. Dave didn't have the patience to tie a boat off properly. It was always floating away when we were married."

Dot frowned at the photograph. "He's not my problem anymore. That's how I need to look at this. Drunk, sober—not my problem. I held him through the shakes and the vomiting, running him hot baths and driving him to meetings because he didn't trust himself behind the wheel and look where it got me. Well it's her turn now. Oh ho!" Dot's eye's gleamed with suppressed triumph. "I should call her to offer my sympathy. If Dave's had a relapse Marlee is well in over her head."

"The police did find an empty bottle of vodka in the boat."

"Hah, I thought as much. They'll find him in a flophouse in Ottawa. I'd stake my life on it. Marlee won't have a clue how to dry him out." Dot snapped the photo. "I'll take this to the police myself and give them a list of his old hangouts. I'll file the missing person's report. That's more my job than yours, don't you think?"

"Yes. Thank you. To be honest, I'm relieved not to have the responsibility."

Alvina moved to go. On the desk a sheet of notepaper caught her eye.

Dot had started a grocery list. It was written in green ink.

IT WAS too much to deal with. Alvina refused to get caught between a runaway alcoholic, his vindictive ex-wife and a seven-year-old crime. As long as Dot filed the missing person's report like she promised, Alvina hoped Dave was okay but there was nothing more she could do for him. She had her own problems. One thing or the other had to happen in the next two weeks—a job or a place to live. Since landlords don't usually rent to unemployed people, the job would have to come first.

Midnight ticked past. She had done everything she could to turn her mind off but sleep still wouldn't come. Alvina left the apartment, following the railroad tracks to the outskirts of Stollerton. The night was fresh with the smell of rain behind it. Where the lights ended, the road split. Alvina took the right fork toward the covered bridge and stepped into utter darkness.

She looked up. The sky opened wide, a black maw shot with tiny brilliants.

Her parents had finally returned her calls. They fretted when she told them about losing her job, worried that they were going to have to house her or pay her student loan. They'd help if they could, but they were staying at a friend's place with plans to go to California for a few months and there was only room for two in the car. No worries, she'd said breezily. I'm fine, *omigod*, I'm totally fine! She hoped they didn't think that's why she'd been trying to reach them. She knew how to take care of herself. They could call her without worrying she was going to ask them for something. Have fun. Enjoy California.

She'd been homeless before and survived. When she was a kid, she used to keep the motel rooms welfare would house them in very tidy. She didn't have to, but she liked a tidy room. Alvina had to admire Violet's trust in God. Maybe trust came easier to kids with houses.

Dark woods crowded the narrow road to the bridge. A half-moon lit the way ahead. In spite of her previous experience with homelessness, Alvina was scared. Without Dave's help, her chances of finding a job were nil. Her clips weren't good enough. The anonymous note—her hot tip—the thing that was supposed to lead to the big story was bogus just as Dave said it was. He must have guessed Dot would pull some trick when the article about Marlee came out. He said the sender was a crackpot. And now Dave was sleeping it off somewhere. Alvina wouldn't mention the cassette tape when he was found. He'd have enough to deal with just getting sober.

*Dave, buddy, if you're there, pick up. I've got a problem.* Trey had a problem all right. Dave-buddy would have been too drunk to save her. Or too weak, too depraved; a pimp, just like Dot said he was. Dot said there was no excuse for what Trey Bremer did, but Teresa was a tough girl to resist when she wanted something. What did Teresa want that Trey had to kill her for? He'd sounded rushed on the phone. His breathing was shallow, like a man running away from something. The good husband in a hurry to get home to the wife and kids after he'd bludgeoned his girlfriend to death? So they were definitely sleeping together. An affair—but rape happens even in marriages. Trey tells Dave to talk some sense into her. But she was dead at that point. What happened that night?

Is it possible Dave supplied Trey with the flashlight and Dot knew about it? Then Marlee wasn't her anonymous note target after all. Dave was. She probably hoped her poisonous question would cause a relapse. Some people weren't happy until the people they loved fell apart. Co-dependency they call that.

The road led to the wide wooden planks of the covered bridge. Her steps thudded hollowly in the long structure. Alvina hesitated, wondering if she should turn back and go home.

There was a sound deep within the bowels of the bridge. She peered into the watery moonlit distance. A man, visible only in silhouette, stood at the far end. He was leaning on the railing looking out over the rapids. He must have come from the other road on the opposite side of the river. It was too dark to see him clearly. A shaft of moonlight caught his profile. His hair gleamed like white gold.

She hesitated before coming closer. "Del?"

Del Musgrave looked up and swore under his breath when he saw who it was. "I don't believe this," he muttered. He straightened and tried to smile but was aware his mouth was pulled tight. Like a snarl, he thought. Like a freaking wolf. You'll scare the shit out of her.

"Hi." No one thinks clearly at a time like that. He let

go of the smile and his panic showed. "What are you doing out this late?"

"I couldn't sleep. I thought if I took a walk it would help. What are you doing here?"

"The same—couldn't sleep. But I went for a boat ride. The bridge is usually busy with people in the summer."

"I came looking for the stars."

Her breathing sounded tight. She was either as scared of him as he was of her, or maybe it was something else. He thought about kissing her to see what she would do. "Did you find them?" Now he was the one out of breath.

"Yes, but I had to get beyond the village limits just like you said. The *Record* is sold. I told you that, right? I have to move away soon, probably to a city to find another job. I won't be free to walk around at night in a city. I might as well enjoy it while I still can."

"You told me about the *Record* but I thought you'd get a job around here."

"There aren't any jobs. Not with a major newspaper. The *Ottawa Citizen* isn't hiring. I'll send a resume to the CBC's Ottawa bureau. Maybe they need a researcher-fact-checker. It's a long shot. My mother used to say when something doesn't work out the way you hoped, it's because something better is coming along." She tucked her hair behind her ears. "My parents have some strange beliefs. They go to palm readers to decide their career paths."

He propped his elbows on the railing. "How long do you have to find a new job?"

"The new owners take over at the end of August and I have to be out of my apartment at the same time.

My roommate Missy won't tolerate even one late rent payment."

Del couldn't help himself. He laughed. "Do you believe in curses?"

"No. Sort of. Do you?"

"I used to. Right up until this moment I believed I was cursed." He laughed again, ruefully. "Curses are bullshit. You're moving."

"Why is that funny?"

"It's not. It's not." He took a deep breath and wiped his eyes. She was leaving. People do that when they have to find work. He used to do it himself. There was nothing out of the ordinary in their meeting at the trailer or in the sudden, odd encounters he'd had with her since, just mundane coincidence. In a couple of weeks, she'll be gone. Problem solved. Crisis averted. He could admit to himself now that for a while there he was worried. The temptation to seek her out was becoming hard to control.

Del sat down on the foot rail and leaned back against the boards. Relief was what he expected. Not this quaking hollow. Alvina stood over him bathed in moonlight. Her stick legs ended in the Converse running shoes she always wore. Tonight she had on a pair of cargo shorts, belted, and a long-sleeved tee-shirt.

"Aren't you hot in that?"

She looked at the shirt as if she'd forgotten she had it on. "No. I like the heat. Can I ask you something?" She sat down and crossed her legs. "When you said I was nothing like Teresa, what did you mean by that?"

He tilted his head back, hoping to disappear in the dark shadow of the boards. "You're nothing like her. That's all."

"What was she like?"

"She was different. Sometimes it's hard to remember what she was like. She was beautiful but she knew it. It made her hard to paint. I got frustrated with her once and she said it wasn't her fault she knew she was good-looking. She said men had been hitting on her since she was twelve. She'd have to be stupid not put two and two together."

"Yuck."

"Hmm. Yeah, I suppose that would be a pain for a girl."

"You don't mind it when you're nineteen, but twelve? Yuck."

"Male attention, you mean." He couldn't see her expression in the dark. "Do you get lots of male attention?"

Her laugh was soft. "Simply loads. I'm fascinating."

"You're funny. Teresa had no sense of humour. Not about herself anyway." Del shifted his legs under him and relaxed, glad that Alvina couldn't see the pleasure in his face. "I bet guys love being with you. You don't talk much."

"Males love a nice, quiet female, do they?"

"Yeah, they do. The female brain moves too fast for us. By the time we've figured out what you're talking about in one conversation, you've moved on to a new subject."

"You'll have to introduce me to one of these mythical males of whom you speak. I've never met one. Not even you qualify. You're with Dagmar and she's pretty lively."

"Who says I'm with Dagmar?"

"She does. Well, she said it was complicated but in a

couples sort of way. She thought I should know. She was trying to alert me, but it wasn't necessary. You can tell her that." Her voice floated to him, eerily disconnected from the girl. "This is a very awkward conversation."

Now the dark was frustrating. He needed to see her expression, to see if she was serious. "Dagmar and I are not complicated. We're not anything. Dagmar is a friend."

"Friends don't sleep together."

Del vaulted to his feet. He reached down and pulled Alvina up by her arm into the blue-white moonlight. Not roughly, but hard enough, startling her. Her thin body, her wide eyes—he could—right now. "I could fuck you. Would that make us lovers?"

"No." She didn't try to pull away. "Don't be angry."

There was something in her words, in his hands on her arms, in the dark privacy of the bridge. A warning. This was too big. This was not manageable. He didn't want to think about it and risk bringing it to life. A cloud covered the moon. Del dropped his hands to his sides and took two steps back, more for his benefit than for hers.

"I'm not angry. I don't like anyone laying claim to me. Dagmar knows that." His hands were shaking. It was like dropping out and coming back into the world again without knowing how long he'd been gone or what set him off in the first place. Del took a slow, deep breath.

"OK, I see what happened," Alvina said calmly. "I misread the message. Dagmar wasn't staking a claim on you by talking to me. She was trying to protect you."

"Protect me—protect me from what?"

"From me. She was angry at me over the article

about Marlee selling the property the trailer sits on. She's worried I'll exploit you. I wouldn't, but Dagmar doesn't know me. I wouldn't do that to anyone." Alvina tucked her hair behind her ears. "That's two warnings I've had to keep away from you. You'd think I worked for the *National Enquirer*."

Alvina's mouth tugged to a smile. Her smiles were unwilling, Del noticed. Not forced, but hard to come by. Life was a serious business for Alvina Moon. She propped her arms on the railing and rested her head on them. Her eyes were dark and weary. Her skin looked like luminous cream. If he could remember her like this, he could paint her, Del thought.

"How did you get your name?" she murmured.

"I was named for my grandfather on my mother's side—Delmar. It means 'of the sea.' I was born in New Brunswick. What about you?"

"I was named for an obscure movie actress from the thirties. My parents are actors. They were at a cast party the night I was born. I think they pulled the name out of a hat. It means 'noble friend.'"

"It suits you," he said.

"So does yours. 'Of the sea.' A cold north sea. A Viking. That describes you."

Del took a breath. "I've built a canoe. I'm taking it for a test run from my place to the base of the Paugan Falls. The water is calmer there and it's private. Come with me."

"You've *built* a canoe? How?"

"With birch bark. An Ojibwa artist staying at the Camp last winter told me how it was done. I wanted a canoe and birch bark canoes are the best. They're strong and light and able to carry heavy loads. The tree is the main thing. It has to be tall and have its branches shed from the lower trunk. I built mine in the spring."

"When are you going to test it?"

"Tomorrow."

She tucked her hair behind her ears, her face considering. The river ticked behind them. "I can't. I have to work."

"Okay," Del said. "Next time." He turned to leave. Walk away, he thought. Take it as a sign.

"Wait." Alvina touched his arm. "I could go if there's a story in it. I'm really stuck for ideas right now. I've sold all this advertising for the last issue and there's not enough copy. I could write about the canoe trip and take a couple of photos. Not an interview—nothing like that." She crossed her arms over her middle.

Be at the cabin early, he told her. He wanted to leave before nine.

# TEN

**D**EL WAS leaning in the doorway, waiting for her. The sun made a glossy helmet of his head. A small red cooler and a backpack were at his feet. Alvina climbed out of the van. The smell of wood smoke was in the air. For a second she thought the forest was on fire until she saw the burn barrel at the edge of the meadow. Strips of bark and wood debris were smouldering inside the heavy metal cylinder, a recovered oil drum.

"Hi," she said. Her stomach was back on the queasy roller coaster. She had skipped breakfast, too nervous to eat.

"You came. I thought you'd change your mind."

"No. I'm here. I'm looking forward to it."

Alvina tugged the camisole shirt she was wearing down over her stomach. White cotton with ruffles—it was the prettiest thing she could find that was clean. She forgot the reason why she never wore it. It rode up.

There was an opening in the forest where stakes had been driven into the ground to secure rolls of bark, the foundation of the hand-crafted canoe. Alvina lifted her camera and zoomed in to photograph it. "What are those logs for?" She pointed to the stack in the meadow.

"My painting studio. I'll chainsaw those logs into six inch lengths and stack and mortar them together into four walls. A guest at the Camp gave a talk about it. I have some diagrams. It's called stack wall construction. It's the easiest and cheapest construction method around."

The field was growing up around the stack. The logs were rotting into the earth.

"How long have they been there?"

"Seven years."

As long as Teresa has been dead, Alvina thought. The studio, the cabin, even Del himself had been halted in mid-stride by her death. Who was Teresa exactly? A misused girl who had gone to the Oasis with Trey because she was vain and gullible? Or a misbegotten schemer. A cuckoo in Marlee's nest. The bastard bride of both Del and Trey.

Teresa and Del. Babes in the wood. Dave got it only half-right. One of them was a wolf. Del Musgrave had been hurt by her. Hurt so bad that he had left off living.

He closed the cabin door, picked up the cooler and hefted the backpack over one shoulder. A blanket was strapped to the pack.

The trees sounded with the staccato call of birds. The heat bugs were already high though the day had barely begun. A gust flapped the laundry on his line. It was a strange quiet at Del's cabin because in a way, it wasn't quiet at all. It was just the absence of human life she was hearing. No radio noise, television, phones ringing and car motors made it seem quieter than it really was.

"I thought we were testing the canoe." She eyed the blanket. Alvina slung her camera case across her body and the camisole rode up.

"We are. We'll paddle upriver to a spot I want to

paint. If the canoe holds together, we'll picnic there if you can spare the time from work."

"I'm on my own again today. Dave is sort of AWOL at the moment. I left a message on the answering machine just in case he comes in and wonders where I am. A hundred and fifty-year-old institution is closing its doors—he'd better be here for it or I'll kill him. The *Record* deserves a better send-off than just me and a cupcake." It was a relief to say it out loud as though it could almost be normal for a person's boss to vanish. She squinted at Del. "What do you mean if the canoe holds together?"

Del grinned and walked past her, his long legs cutting a path across the meadow that was wet with dew. A thin mist rose up and drifted about his knees. Sunlight dappled across his back. Alvina watched him. The vision was so familiar it dazzled and half-frightened her to tears. Coral would say the *déjà vu* meant Alvina had known Del in a previous life, which could explain a few things, but did nothing to release her from the painful obsession she had with getting to know him in this life.

Alvina broke into a run and caught up with him on the trail that led through the forest to the dock. Her shoes were soaked. They walked side-by-side in silence to the riverbank. The canoe was stowed upside down several feet onshore under some cedars. Del handed her his pack and then lifted the canoe over his head, like a *voyageur*, *portage*-style. He carried it to the dock and gently slid it into the water. Birch bark seemed like an insanely fragile material for a boat. Del's first instruction when she climbed in was to sit perfectly still, absolutely no fidgeting or shifting allowed.

Traditional canoes were narrow and tippy. There were no life jackets. Del knelt behind her on a thin piece of foam and pushed off from the rock.

The air smelled like fresh water. Morning was the sweet spot in a summer day. "It'll take us an hour to get there," said Del. They were paddling to a section of the river where there was not another living soul around. Between them sat his backpack and the cooler that held their lunch. The cooler would be used as a stool when he painted he explained. Otherwise he'd have packed the lunch in paper, something he could burn.

"Whatever we bring in, we have to bring out."

The paddle cut the water noiselessly. There were continual changes in the current. Whorls and bends in places where the river seemed to turn back on itself, and even its personality changed from mudflats to shallows to deep dark water. Del answered her questions about the canoe, the river and the groups he guided. He told her how the Europeans would hike to the top of the mountain and instantly fall asleep. "It's the air. They aren't used to it."

A mother duck led her babies into the water. They canoed past a fallen barn; aspens and lilac bushes were growing in the abandoned pasture. The farmhouse had been cut off from the barn by the old highway decades ago. Del told her that at one time the ribbon of asphalt was the only route to the Hills from the Ottawa Valley. And she'd find, if she travelled it, that every five miles or so there was a village or a general store or the crumbling remains of an inn. Five miles being the distance a horse could travel before it needed to stop and be watered. Like a skeleton, the region hadn't prospered to the point that the pioneer life was padded from view.

The pool below the Paugan Falls was as still as one could hope to find on the Gatineau River. Before the Paugan Dam was built, millennia of falling water had carved a deep basin in the river bed. With the falls stopped, the water here was smooth as glass and hushed. The land was wild, though not especially remote, a corridor of bush lots inhabited by birds, chipmunks, squirrels, rabbits, fox, deer and wolves. Pale green aspens and poplars crowded with dark green pine, hemlock and spruce.

The rock face of the Paugan Falls was rounded smooth. Above the dam, Del told her the water sprawled over hillsides, between trees. Fifty farms and a portion of the village of Lac Ste. Marie were swallowed up by the rising river when the dam was built. Alvina couldn't visualize farms under water. Drowned pastures, fields and farmhouses.

"What a mess," she said. "What a waste."

"But we have electricity."

The world had changed in 1920. West Québec needed electricity. There was no other way. The world is always changing, Alvina thought, and it always leaves a mess.

"The headwaters are near Parent, in the Haute-Mauricie region. Five hundred and twenty kilometres of river, eighty percent of it is forested."

For a century, logging companies used the river to float logs downstream to pulp and paper mills in Hull. Logs were guided over the thirty-five meter drop at the Paugan Falls by *draveurs* clutching long poles with spikes on the ends, dancing over log jams with speed and agility. After the dam cut off the fast moving waters, a sluice was devised to send the logs over the mountain and down to the river below. The Paugan Falls were gone now, dried up, killed by a curve of concrete. Its rock face was rudely exposed. The skeleton of the mighty cliff loomed. Smooth, white, rounded granite like the white bones of an old woman.

"It's sort of obscene," Alvina said. "We're not supposed to see this. It's supposed to be hidden by water."

This far upriver civilization seemed to disappear altogether. Even the power lines that were the reason for the wholesale flooding in the first place were hard to find. Del steered the canoe to a smooth rock shore. Alvina moved to get her camera and the canoe tilted under her. "How do I get out?"

"Give me a minute."

He beached the prow and shoved the paddle hard to pull alongside the rock. Del leapt out easily and quickly and reached down to help her. The wind was in the pines and the sky was cloudless. The river lapped peaceably against the canoe.

"This is it. It's usually bad here in the summer with the bugs. But if the day's hot enough, the bugs die off and it's tolerable."

He pulled the canoe well up on shore, shouldered the pack, and then turned, following a faint trail into the forest. Alvina snatched up her camera and the cooler and hiked after him, realizing that she'd have to rush to catch up or she'd be left behind.

The forest thickened around them. Her camera swung from her shoulder. She mustn't forget to take photos of the canoe or the whole trip would be for nothing. The day was sticky with humidity and the forest didn't offer much relief. The heat thinned a little under the pines, a thick carpet of leaf litter and needles cushioned their steps. The soil was too thin and the tree canopy too thick to encourage growth on the forest floor. The way ahead was uncluttered and well-trod. The hot sharp scent of dead spruce needles filled her nose. She breathed deeply, a smell she remembered from childhood. "It's like playing in the woods when you're a kid," she said. "Is that why you like being a guide?"

"I like to paint. I guide because it pays the bills. Tourists don't understand the wilderness. If I don't have something planned like cliff diving or climbing, they get bored. They're enthused by how rough it is at first, figuring the wilderness is an extreme sport. But then they get uneasy. Their heads snap around but they can't see anything. They think if it's in a painting the wilderness must be worth something. But they can't see it and it makes them nervous. They like nature but they have to drive a spike into it."

Alvina was panting a little from the hike. The camisole clung to her back. "To be fair, human beings have a reason to be nervous. There are predators and bugs and getting lost and going hungry and exposure to the elements—basic survival is at stake. The pioneers cleared the forests just as soon as they could for that reason."

Del looked back at her. He wasn't even breaking a sweat. "Are you nervous?"

"No." But she was and she had a feeling he knew she was.

"We're here," he said abruptly as they entered a grove of soaring pines.

The trees, ten or more of them, lifted to the sky

on wide trunks, straight as arrows. They had grown in a circle leaving a clearing below. Del said. "These trees wouldn't have survived if the dam hadn't been built. The logging company would have taken them."

Alvina gazed up at the green canopy. She lifted her camera without seeing what it was he saw or how this rugged landscape could become art. Del untied the blanket from backpack and spread it out on the ground. He sat down and flipped open the cooler, which was the last thing she expected him to do.

"I thought you were going to paint."

"I have to eat first. Breakfast was a long time ago. Want one?" He lifted out a sandwich wrapped in waxed paper and offered it to her.

The cooler was filled with sandwiches, cartons of cold milk, fruit and cakes, enough for two. It was only ten o'clock in the morning. Men who worked out-of-doors were always hungry. They burned through food. Alvina accepted the sandwich even though she was too jittery to eat it. Del had no problem. He devoured his in a half-dozen bites. Starving after paddling the river, he told her between mouthfuls.

When he was finished, he lay back on the blanket and closed his eyes.

"Now what are you doing?"

"I'm listening. Stop talking and listen."

Alvina closed her mouth and heard the wind in the pines. She remembered Del telling her this piece of Earth was Precambrian, the earliest geological era. It had been in existence long before humans and it would exist long after humans were gone. There was comfort in that. Being here, in a fixed place that wouldn't move or shift or toss her off was very reassuring.

She stretched out on the blanket beside Del, aware of what she was doing, but not really. Her mind had moved to a distant place, pulled by something that was completely new to her. It was the sharp bliss of desire.

"Can I ask you a personal question? You don't have to answer, I won't be offended."

Del twisted his neck to look at her but didn't speak.

The courage to ask seemed to come out of nowhere. "How did you get those marks on your back? I saw them the other day when you were painting."

"I had an accident when I was a kid," he said automatically. "I got caught in some barbed wire."

The air blew over them, warm and sweet smelling.

"No, I don't think that's true. I've seen a barbed wire injury. It doesn't look like that."

Del sighed, irritated. "My dad hit me with a bicycle chain when I was fourteen. What difference does it make?"

"No difference to me. Why did you lie?"

"I get asked about those scars at least three times a month. I don't want to get into it every time I take my shirt off." He bent one arm across his forehead, shading his face.

"I'm sorry I asked. I didn't realize you walked around with your shirt off as a regular thing." Alvina rolled to her side and propped her head in her hand. "I thought you were trying to put me off because I'm here for a story and you want to get rid of me."

"I don't want to get rid of you." Del gazed at her.

Her stomach dipped. Alvina looked at the trees. His hair smelled like the wind. "I don't need the truth in every situation," she said. "It's okay to lie to me a little."

There was pause. Then Del sighed. "My dad was

trying to start a small side business out of our garage fixing bikes. He had a couple of bikes to fix that afternoon and I was helping him. I thought we were doing pretty good, we were enjoying the work, at least I was. Something happened to piss him off. He got easily frustrated, my dad. The chain fell off the bike he was working on. I didn't notice. He picked it up and swung it. It hit me on my back. I thought it was an accident at first so I didn't move. He hit me twice more before I figured it out."

Alvina felt her lungs give out. "What did you do?"

"I ran like hell to the woods. Same thing I always did when he got like that. He never followed me there. He lost his power in the forest and I found mine. He was afraid of any place he couldn't control. The house was his kingdom. The woods were mine."

Del crooked his arm over his face. The wind moved through the trees high above them.

"What about your mom? Where was she when all this was going on?"

"If she wasn't at work, she was slaving away in the kitchen, trying to keep the peace. My mother worked days as a receptionist at a hotel. Dad worked nights as a security guard. The fireworks went off in the hours they overlapped. The first time he hit me I was eight or nine. I was trying to stop him from beating my mother. The last time was with the bicycle chain. That was the year he died."

Alvina rolled away from him and stared at the sky. She felt like crying. It would disgust him if she did. "How do people get like that? What makes a person so vicious that they could hit a little kid?"

"Owen Musgrave was a sadist. It's not worth trying

to understand why. My Dad had an insurance policy with the security company he worked for. When he died, my mother was finally rid of him and she was well-provided for. Some people only serve humanity by dying."

"Living with that—I'm glad he's dead and he's not even my father. That's like a happy ending, actually. The moral of the story. How did he die?"

Del wouldn't look at her. "It was a freak accident. He filled the lawnmower with gasoline and then decided to blow off the grass clippings with the compressed air hose. The force of the air and the gas fumes sparked and burst into flame. His clothing ignited in seconds. Eighty percent of his body burned. The paramedics said my dad let the fire take him. Burn victims are usually survivors; human beings have a strong survival instinct, even in pain. Not my dad. He inhaled the flames."

"My god. Oh my god. Del, I'm sorry. That's a terrible way to die."

"It's a worse way to live. People said he was handsome. That's all he had going for him and in the end he didn't even have that." Del sat up and eyed her over his shoulder. His brow was clear and untroubled. "I'm going to paint now. Do you want to come with me or do you want to stay here and write your story? The spot isn't far from here."

To reach his painting site, they had to hike through the woods and then climb a small but steep hill. Once at the top, the Gatineau Hills rolled out before them in smoky greens and soft blues. Tough grasses grew between the boulders. "We're on Canadian Shield," he explained. "The soil cover here isn't deep enough for tree seedlings to root." Low clumps of juniper bushes managed to thrive.

Alvina sat on an ancient stone and opened the sandwich he'd given her. Roast beef on white bread with ketchup. The heat bore down, stunning the Québec wilderness into silence. The ground was crunchy with dry lichen and moss. Below them, the river looked like a chunky band of silver. She asked to see what he was working on and he showed her a forest thick with pale green birches and green black pines. A small portion of the scene was unfinished. Ghostly lines, sketched in the right-hand corner still had to be painted. Del stood close behind her as she examined it. His flesh smelled of linseed oil and clean sweat.

"I'm running out of paint. I'll have to learn to work with less if I'm going to get through the summer."

He set up the cooler as his stool and propped the plywood square against a rock. Then he pulled the paint box and palette out of the backpack. This is his ritual, she thought as she watched him. Del's expression was as solemn as a priest's.

Once he started painting, she knew he was no longer aware of her or even himself. His movements lifting brush to palette to canvas were abrupt, decisive and exciting. Oils stretched over the plywood became trees. Colours were blended or shot out from the view. The surprise when minor daubs of grey became rocks and smudged lines became distant hillsides. And within the whole was something more—a longing for a place, as if he was trying to live through the landscape and could never quite pull it off. He worked as though he was in a fight to the death with the paint. It was a terrible calling.

Or maybe that was just her interpretation, Alvina

thought. Maybe she was projecting onto Del qualities and feelings he didn't possess because he was handsome. It was hard to see past his beauty. Hard to know who he really was. His muscles bunched under his pale blue tee-shirt, with its neckline that had been stretched from being washed too many times. He wore long pants of army cotton and thick hiking boots.

Along his back were three white scars.

Del Musgrave needed this, she realized. He needed the wilderness. Painting was the delivery system, the excuse to leave the civilized world, the way some people use bird-watching as an excuse. It was the trees, stone, wind and water that he came here to be with. The shape of what he had inside him needed breathing room to grow.

It seemed to Alvina that the only way to really see Del Musgrave was from behind. He blinded one face-to-face. His body was long and lean, though his shoulders were broad from years of manual labour. He was brown from the sun. Not a good thing, Alvina thought. He should watch that. Skin cancer. His blonde hair was getting long. It curled below his ears. It amazed her that he could be so unselfconsciously beautiful. Not using it and not interested in it, tossing it away like it bored him.

The effect was osmotic. In Del's company, for once she wasn't tracking her every inadequacy. Maybe it would be different if they were out in the world. If they were at Café Trémolos with Dagmar, Missy and Stu she would notice everything. It was being alone that separated them from judgment.

"Last night on the bridge, you said you received two warnings about me. One was from Dagmar. Who was the other one from?"

"I can't remember." Alvina's face went hot.

"Now who's lying?" Del set his brush down and wiped his hands on an oily rag. "Was it Dave?"

Actually it was Dave on one occasion. Alvina recalled he had given the same warning Dagmar did: leave Del Musgrave alone. But that was to do with her job. Marlee's warning was different. It was personal and as it turned out, embarrassingly prescient.

"No, it wasn't Dave." She fumbled with her sandwich. "It was Marlee Bremer."

"When was this?" he asked casually.

"Last Sunday. I was following up on the story I'd written about the trailer being sold and I had some questions about her husband's appeal. She wasn't happy about it. She probably said it to get revenge because I intruded on her privacy. People hate reporters. It wasn't important."

Alvina's neck burned. She felt prickly bringing up Trey Bremer to Del. A ridiculous over-sensitivity, she thought. A bad habit she'd picked up from her parents, dramatizing feelings in people that probably weren't there.

"What did she say exactly?" He lifted a brush coated in ochre and began to clean it.

"That you were unpredictable and to stay away. It was presumptuous of her. I'm embarrassed we're even talking about it. All artists are temperamental. My parents, Coral and Oliver Moon are prime examples. I grew up with creative genius. I know what to expect."

"But she said I was unpredictable." Del's expression was bland. "She wasn't talking about artistic temperament."

She couldn't look at him. "I don't know what made her say anything in the first place. I didn't ask for her advice. I never gave the impression you were more than a friend. I told her you were with Dagmar. Sorry, but I thought you were. That seemed to make her happy."

"So it was okay for Dagmar to be with me, but not you. It was you she warned against getting too close." He wiped down each of his brushes and set them in the box.

"Yes. I guess that's true. It was just me."

"It makes me feel like a predator, bringing you here." He slammed the paint box closed. "People told you I can't be trusted so why did you come today?"

"I can look out for myself. I've been doing it since I was ten."

"We have that in common." He rubbed a hand through his hair, dismay in his face.

Alvina held her breath, distantly aware that something she didn't want to happen was about to happen.

"Marlee is not wrong about me," Del said. "I know what I'm like. Maybe she saw it in me years ago and it's still there. This is hard for me to say. I wish you knew how hard. See, this is the difference between you and Dagmar. I wouldn't have to have this conversation with Dagmar."

"It's fine." Alvina set her sandwich in her lap, her appetite gone. "I get it. You don't have to let me down gently or anything like that. I'm tougher than people think. It really is okay. I'm leaving town soon anyway. We can just be friends."

"You don't understand." Del crouched down in front of her. His hands wrapped around her calves just as he had done when he first met her and she'd scraped her knees. "I met a woman once at the Camp, a sculptor from Chicago who had a pet python. She'd raised this python from infancy, nurtured it and loved it. One day she noticed it was acting strange. She told her friends the snake seemed lethargic, it wasn't interested in eating. She thought it was ill. One morning she woke up and the python was stretched out in bed beside her, stretched out the full length of her body. She called the vet's office, frantic, her snake needed help. The vet came on the phone as soon as his assistant relayed her message. He told the woman to hang up and leave the apartment immediately. He was sending a team to collect the snake. The woman asked why, convinced the vet was going to say her pet snake was dying. The vet told her bluntly—her pet was getting ready to kill her. Pythons measure their victims before consuming them."

"That's disgusting. Are you saying that's me?"

He gazed at her. "I'm saying I want to fuck you, Alvina. I don't want to be your friend. That's what Marlee was warning you about. That's what I'm like."

Her brain fogged and then reassembled as her body responded. And then she felt sick, fearful he was going to change his mind or that through a horrible mistake, the wrong words spoken, she was going to lose this chance forever. Lust was a little like going insane. Reason didn't stand a chance against it. She literally couldn't think.

He released her abruptly and got to his feet, slapping the dirt from his knees. The sun was hard and brilliant behind him, blinding her. "Talking about it makes me want it so we're not going to talk about it. I'm not going to see you anymore. Don't try to see me. I don't want to get into something I can't get out of."

"Is this because I asked you about the scars?"

"No, it's because I wanted to tell you about them."

Del stooped to pick up his paint box. Shadows were falling and he was avoiding eye contact. It was hard to read his expression. But his words had given her hope, which was never a good thing and she should have known better.

"You don't want to get hurt again. I get that. You loved Teresa and she hurt you."

He leaned forward, growing more handsome as he became earnest. "She hurt me?"

And then Alvina realized her mistake. Del didn't know what Teresa was up to. He wasn't hurt. He wasn't psychologically scarred, afraid to fall in love or any of the scenarios she'd manufactured in her brain. He meant exactly what he said: he didn't want to get into something he couldn't get out of. Because Del Musgrave knew, as all the guys Alvina had been with knew, that the day would come when he would definitely want out.

She ought to pull the anonymous note out of the camera bag and shove it in his face. Dot's green poison dragged out in the open, forcing him to see the girl he was so bloody obsessed with. Why not? Why shouldn't he hurt like hell? Show him the cassette tape too, let him hear what he would've suffered until he was a dead old man if Teresa had lived. Alvina had the proof. She could do it to him. Right now.

"Come on, Alvina. Tell me. How did Teresa hurt me?"

"She hurt you ... by dying. That's all I meant." Alvina quickly looked away. Of course she couldn't do it. Was there ever any doubt?

A siren pierced the air with an unholy wail.

Alvina slammed her hands over her ears. "What the hell!"

They spun in unison and faced the river. Del cupped his hands over his eyes and looked down. "It's the warning siren. They're going to open the dam!" He turned to her, his face suddenly alive. "Come on!"

She held back, letting him run ahead so she could pull herself together. She had to get her camera anyway and made a detour to the blanket where she'd left it. There was a second wail—a blast so loud Alvina's eardrums rang. Del scaled a mound of rock at the river's edge. When she got there, he grabbed her hand and pulled her up behind him. They were very close to the white rock face of the Paugan Falls.

"What's happening?" she gasped.

"Look." Del pointed up. "The rain we had on Monday must have filled the reservoir. Hydro Québec schedules these openings when the water level gets too high."

At the top of the Paugan Falls cliff, the spillway compartments were noisily rising, metal grinding, an engineering marvel of switches and gears—men in hardhats were overseeing the release of the Gatineau River. Alvina stepped to the edge of the rock and lifted her camera.

"Get back here! You're too close. If you lose your balance you won't be able to fight the current and you'll get swept away. Alvina, I'm serious. It's too dangerous. Put your camera down and get back here."

A hot geyser of rage boiled up in Alvina's chest and shot out uncontrollably. "I'm taking the fucking picture! You've warned me about the danger—thank you. If I fall in it's on me, but I'm getting a photo of the goddamned Paugan Falls for the *Record!*" Her limbs quivered and her eyes burned. *Don't you dare cry, Alvina.*

There was a roar above. Del's eyes moved to the smoothly rising dam.

"Okay, okay. But wait. Don't move." He took off his belt, fed it through one of the belt loops on her shorts and twisted the other end around his wrist. "Okay, I've got you. Go ahead, but I want you to know there's a huge fine if they catch us. No one is allowed in this area after the second siren. They won't give you a break even if you say you're from the *Record.*"

He gripped the end of the belt.

Alvina turned away. She couldn't bear to look at him. She'd exposed her feelings and he didn't want the hassle. That's what it came down to. In two weeks she'll be homeless and unemployed. Concentrate on that. Give yourself another stale pep talk.

The waterfall trickle became a surge of white foamy water and then a mile high breaker. Alvina raised her camera, leaning her body out over the edge as far as Del could hold her. She looked through the viewfinder. The calm waters above the dam were unleashed with deadly force, pounding over the concrete spillway, hurtling off the cliff face and crashing into the river below them. The roar was deafening.

Alvina lifted her camera before the spray reached them. Her eyes were blurry with tears. She leaned out further, wondering what she was doing even as Del strained to hold her.

She twisted to meet his eyes. The leather belt had darkened and the blood had left his wrist. One slip and she would fall into the rushing current. He could let go and she would fall. It would be no one's fault. She'd heard that drowning was pretty painless.

His blonde hair was netted with rainbow spray.

"A death wish leads to death, Alvina."

His voice held a warning. Reading her mind.

# ELEVEN

THE MUNICIPALITÉ régionale de comté des Collines police force wasn't large but it was impressive in action. A convoy of police cruisers and the MRC des Collines CSU van stopped at the lights. One after the other turned left into the village. No sirens.

They were going to a body.

Alvina was in Dave's office when she saw the procession go by. She jumped to the window. Bringing up the rear was a black unmarked sedan. The man in the passenger seat was Detective Sergeant Rompré.

Alvina dropped the load of files she was sorting and broke into a run. At the bottom of the stairs she realized she'd forgotten her camera and dithered, debating whether it was worth getting photos. Ingrained training made her pound back up the stairs. Dave would be pleased. *That's using your head, Moon.*

A crowd had lined the train trestle bridge despite attempts by the police to move them along. Crime Scene Unit investigators were combing the riverbank below. DS Rompré was among them, deep in conversation with his team. The village street had been blocked off to traffic. Five or six beat constables bundled in black vests and weighted down with guns, sticks and radios stood about gossiping, already bored. The main thrust of their calling was to prevent crime and it was too late for that. A crime had already been committed.

"What's going on?" Out of breath, Alvina joined Mavis Brant who was watching the action from the north end of the bridge. Finding Mavis was a lucky break. She could always be counted on for a juicy quote. Alvina lifted her camera and fired off some shots of the scene.

"Those kids were pushing their bikes over the bridge." Mavis pointed to a clump of chattering, hyper nine-year-olds. "One of them glanced down between the railroad ties and saw something in the river. So they went down to investigate the way boys do, and it turned out to be a body. The panic to save this man who was so obviously past saving wasn't even funny. I don't know what they're teaching them in schools these days. Whatever it is, it isn't common sense. The kids screamed for help and a gang of municipal workers dropped their shovels and came running. Any excuse to stop work for all the use they were. Three of them threw up in the bushes when they got a look at the body."

"Why is Detective Sergeant Rompré here? Is it a homicide?"

"I wouldn't be surprised. It's a wonder we're not all killed in our beds. That young cop, what's her name— Constable Fournier, she's taking statements. She's quite tiny, don't you think? She wears that bullet proof vest and so forth, but she's still too small to defend a person in my opinion. If I'm being attacked, I would prefer a male officer to come to my defense, not another woman, wouldn't you?"

"I think the gun balances things out." Alvina peered through her viewfinder.

Constable Martine Fournier was the officer DS Rompré assigned to take witness statements from *les anglais*. Her mother tongue was English. The population of West Québec spoke enough French and English to get along, but in a crisis people can barely get the story out, never mind get it out in translation. Rompré was not interested in politics; he was interested in getting an accurate statement. If the witness's mother tongue was French he sent his French officer; if English, he sent Fournier.

"Have they identified the body?"

"They think a fisherman got swept away when the dam opened. You know how quiet it is up there for fishing. They tell these guys to stay clear but do they listen? His boat must have capsized. No life jacket as usual. I heard one of those forensic fellows you see in the white coverall there say he's been in the water for a few days."

Constable Lemen had finished interviewing the municipal workers and approached Detective Sergeant Rompré. Their exchange was brief and in French, although Alvina remembered Lemen's English was good. He was the constable who had responded to her call when Dave went missing.

Her breath caught.

Detective Sergeant Rompré looked up, scanning the crowd on the bridge until he found her. She met his eyes. He was wearing a light linen suit and a tie, loose at the neck, a blue tie with green flecks. His sympathetic brown gaze didn't miss much. Rompré gave a slight shake of his head and walked toward her.

Alvina's legs gave way and she fell to the ground.

HYDRO QUÉBEC issued a statement. When the sirens have sounded, fishermen, swimmers and other recreational users of the river are to leave the area immediately. A boy drowned a few years back after a dam opening. Despite posted signs warning of danger, the boy's mother thought it was a great swimming location. Since then, Hydro Québec ran frequent public service announcements to inform the public of the danger.

No one could blame Hydro Québec for this one. Dave Gomer was good and dead before the dam opened and shot him downriver like a watermelon seed. CSU determined that the victim had floated a distance downstream before getting caught on some debris where he might have stayed if the dam hadn't opened. The sudden influx of water raised the river level and tossed the corpse violently downriver—a washing machine with rocks as one CSU investigator described it —until it reached the rapids where the real damage was done. By the time his body floated into Stollerton Bay, Dave Gomer was unrecognizable. Dental records were used for the identification, the only evidence his ex-wife Dorothy would accept, although his wallet was still in his back pocket.

Dorothy Gomer became regarded as Dave's widow based on her recent appeals to search for the man, a role she embraced with alacrity. Dead, her ex-husband had elevated Dot to a minor celebrity. There was heady prestige in making the funeral arrangements; a shiver of glory when she accepted the condolences of her colleagues at the dental clinic. But when asked if she'd ever remarry, the answer was an unqualified no. Fool me once was Dot's view of marriage now.

Marlee Bremer was in the hairdresser's when she learned that the body found under the trestle bridge was Dave Gomer's. She happened to be looking at her reflection in the mirror at the time. Other than a rapid blink of the eyes, her reaction was appropriately dismayed. She asked how it happened and expressed concern for her old colleague, Dotty.

Then she gave instructions for the highlights she needed.


MAVIS BRANT gossiped about it later, how without any warning at all, Alvina Moon had collapsed at her feet. "As it turned out, the drowned man was her boss Dave Gomer. They'll find a bottle of scotch in his system," predicted Mavis with grim satisfaction. "It's not called dead drunk for nothing."

Everyone who knew Dave, even those who liked him, agreed with Mavis Brant, which explained why so few volunteers had come forward to search for the missing man in the first place. Interest in the disappearance of the larger-than-life publisher of *The Stollerton Record* had waned at the exact moment his body was spotted under the trestle bridge.

The preliminary exam couldn't offer a precise time of death nor could investigators determine where the accident occurred. It wasn't certain that the victim was fishing at the time, although that was the most likely explanation for why he was in the water. However, his fishing rod and tackle box had not been touched.

The regulars at Keefer's were happy to offer up their theories to Constable Martine Fournier. Clearly, Dave had stood up in the boat to take a leak and fell in. Drowned fishermen were almost always found with their flies open—the final indignity. Dave didn't believe in lifejackets. You either believe you're going to drown or you don't, said his buddies, and Dave didn't believe he'd drown.

"Did you see him that morning?" Constable Fournier asked with remarkable patience. "Did anyone witness Dave Gomer on the river last Monday?"

Whether anyone saw him was of no importance. Something happened to him. He stood up, lost his balance, and knocked himself unconscious. That was one theory and a good one. The other was that he was reaching for something and lost his balance. Dave's friends enjoyed discussing variations on the lost-balance theory; the many ways and means a guy can lose his balance in a boat and drown. Dave, drunk as a lord, passed out and took a tumble. Dave used to know how to tie one on.

Constable Fournier sensed she was losing control of the interview and tried to bring the men back around to the main topic. "Did any of you see him at all on Monday? Even a brief sighting can help us establish the time of death. A simple yes or no will do."

They frowned in their beer. None of them had seen him that day and they were genuinely sorry that they hadn't. Speculating about his disappearance and death had made for long and satisfying conversations.

Then one of the men piped up, reluctantly. He'd seen Dave's boat on the river a few days ago. Typically, (Fournier was familiar with the type) he then reversed himself and said he couldn't say for sure it was Dave's. When was this, she asked, knowing these guys recognized each other's boats and pickup trucks like they knew their own children.

"Monday morning. It was raining so I didn't get a good look. I saw him from the highway. He was on his way back from fishing. That's what it looked like to me. He was coming downriver at a good clip in the direction of Stollerton."

The same day he disappeared. The witness didn't come forward earlier when Dot was organizing the search because he thought it was nobody's business if Dave wanted to disappear for a few days. Constable Fournier knew the drill. Stoicism and gritty independence might be great survival skills, but they made her job harder than it had to be.

Still, it was a successful interview. Dave Gomer was seen alive and travelling downriver on Monday morning. The information offered a starting point for the investigation which was better than nothing.

DETECTIVE SERGEANT Rompré was always the same, no matter what the situation: calm, with an intensity that hummed below the surface. Ray had warned Alvina not to be fooled by his seemingly restful persona. The man was not at rest. He sat at Alvina's desk studying the contents of the red file folder Constable Fournier had handed him. Very little was known about DS Edouard Rompré. No one could understand why a career cop of his ability would join an infant regional police force in the least glamorous corner of Québec. The police had more or less commandeered the *Record* offices for their investigation. Ray told her to give them anything they wanted. Hester had said the same. Alvina was trying to be cooperative but she didn't know what it was they were looking for. Dave's office had been sealed off.

"*Mademoiselle, je suis désolé. Nous connaisson, oui?*"

Alvina nodded, her throat tight. "Yes, we have met before. I came to the station a few weeks ago. I reported finding blood in an abandoned trailer. You said it wasn't a police matter."

"*Je me souviens. Merci beaucoup.*" Rompré removed a black notebook from his jacket pocket. "*Parlez vous Français?*"

"*Mais oui.*" Alvina glanced at Constable Martine Fournier. "But my vocabulary is limited."

"English is fine," said Fournier.

Alvina watched them, the police; a dark blue sea moving in and out of the office. Her heart was as dry as a bone. Why wasn't she crying? Her irascible boss was dead and here she sat as unresponsive as a rock. Even Ray had cried. He was the first person Alvina had called when Dave's body was found. A middle-aged man breaking into tears had to be the most tragic sound on the planet. Her second phone call to her parents was less moving. They asked who Dave Gomer was.

Rompré looked up from the report Constable Lemen had filed on the missing man. "The deceased spoke with you on Monday morning by telephone. Is this correct?"

"Yes. He said he'd be late. It was raining so I said you aren't fishing in the rain, are you? And he said it was the best time so I thought that's what he was doing. He always goes fishing in the morning."

"What was his state of mind? You told Constable Lemen that your boss was on edge lately."

"He was anxious about a deal going through with MetMedia and at the same time he blamed himself for the paper going under. Our advertising had gone down.

We couldn't compete with the Internet. Dave said he wouldn't even try. He said he didn't sign up to tweet the news for people too lazy to think." Alvina tucked her hair behind her ears. "I think he was relieved to get out of the business while he still could."

"We'll need the names and coordinates of the MetMedia people," said Constable Fournier.

Alvina moved to the Rolodex sitting on her desk. So this was really happening, she thought. This wasn't a dream. Dave who used to help her do her taxes and made sure there was windshield washer fluid in the van before she took it out, Dave was really dead. She found the card with her boss's handwriting scrawled across it (*Make a file for these guys, Moon. You never know*) and handed it to Fournier.

"Was Monsieur Gomer a heavy drinker?"

"No, he's been sober for seven years. Ray Milligan knows more about that than I do. He's the *Deeper Vibe* editor. It was Dave who got Ray into A.A. He found him passed out in the park one morning and asked him if he wanted to stop drinking. Ray said he did and Dave took him to a meeting. They've been going ever since." Alvina gazed blindly at her hands. "I think this was my fault."

"How so?"

The time had come. She had to say it. "An anonymous note came to the office addressed to me. Dave told me to shred it. He'd been under so much stress. I didn't think. I hoped it'd lead to a story I could show an editor. What happened was, I asked Marlee Bremer about the flashlight that was used to murder Teresa Musgrave and I think because of that she pulled the contract with MetMedia. She warned me our conversation was setting something in motion. MetMedia was Dave's last chance to get out of the business and retire. When he called the office on Monday he asked me if I'd destroyed the note like he asked. I lied and told him I did. Then he disappeared and a bottle of vodka was found in his boat."

She felt sick. Dry. Hollow. It was a kind of suicide what Dave did. A sober alcoholic pushed to the limit because everything he'd worked for had gone up in smoke. He was dead. It was too late to make it better. Too late to ask Marlee Bremer to reconsider. Too late to tell Dave she was sorry. From the moment they found his body the only thing Alvina was sure of was that it was too late.

"Do you still have it?" Rompré's expression had not changed.

She took the camera down from the shelf above, withdrew the envelope and set it on the desk. Constable Fournier pulled on a pair of latex gloves. The notepaper was carefully removed from the envelope and unfolded on the desk.

*Where did he get the flashlight?*

The constable made eye contact with Rompré who nodded. She stepped out into the hall. Moments later, Alvina heard Constable Lemen's footsteps on the stairs exiting the building. Fournier returned to the office and bagged the note and the envelope.

"Did you show the note or discuss its contents with anyone other than Dave?" said Rompré.

"I asked Marlee Bremer the question but I didn't reveal my source. Dave said it was from someone with a grudge against her. We ran her interview the week before. He said it had flushed out the crackpots." Alvina flopped to her chair, hugging the camera case to her body. She felt deeply exhausted, like she'd been awake for days.

"You believed the message referred to the flashlight Trey Bremer used to murder Teresa Fillion."

"Not right away. I found the story in the archives and then Dave told me the rest."

"And if you had shredded the note there would be no possibility of tracing the sender."

Rompré's brown eyes held a light that puzzled Alvina. "Yes. I suppose so. But Dave already knew who the sender was—his ex-wife, Dot. Her name is Dorothy but everyone calls her Dot. I went to her place on Wednesday to ask her to file a missing person's report and I noticed she had a grocery list written in green ink. What are the odds of two people with a grudge against Marlee Bremer using green pens for their correspondence?"

"Was Dave able to confirm the handwriting was the same?"

"No, he never saw the note. I told him about it on the phone. But he knew it was from Dot. Whoever asked this question already knew the answer and the logical person to know such a thing was Dave's wife at the time. I think he realized instantly she was trying to mess him up." Alvina reddened. "It's just a theory I have."

Rompré leaned forward. "But how did Madame Gomer know this question would upset her husband?"

Alvina lifted her face. Sweat had glued her hair to her cheek. "I'm sorry?"

"How was Dave Gomer connected to the murder of Teresa Fillion?" The question hung in the air.

"Well, Dave got Teresa the job with the Bremers."

Alvina tucked her hair behind her ears.

"Yes?"

"Well." She took a breath. "Dot suggested Dave might have been more involved in that situation than he let on. I don't mean in a criminal way—but morally, for financial gain. He sobered up after Teresa was murdered. He felt responsible. Whatever he did, the amends he felt he had to make to Mrs. Bremer ended his marriage to Dot. According to her."

Rompré leaned back in the chair. He pressed the palms of his hands together and rested his chin on the tips of his fingers. "What did you think when you heard this? Did you believe your boss could be connected to a murder seven years ago?"

Alvina was beginning to understand what Hester meant about DS Rompré. He had a way of hearing everything. Whatever you thought you were hiding. The camera case was in her lap. If Ray were here he'd tell her there was no Dave to ask so what difference did it make—give them the cassette tape. Ray was pragmatic when it came to journalistic integrity. "I thought he might have done something stupid when he was still drinking. It was obvious something was wrong when I told him about the note and he flipped out. I wouldn't have judged him. We could have dealt with it. Anything would have been better than this."

Rompré turned to Fournier. The conversation that followed in rapid French was too fast for Alvina to interpret. Constable Fournier stepped to a corner of the room to make a phone call. "Regarding the vodka bottle," he asked. "Was this your boss's usual drink?"

"I don't know. I never saw him drink. I did find an empty scotch bottle in one of the file drawers though.

It was old; it hadn't been touched in years. Ray told me Dave drank scotch before he got sober."

"We will need to speak to him."

"He's on vacation in Prince Edward Island." Alvina wrote down his contact information. Her hands shook badly. She pushed the slip of paper across the desk. "I'm sorry," she said. "I hope you can read that."

"*Merci*. We won't keep you much longer."

Alvina nodded. Her head felt stuffed and hot. "Does it have to get out about the vodka? The only thing this town is going to remember about Dave is that he was wasted when he drowned. It was a terrible accident. I don't see why the cause of death has to be made public."

Rompré's brown eyes met hers. "The preliminary examination of the body indicates Monsieur Gomer's skull was crushed. He was dead before he went into the water."

The detective's voice was so low and calm that Alvina thought she must have misheard. She frowned. "No, that can't be right. How did he get in the water if he was dead? No, you must be mistaken. He was drinking. Maybe he fell?"

"There were no fingerprints in the boat, on the tiller, nor on the vodka bottle. There were no prints in the places we would expect to find prints. The victim did not wipe his fingerprints before hitting his head and falling overboard. We are treating his death as suspicious."

"Suspicious," Alvina repeated slowly. Her lips felt dry and papery. "You mean murder. Someone murdered Dave. That's insane. No one would murder Dave. You mean like for money? He didn't have any." The office air was choking her.

"Are you all right?" Fournier asked. "Is there someone we should call to stay with you?"

"No. No, I'm fine." Alvina wiped her eyes on the hem of her blouse. "I'm just scared about what to do about the paper. We have the final issue to get out and I've never done it on my own before. But I'll be okay. I can manage. Thanks anyway."

DS Rompré handed her his card. "Call me at any time, day or night. I will answer. We are here to help you."

Alvina nodded and felt weirdly grateful. Fournier gave her a tissue. Instructions were issued to keep everything she had told them confidential or she risked compromising the investigation and a potential arrest. This included the details of the anonymous note. Was there a young man in Mademoiselle Moon's life that she might be tempted to confide in?

"No, there is no one."

Rompré slipped his notebook in his jacket pocket. A smile crossed his face.

"What?" Alvina asked, alert to insult.

"*Mademoiselle Moon* is the title of a children's book. In the story, Miss Moon is permitted to see her hero the Sun for only a few minutes each dawn before the brilliance of the Sun overwhelms her."

"Sounds sad for a kid's book."

"It is. It is a tragedy. But the children don't know it."

# TWELVE

THE TEENAGED waitress handed him a menu. Del glanced at it and handed it back to her. "I'll have a hamburger and a beer."

The girl frowned. "You mean like the Veggie Burger? Cause we don't have meat, right? We're vegetarian so, like, there's no hamburger on the menu."

Del's face muscles tightened. "Fine, yes. I'll take the Veggie Burger."

The girl left him alone on the patio. Café Trémolos was filling up with workers stopping in for Happy Hour on their way home from jobs in the city. There weren't many kids on the raft. They were still ranged along the train trestle bridge checking out the accident. Del had seen a crowd gathered there when he boated by but he didn't stop to find out what happened. Whatever it was, the excitement was almost over. The police were already clearing the scene.

Alvina's building was across the street on the corner. A black sedan was pulling away from the *Record* parking lot just as he sat down. There were two cops inside.

The waitress brought a glass of cold beer to his table and set it in front of him. "What was that all about on the bridge?" he asked.

"They found a body under it, a drowned man, and

the cops they like blocked off the road for *hours*. We had customers calling from their cell phones saying they couldn't get through because of the blockade so they were going someplace else, like it was our *fault*. So now we're wondering, the owners I mean, we're wondering, you know—who's going to pay for that? The lost business, right? I mean, there should be some compensation."

"Who drowned? Do they know?"

The girl shrugged. "Beats me. Some fisherman. It'll be twenty minutes for your Veggie Burger."

Del's eyes lifted to *The Stollerton Record*'s window. He remembered the night he took Alvina to the raft. How she had gripped the sides of the motorboat, shaking all over as if she were cold. She probably was, thought Del. The air was always cooler on the river. Wind sheer had pinned her hair over her face but whenever she turned to see where they were going, her hair would catch and flap wide, revealing narrowed eyes, slim jaw and her pretty mouth. Alvina was pretty. Her hair was a colour Del had never seen. If the Sun and the Moon had a kid, it would have Alvina's hair colour.

"I thought it was you. What are you doing here?" Dagmar Weibe slipped into the chair across from him. She smelled of sandalwood.

"Having a beer." Del made himself smile. "What are you doing here?"

"I'm meeting Stu and some others. We're going into the city to see the Jackson Pollack exhibit. There's a discount on Monday nights. Hey, you should come." Her chain necklaces jingled. "There's room in the car."

He shook his head. "I only stopped for a beer and a burger."

"You left your natural habitat to get a Veggie Burger? Hmmm, I don't think so, Musgrave." She reached across the table for his beer glass, smiling her secret smile of sexual conquest. "I'm pretty sure it's not a vegetarian patty you're hungry for," she said and dipped her tongue into the head of foam.

This was Dagmar Weibe at her most attractive. Who she was and what she wanted, Del understood perfectly. He had explored her depths, sounded her out and was no longer interested. But here she was, perched across from him, tapping away, still trying to break in.

"What were the cops doing at the *Record*?"

Dagmar followed his eyes. "Some kids found Dave Gomer's body under the bridge. Alvina Moon passed out when they told her. We all thought, hmm, that's a bit over-the-top, don't you think, chick? She makes herself ridiculous. He was just her boss. The cops took her to the *Record* to talk to her."

"Is she okay?"

"The paramedics revived her. I don't know. It's hard to tell with Alvina. She always looks like she's about to fall down. Hey, did you ever confront her about that article she wrote? You must have been so pissed. I know I would've been. It was a total betrayal of trust."

Dagmar heaved herself back in the chair. Del fixed his eyes on her breasts moving softly under her tank top, trying to feel horny rather than this other thing. He had an overpowering urge to cross the street and find Alvina. Just to look at her, make sure she wasn't hurt.

He said: "She apologized. That was the end of it. I won't be seeing her again."

Dagmar chuckled darkly. "Oh, I wouldn't be so sure about that. She'll find an excuse. You're big news to a girl like that. Well you are! Don't look so offended. You'll see." Her blonde head tilted to one side, considering him. "God, you're naïve when it comes to women."

"Am I?"

"You don't believe me? What did you think was going to happen when you took Alvina Moon for a boat ride? Dude, she's in love with you. She wants to have your babies. It's written all over her face. You're never going to shake her. You might have to leave town." Dagmar's eyes danced.

Del swallowed his beer slowly. The word *love* had never stood for anything Del thought he needed to take seriously. He believed he loved Teresa once, but obsession wasn't love. Desire, lust, all those emotions that go through a young man when he looks at a girl, he thought that's all there was to it. No one had taught him. The nature of lust and obsession is to breed more lust and obsession until there is nothing left but the worm itself.

Alvina loved him. Dizzy and sick as with vertigo, Del got to his feet. "I have a better idea." He snapped a look at the *Record*. "Instead of leaving town, how about we go to my place and fuck each other's brains out."

Dagmar protested with a laugh that he was using her to throw cold water on Alvina Moon. She was wrong but Del couldn't say so. Alvina was a message, not perfectly intelligible, that woke in him a buried longing. He despised himself for trailing her here like a mongrel dog. He despised himself for the loneliness he felt that just wouldn't let up.

"Think of it as your good deed for the day. She should know what I'm really like."

Dagmar didn't object and if he had more affection

for her, he'd be grateful she didn't object. She texted Stu that she was cancelling and Del threw a twenty on the table. He jogged across the street to the boat before he could change his mind. If he could go back to being the man he was before Teresa started working for the Bremer's maybe he'd risk something more with Alvina. But there was too much he couldn't remember and what he did remember, he didn't understand. Like a puzzle he didn't know how to assemble, he was frustrated by his ignorance and his inability to figure anything out.

This much Del did know:

Teresa was a fool who'd lived in a bubble of comfort her whole life. Violence couldn't be manipulated. Evil had a mind of its own. Sexual masochists were like tourists dipping their toes in brutality. It was a whole different story when you lived in it on a permanent basis. Violence changed a person.

Del took Dagmar's hand and helped her into the boat. He cast a last furtive glance at the window where Alvina might be watching. He hoped she was. It was better this way. He fixed his mind on the journey home, the long night ahead, and the release he'd find in Dagmar's body.

ALVINA WATCHED them leave from the window in Dave's office. It was a big window that looked out onto the street and Café Trémolos's patio. They couldn't see her. She'd stepped back from the glass so they couldn't see her. Dagmar sat in the same place in the Harber Craft that Alvina had sat when he took her to see the raft. The two of them together were strikingly beautiful. It hurt. It was incredible how much it hurt, considering she hardly knew him. She tried to impose logic, common sense. Walk away from the window. It was like her mind was trapped in a cage.

She should call her parents.

Would they listen? Be honest, Alvina. Do your parents *care* to know what you're feeling right now? I mean it's one thing to not expect their interest—it's another to discover you were right not to. Coral and Oliver will cringe. What parent wants to hear their daughter has so little going for her that one date with a good-looking guy has completely messed her up? Huh? Think about it. You have to love yourself before anyone else can love you. That's what Coral would say.

Doesn't sound fair. How was she supposed to pull that off?

The office was silent, no help at all. Stu and some other artists Alvina recognized from the Arts and Letters Festival arrived on the patio. They ordered food and drinks. Little white twinkling lights came on at the café; purple dusk was falling.

This wasn't depression then. With depression she'd be lying in bed, curtains closed, sobbing or not sobbing; hair greasy, skin breaking out from excess oils. The needs of her flesh untended. What would it be like to really let go? A body rotting on the vine. That sounded biblical. Rotting on the vine. A wholesome piece of fruit left to rot, clinging to the vine in the hope that someone will pick her. And no one does. All around her, the fruit is harvested and she is left in the hot sun getting riper and riper until it's too late, she's turned to rot. She'd bitten into a rotten plum once.

She wished Dave were here. He wouldn't mind hearing about her crappy future and her pointless mad love for Del Musgrave. That was the funny thing about

Dave. For a guy with no patience, he had a lot of patience with her.

Alvina plunked down in his old swivel chair. "It was going to be a great last issue, Dave. Tons of businesses bought advertising. We were all depending on you to get the historic final edition out. You know I can't do it. This was not a good time to die."

And then the shocking fact of Dave's death broke in on her. Alvina tipped her head back, fists clenched, eyes tight, fighting it, but tears poured out of her like a faucet, cramping her stomach and choking her throat. After a moment she tried to regain control, distantly aware these were tears of self-pity and not for poor Dave but she couldn't help herself. A fresh storm boiled down her face. He was supposed to write her a reference. He was supposed to help her find another job.

"Who would be so selfish as to kill you when I needed you to—to—" She was going to say 'be the adult' but she wasn't sure what she meant by that, except that she felt suddenly bereft. Detective Sergeant Rompré's card was still in her hand. But he meant she should call if she needed help coping with Dave's death, not help coping with her whole life which was evaporating before her eyes.

*You could give them the cassette tape.*

We like to think we'll do the right thing in a criminal investigation until doing the right thing involves someone we care about. Dave Gomer wasn't always easy to work for, but at least he was consistent. Alvina Moon knew where she was with him. Dave had liked her whether she liked herself or not, and because of that, the cassette was still in her camera case where it would stay. She wiped her eyes on the tissue Constable

Fournier had given her. Anyway, it was unlikely that a phone call seven years ago would have anything to do with Dave's death. The man was not himself back then. He made mistakes. People would misinterpret. Trey calling him that night didn't change anything.

*Use your head, Moon. If that was true, then why was he killed?*

She hadn't thought of this. Why *was* Dave killed?

If he was there the night Teresa was murdered, he could have knowledge of the crime. Could he have been blackmailing someone? Was the flashlight his or did Dave know who it belonged to? What was he looking up in the archives the day he disappeared? One of the books was open on his desk when she came in that morning. Constable Lemen said his fishing hat and jacket were found in the boat, but it was raining, so why would he take them off? Ray said a scotch drinker doesn't go to the liquor store and buy vodka and Ray would know. That wasn't Dave's bottle. So who brought the vodka?

No answers from the ether.

Alvina sighed. She'd been in the office alone for too long, too full of emotion and questions—pointless, repetitive questions. The saddest thing of all was even if the police did figure out who killed Dave, it wouldn't change a thing. Not for her anyway. He was dead. Somebody took him away. She'll never get another Dave Gomer in her life.

Her eyes were drawn to the green chair behind the office door. The chair was hunched in the corner, made nearly invisible by deep shadow. Alvina peered harder, straining to see. It looked like somebody was sitting there. Which was ridiculous. She was really starting to lose it. *Be sensible, Moon.* Alvina walked over to the chair and sat down. It felt like hiding in a closet: dark, stuffy and safe. Dave's desk looked much more imposing from this distance. The police tape was gone. She should box up his personal belongings and give them to Dorothy Gomer as a sort of peace offering. Alvina felt guilty about Dot and her green pen and her sad marital history. She might appreciate getting custody of her dead husband's stuff. There were also the archives to dispose of, forty bound copies of *The Stollerton Record*. The man from the Historical Society would take those off her hands. MetMedia said under the circumstances they would give the *Record* an extension to clear out but Alvina wanted to get it over with as fast as possible. No idea why. She had nothing waiting for her.

Night was falling outside the window. Alvina sat back in the green chair. Dave Gomer was still with her after all, giving her something to think about other than Del Musgrave. Emotion clogged her throat. Her eyes swerved over the room, over the shadows, the gloom, the heat stifling the air. Marlee Bremer's ominous words came back to haunt her: *This conversation is setting something in motion. Something none of us might like.*

On impulse she picked up the phone and called Missy. Maybe they could order pizza and Alvina could talk over the case with her? Alvina could pick up it on her way home, her treat. But Missy was hosting a dinner party. "Honestly, if I'd known, Vinny, I'd ask you to join us but I didn't cook enough for an extra person. You're better off with your own friends tonight anyway, don't you think? I'd help if I could but I'm in a really good space right now and talking about death will only bring me down. Be honest, Alvina, do you really need to talk, or is it just attention you're after...? I'm not judging, I have no opinion, but he was just your boss."

Alvina wordlessly hung up the phone, cutting Missy off.

*Now you've done it. Now you really will have to move.* Missy was universally sweet to everybody. Living with Alvina Moon had driven Missy Cooper over the edge.

Her stomach growled. *The body has no clue.* Even when there's no discernible reason to support life, oh how the body insists on going on. Stomach wants food, blood wants warmth. She would have to find a way to live, even if she had no idea how and the thought of it made her sick.

Alvina slung her satchel across her body and locked the door on her way out. Since she wasn't dead, she didn't want to be uncomfortable. She'd get a hamburger from the *dépanneur* before they closed.


DOT WASN'T best pleased. She expected the police to interview her the longest, considering she was the widow, but that Constable Fournier appeared to be in a hurry. She kept pulling at her collar. She could have taken that bullet-proof vest off if she found it too stuffy in the house. The windows had to be closed during the day to keep out the heat. They were opened at night. This was just common sense. Dot didn't have an air conditioner. Not everyone can afford air conditioning. Not everyone has salaries paid by the taxpayers.

DS Rompré asked very few questions for an officer of the law in her opinion. No interest at all in how Marlee Bremer drove a wedge between her and Dave. He seemed more concerned with what Dave had done to Marlee than what Marlee had done to Dot. Well, that's the French for you. An English detective would have been alert to that piece of information. He asked her to write up a brief statement which she was happy to do until he handed her a scrap of paper and a pen from her desk! Now what police department in the world records official statements in *green* ink? Very haphazard and disrespectful in Dot's opinion. But Dot gritted her teeth and did what was asked of her, as any good citizen should.

For all the thanks she got. Detective Rompré barely looked at it. He wanted to know if Dot remembered where Dave was the night Teresa Fillion was murdered. *Who?* Teresa Musgrave. Well, why not say so in the first place? Why complicate things? Of course she knew where Dave was the night Teresa was murdered. He was her husband wasn't he? Dot had awakened in an empty bed and looked out of the bedroom window.

"He was passed out drunk at the end of the dock. My husband was a blackout alcoholic. That is what I had to live with."

DS Rompré asked her what Dave Gomer drank. Adding insult to injury.

Dot had had to take a very deep steadying breath. "Scotch," she'd said, bravely.

They ought to be ashamed of themselves. She expected a little more sensitivity from the police.

IN DIRECT contrast, Marlee Bremer was determined to get straight to the point. "A poison pen? Well, I've more than my share of those. What did it say?"

DS Rompré declined to answer but requested a handwriting sample, defeating the purpose as far as Marlee could see since she was aware of the reason he was asking. If she did write the note, she would be careful to change her hand.

"I think you'll find plenty of poison pen suspects. A whole village of them, in fact. Do you intend to get handwriting samples from them all?"

On the question of what Dave drank, she responded "I have no idea. He didn't drink as far as I knew. He stopped seven years ago."

The interview would have ended there if Violet hadn't come into the room and told the officers she'd seen Dave in his boat the morning he went missing. She was sitting on the dock and Dave had waved at her as he passed.

"You were out in the rain?"

"I had an umbrella."

Marlee was asked to produce the large yellow umbrella and Violet was made to demonstrate for the officers where she was positioned on the dock when she saw Dave pass. A mountain out of a molehill in Marlee's opinion. Violet was then asked to go to her room and write out everything she had seen. DS Rompré seemed to think it was important even though she was only twelve and hardly a reliable witness.

They were perfectly civil and apologetic, but Marlee resented the intrusion. She was very sorry Dave had drowned, he was a friend, but she doubted a poison pen was the cause. Dave was a tough-as-boots newsman; nothing rattled him. Now, if they'd excuse her, she had to get dinner ready. There wasn't time to prepare a proper meal. Cold chicken and salad would have to do.

DAVE GOMER wasn't the region's usual sort of victim. The majority of homicides the MRC des Collines investigated were alcohol or drug-related. People in their right minds rarely killed one another, which was a blessing as the regional police force operated on shoestring budget to carry out their work. Handwriting samples, topographical maps of the Gatineau River, interviews and witness statements were spread out on the table in the Incident Room. The investigation into the death of *The Stollerton Record*'s publisher had subtly shifted from 'Suspicious' to 'Homicide.'

"The handwriting analyst got back to me," said Constable Fournier coming into the room. "Marlee Bremer isn't a match. He's still working on Dorothy Gomer's sample but so far he's not convinced she's the author of our poison pen. You also gave him Violet Bremer's statement. He hasn't got to that one yet. Is she a candidate?"

"*Mais oui.* She was sitting on the dock in the rain. This is the temperament to write an anonymous note in green ink and shove it in the letterbox of the local newspaper."

"If you say so, sir. The interviews weren't very helpful. Maybe the reason we can't get a lead on Dave Gomer's killer is because nobody killed Dave Gomer. We didn't learn anything today that suggests he was murdered. Gomer was an alcoholic who had a relapse. He stood up in the boat, lost his balance and fell. He hit his head, tried to stand, fell again which was the killing blow and he slipped overboard."

Rompré settled in a chair, crossing one leg over the other. "Why did the victim remove his hat and coat? It was raining."

"But it wasn't chilly. A July rain is more humid than refreshing. The victim stood up to take off his jacket.

He'd been drinking. He was overheated. The hat came off when he slipped."

Rompré nodded. His eyes drooped. "And the absence of fingerprints?"

"Degraded by the rain. Our equipment wasn't sensitive enough to pick them up."

"*C'est bon.* Now explain why his body was not discovered until Saturday. He was last seen alive by Violet Bremer and by our witness downriver of the Bremer dock on Monday. Why was his body not discovered earlier? Six days is a long time for an object to make the trip into Stollerton Bay. The distance is only seven kilometres."

"His body was caught on some debris. When the dam opened on Thursday, the water level was raised and the body floated free."

"It is possible but unlikely given the extent of the damage to the corpse. However, police divers are searching the area between the Bremer dock and the rapids for physical evidence of this."

"You don't sound convinced they'll find any."

Rompré bent over the topographical map of the Gatineau River. He sipped his coffee, tracing the line of the river from the bridge at Martingale to Stollerton. "He was killed here," he said, pointing to a section of the river that was furthest away from the highway.

"Upriver of the bridge at Martingale," the constable mused. "Not much there. The old highway runs along one side the river, overgrown in so many places the bank has gone back to the wild. On the other side it's even more isolated. There are some privately-owned hunting camps and the Martingale Camp is further up river. The killer could do what needed to be done without fear of being seen." She frowned. "But we have two witnesses who saw Dave returning downriver that morning."

"There were two people riding in Dave's boat on the journey upriver. Only one returned. This is the person our witness and Violet Bremer saw. The girl's memory *c'est exceptionnelle*. She said the boat was almost level with the surface of the water as it passed the dock. Dave Gomer weighed ninety-five kilograms. His weight would have angled the prow out of the water by lowering the stern of the Princecraft."

"She's a twelve-year-old kid, sir."

"An observant twelve-year-old kid. Alvina Moon said Dave Gomer fished every morning in the summer. Violet Bremer spends her summer holiday sitting on the dock. She has witnessed Mr. Gomer in his boat many times. On this occasion she observes something is not right. The boat is not riding the same because the person in the boat is not Mr. Gomer."

"What if she's just trying to ... as kids will do ... you know, look important? If she retracts later, we'll have wasted time and resources on an accidental death."

"You are not convinced this is murder."

"I just wish we had a witness who could put someone in the boat with Dave. Could the assailant have taken his own boat, met Dave, killed him and then travelled downriver disguised as Dave?"

"For what purpose? Why not return to one's boat, motor away, and let the victim's boat float free as it would in an accidental drowning. *Non*." Rompré added thoughtfully, "The killer needed M. Gomer's boat to leave the scene because his assailant had not planned to kill M. Gomer when they set out together. But once the deed is done, he or she has no choice but to use the boat to escape. The blue windbreaker and beige hat is donned to confuse any possible witnesses. There would not be many at that hour of the morning. And the rain reduced visibility."

"Why would someone spontaneously kill Dave Gomer? Could the vodka have anything to do with it? If he was drinking with his assailant and a fight broke out, that makes this manslaughter, not murder."

"The vodka bottle was the mistake. Dave Gomer drank scotch. We must accept Ray Milligan's expertise in this area. Where did the vodka come from? Either Dave brought it with him, intending to get drunk. Or someone else brought it. As Ray Milligan pointed out, a scotch drinker does not go to the liquor store and buy vodka. Dave did not bring the vodka onto the boat with him. His killer made a mistake."

"The vodka was meant to get Dave to start drinking again. It didn't work so the killer resorts to plan B. The guy had no money, no natural enemies, no lovers to piss off." Constable Fournier hunched forward, thinking. "He's not the usual sort of victim, is he? He was a sober alcoholic so we can't even blame it on the booze. Why was he killed?"

DS Rompré looked as close to excited as the constable had ever seen him. He wasn't what she would catalogue as an expressive. Martine had her own private method of profiling the people she encountered in her line of work. 'Expressives' telegraphed their feelings through their hands, faces and voice. They were most often the artists, activists and the francophone population. 'Flatliners' were the opposite. They gave nothing away. It was easy to mistake their stoicism for a lack of feeling. Farm people and blue collar workers were most often in this group. Rompré was in a category all of his own. He didn't express, but he wasn't a flatliner either.

"Why was this man killed?" he asked. "His life was unremarkable. His business was being sold but this is not a tragedy. A sorrow perhaps, a regret, but not a surprising outcome given the times we live in and not a bad result for a man his age. He could retire. All is well until the note arrives. *Where did he get the flashlight?*"

The constable suppressed a groan. It was almost quitting time. She had plans to spend a couple of days at a friend's cottage in Lac Ste-Marie, a forty-five minute drive and she still had to pack. She pulled Teresa Fillion's murder file toward her. "The Crown contended that the flashlight came from the service bay at the dealership."

The DS tipped his head back and closed his eyes briefly. "Alvina Moon had a journalist's observation about this anonymous tip. She said it came from someone who already knew the answer. She was wrong in thinking it was Dorothy Gomer, but the premise is sound. Whoever wrote the note knew that Trey Bremer did not have access to a flashlight on the night of the murder. Tell me about the other husband, Del Musgrave. Was he ever considered a suspect in his wife's murder?"

"He was eliminated from our enquiries almost immediately. Musgrave was guiding five fishermen at the Martingale Hunt and Fish Camp that night. The camp is thirty kilometres upriver from the scene and he didn't have a vehicle. Do you want to talk to him?"

The DS waved his hand. "*Je pensais à autre chose.* It is not important. We have an anonymous note that connects our victim to a seven-year-old crime. This is where we begin."

"Well," said Fournier, consulting her notes, "on the night of the murder, Dave didn't come home. His wife, Dot found him passed out on the dock. Ray Milligan gave Constable Lemen quite an education in alcohol-induced blackouts specifically, and alcohol-related brain damage in general. His report is in the file." She passed it to Rompré who nodded but didn't look at it. "If Dave was drinking that night, he might have gone to the trailer, witnessed the murder and blacked out. The night was erased from his mind. But years later, as he regains his faculties, something might have come back to him."

Rompré sat forward, his elbows resting on his knees. "A recent convergence of events could have forced the memory back to our victim. A few weeks ago Alvina Moon came to the station to report finding blood in an abandoned trailer on the river. It is certain that she would have mentioned the finding to her boss."

"And then the note arrives. That is a remarkable coincidence, sir."

"I would say it is a case of one thing leading to another."

# THIRTEEN

THE MARTINGALE Hunt and Fish Camp dated from the 1920's when the paper mills were still in full operation. The main lodge was built in the style of the Great Camps of the Adirondacks, common at the time for ersatz outdoorsman explained Gerry Dunn. "But not on that scale obviously."

He looked at her expectantly. Alvina dutifully raised her camera to her eye and took the photo.

"The paper companies built these camps all over Québec for their employees and their families. They'd come here on holiday, all on the company dime. It must have been a dream for those workers coming to this place after the noise and dirt of Hull. When the mills closed down so did the camps. I rescued this one in 1995 for a song. It took years of money and labour to get it where it is today—but it was a labour of love, right?"

Gerry Dunn was a short and stocky man with thick muscles and red hair that was dulling to grey. He bounced from room to room, rolling off the balls of his feet, jabbing the air with his finger to make a point.

Alvina snuck a look at her phone to check the time. It was after twelve. The *Record* hadn't missed a deadline in a hundred and fifty years. She should make her excuses and go. She wouldn't have come except that Missy was at the apartment giving her the silent treatment. When she pulled into the parking lot Gerry Dunn had greeted her with sharp rooster eyes and talking a mile a minute, propelled her on a tour of the main lodge.

It was pretty impressive—fat log walls and a high timbered ceiling; a stone hearth at one end and a screened-in porch at the other. A rack of moose antlers hung over the hearth. Furnishings were spare. There were three brown leather sofas arranged around the fireplace, a huge multi-coloured rag rug and a large square coffee table. Refectory tables with benches on either side claimed the rest of the room.

"This is where the guests take their meals. I worried it was too rustic at one point and introduced chairs. The uproar! They hated it. Demanded we go back to the benches. It's like a kids' summer camp in here at night. The lighting is lousy though. It's always dark inside a log structure, eh? The logs suck up light like a sponge. I had to rig something special to show off Del's paintings. That's his work you see on the on the wall there. I handle the sale of his work. We sell at least one for every group booking we get, especially to the Europeans. The Americans are catching on too. He grows on you. Musgrave's got something. I'm not an art lover—I don't know what it is he's got—but he's got something."

The artist was in the kitchen fixing a leaky sink, Gerry told her.

"He isn't the reason I'm here," Alvina muttered as she fumbled with the settings on her camera. "A feature on the Camp was a good fit for the historic final edition of the *Record*."

Gerry led the way to the screened-in porch. Cushions printed with mallards and elks on Adirondack chairs. He waited for Alvina's nod of appreciation, the taking of the photograph, and then it was down the steps for a tour of the grounds. The lodge was flanked by smaller log cabins tucked under huge white pines that dotted the campground. The trees contributed shade, damp and pine needles that covered the ground an inch deep.

"Come on. I'm going to show you something that will knock your socks off. You want history? I'm gonna show you history."

She followed Gerry along a packed dirt path that had been neatly swept and wondered how much advertising she had. Enough to go to twenty-six pages?

Gerry pointed up. "These trees were saved by the paper mills to be enjoyed for recreation. How's that for hypocrisy? Sacrifice the forest for capitalism and now those same capitalists spend thousands of dollars two or three times a year to escape to a forest."

"We all use paper."

"Yep, yep, we all use paper. You can always count on a Canadian journalist to see the other side of the coin. You'd think for a nation of wilderness dwellers we'd have some hard opinions about saving the environment but no—Canada is philosophic about the loss of trees."

"Nothing stays the same. Everything has to perish for the greater cause."

Gerry gave her a sharp glance. "It's a cold comfort when they do."


DEL SMELLED lavender. He pulled out from under the sink and glanced over the camp kitchen, spacious and utilitarian, designed for men to be used by men. The corners and awkward spaces had become dirty catchalls for anything Gerry didn't want to throw out.

Teresa's skin had always smelled of lavender. It was the soap she used. He looked harder into the shadowed area behind the industrial-sized gas range. There was nothing there. He was imagining things.

The kitchen telephone was mounted on the wall over the desk that Gerry still used to take bookings and do business. He had an office but Gerry liked to be close to the action. The desk was an antique salvaged from the old paper mill when it went out of business. Phone calls could be picked up in the kitchen and then transferred to Gerry's office.

The scent of lavender was stronger now.

"Teresa?" He heard his voice whisper her name. He hoped it was his voice or he was hearing things as well.

Teresa used to have a green dress made of light floaty material and wedge-heeled shoes with the laces that tied up her calves. Heels made of jute. A memory flickered of watching her walk around the cabin naked, looking for her shoe. He had liked watching her. He like the way she smelled fresh from her shower, the lavender soap she used on her skin. She had beautiful skin, pearl in colour and luminosity.

Teresa wore the green dress that morning and tied up the laces of those silly shoes. The outfit didn't make sense for babysitting a couple of kids all day. He had laughed at her. His father's laugh. He was often cruel to her because he loved her so much. Because she made him feel helpless. Was it like that for his father? Helpless with love, Owen Musgrave would shove Del's mother into the wall.

He closed his eyes following the memory as far as he could into those grey recesses where Teresa held court over his mind. She was dissatisfied with him and lonely. She was lonely.

Why are you wearing a dress and heels to babysit a couple of kids?

I'm taking them to the library today. I like to look nice when I'm in the village.

She said other people have lives, Del, and it wouldn't hurt to be more involved and social. Everything she said on the subject froze in his ears like a doctor's diagnosis. He didn't want to do anything more—he couldn't be rushed. He had to paint—he was so far behind—so much to learn.

It takes time Teresa. It takes time to get really good at something.

But what is it? What good is it?

He didn't have an answer. Art wasn't good for anything. You hung it on a wall.

She wore a green dress that floated about her thighs. The day she died was a hot, hot day. There was a group coming in from Chicago that weekend. Del was lying on the bed in the cabin watching her get dressed.

You going to take me to work or what? Eyeing him warily.

He wanted sex but she'd already taken a shower and didn't want to get mussed. She was dressed, looking pretty and sweet and she was his wife. He was horny. He wouldn't be seeing her for two days.

I have to get going so don't get any ideas. I'm late for work.

You must be getting it someplace. Sly, using his father's words but denying this to himself even as he said it. A dual creature within the same mind, in unison recognizing the source of the abuse and denying it at the same time.

He remembered the look on Teresa's face. Her eyes had flicked slightly to the left, there was a minor twitch in her jaw; an imperceptible change in her body and mood that if he had not been a painter he would not have seen it. Coming to that memory was like standing on the ledge of a four-storied building. The fall wouldn't kill him but it would break every bone in his body.

Teresa was leaving him.

People fall out of love all the time, she said, slipping into her good underwear. Shit happens.

The morning shit happened, Del was lying on the bed staring at the water stain on the ceiling while his wife laid it out for him: Call the bank to get this place appraised but don't tell them it's for a divorce or they'll screw you. When you have the money to buy me out, I'll file for divorce.

Her eyes had gone to his penis, soft and vulnerable in its stiff nest of pubic hair. She said a lot of meaningless things about wishing him all the best, parting friends and getting on with their lives. Every word of it bullshit because she knew he couldn't go to a bank or call an appraiser. He couldn't do anything but work at the camp and paint.

Who's the guy?

There is no guy. Why does there always have to be a guy? I'm just not happy.

Del had repressed knowledge of that day for seven years. That's what made reliving it so vivid. Time hadn't dulled the shock. The morning she died, Teresa said she was leaving him.

Don't do this, he'd said, helplessly.

Teresa had said: I'm already doing it, stupid.

HEAT INSECTS whined above the trees.

"These are the cabins." Gerry Dunn bobbed his neck. "This is real history here."

Twelve cabins flanked the path at irregular distances, their miniature porches protruding. Squat log boxes, fitted and furnished as they had been in the Thirties.

"This is where wives and kids would stay when they came out. The men would fish all day and then head over to the main lodge for cards and booze, see. So it was a real vacation for everyone."

The sun was high but the trees kept the cabins cool. The pines brushed together in the hot dry wind and scented the air. The main path branched off in various directions: to toilets and shower stalls, a horseshoe pitch and croquet lawn, each were marked by wooden signs pointing the way.

"We keep them furnished as they were back then. The guests come here for the historical atmosphere. You getting this for the paper? Only I thought that's why you were here, to do a story on the Camp for the last issue of the *Record*."

"Yes, that is absolutely correct." Alvina dug her notepad and pen out of her satchel and scribbled down the facts and dates she could remember. "Dave assigned the story to me a few weeks ago but I could only get to it now."

"It's got to be hard over there at the paper without Dave." Gerry clucked his tongue. "I hope I'm dead before print disappears completely. I'm not much of a reader but I like a catalogue to be a catalogue. Losing the *Record* is what killed Dave Gomer and I've said so. People have died for less. A tragedy, such a tragedy. It hurts when a way of life goes, we can't pretend it doesn't. We all thought he'd given up the booze for good."

Gerry Dunn was taking care to not come across as judgmental, but Alvina knew he was curious. He was a gossip, the same as the men he drank with at Keefer's. He had liked Dave Gomer, he wouldn't stand for Dave Gomer's name to be dragged through the mud but he wanted to gossip about him all the same.

"Dave wasn't drunk when he died. The police are treating his death as suspicious. I'm not allowed to discuss the details."

Gerry's eyes had widened. "You don't say. Well, I guess the same shit happens here as in other places. The difference here," continued Gerry as he led her along the path, "is we have time to examine the shit that happens and think about it and maybe do something to change if change is needed. We're alert to change here. That's the big difference between rural and urban. Change doesn't wash over us. It crashes in to the very core of how we live. We feel it. We suffer it. We respect it the same way we respect a barking dog. Consequently, we're slow to open the door to it. Developers think we're backward or stubborn. I'm not denying we are, but only because when something changes here it changes the entire organism. One fast food restaurant can wipe out three family diners. You see what I'm saying?"

Alvina nodded. Gerry Dunn could talk a blue streak as Dave used to say. He had sharp blue eyes, intelligent and inquisitive, and an energy that meant he was always in motion.

The Camp had certainly done its best to resist change. It was Del's job to scrape, stain and seal the logs of every building each year. For this he earned minimum wage, unchanged from the day he was hired.

"I'd go broke if I had to pay union rates. Don't put that in the paper. That's off the record. Del came here looking for a job when he was nineteen or twenty. Men of my generation don't come across lads like Del Musgrave anymore. Good with their hands, not full of themselves, not stoned. Young people have no maturity nowadays. I hear of high-school kids still bullying classmates like they're a bunch of sixth graders. Makes me sick. I took one look at Del Musgrave and thought 'he won't last long.' He proved me wrong but he's a different one. I don't want to say backward, but he's got some funny ideas. I order his painting supplies for him because he won't get a phone at his place."

"Why's that?" She picked her way over a thick tree root.

"He got rid of it after Teresa died. Reporters wouldn't leave him alone. I got fed up with them myself here at the lodge. Something like twenty calls a day. Same asinine questions over and over again." Gerry jerked his chin at her. "One of them wanted to know if Del had been offered a book deal. A book deal for what, says I. The dead wife, the guy tells me, the trauma; the triumph of the human spirit. Triumph of the human bloody spirit! I said where in the sweet hereafter do you see *that* in what happened here? Triumph of the flaming bloody spirit is don't rape and murder in the first place! That would be a flaming story—not this tedious shit we've been doing to each other for centuries."

"Del told me he doesn't remember much."

"It was a shock. A hell of a shock. The mind can't recover from a shock like that. I've read up on it. Oh no.

The brain is a masterful organ. Even when the trauma has passed, the memory is impaired. It's like a rupture."

"He said you told him about the thin place in Celtic mythology. We live in a thin place here because of the mountains and water. Do you really believe that?"

"Oh, he told you about that, did he? I was trying to make him feel better. He believes Teresa's here, see, and whether we think it's rational or not, Del needs to experience her again in order to let her go. You see what I'm saying? That girl has a hold on him that for the life of me I cannot understand." Gerry said this ruefully with a shake of his head as if he were referring to an unfortunate appendage. "He has a lot of funny ideas, does Del. Good-looking guy, but strange. Last year, a man came from New York who had a pal who owned a gallery. I'm shipping this gallery owner something like a painting every six months. The cheques come to me. I cash 'em and give the money to Del because Del doesn't do banks. Hates 'em. I tell him we all do, buddy, we all do. But we're chained to them and I won't be around forever. Maybe he's got a bankroll hidden in his mattress, I don't know, but I worry about that boy. Art does not pay steady."

DEL MUSGRAVE shoved his body under the sink. He pounded on the steel sleeve fastener with the wrench but it wouldn't budge.

One fucking memory. It was like dropping a pebble in stagnant water, releasing ring after ring of memories polluting his brain. She was always coming home from work with bruises. She said she got them from playing with the kids in the park. Bruising on her inner thigh?

No, no, it's not like that, Teresa had said, laughing.

It's only a game. It's not real, Del, for Christ's sake. Don't be such a prude.

He remembered now.

Del dropped his wrench and stared deep into the corners of the room. A sigh or a whisper came from Gerry's desk as though someone were sitting there, swivelling in the chair. Or maybe it was the wind moving through the giant pines. The kitchen was filled with cool shadows and mingled smells of pine needles and musk. Her lavender presence tightened into a physical entity. Del closed his eyes and felt Teresa's fingers on his lips as she did once to wake him up. She had put her hand over his mouth, jolting Del awake, his fists punching to keep from being suffocated.

What are you doing? I could've hurt you, you fool.

She slipped her naked body under his, suddenly horny. I'll do anything you want. Just don't hurt me.

What are you talking about?

Try it just once. You might like it.

No. What's wrong with you?

Del didn't understand. That was the main problem. His frustration at not understanding angered him at once. It was like a light sensor going off in the wind, dropping him in and out of consciousness. He was revolted by her and that made it easier. She had made herself revolting to him, less than human, and that's what she wanted, right? She was too vain to know what she was playing with.

He pushed back against the memories that emerged from the corners of his mind. Flashes broke through of walking through the forest, taking the cool green path to the bright hollow of light on the dock where Teresa was sunbathing in a tiny two-piece bathing suit.

Creeping toward her, careful not to make any sound. Give it to her. She deserves it. She screamed when she saw him and he had to clamp his hand over her mouth. She fought him hard, pushing his hands away. He twisted her flesh, bruising her arms and pinned her thighs apart. He closed his eyes so he couldn't see her face and tugged on the crotch of her bathing suit, wrenching it to one side to enter her. She wasn't ready but he forced himself inside her anyway. This is what she wants.

It was like asking a grizzly she thought was a teddy bear to pretend he's a grizzly.

Teresa thought it was hilarious that Del was so messed up about it later. To her it was just a game. But Del. Del heard a creature wake inside him. A dark little troll who lived under his bridge, stirred awake by her helplessness, by her screams, by his weight crushing her, by his self-pitying justification: *you had it coming*. And she did. She said force was what she wanted. Del knew he couldn't trust himself in that place but he went there anyway and once he was there he was lost.

He paced the Camp kitchen in a cold sweat. Recall came backwards from the day they found her body. Del remembered riding in the back of the police car to the morgue to identify the body and having a fantastically real premonition that it wasn't Teresa they'd found. The relief he felt had left him unprepared for the moment they wheeled her out on a stainless steel table.

The memories were piecing together so rapidly, he began to believe he understood why it happened and why he couldn't remember for so long—a trick of his brain to make him believe the worst of it was over.

The truth was his memory was only just getting

started. Del sat in the kitchen, pipe wrench dangling between his fingers, immersed in recalling what it was he didn't know.

A long way off and a long time coming, but it was here now.

THE DRY scent of pine needles lifted on the breeze. Alvina breathed deeply. Her eyes travelled to the soaring pines, to the sun-spackled river, which made her think of fishing and suddenly she missed Dave. Everything about him—the way he'd shoot out of his chair when something happened in the village below his window, snapping his fingers and yelling "Moon! Moon! Get over here!" Dave was so alive in her mind she found it hard to believe he wasn't waiting for her at the office. He wasn't going to call her on the cell phone and demand to know where the hell she was. Del had none of that with Teresa. Her death was more final than an amputation.

"You interested in history for the historical last edition of the *Record*?" asked Gerry. "I got history. I got something you have to see. You will not believe your eyes. Just follow me—watch your step."

They walked until they were out from under the pines into the blazing sun and a rougher, wilder stretch of the property that ended at a fence, more or less new black wire mesh, about six feet high. The gate in the fence was padlocked. Gerry hauled a ring of keys from his pocket, selected one and opened the lock. "I fenced it in for insurance reasons. It'll come down when the restoration is complete but for now, if some asshole trespasses and breaks a leg, I'll be the one who gets sued. After you," he said.

Alvina stepped into a wilderness. The dirt path had

ended abruptly at the fence or appeared to. In fact, it was still there, just wildly overgrown. Gerry trotted nimbly ahead of Alvina through wild raspberry cane and thistle that encroached on a walkway of boards, some missing, some rotted away.

"This old boardwalk leads to the tennis court at the edge of the property. Oh yes, a tennis court. They knew how to do recreation back then. But first, look here. See that?"

An abandoned swimming pool. They stood side-by-side at the cracked tiled edge and peered over the side. The mosaic tiling at the bottom of the pool had been prised up in places leaving gaps in the overall design which Gerry said was a depiction of the Gatineau Hills. The deep end was clogged with leaves, fallen branches and dirt. There were curving concrete steps in the shallow area that suggested a grotto.

"A pool," Alvina said, fully astonished. "Why would they build a pool when the river is right there?"

"Well, you got to remember the river was a commercial waterway back then. Logs were floated down the river. Not recreation-friendly. This pool was for the kiddies and the ladies. Pools like this were all the rage for the working class. The bathing house is a miniature of the Sunnyside Bathing House in Toronto."

Gerry pointed to a shattered *cabane*, constructed of pink granite and wood. The wood had flaked and peeled its paint decades ago. The roof was caved in. "That's where they would change into their bathing costumes."

Alvina lifted the camera to take a picture. Gerry beamed.

"I'm planning to restore it, see, this whole section, pool, bathhouse, the gardens. See those lilac shrubs and peonies? They're still thriving from when they were planted ninety years ago. All this here was landscaped back then. I still have the photos. I'm going to bring it back. Open the pool. Put some wicker lounges out here. The guests will go nuts for it. History—that's what sets the Camp apart from other resorts."

They moved on, over the decaying boardwalk. "I'll show you the tennis court," Gerry was saying, leading the way. "You won't believe it."

Alvina shoulders were burning. She should have worn a hat. Bees buzzed through the wild raspberry cane. She was wearing her orange dress and it caught on every thorn. The boardwalk opened to an antique tennis court and she didn't believe it, just as Gerry predicted. It was badly neglected. Vegetation poked up between the cracks in the concrete. The net was gone but there were spectator stands—actual stands for spectators—that were in need of repair but Alvina marvelled that the Camp had taken the trouble to build them in the first place.

"They were mad for outdoor activities," said Gerry. "Everything had to be out-of-doors unless it was pouring rain. For health, you see. They believed the fresh air was good for the lungs. Lots of lung disease in the old days."

"Will you restore this too?"

"You better believe it. The Camp is a natural for recreational development. It'll be worth a fortune when I'm finished."

Alvina took several photos. She could see traces of the old garden. The walkway led into the woods. "Where does it go from here?"

"To the old highway. Guests would get off the train

in Stollerton and the buggy would take them the rest of the distance along the old highway. The tarmac is still visible here and there, mostly grown over now but the corridor is still clear. Del travels it in the winter to work and back. I'm going to apply to the Ministry of Transport to see about accessing it for a bike path in the summer and cross country ski trail in the winter. Skidoo club business isn't sustainable, see. It goes down every time fuel prices go up."

Gerry glanced at her expectantly. Alvina wrote it down: *Year round.*

The tour ended back at the main lodge. Alvina's legs were scratched by the raspberry cane. Gerry deposited her at the van which was parked in the tradesman's lot nearest the back door. Guest parking was a groomed gravelled lot to the right of the grand main entrance. The passenger side window of the van was down. She leaned in and set the camera and notepad on the seat. Alvina glanced surreptitiously at the lodge. The back entrance was approximately ten steps away. Gerry nodded and smiled, eyebrows lifted. Alvina panicked. The longer the seconds stretched past without seeing Del, the more worried she became that this was it. She would leave town without ever seeing him again.

Gerry Dunn thrust his hand in her face. "Well so long, Alvina. Thanks for doing this. I'll be watching for the article in the paper on Monday morning. The last edition, eh? Can't imagine what we're going to do without our little paper."

"I'll do my best. I can't guarantee I can even get into the office. The police have it sealed." Alvina bristled. "It's funny. No one cared about the *Record* when Dave was alive and we were still in business, but now that it's gone, suddenly everyone's upset about losing the paper."

Gerry clucked his tongue reprovingly. "It's not as bad as all that. You're too young to be so cynical."

Alvina found people were always confusing truth with cynicism and cynicism with truth. She bent over her satchel pretending to search for the key to the ignition. The screen door behind them squealed open. Del came out on the porch, bare-chested, wiping his hands on a dish towel that became black with gunk. His skin was shiny with sweat. He stopped when he saw her. The yellow porch light over his head was webbed with moths.

She steadied herself against the van.

"Hey up boyo—what's wrong?" Gerry faced him. "Ah, Jesus, you aren't going to tell me it's a major renovation because by the look on your face, it's some kind of bad news."

"It's not great news. You need to call a plumber. I gave you a patch job that'll hold until after Labour Day but don't count on it after that."

"Well, okay then, okay, we've seen worse. Don't pull a face. I'll hire a plumber if you think I need to. It'll all come to right in the end." Gerry turned to Alvina. "My friend Del here could be running this place for triple what I'm paying him but he refuses to see the light."

"I've seen the light—it's paperwork, customers, suppliers, ulcers and a drinking problem."

Del Musgrave had a thousand small expressions that Alvina was only beginning to learn to read. He was a northern man with the heat and ice of the north on him, but he was not made of ice. Something was wrong. His eyes had changed.

Gerry clamped his hand on Del's head and rubbed it. "He gets like this. Frets like an old woman when things break down. He works his tail off to make sure everything runs smooth but something always happens. Isn't that right, Del?"

"Something always happens."

"What the hell—it's only money," said Gerry. "See you in the funny papers!" He turned away with a jaunty wave and left them standing alone in the parking lot.

"Hi," said Alvina, cautiously.

Del didn't move. "Hi."

"I was here doing an interview with Gerry. He took me on a tour of the Camp. It's beautiful. I love the history."

Del wiped sweat from his face. His eyes were dark.

The sky closed in, fogged in shadow. The sun disappeared behind a cloud. She didn't know what to say to hold him there. And then she did.

"Dave is dead."

"I heard. Gerry told me he drowned in a fishing accident."

"Well. Ah. He called me that morning and said he'd be late. It must have happened soon after that. They found his body in the bay. The police have sealed off his house and his office. I was trying to pack up but they won't let me and the MetMedia people want it empty when they move in. So it looks like another delay."

"When are you leaving?"

Something broke inside her, a hope or the breath she was holding. "Oh...." She frowned at the ignition key in her hand. "On Monday I guess. After the *Record* is distributed, I'll hit the road. So if I don't see you, good-bye and good luck. It was nice to know you. Really nice."

She meant it for once and it was good that she actually meant it because then she wouldn't cry. Her heart was still. There was the break and then stillness.

Alvina turned and opened the driver's side door. Del stood, a stone, watching her. Her body was shaking. It didn't matter what she told herself about the futility of reacting this way, her body experienced the separation before her mind could cope. Her thighs were jelly. The air smelled of hot metal. She concentrated on climbing inside and turning the ignition. Don't think. Just do it. The engine rumbled to life.

Del came to the window. He put his hand on her arm, on the fleshy part nearest her underarm.

"Don't leave right away."

She sucked her lips. "No?"

"I'd like it if you stayed." His eyes were serious. "I need you to stay."

"All right. I will."

A flare of sunlight flashed over them as the sun cleared the cloud and Alvina was blinded for an instant. She closed her eyes and Del disappeared behind her red lids. When she opened them again he was waiting for her in the white hot light, blasting happiness to her core.


DEL YANKED on the starter cord, waved a salute to Gerry and revved the motor. He accelerated, pushing the old Harber Craft to a speed he rarely used on the river. The prow lifted and the wind watered his eyes but he didn't let up. It took all of his concentration to navigate around the rocks and protuberances. The boat was willing to cooperate, rocketing over the swells and darting around submerged logs.

Going back to the cabin frightened him. Del had too much respect for fear to ignore it. His life was going to collapse out from under him on this day or the day after that, or in the split second in between. Asking Alvina to be around when it did was only going make it worse. That was not his intention when he came outside to say good-bye and saw her leaning against the van. The sun setting was hard in her eyes reflecting chips of amber. The look she gave him was so wholly heartbreaking that Del was convinced she'd lost sight of the good in him and could see only the refuse, the bits of him that could never be reclaimed. From the beginning it was worse with her, and better.

Del remembered what he was like before he cared about her: a tiny shrunken man, blackened with sickness, muttering incantations to keep from being saved. He was changed. Not the same man anymore. But he couldn't have her. He had to get that through his head.

The horizon was fringed with mauve. Sunset was coming on earlier and earlier. His dock and the path to the cabin were directly ahead. The river rushed past the sides of the boat, a waterfall noise that wasn't soothing. Del swerved a bank of flotsam, leaving behind a white wake that crashed up on shore.

# FOURTEEN

THE INTERVIEW room was comparatively quiet in Montreal's Bordeaux Prison, a male correctional facility enclosed by thirty foot walls. The corridors, on the other hand, rang with a masculine din that never seemed to let up. Trey Bremer often thought that the noise alone was punishment enough. He sat down across the table from the MRC des Collines police officers, arranging his expression to exhibit a complete lack of reserve. Ask me anything, his face told them.

Detective Sergeant Rompré appeared to be comfortable on the metal chair he was given. The detective was dressed well for a cop. Trey used to own suits like that—a summer suit, the colour of beach sand. The blue shirt and matching tie were a good contrast with Rompré's dark brown eyes and light, almost oatmeal-blonde hair. Possibly thinning, Trey noted.

Trey's own looks had held up despite seven years in a maximum security prison. He wore glasses with thick black frames. He often thought looked more like a professor than a convict.

Rompré's black notebook was open on the table in front of him. He and his constable didn't waste time on pleasantries; it was a two hour drive back to Stollerton.

"We have read through your initial statement to

police but I would like to hear the whole story from you directly, Mr. Bremer. Describe the morning Teresa Musgrave did not show up for work."

Trey crossed one leg over the other. His gazed rested on Constable Fournier's pretty face and he smiled. "I would ask what brought this on but you wouldn't tell me, would you?"

"No sir. Please just answer the detective sergeant's question."

"I'm already in jail. I suppose it can't get any worse."

He tried to sound cheerful. Like an innocent man would. His freedom was riding on convincing DS Rompré of that. Marlee had fired his legal team. The interview she gave *The Stollerton Record* made it clear she was leaving him here to rot. The trailer was going to be hauled away and destroyed. The sexual behaviours expert was his last hope and now even that was gone. The world was rapidly changing on the outside. His kids were growing up. Everyone would forget he was in here if he didn't do something to save himself.

"It was a normal Monday morning," Trey said. "Marlee had come out of the shower. I was feeding Harry his cereal in his highchair and my daughter Violet was eating her toast at the table. Everything was under control. That's why we didn't notice Teresa was late until it was time for me to leave for the dealership and she still hadn't arrived. Her husband Del was away all weekend on a fishing trip; he was supposed to be back in time to get her to work. I thought he must have got hung up and couldn't get her to our place." Trey addressed Fournier who was taking notes. "They travelled by boat. They couldn't afford a car or Del didn't have a license—I can't remember which. The lack of wheels was one of the many things Teresa complained to me about with regard to her marriage. Her life was confined to the river."

"When did you see her last?"

Trey said clearly and firmly. "The last time I saw Teresa Musgrave was on Friday at about nine-thirty p.m. at the trailer. She was angry but otherwise in fine shape when I left her. My story hasn't changed and it never will change. We were having an affair. A sexual affair," he said with a pointed glance at the female cop. "My lawyers were working on proving it until my wife fired the whole crew. I don't know why. I haven't had a chance to talk to her. I thought that's why you were here, actually. I thought there was some new information."

"This interview is in no way connected to your conviction, Monsieur Bremer. We are investigating another matter that may or may not be connected to Teresa Musgrave's death. On the witness stand you admitted to quarrelling with Teresa on the night of the murder. Can you tell us what about?"

"I told her I loved her. A man says things in the heat of the moment." He appealed to Fournier. "That makes me an asshole, not a murderer. Teresa thought—well, she thought we were going to run away together. I had two kids and a third on the way. I couldn't leave my wife. We argued. Teresa sulked and refused to get in the car like a fucking child. I had to get home, so I left her there. I called a buddy from a pay phone to go pick her up and take her home. What harm could come to her in the twenty minutes or so it would take Dave to reach the trailer? I don't know what went wrong. Honest to God, I thought she was safe at home until Marlee called Del on

Monday morning. When she got off the phone she told me Del had been home for an hour and there was no sign of Teresa. He thought she was with us."

"So you went to the trailer to look for her."

Trey rubbed the back of his neck. He was lightly perspiring. "I did. I don't know why I did. I should have called Dave first to find out what happened on Friday. I'm impulsive, that's always been my problem. But when she was suddenly missing, I freaked." He grinned sheepishly, trying not to make eye contact with the female cop. "She wasn't playing the game, if you know what I mean. We weren't supposed to attract attention to ourselves. She'd gone off script."

"No, we do not know what you mean, sir. Please explain."

Rompré crossed one leg over the other. Energy seemed flow from him that had nothing to do with the coffee he was drinking. Trey bet Rompré's impulses never got the better of him or were something he had to control. He envied that containment. He wished he had it.

"My lawyers advised against going into detail when I was arrested, but with regard to this accusation of rape —well, there's an explanation. Technically, I did rape Teresa that night, but it was with her consent. It was a game we played. I was driving Teresa home one night and she told me about a rape fantasy she had. It was so ... ah ... compelling that I couldn't stop thinking about it. I didn't know girls her age could have thoughts like that. Well, one thing led to another and the next time I had to drive her home ... well, I took her to the trailer instead." Trey squirmed. "And I, ah, assaulted her. We both liked it, so we did it again the next chance we got, ah, role playing different scenarios. All consensual, you see? There was one occasion she brought Harry and Violet along to go swimming for the babysitter scenario." Trey stopped. "I tried to explain it to the jury but they didn't get it." His face was hot. "I didn't get it myself. That kind of thing was completely out of character for me. Marlee was the only woman I'd ever been with. Teresa was ... wild."

"It was a game until you told her you loved her and then it was no longer a game to her. You went to the trailer on Monday morning believing Teresa had gone 'off script'. Correct?"

"Yes," Trey exhaled, relieved they understood him. "I had no idea what to expect. Teresa was kind of insane —high-octane passion crazy. I thought I had it under control. Disappearing like that was not a good sign. She was hell-bent on leaving Del. If I didn't leave Marlee, Teresa would make sure Marlee left me."

"And then what happened?"

It wasn't hard to remember every detail. Trey Bremer had relived that day almost every day for the past seven years. In prison, there was little else to occupy his mind.

It had been surreal listening to the plans that came out of Teresa's mouth that night. The same mouth that only minutes before had been filled with his penis now wanted him to go home, talk to his wife—*break the news*. How was he supposed to respond to that? Was he supposed to tell Teresa it was all a joke? That he only loved her because they had hot, naked daylight sex and he never wanted to give it up? That she wasn't the fucking heart attack he'd have one day? Driving to the trailer on Monday morning, his chest was so tight he could hardly draw breath down his windpipe. When he found her dead, it was almost a relief. He was so fucking relieved to be safe from getting caught that he never saw the other danger coming.

Heat had shimmered off the pink and white trailer. Their oasis, Teresa had called it. A bloom of pollen lay on the river like a skin. The milkweed and pink sweet pea blooms. The Manitoba maple sprawled over the water. Trey had fixed his eyes on the things he'd seen a thousand times before but had never really seen, and tried not to think of the smell that grew stronger and stronger the closer he got to the trailer. He pulled down on the chrome handle and the door opened with a pop of released air pressure.

A stench mushroomed out, knocking him back. He stumbled across the gravel, bent over at the waist, gulping in air to control his stomach. The stink of rotting flesh stuck in his nostrils.

"I should have driven her home," he said. "I should have forced her to get in the car with me. I couldn't have stayed the night even if I'd wanted to! Marlee was already pissed with me for missing dinner and the kids' baths. She said she wasn't but she didn't wait up for me, she spent the night on the spare bed in Harry's room."

"You opened the door to the trailer. And then what?"

"The smell was overpowering. I wrapped my tie around my nose and mouth. There's not a lot of light inside that trailer because of the trees. It took a few minutes for my eyes to adjust. I thought maybe a raccoon had got trapped and died. I saw a flashlight on the table. I assumed it was my buddy Dave's so I picked it up. It was heavy. There was something stuck in the lamp where it twisted into the handle."

He uncrossed his legs and leaned forward. His eyes were fixed on Rompré's notebook.

"It was a long brown hair. There was blood and what looked to be a patch of human scalp. I dropped it—threw it away actually and it rolled under the table. There's a galley kitchen that separates the dinette from the foam couch that folds out into a sleeping area. The sheet we'd had sex on looked like it was bundled against the wall. I had a bad feeling. I knew what was under it but I was praying hard I was wrong."

Trey sat back. "I don't have to tell you what was there."

But he did. They said they needed to hear it from Trey exactly what he saw.

Teresa's body lay crumpled on the bed. Her legs were bent at an impossible angle. Blood was splattered up the birch-panelled walls, stuck in the window screen, pooled under her head. Her face was untouched and impossibly young. Her eyes were open. Cloudy green eyes. A breeze puffed under the sheet, as though she were still breathing. Trey half-expected her to lift her smashed body, rising to a sitting position and stare at him with those blank green eyes.

"I'm not a brave man. I panicked. I thought the guy, or the gang—whoever did this to her, might still be around. I got the hell out of there. I didn't check to see if she was still alive or could be helped. She couldn't but I should have checked anyway. Of everything I've done, that part bothers me the most. I should have checked for a pulse at least."

Instead, Trey had hurtled himself to the riverbank where he collapsed and wept, not for Teresa whom he did love in his way, but for himself and the unfairness of having something that was just his taken away.

"I called 911 from my cell phone and you know the rest."

Trey's eyes trailed over to Constable Fournier's face. She was blonde. Very pretty. Teresa had told him once he was handsome in a broken-down old movie star sort of way. Attractive to women and some men too. Trey managed to be wildly popular and wildly unavailable at the same time. The prison psychiatrist said it was because he was adept at sidestepping intimacy.

"From which pay phone did you make the call to your friend on Friday?"

"There's a phone booth in St. Jude at the Outpost. It's a corner store but you know what it's like in the country. It's a long way to the corner of anything. It took me out of my way but I couldn't risk calling from my cell phone. My wife was always going through my phone. She would question a call to the newspaper office on Friday night when I was supposed to be up to my ears in work. I talked to Dave but he was pretty well gone by then into the booze. He must have blacked out because he told my lawyers he didn't remember getting the call."

Rompré was silent for several seconds. And then he asked:

"Did you ever consider that Mr. Gomer could have killed Teresa?"

Trey mouth sagged open. "No. God no. He didn't, did he? We weren't close friends, but he was always willing to help me out. He was an old booze hound. He wasn't a violent guy."

"Yet you thought it was his flashlight that had been left behind."

"Yes, but that didn't mean anything. He could have

left it for her if she refused to let him take her home. I mean, Teresa was determined to spend the night in that moldy dump with or without me. Maybe she believed my leaving was part of the game. I don't know." Trey sighed. "Why would Dave kill Teresa? He—I mean—he knew what was going on with her and me. It doesn't make sense."

"Where did the flashlight come from?"

"I don't know," he said, wearily. "It wasn't there when I left on Friday. I'm sure of it. I've been asked and answered that question so many times. I never saw it before that day."

Rompré nodded slightly at Fournier. She made a note in her book.

"Monsieur Bremer, do you have an explanation for how the clothes you were wearing the night of the murder came to be incinerated in the fire pit?"

Trey lifted his brows but couldn't bring himself to make eye contact. Even now, with everything riding on this, was he still going to protect her? "They found remnants of a suit. It wasn't mine. I was wearing a grey suit which I hung in the laundry room. I realize Marlee told police she didn't find the suit in the laundry room but my wife led a very busy life. She was tired and probably distracted. She must have taken it in without it registering on her consciousness. Do you know what I mean? When we perform a mundane task over and over again, we half-forget we are doing it."

Rompré nodded. "This is true. For us, of course, it is difficult to accept that your wife would not make every effort to recall the suit when it could prove her husband's innocence."

Trey's mouth thinned. "If I had a better explanation,

I wouldn't be in prison."

"It is of no consequence. The clothing fibers recovered from the fire pit matched the clothing fibers found in the trailer. We have read the lab reports. They were one and the same. Did Mrs. Bremer take her own vehicle to run the errands?"

"Yes, as a usual practice. But on that morning I had blocked her in so she took my car instead. I remember because my son came into the bedroom asking for cereal. It was very unlike her to leave me with the kids on Saturday because it was my day to sleep late. I looked out of our bedroom window. It faces the driveway. My car was gone."

"You did not see your wife get into the car."

He hesitated for a fraction of a second before answering. "No."

"You did not attempt to contact Teresa?"

"No. I might have if we had a boat and I could've got to the trailer without taking the car out on a Sunday. Sunday was family day. I was going to talk to Teresa on Monday when Marlee was at her doctor's appointment."

Rompré leaned forward. "To the best of your knowledge, your wife left home on Saturday morning with two suits for the dry cleaners. One came back. The other was found in the fire pit. Is there anything you would like to add, Monsieur Bremer?"

Trey remembered with a sharp pang, his wife materializing in their bedroom doorway on Saturday night, before he knew Teresa was murdered. The light from the hall had shone through Marlee's night gown. His wife's body was different from Teresa's but Trey didn't compare them. He never had. Part of the fun was the novelty of each woman's shape.

"Everything okay?" he'd asked cautiously. "Can't sleep?"

She had been in a strange mood all that day, returning home from the grocery store without any groceries, silent and withdrawn. Trey had gone to bed alone, feeling resentful that he was being punished for nothing. She was pissed with him, that much was obvious. Marlee had a trick of not looking him in the eye when she was mad. He should have tried to talk to her but he was tired and not up to a big discussion on how he was failing her as husband.

Marlee had climbed into bed beside him. "I'm worried. About us."

Trey remembered sighing and saying something like we're fine, we're just going through a rough patch, but we'll be fine. He had meant it when he told her he wasn't going anywhere.

Then his wife did a strange thing. She placed her hand flat in the middle of his chest and said: "I'm glad it's over."

At the time, he didn't dare ask her what she meant. But times had changed. The baby was born, his son, Stanley. Terrible name. Marlee's father's middle name. Seven years in prison was a long atonement for screwing the babysitter on literally a handful of occasions. He'd waited this long for his wife to forgive him and tell the police what she'd done. He couldn't wait any longer.

"I have something to add to my statement. Something I haven't told anyone. I lied to you just now. I saw my wife getting into my car on Saturday morning. I was awake. I saw her from the window. She was carrying a slate blue suit and the grey suit I had worn on Friday. Within the bundle were several of my shirts. She had a schedule that she stuck to like glue. Every Saturday my suits went to the drycleaners. Groceries and drycleaning were done on the same day at the same place. The IGA had a service."

"Why didn't you report this to DS Giroux?"

"Because I didn't want my kid to be born in prison! Marlee was pregnant. She wouldn't have done it if she wasn't desperate. Me and the kids, we were all she had. She was only trying to protect her family."

"Monsieur Bremer, do you believe your wife murdered Teresa Musgrave?"

"Who else could have done it? She had my suit in her arms and then they find it burned in the fire pit?" Trey swallowed. "There's something else. I didn't see her on Friday night, the night of the murder. She slept in Harry's room but she could have left and come back without me knowing. Look, I'm not proud of doing this! I don't want the mother of my children to go to prison. But I have to get out of here. If I were guilty, I could take it—I really could. But I'm innocent and no one will help me."

Rompré nodded. "One last question, *monsieur.*"

For a heart stopping moment, Trey thought that this was it. It was a sickening flash of hope—a rare one.

"What did Dave Gomer drink?"

He usually didn't get sucked in like that. Prison must be getting to him. "Scotch," he said in a flat voice. "Dave loved his scotch."

They weren't interested in helping him. Trey was never getting out of here.

THE RETURN drive from Montreal to Stollerton

would be painless if they didn't encounter highway construction and Constable Fournier couldn't remember a time when there wasn't highway construction in Montreal. She merged onto the freeway, braked and swerved, cutting off a transport truck in the middle lane. Her eyes were locked on the traffic ahead.

"In my opinion, sir, Bremer's good-humoured sincerity was just an act. Did you see his eyes light up when we walked in? He saw an opportunity to get his case reopened and he grabbed it. His story of picking up the murder weapon to examine it was bizarre. Who walks into a crime scene and starts handling the weapon? Innocent people usually can't wait to get away from the body and turn the problem over to police. Bremer is no fool. He knew we'd find his semen and prints in the trailer; it would have been suspicious if there were none on the flashlight. It'd look like he wiped it down."

"You did not believe his story."

"Not a word of it, sir. I think he was making it up as he went along. Trey never told police he'd called Dave Gomer that night. It isn't in any of DS Giroux's reports. Bremer lied more than once during that investigation, there's no reason to believe he's telling the truth now. He's a narcissist with a serious sexual dysfunction. Rape is recreation to him. I thought I'd heard everything until I heard rape described as a sex game."

"The world is corrupt and all human beings are complicit to some degree in its corruption. Our job is not to judge but to redeem our small corner of it."

Fournier glanced quickly at Rompré. "What prompted you to ask how him how his suit came to be burned in the fire pit?"

"It was the image of Trey Bremer driving the roads in his underwear."

"He wouldn't have been the only one. It was a hot night in July. Sir, even if everything he said was true, even if it wasn't rape but an affair, that doesn't remove motive. Bremer murdered Teresa because she was going to tell his wife."

Rompré rubbed his eyes. "Whatever else Bremer did that night, he did not burn his suit."

"Because of the alleged phone call? You think it unlikely he walked into a phone booth in his underwear."

They had put in a request for a warrant to access the record of calls made from the pay phone in St. Jude. It was a long shot. After seven years, the odds were against Bell Canada having kept records on a little-used, forgotten pay phone in rural West Québec.

"No, I think it is unlikely Bremer walked into his house at nine-forty-five in the evening wearing only his underwear. He anticipated seeing his wife—an angry wife who had been waiting impatiently for several hours for his return. She would certainly notice if he were to walk in wearing only his briefs."

"Bremer said Marlee was asleep in their son's room when he came home. She didn't hear him come in. She wouldn't know what he was wearing."

"*Oui. Je me souvien.* But he did not know his wife was asleep in his son's room when he came home. This was an event Bremer could not have foreseen when he left the trailer."

Fournier nodded slowly. "Yes, I see. He came home wearing the suit."

"He was wearing the suit."

The constable maneuvered around a semi-tractor trailer. The scenery changed from flat tracts of housing developments to rolling hills and scruffy farmland dotted with hay bales.

"Then how did it get in the fire pit? Trey saw his wife put the suit in his car. Could someone have intercepted it? What about Dave Gomer? He was drinking heavily at the time. He got the phone call, went to the trailer. Maybe Teresa decided to stop playing the game and threatened both Dave and Trey with the police. Dave loses control, kills her and then frames Trey for the murder. He was a blackmailer. Dave was the reason Teresa was working for Trey Bremer in the first place. Years later, a note surfaces and Dave thinks he's been found out. His wounds could have been self-inflicted, the result of being bounced over the rapids. He could have been drinking vodka instead of scotch. He could have had a guilty conscience."

"He could have been many things, but he could not have burned M. Bremer's suit in the fire pit. He was seen passed out on the dock on Saturday morning by his wife, Dorothy. Only one person could have burned the suit if it was not Bremer."

"Marlee Bremer."

"*Oui.*"

"I don't understand, sir. Did she find blood and then destroyed the suit to try and protect him?"

"Her husband is in prison. Marlee Bremer did not take steps to protect her husband. She took steps to make sure her husband was convicted. She destroyed a piece of evidence that could have led to reasonable doubt. You saw the crime scene photographs. It would be difficult to get a conviction if CSU discovered no blood on Bremer's clothing. We have established he did not return home in his briefs. He was wearing his suit because there was no blood on his suit. Marlee Bremer burned it to make investigators believe there was."

Fournier nodded. "It worked. Finding the burned remnants convinced investigators Trey Bremer was guilty. It was a slam-dunk at that point."

DS Rompré was on leave in Québec City at the time of the murder. Detective Sergeant Giroux had been assigned to the investigation. The case was a career-maker for him as it turned out. Giroux had gone on to make lieutenant with the MRC des Laurentides in Ville de Mont-Tremblant.

"If Marlee took his vehicle on Saturday morning that would explain why no other tire treads were found at the scene. The lab was able to narrow the time the suit was burned to a twelve hour period between nine p.m. on Friday and nine a.m. on Saturday morning. She had means and opportunity. But what did Marlee Bremer gain by sending her husband to jail? No, it doesn't make sense to me, sir. Trey could be lying about seeing his wife leave."

"He could be lying or Marlee Bremer could be lying about her actions that morning. We could spend many hours trying to determine which of them is telling the truth. More useful to our purpose is to determine who stood to profit by destroying the suit?"

"The first and most obvious person was Trey Bremer, but since he had it on when he came home, the only other person who had access to the clothing was Marlee Bremer. She must've done it to help him, sir. From the beginning she supported her husband's story, even claiming she took it to the drycleaners. It wasn't until after she recanted and CSU did another search of the scene that an arrest could be made. Because there was no criminal intent, Giroux said it was an honest mistake and no charges were laid for obstruction."

"*C'est ça*. An honest mistake that delayed her husband's arrest by a week."

Rompré leaned back against the headrest, deep in thought.


TREY BREMER lay in his cell trying to remember what Teresa Musgrave was like and couldn't. Was it terrible he could only remember the sex they had? Episodes bloomed in his mind, jumbled between his legs, and held on with an iron grip. He didn't know he had that in him, to be less than a perfect gentleman with a girl. He loved it.

But he loved the game, not the girl. As soon as Teresa stopped playing he had no use for her. He already had a wife. He wanted a slut. Why do things have to get so serious and complicated for women?

That's what this whole madness boiled down to—a moment of sincere appreciation—that's all it was. Trey thought a nineteen-year-old would be cool enough to understand his meaning. Teresa wasn't. She asked him what he dreamed of being. He had no answer for her. He already was what he dreamed of being. He wanted to run the family business, have a wife and kids and be respected. He wanted his house showcased in *Ottawa Life Magazine*. He wanted to be a success like his father before him. He did not want to run away with a teenager to live in obscurity while another man raised his kids.

He regretted those few weeks in July, but not for the

sex—he was grateful he experienced hot freaky sex at least once before he became a limp-dick old man. It was the addiction he regretted, the helplessness, the loss of self-control that shamed him to his core. If Teresa hadn't been killed, he never would've stopped. He would have lost everything for the sex games they played in the Oasis.

That day at the trailer with the kids though ... in spite of it all, he had the impression she was good with Harry and Violet. He didn't know what made him think of that. But it was nice memory of her. Trey was glad then to have a good memory of Teresa at last.

# FIFTEEN

AS IF on cue, the temperature dropped and cleaning the office wouldn't be as unpleasant as Alvina had anticipated. She set her satchel on the reception desk and glanced at the answering machine. No flashing red light. No messages.

No call from Del.

It's only been a few days, she told herself. He's busy with work and his art, his art and his work—a mantra that became less reassuring the more she had to repeat it. Maybe his deal was the same as her parents. Del said he wanted her to stay. Coral and Oliver Moon always said the same thing right before they left town. Maybe he needed her the same way. He liked having her around so he could forget about her.

Alvina unplugged the answering machine and stuffed it into a box for the Déjà Vu thrift store in Innes. There. That solved that problem. No answering machine meant no reminders that Del Musgrave didn't call.

Everything else was already gone from Dave's office, including Dave's leather chairs from 1985. Ray Milligan from *Deeper Vibe* had tears running down his face when they hauled Dave's desk away. The reception desk was staying though. MetMedia's managing editor wanted it. He had also asked for a meeting with Alvina to brief him on the local customs and generally bring him up to speed on how things worked in the country. It gave her a legitimate reason for sticking around.

She stepped into the rear office where the stringers used to work back when the *Record* made enough money to hire stringers. There were two desks in the room, a filing cabinet and a window that looked out over the roof tops of the neighbouring businesses. A cheerful view of a quaint little town, the Huck Finn raft, the brick-red covered bridge, its hills and river— Alvina hated it. She hated everything about it. The town admired Del and had no use for her. And now Del didn't want her either. They could both go to hell.

She turned away from the dingy window and pulled open the top drawer of the metal filing cabinet. Thirty years of photos were stored there, neatly filed by some efficient office secretary back when businesses still employed secretaries. Alvina sifted through one of the files. The photos had been taken the old-fashioned way, with cameras that used film. Some had tiny time stamps in their white scalloped borders. Black and white images of fathers who had passed away, parents celebrating anniversaries, children who had graduated from university. Years old most of them, their subjects long gone.

We must all have holes in us by the time we die, she thought, turning the photos over. Large holes. Pin holes. Slashes of holes; ragged, gnawed holes. Del's rejection had left a hole in her. She didn't know how to compete for love. She'd tried that once with her parents and they picked the theatre so she gave up.

Dave's weathered sardonic face stared back at her from one photo she held in her hand. His blue eyes full of blame and so they should be. She'd pretty much given up on him too. Dave Gomer the murder victim was too strange to accept, never mind solve. The police would figure it out. And anyway, maybe his death wasn't a murder. Maybe this was a straight-up, old-fashioned boating-and-alcohol tragedy. The kind police warn the public against every single summer and the public cheerfully ignores.

She lined up the photographs in neat, evenly spaced rows on the desk. Like a gang of affectionate friends keeping her company. She couldn't deny it. Those smiling faces were cheering her up, filling her with hope. Thin icy fingers of hope rising up, treacherously leading her back to thinking Del could've meant it when he said he needed her to stay. *Use your head, Moon. He'd have called by now.*

There was a noise in the outer office.

Alvina looked up from the photographs and listened. It sounded like someone was going through her desk. The *Deeper Vibe* was still on holiday, though Ray had flown back for Dave's funeral. Alvina had locked the street-level door when she came in. The *Record* was no longer in business; she didn't want the public wandering in to gawk while she finished packing. Maybe MetMedia's managing editor had arrived a day early.

Alvina stepped into the room and started. "What are you doing?"

Violet Bremer gave a little scream and jumped away from Alvina's desk. "I didn't think anyone was here."

The girl was wearing a cotton dress patterned in orange and hot pink flowers, cinched at the waist with a wide shiny yellow belt. Her mother must have taken her shopping for new school clothes, Alvina thought mechanically. A tall, serious girl.

"How did you get in here? The door was locked downstairs. I locked it. We're closed."

"I used the spare key under the flower pot outside. I saw you look under the pot once a long time ago and I wondered what was there."

"So that gave you the right to break in?"

"No. I didn't break in. I used the key I said. You were at Mr. Gomer's funeral. You seemed upset so I came to pay my respects. It should comfort you to know that he's gone to a good place. He's gone to God."

Alvina felt cracked inside, chipped and brittle. She was one bad conversation away from losing it. "He's gone to the crematorium, Violet. You didn't know Dave at all."

"Yes, I did." Violet's eyes were wide and grey. "I've known him since I was a kid."

"You still are a kid. Where's your mother? Does she know you're here?"

She shifted her weight. Violet's yellow sandals matched her belt. "She's at Sur la Lune with Harry and Stanley. I told her I had to get a book out of the library."

Alvina extended her hand, palm up. "Give me the key."

Violet dropped it, unconcerned, on the desk, enraging Alvina further. Another privileged kid insensible to anyone's feelings but her own. Another kid who had everything and felt entitled to more. "Who do you think you are? Do you think because your mother bought some crappy advertising once upon a time that gives you the right to do what you like on private property? I heard you going through my desk. You were stealing. Yes, you were. Don't lie to me. Get out before I call the cops. Go home to your mother. Go on, get out. Maybe she'll have me fired." Alvina dashed hot tears from her eyes.

"What's wrong with you? Why are you crying?"

"*Guess*, you little idiot. Selfish brat. *Thief.*"

"Don't call me names." Violet's face turned red. Her wide grey eyes filled with tears. "I wasn't stealing. I was looking for something I left here a few weeks ago and I need it back."

"What is it? I didn't see anything of yours here."

"You wouldn't recognize it. I thought you might have left it lying out or in a file."

Alvina narrowed her eyes. "Would this thing of yours be a note by any chance? An anonymous note written in green ink, stuck in an envelope with my name on it?"

"No."

Violet's gaze shifted.

Green ink and a little girl's handwriting. The anonymous tipster was standing right in front of her. Not Dot. Not someone with a grudge. A kid. Twelve-year-old Violet-fucking-Bremer. "Oh yes, it was. It was you. Where did he get the flashlight? You hurt a lot of people with that question. You caused a lot of pain for a lot of people and you didn't even have the guts to sign your name."

"It wasn't me." Her jaw trembled.

"Either tell me the truth or I'll talk to your mother. Why send it to me? What did you think I was going to do with it?"

Violet's mouth tightened belligerently. "I thought because you were new in town, you wouldn't have the same prejudices against my dad that the rest of them do and you'd look into it. It was a clue to get you interested in his case."

It turned out Marlee Bremer had pulled into the post office that day to mail a bunch of packages. The *Record* was a short hop down the street and Violet saw her chance. "I stuck it through the letter slot. So now you know. So what did you do with it? If I'm allowed to ask without you biting my head off or calling me names."

"I put it in the shredder. A newspaper doesn't chase after anonymous tips. Why do you need it back? If I'm allowed to ask without you being arrogant and disrespectful."

Violet twisted on her toes and her skin pinked. "I don't want anyone to know I wrote it, especially my mother because she'll think I'm going behind her back. I'm the only one that gets it that my dad is innocent. He told me he is and I know he's telling the truth because I was in the trailer seven years ago and I know there was no flashlight in there. But see, if I tell them that, they'll say I'm making it up because I'm twelve and how could remember that far back."

"You can't remember that far back," Alvina said without interest.

"I can! I do. I remember the whole day. Not at first. It took awhile but I can tell you everything about that day. Teresa took Harry and me to the library to return our books and then a man came and drove us to the trailer. He didn't have a car seat for Harry. I remember that. He said Harry was big enough for the seat belt, which he wasn't." Violet raised her eyebrows, expecting outrage.

"You're making this up."

Violet persisted, her face getting pinker. "Teresa

told us we were going swimming but I didn't have my bathing suit. Harry didn't care because he was practically a baby, but I wanted to go home and get my bathing suit. Teresa said not a chance in hell, so the man said we'd have a treasure hunt instead. He gave me a blue jay's feather. There was a big rock that we sat on."

Violet left out the part about Harry falling asleep in the car and how she had tapped him on the nose with sharp, sneaky force to wake him up, and then gazed out of the window as if she didn't know why he was crying. She was always doing things like that for no good reason. It was a hot day. A real scorcher. The weatherman said it on the car radio. Teresa's hair was stuck to her neck. She gave Harry a bag of ketchup chips to shut him up.

"We turned down an old road where there were big trees growing around and then we stopped in front of a broken-down old trailer. I said it was a rotten, scabby spider house. Teresa said it was an oasis. She and the man got out. Harry escaped from his seat belt—Harry Houdini, my father used to call him, and I got out too. Harry sat down in the middle of the road to play but I ran toward the river and Teresa raced after me, grabbed me and squeezed me super tight. I was kicking and screaming and Teresa was furious. She pulled Harry up by his arm and yanked both of us to the trailer's tow bar and made us sit down. She said: Don't move. This was not the day to tempt fate. I asked her what 'tempt fate' was and she said she'd tell me when I was older. The man who drove us stayed on the swimming rock. He put six cans of beer in the river to keep them cold. When I was five I didn't know they were beer cans. I only figured that out last year. They looked like big silver bullets."

Violet bent down to scratch her leg and squished a bug that was crawling up her calf. "I thought it was pop. Our mom didn't let us drink pop."

"Who was the man?"

"Mr. Gomer. I didn't know it was him at the time but when I got older, I felt like I'd met him before. I figured it out when Mom took us with her to the trailer. She was cleaning it up to sell it and we were swimming in the river. And then I remembered when I was there before, exactly as it happened. I just had to get older. You see, the memory got locked in but I didn't understand what it meant. It's hard to explain. Everything was stored in my mind—who was there, what they said, what they did—but I didn't know what it meant until now." Violet looked at her anxiously. "Do I sound like a weirdo?"

"Your mom told us you have a photographic memory. I guess it's not something you can control. You can't help having it. It doesn't make you weird. It's sort of a gift."

Violet stared at her, amazed. "That's what Pastor Henry says. He says it's a gift from God. But it feels more like a cross. I wish I didn't have it."

FIVE-YEAR-OLD Violet had left the tow bar and leaned in the doorway of the trailer wanting juice. Their carry-all was in the trunk of the car along with Harry's stroller. Teresa pulled it out, set it on the hood of the car and unzipped it. There was a package of disinfectant wipes in a side pocket that Violet's mother had insisted she use before handling their food. Violet thought a rule was a rule and asked Teresa to wipe her hands first. Teresa pulled out a wipe and carefully cleaned her fingers and then Violet's.

"I want the pink straw."

Teresa inserted the straw and handed it to Violet. "What do you say?"

"Thank you."

Harry had not moved from the tow bar. He was a docile and obedient little boy who did not tempt fate. Teresa picked him up and carried him to the rear of the trailer. High above was a shiny patch of metal that she showed him as she wiped his nose with the disinfectant cloth.

"What is it?" Violet said. "What are you looking at you guys?"

Harry was tugging on the straps of her bra so Teresa had set him down on his feet. Her little brother wandered a few steps before plopping down in the gravel and pine needles.

"What is it, Teresa? What is that thing? I want to see it too."

It was a palm tree. A shiny silver palm tree that bent over some letters that were also shiny. "Let—me—see!" Violet punctuated each word with a scream.

Teresa lifted her up. Violet traced the chrome palm tree with her small fingers. "What's it say? What's it say on this thing?"

"It says the name of the trailer," Teresa answered. "This trailer is called 'Oasis.'"


IT WASN'T funny anymore. Alvina felt creepy, a voyeur spying on a dead teenager taking care of couple of little kids while Dave sat by the river drinking beer. She could see the scene in her head and she didn't want to. "So the man who brought you to the trailer was Dave Gomer. Okay. Well, he told me he got Teresa the job as your nanny so it could be that he offered her a ride that day. I'm not sure why he would do that. But all right. I believe you were at the trailer with Teresa and Dave."

"There were strawberries on the table. I think we were supposed to have a picnic but Harry and I didn't get any. Teresa let me play inside the trailer but I wasn't allowed to touch the berries. She had to stay outside and keep an eye on Harry because of the river. He was sitting in the laneway heaping pine needles into little mounds. Harry was still practically a baby then, only two years old. He doesn't remember anything."

The pink dining table with the gold stars was the first thing Violet saw when she climbed the metal stair and entered the trailer. Violet poked into all the cupboards and drawers, opening and closing each one. "It had a little sink like in my playhouse," she said unperturbedly. "I wanted to live there."

"Now I know you're lying. The drawers were swollen shut. I couldn't open them, how could a little kid."

Violet raised her brows. "I couldn't get two of them open. The cupboards were okay but the cutlery drawers beside the sink were stuck shut. But if you go in the cupboard under the sink, you can see what's inside them. They were empty. I looked in every corner of that trailer and there was no flashlight. Then my dad arrived and Teresa told Harry and me we could go swimming and she closed the door. Mr. Gomer was keeping an eye on us so it was perfectly safe. My father would never have let us near water unsupervised in case you were wondering."

"I wasn't. What was your dad doing there?"

"He had to show Teresa around the trailer," Violet said. "Daddy said she was moving out of the house she was living in and coming to live in the trailer. He had to show her how everything worked. My father was helping Teresa, get it? He was her friend. And he didn't have a flashlight."

"The flashlight wasn't in the trailer which is not the same thing as saying he didn't have one. Everyone says he took it from the service bay at the dealership. Violet, you better stop making this your problem or it'll drive you crazy. You're a kid. Go enjoy being a kid. You remembered the trailer and you told me about it—that's good. But that's the end."

Violet shook her head firmly. "No, no it is *not*. You don't know. My dad didn't do this and no one will help him. My mother fired Monsieur Nault so now he's all alone. I'm the only one who believes him. I don't care about being a kid. I care about getting my dad out of prison. If everyone is so sure where the flashlight came from, then why did the note upset people? Huh? Why did it cause trouble? Because somebody knows the truth, that's why. Someone knows my dad didn't kill Teresa and Mr. Gomer's murder proves it."

"You're delusional."

"Don't say that. Do not say that! I am not! Mr. Gomer was at the trailer—he knew my dad wouldn't hurt Teresa. He believed in my dad and he stuck up for us in the paper. Why would he do that if he didn't know my dad was innocent? My mother said Dave Gomer was our champion. Mr. Gomer found out who really killed Teresa and this person killed him to shut him up."

"Violet, relax. This isn't a Nancy Drew novel, these are real people. You can't accuse innocent people of double homicide just because it suits you. Dave wasn't murdered. He was an alcoholic who had a relapse. He must've hit his head and fell overboard."

"No, he didn't and I can prove he didn't because I saw him—I saw his killer. He went right past me in Dave Gomer's boat. He was wearing Mr. Gomer's hat and jacket but I knew it wasn't him because of the way the boat was in the water. The boat was like this." Violet held her arm at a 180 degree angle. When Mr. Gomer goes fishing in the morning, his boat is always like so." The arm was adjusted to 90 degrees. "It wasn't the same man. I thought it was strange but I didn't get suspicious until they found Mr. Gomer's body."

"What are you talking about?"

"It was somebody wearing his jacket and hat. I put that in my statement to the police. They think he was killed upriver, really far from where they found his boat."

In her mind's eye Alvina saw Del Musgrave standing under lettuce yellow trees. The sun full on him and his eyes full on her. "Liar. You don't know that. You don't know what the cops think."

"Listen—listen to me! Why did it take his body so long to float into Stollerton Bay? It's only seven kilometres and he wasn't discovered for six days. That's too long! I researched it."

"You don't have to yell. I'm standing right here. I can hear you perfectly. Dave's body got must have got tangled in debris. The police probably have this all figured out by now. They have labs and forensics. There's nothing to prove Dave was murdered or they would have told me."

"You're making that up." Violet twisted away, her long limbs seeming to fly out from her body. "If you aren't even going to be serious—you'll be sorry one day.

You could have helped solve a murder case but you were too stupid. Everyone will say so."

"Violet, don't be a brat. I'm leaving town in a couple of days, I couldn't help even if I wanted to. Your dad is in prison because he's guilty—that's how it is. The Crown had a mountain of evidence against him; the flashlight was just a tiny question mark. So watch who you're calling stupid, you little toad. I could still tell your mother about that note."

"Ask me if I care! I don't care what you do. You think you know everything. Go ahead and tell her. I'll just deny it. You shredded the note so good luck proving it was me." Her eyes reddened and narrowed. "Did anyone even see it? It'd be easy to make it look like you're the one who's lying and not me. It'd be your word against mine. It's not just guilty people who go to jail. Jesus was innocent too."

"Leave Jesus out of this. Your dad is not Jesus."

Violet flushed scarlet, gripped her stomach and burst into hysterical tears. Unabashed wailing as only a kid will do. Her nose ran. Alvina opened the top drawer of her desk and reached for a pack of tissues "Here. Here —take it. Don't cry. I'm sorry I said that about Jesus. I ought to show more respect."

"It's not that." Violet jammed a ball of tissue over each eye. "It's ... it's ... what if I'm wrong? What if my dad really is guilty and I'm the only one who is fooled by him?"

"You'll know the truth when the time comes. You're doing the best you can to make your parents happy. One day this will all make sense. I think. I'm not the best person to give advice when it comes to parents. I still have no clue about mine."

Violet nodded and dabbed her nose. "Is Del Musgrave your boyfriend?"

"No." Alvina moved behind the reception desk. Cool terror danced up her spine. "You saw us in a boat all of one time. You have a big imagination, Violet."

"Yes. I know I do. But he could have been so it made sense to ask. I'm glad he's not because you'd be really upset to find out it was Del Musgrave I saw going past in Mr. Gomer's boat. My mother bought a couple of his paintings once. It was him. He was wearing Mr. Gomer's beige hat but I could see blonde hair poking out under it."

Alvina found it hard to follow what Violet was saying. "Del Musgrave was in Dave's boat. Have you told the police?"

"No, because I thought he was your boyfriend."

"Thank god." She sat down in the chair and dropped her head to her desk. "Don't mind me. I'm just tired. I didn't get much sleep last night."

A bird was singing. The sweet scent of dirt and damp floated in through the open window. Alvina was aware of heat on her neck and behind her eyes. Violet was quiet now too, waiting for her to say something.

This was no time to fall apart.

"I'll tell them, Violet. DS Rompré gave me his card. I'll call him and tell him what you've told me. You'd better get going now. It smells like rain. You'll get caught in it. Here, give me that tissue. It's no good to you now. Take a fresh one."

Minutes later, watching from Dave's window, Alvina saw Violet race off down the street just as the first big drops fell. Dark green mountains closed in, lining the river basin like walls. Her ribcage hurt. It hurt to breathe. Like an old person, a retiree, bones aching before a rainstorm. An anxiety attack. It's not like the feeling was new to her. If she had a friend she could call it would help. Not Ray. He'd want to call the police.

She wished she could tell Del about the rain and the smell of the jack pines and dust. She wished he knew the spaces she had inside her, her depths and interesting twists. Alvina fingered the hem of the pretty orange dress she'd put on in case he called. That she still wished he would fall in love with her knowing what she knew about him ... roused her to fear herself.

# SIXTEEN

THE STORM broke at one o'clock in the afternoon. Black clouds had been threatening all morning, settling in low over the village. It was a summer storm, fast, hot, and white with lightning. Rain fell in sheets. Del had been caught out on the river coming home from the Camp. Gerry had been tracking the weather report all day. He cancelled the fishing group that was scheduled to go out that afternoon when they issued the storm watch. Gerry sent Del home, telling him to get his ass off the river before it broke. Del had done his best. He pulled up to his dock, jumped out and tied the boat off quickly. The path through the forest was taken at a gallop. Lightning sparked and a thunderclap boomed overhead. He ran, reaching the edge of the wood where the meadow began. The cabin was just ahead. Del skidded to a stop and blinked the rain out of his eyes.

A brown van was pulling into the yard. Alvina Moon was behind the wheel.

He drew back out of sight and watched her from the edge of the forest. She climbed out, slamming the door hard, probably hoping the noise would draw him out and she wouldn't have to knock. The rain was soaking her to the skin. She walked around to the front of the van and stood looking first in one direction and then the other. Her hair was glued flat to her head and neck. The orange dress she was wearing clung to her skinny body.

The meadow was between them. Its flowers were brilliant, their colours popped against the grey. Alvina hugged her arms across her middle and stared. Del thought she must have seen him or figured out he was there because her eyes were fixed and she strained forward as if sensing him hiding in the trees. And then she turned and began walking to the driver's side door of the van.

*Let her go.*

His chest clamped and he lunged out the forest, walking briskly with his head down as if he were hurrying back from the dock. She looked up and saw him at the same time he saw her. He stopped in the middle of the meadow.

Her voice reached him, thin in the rain. "Did you kill Dave?"

They were soaked through, the both of them. Del shoved his hair out of his eyes. Thunder rumbled. "I thought he drowned in a fishing accident."

"It wasn't an accident. Somebody cracked his skull with a mallet and then tossed him over the side of the boat." She held her side, crumpling a little, like she wanted to shrink into herself. "I'm sorry. I have to know."

Del crossed the meadow in three long strides and caught her hand. "Come on." He drew her to the van, opened the driver's door and helped her inside. She slumped limp and blank-eyed in the seat. He jogged around the front of the van to the passenger side, hopped up and slammed the door behind him. The rain pattered on the roof.

"Are the cops sure about this or are they just being cautious? I've seen fishermen drown with the same injuries. They're usually drunk when it happens."

Alvina's hair ran in rivulets. "There was a vodka bottle in the boat. The killer didn't know that Dave drank scotch." The look she gave him was chillingly vacant. "The police told me to keep what I know to myself."

"Then I guess you'd better not say anything."

Del waited. Her body was stiff, a wire of tension; her eyes stared straight ahead. The reflection of the rain on the windshield ran down her face.

"Do you remember when you told me the story of the woman and her python? I thought about that story a lot." She rubbed her eyes. "You shouldn't have asked me to stay."

He held her face with his eyes and the graceful white length of her neck. "Tell me what happened."

The tension gave way. She leaned her head against the bucket seat. "An anonymous note came to the office a few weeks ago addressed to me. It said: Where did he get the flashlight? It was a clue about the flashlight used to kill your wife. Dave told me to destroy it and I didn't. Then Dave was killed." She took a breath. "The police have the note now because they think there's a connection between Dave's death and your wife's murder. Del, I know you're the connection. You blamed Dave for your wife's death. You met him on the river, killed him, then put on his jacket and hat and boated downriver. Someone saw you. This person came to me with the information because I'm a reporter. I said I would go to the police. And I have to; I have to turn you in. So you see? It was me all along. I was the python in the story. I was the one measuring you for the kill."

And then unexpectedly, terrifying him, she collapsed over steering wheel. Her shoulders shook violently; her throat howled real grief that sounded like it couldn't be stopped. Del put his arm around her, not knowing what else to do.

"What do you need me to do," he urged. "I'll do whatever you need."

"That's the first time anyone has ever said that me." She wiped her eyes and laughed. "It's usually the other way around."

Del took her face in his hands and kissed her lightly.

"I wish you wouldn't." She wouldn't meet his eyes. "You don't mean anything by it so I wish you wouldn't."

He released her and opened the passenger door. "You're probably right. Come on. We could both use a drink." He hopped out.

Alvina watched as he came around to her side of the van and opened the door. His hair and skin were wet. His face glistened.

A rod of lightning flashed overhead, splitting her optic nerve with needle sharp pain. She raised her arm in front of her face, partially blinded. Del put his arms around her and lifted her down like she was broken or made of something fragile. Rain trickled down his hair and dripped from his eyelashes. He took her hand. "We'll have to make a run for it."

They raced across the grass to the cabin, hurled themselves inside and slammed the door. The wind roared around them. Summer storms were more violent than any other, but shorter too. Del said this one would probably blow itself out in less than an hour.

Then he disappeared into the bathroom to round up some towels.

Alvina stood at the door, dripping water. The cabin smelled of cooking oil and damp wood. There was a brown stain on the ceiling from a long ago leak and oily cobwebs laced the overhead light. Del's house was a tarpaper shack constructed out of plywood and two by fours, fitted with a window and a shingled roof and plunked in the middle of the bush.

She turned back and almost jumped out of her skin when she saw the gleam of his hair. He was standing in the shadows, watching her.

"I scared you. Sorry." He handed her a towel. "The cabin is not much to look at but it's all mine. I wanted to own land from the time I was twelve; I didn't care about the house. I could live in a cardboard box if I had to. I'm pretty self-sufficient here. The fridge, radio and lamp are powered by solar batteries. Hot water comes from a propane tank. I don't need anything else."

The walls were painted slate blue. His wife had long ago fixed a red curtain over the window that was pulled back. On rainy days the bruised world outside matched the colour of the walls. Del said it was like being in the hull of a battleship.

"I'll get us some dry clothes."

He was talking to fill the space. Alvina could hear it in his voice. After high emotion there was always awkwardness. Her head throbbed. "I wasn't supposed to tell anyone about the anonymous note or what it said. Don't repeat it, please?"

"Who am I going to tell?"

"I don't know," she said dully. "You might tell someone."

He wordlessly handed her a tee-shirt and a pair of sweat pants and directed her to the tiny bathroom to change. Alvina stripped off her sopping dress and flung it over the shower rail. There was no hope it would dry out before she left. The tee-shirt smelled like him and was big enough to be his but not the sweatpants. They belonged to a woman. Alvina registered this fact without emotion. They were probably Dagmar's.

Her head hurt a little less now. Alvina opened her eyes and met her reflection in the mirror. Her colour was good and her eyes were dark and healthy. She wasn't losing it. She almost wished she was; it would explain what she was doing here. She'd better not be crawling after a killer because that was the kind of thing girls with low self-esteem did. She could almost hear the tut-tut of contempt from Missy and Dagmar.

Alvina came out of the bathroom to find Del in the kitchen removing two cold beers from the squat bar refrigerator. He had changed his shirt and found a pair of dry shorts. The kitchen amounted to a propane stove abutting a makeshift counter and a shelf for dishes and tins of food. The two person dining table was crowded with paint brushes and tubes of oil paints. Her gaze lighted on the tools of an artist—a gummy plywood board that served as his palette and a stack of art books piled on a three-legged stool. His work was neatly stowed in the loft above the bed.

"Can I see?"

Del pulled down three paintings. "I do oil on wood mostly, canvas when I can afford it." His supply of paints and brushes were seriously depleted. "I had a busy spring. Gerry's behind in the order from Wallack's." The premier art supply store in Ottawa.

She stepped back. Nature's violence was more evident in these works than in the one he brought with him on the canoe trip. Each painting was a landscape at war with the elements, lonely and defiantly alone. She wondered which came first: the fury of the storm or the unexpressed rage of the painter. "I had no idea you were this good." He was good—the kind of good that made mortals uneasy. Alvina handed the paintings back to Del. He slid them in the loft.

The bed below was made up with a red comforter and two pillows in blood red casings to match the curtain. A blue armchair was tucked in the corner of the room with a lamp stand behind it. Alvina sat down. Her ribs ached. Her eyes drifted to the bed. There was a charcoal sketch of a naked woman pinned above the headboard.

"Is that Teresa?" Silly question. Of course it was.

Del uncapped the beer bottles. "I sketched that before she woke up. It was the only time she wasn't aware she was desirable."

"How come you don't hang your other paintings on the wall?"

"I don't want to look at them." He reached over her to turn on the lamp. The window for all its size couldn't compete with the deep blue-grey of the walls. She caught his scent—Irish Spring soap. "You look wrung out." He handed her the beer. "Here, drink this."

The cabin was tiled with green and grey linoleum, worn down with ground-in dirt. He must have given up washing it years ago.

Del caught her looking over the place. "Teresa wasn't happy here. I installed a bathroom the year we were married but she wanted something better."

"I think it's cozy."

"Don't," he said sharply. "Don't try to be what she wasn't. Don't try to fit yourself in a place before you even know if you want to be there."

"I'm not." Alvina shrugged but was stung almost to tears. She said with deliberate cruelty, "Was the cabin the reason Teresa was going to leave you?"

His body stilled. "Where would you get an idea like that?"

Instinct told her to leave Violet Bremer out of it. "From Marlee Bremer the same day she told me to stay away from you. According to her, Teresa was looking into renting the Oasis because she was planning to leave you." The jab wasn't delivered with sufficient force to wound him and Alvina had already lost the stomach for revenge.

Del's eyes flickered. "Dagmar warned me you would do this. She said I was big news to a girl like you. Are you using my wife's murder to get close to me? Dagmar says you've fallen in love with me. Is that why you came here to warn me about this eyewitness instead of going to the police?"

Blood roared in Alvina's ears. Her breath came in short gasps. She couldn't defend herself, she couldn't breathe. "I came here because I wanted—I wanted to give you a chance to explain. I know why you did it and I thought—I'm not—I haven't—what business is it of Dagmar's or yours how I feel? You are nothing to me. I don't love you at all. I hate you."

A dark tension came over Del's face. "Dagmar said you would deny it."

"Go to hell. Both of you." She set her beer down and rose unsteadily to her feet. "I'll return your clothes to

Dagmar. She can give them to you the next time you see her."

"Where are you going?"

"I don't know. Some place else." Alvina blindly searched the floor for her camera bag until she remembered she didn't bring it.

He nodded to the window. The storm was fully upon them. The view beyond was spitted with rain. "You can't see three feet in front of you in this. Stay here and wait it out. Don't try to drive in this."

Her teeth began clattering in her head. Her jaw trembled violently. "What's it to you? I'll do what I want."

"You're shaking from head to toe. You're too damned skinny, that's the problem. I'm going to make you something to eat." Del moved to the kitchen. "Is there somebody you should call; someone who'll be worried about you?" He dug out a loaf of bread and fumbled the bag open.

"No."

"You'd better stay then."

Del loaded the bread with salami, mustard and lettuce, sliced them in half and set the sandwiches on plates on a TV tray between them. The tray was printed with a picture of mallards nesting in a marsh. "Eat," he instructed. "You need it."

They ate in silence in their respective places, she in the armchair; he on the bed. She ate ravenously either from the chill or emotional exhaustion or because she was desperately hungry. She had skipped breakfast. Missy looked daggers every time Alvina opened the cupboard. It wasn't worth the aggravation for a bowl of Cheerios.

"What's the Oasis?" Del's voice cut the silence between them.

"It's the model name of the trailer. It's written on the back in chrome letters with a palm tree." Alvina lifted her eyes to his briefly. "I thought you knew."

"I don't know anything about the case. A cop dropped off a copy of the transcripts from the trial and told me to call if I had any questions. I burned them in the woodstove." Del's eyes were hooded. "But just now when you said oasis, I remembered Teresa used that word once. I was painting, ignoring her—according to her I was ignoring her, but I had to if I was going to get any work done. She said I could paint all I wanted; she had a little oasis of her own."

"Maybe she meant an oasis in general, like an oasis of calm or how this cabin is like an oasis."

"No, that's not what she meant."

Del seemed to be hearing or seeing something that was deeply interior, beyond Alvina's comprehension. His expression was fixed, and yet in its rigidity, he communicated more pain than if he had broken into tears. He knew his wife was cheating on him, Alvina thought. He knew.

Her stomach rolled.

"What does it matter now?" She let hair fall in front of her eyes so he wouldn't see that she was stricken with fear and pity. "She's been dead for seven years. Let it go."

Del pushed his sandwich away and rose to his feet. He stood at the window, his back to Alvina. The view showed a black forest bending under the rain. "She'd been to the trailer with him before, before she was raped." The muscles in his face were held so tightly in place he could have been made of marble. "That guy

Bremer, he probably figured he had it all worked out—a wife, a couple of kids and another man's wife to screw on the side. He was just as trapped as I was, he just didn't know it."

Alvina's lips were numb. The words tumbled out of her in a flat monotone. "I'm not going to respond to that because there's no proof and she's not here to defend herself. Even if she was sleeping with him, it doesn't mean she didn't love you. She could have made a mistake that she regretted. Maybe that's why Trey attacked her, because she was ending it with him. We all make mistakes."

Wordlessly, he carried their plates to the tiny kitchen sink. Alvina joined him, taking a dish towel from the peg. They stood side-by-side, doing the dishes in silence. The storm sounded over them, already on its way out. When it passed, the sky would be blue and serene again, as if nothing happened.

Del turned to her, half-smiling.

"What?" Alvina asked.

"Nothing. Just you being here."

She dried her hands on the towel, smiling too at the randomness of fate. I mean, you had to laugh. She was standing in Del Musgrave's kitchen washing dishes because she took a wrong turn one day. Given a couple of weeks and Alvina Moon would have moved away from Stollerton, never having laid eyes on Del Musgrave.

"I'm leaving town tomorrow." Suddenly, she found it hard to speak. "I won't go to the police. I think I knew from the beginning that I wasn't going to. I won't say anything, I promise."

"I know you won't." He took the towel from her

hands. "Do you hate me so much that you won't stop thinking about me when you're gone?"

"No."

"Then you only hate me a little. But you don't love me either. That's good."

He didn't object to her hate but her love wasn't wanted, not even as an idea that couldn't touch him. Her eyes burned a little. "No one talks to me like you do. I don't understand what you mean half the time."

"People don't say anything worth listening to half the time."

If she wasn't so desperate it probably wouldn't have mattered what he felt about her. But she was a girl who needed to be loved and she knew she was and Del Musgrave wanted no part of that. The position they were in was not a criticism of him or of her, but for the first time in her life Alvina realized indifference wasn't good enough.

Del moved toward her.

"I have to leave now," she said quickly to stop him from touching her.

He hesitated. "Is that what you want?"

"I want something I can't have." Mortified, Alvina realized her eyes were filling with tears. "Oh God, here I go again. Oh shit. I'm sorry." Her throat closed. Her body shook with sobs. "This is ridiculous."

Del went to the bathroom. He returned carrying a wet hand towel.

"It's the shock. Somebody should've taken you to a doctor. Here, this'll help." He settled the cold terry over her face. "Feels good, doesn't it. It's okay. You're okay. No need to cry. Everything's all right now."

Alvina nodded—mute, not believing him, but trying

to be cooperative. The towel was clammy and scented with fabric softener. The chilled damp soothed the hot salt from her eyes. She felt hollow as though crying had washed her away, like the rain disappears the sun. She must have said the words out loud because Del said:

"The sun hasn't gone for good, Alvina. It's still there."

"For God's sake, don't be nice to me. It'll give me ideas."

"Come here." He caught her by the hand. "I'm going to show you something. I want you to understand something." Del flung open the cabin door and dragged her out, shoeless, into the teeth of the storm.

He hauled her across the meadow to the edge of the forest. Brittle leaf litter and spruce needles crackled under Alvina's bare feet. The rain, though heavy and hard, had not penetrated the dry earth. Droplets bounced and rolled off the dead leaves, turning them slick and shiny. Del pulled her to the stack of logs in the far corner of the meadow.

"You see this?" His voice rose to a holler. Milkweed and thistle choked out the site where his studio would be. "Logs rotting into the earth, bleeding out just like my fucking life." Rain rolled down his face. "I have to paint. I don't want anything else. You'll say that's great, you want that too, until it bores you and you want something else. And then you'll want me to feel like you do. To care about the same shit you care about and I won't. I never will. You'll demand something of me that I can't give and  don't care about giving, but I'll waste energy trying to. I need *space*. Do you understand? And no matter how hard I fight to get space, life crowds in. My work is small and it'll stay small if I let this thing with you go any further."

Rain dripped in her eyes, half-blinding her. "You don't have to explain. You don't owe me anything. It's okay. I understand." Alvina drew away from him. "I'll go now. It helped me to see you and talk to you—it really did. And to talk about Dave. I know that makes no sense but it helped. You were a friend. I won't go to the police. I feel better now—so thanks. I mean it."

"I'm glad I could help."

"You did. You have. And thank you for the sandwich and the beer."

"You're very polite."

"Are you laughing at me?"

"A little."

He touched her mouth with long square fingers that were shaking. But then so were hers. She could hear her teeth chattering as if in a tunnel.

Del drew her out from under the cover of the trees to the meadow where the rain fell hard and drenched them both. "You're soaking wet. I think you'd better stay."

He kissed her eyes and her hair and then her mouth.


IT WAS easy after that. He took her by the hand and led her to the cabin, lifted her up, his arms locked below her buttocks. Alvina wrapped her legs around his middle and allowed him to carry her inside.

Del undressed her as soon as they were over the threshold, the door standing open to let in the rain. Her body was under his hands. He closed his eyes trying to paint her in his mind, the silk of her skin, the fluted bones of her shoulders and the long curve of her back. A skinny girl, but strong. Contradictions and no straight lines.

Her fingers traced the scars on his back. Del yielded wordlessly to the moment when everything became clear. Clear as the thin, clean air on a winter morning and bitter too because there was always a cost to a new beginning. Certain pieces of him, certain shields, would have to be severed. Alvina was not Teresa and as long as he reminded his other self of that fact, it was possible they could be happy. It was possible something could change.

IT WAS very dark. Pitch black in the cabin. Alvina lay still, listening to the wind moving over the walls and the sound of Del Musgrave's breathing. The storm had blown out, bringing humidity and no break in the temperature. Their skin stuck together. She waited for him to roll away but he didn't. His hand was fixed to her hip. Her eyes watered like she'd been snared in a light too bright. Behind her was black nothingness. Life had crowded in, just as Del Musgrave said it would.

# SEVENTEEN

MARLEE BREMER'S living room was impressive, tastefully decorated but not luxuriously.

"She won't break," remarked Constable Fournier, glancing around her. "She'll stick to her story."

They were waiting for their hostess to reappear. Marlee had gone to fetch Violet at Rompré's request and like most twelve-year-old kids Violet was taking her time in responding. Mrs. Bremer had been surprised to see them but she answered their questions, careful not to add anything to what they already knew. Dave Gomer had been a good friend to her and she was sorry to lose him. No, she didn't know anyone who would want to kill him.

Fournier observed mother and daughter from the living room window. Marlee followed Violet through the garden to the house. She stooped to pull a weed from the peony bed. The boys, Harry and Stanley were building a fort in the lower garden. "She was six months pregnant at the time. I'm trying to imagine her swinging a flashlight with a baby belly." Fournier turned to the DS. "The impossibility of proving any of this—that's what worries me. Trey Bremer's testimony is suspect. Prison could be getting to him and he's looking for a way out."

"When we know what we have to prove, we will find

the proof."

Their hostess stepped through the French doors, smiling and smoothing her hair off her face. "Whew! It is hot out there. It's just as well she came in now anyway. Violet, you remember Detective Sergeant Rompré and his assistant." She settled herself in a compact striped armchair and picked up her cup of coffee. "Where were we?"

"Violet, my name is Constable Martine Fournier. I'll be taking notes during the interview. Please answer every question as fully as possible and truthfully."

"My," said Marlee with a flashing smile, "we are very serious all of a sudden."

Detective Sergeant Rompré looked at Violet and nodded at her to sit. He linked his fingers together. He had a musician's hands, long fingers and strong. Violet heard a rumour that he played the cello although she couldn't imagine why a person would play the cello outside of an orchestra.

"We spoke with your father a few days ago. He informed us of an occasion you were at the trailer with your brother, Harry. You were quite little at the time. Do you know which trailer I am referring to?"

"Yes," said Violet. "It has a silver palm tree. Mr. Gomer drove us there in the car with Teresa. We were having a picnic and going swimming. Teresa brought strawberries. It was the day we went to the library."

The skin around her mother's eyes was pulled tight at the corners.

"Mrs. Bremer, were you aware of this visit?"

"Absolutely not. I'm not sure of the day in question but I do remember dropping the children and Teresa off at the library to return their books. They were to arrive for story time at the library, then visit the park and have lunch. I picked them up at three o'clock in the afternoon. We had this arrangement at least once a week to allow me to catch up on housework. I don't know why Dave Gomer would have taken them to the river. He certainly didn't have my permission to do that. Children have to be watched around water every minute."

"He watched. He didn't take his eyes off us when we were in the water." Violet said this in an accusatory tone she knew her mother would hate. Not on purpose. The words just came out that way. "He kept an eye on us while Daddy showed Teresa around the trailer."

Her mother's face went white.

The room stilled.

"What else do you remember about the visit?" Detective Rompé said.

Violet examined each of their faces warily. This could get her into trouble but she had no choice. "Before my dad got there, I was playing in the trailer on my own."

"Yes?"

Violet's heart was beating very fast. "I can say for a fact there was no flashlight in the trailer."

"This was a very long time ago. How can you be certain? You were a little girl."

"I remember perfectly." Violet avoided looking at her mother. "I can tell you something else too. I was in my father's car many times. I looked in all of the compartments. I knew all the stuff in our house and cars, and in my cubby at school and my desk. I'm like my mother that way; I keep track of things. I don't like it when my things go missing. Harry is usually the cause when they do. My dad had a flashlight in his car. I remember it because it was a big orange and black flashlight with a big square lamp that shot a beam of light for miles. It didn't look anything like the flashlight they said he used to kill Teresa."

Detective Sergeant Rompré gave Violet a very solemn stare. A delicious shiver went through her.

Her mother pushed her body forward. "Violet, please."

"How do you know what the flashlight looked like?" Constable Fournier tilted her head and met Violet's eyes, encouraging her it seemed to Violet to tell them everything.

"I saw a photograph." She glanced quickly at her mother. "I wasn't snooping. You were talking to Monsieur Nault in his office and I was keeping an eye on Harry and Stanley in the waiting room. Daddy's file was on the legal secretary's desk. The photographs were sitting right there out in the open. I didn't look at any of the other pictures, just the flashlight."

"Thank you, Violet," Constable Fournier said. "If you will excuse us, we have a few questions for your mother now. You've been very helpful."

Violet Bremer rose to her feet and tugged the towel tighter around her chest. She looked from one adult to the other. Worry balled in her stomach. She thought they had gone to see her father because they'd found out there was no flashlight in the trailer and only Violet could confirm it. But it felt like something else had happened instead, and she'd made it happen.

Marlee Bremer abruptly left her seat and marched to the French doors that were opened to the patio. "Harry and Stanley!" she shouted. "You're covered in dirt. I'm taking you shopping for camping supplies in an hour and I'm not taking you looking like that. You need a bath."

Harry's young voice carried through the windows to the adults in the living room. "We'll take a swim. We don't need a bath every day."

"You do in the summer!" Marlee's voice echoed shrilly across the river. She turned to Rompré and Fournier, her face pink. "They don't need a bath every day in the winter, but in the summer they do unless I want to wash sheets four times a week." She turned back to her sons, her temper completely lost. "Stanley! Harry! I will not tell you again!"

The boys came running up the path, skinny legs pumping. Stanley's face was sweaty and grimy, his eyes shooting alarm. Harry appeared unconcerned, sensing perhaps that with the police there, his mother lacked the authority to rule. The boys tumbled into the house, kicked off their shoes and filed up the stairs, eyeing Constable Martine Fournier's gear with awe.

The adults were alone in the room.

"We interviewed your husband, Madame Bremer. He claimed David Gomer knew about the affair he was conducting with Teresa Musgrave in the trailer. It was necessary to confirm the truth of this statement."

"I see." Marlee's face was frozen.

"There are some issues he raised that perhaps you can help us with. You said you left that morning with the drycleaning. His suit was with the rest of the things. Is this correct?"

"No. It was very difficult for me to have to tell the Crown investigators this, but Trey did not leave his suit in the laundry room. He said he did but it wasn't there."

"He had burned it."

"That is what the Crown contended. Yes."

"Yet in the beginning, you were convinced of your husband's innocence and you corroborated his story."

"Yes. I thought I knew everything about him."

"What happens to the business if Trey divorces you?"

A flash of alarm, quickly mastered, crossed Marlee's face. "What a question. I imagine his mother Freesia Bremer would come back and take it over. I have no legal right to the dealership; I'm CEO by proxy. Trey made the arrangement just before he was arrested. At the time, he was confident he wouldn't be convicted. But why would Trey divorce me? I've stood by him in spite of everything he's put me through. I'm the mother of his children. That still means something to some men."

Rompré made a note in the small black notebook he carried. "On the night of the murder, you slept in your son's room. Is that correct?"

"Yes. Harry had been fussy all day; he developed a fever around five o'clock. I put him to bed and then Trey called. He had dropped Teresa off and was going back to the dealership to catch up on the invoicing. I went to bed early to get as much sleep as I could before Harry woke up and needed attention. I slept in his room so I wouldn't disturb Trey."

"You did not see your husband come home? You didn't hear him arrive, or speak to him?"

"No, I did not."

"It was fortunate for your husband that his son contracted the flu, or he would have had to explain where his expensive grey suit had disappeared to between the dealership and his home. You were angry with him for missing dinner and the children's baths. You were angry because he said he would be home by seven and it was now almost ten o'clock."

"Yes, I was angry. To be perfectly honest, I slept in Harry's room because I didn't want to see him. I was angry and I didn't want to talk to him or look at him. I was hormonal and exhausted. I felt better after a good night's sleep."

"What was your husband wearing when he came home that night?"

"I believe I've already answered that question. I wasn't awake when he came home. I don't know what he was wearing."

"*C'est ça.* You go into the laundry room as usual the next morning, Saturday. Where is your husband's suit at this point?"

"I don't know."

"This is strange. Perhaps he removed it in the bedroom when he came home and left it on the floor?"

"Is that a question? Listen, if you were a woman with small children you would know that I didn't have time to search for a grown man's drycleaning. If it wasn't in the laundry room, it didn't get cleaned. I took what was there."

"It is difficult. We have a man who claims he called his friend that night. This friend is now dead. We have a suit this same man said was left in the home. A wife leaves the house in the morning with the drycleaning. No suit."

"I don't know what to tell you."

"Your husband said the same thing. But as it turns out, this was not entirely true. I have a copy of a statement he made recently to his lawyer, François

Nault. On the morning of July 13, Mr. Bremer was awakened by the sound of the front door closing. Shortly thereafter, his small son came into the bedroom. Monsieur rose from bed, looked out of the window and observed Mrs. Bremer leaving the house carrying a bundle of clothing. She set it on the back seat of Mr. Bremer's car and drove off. Bremer identified a slate blue suit, a light grey and three shirts in the bundle." Rompré set the statement aside. "You took his car because he had parked behind yours."

Marlee sat very still.

"Trey didn't witness any such thing, detective. He was still sleeping when I left. I'm sorry, but his only defense is to lie about what happened."

"He was not asleep. A man who is fast asleep does not know which car is in the driveway and which is not. We see from the layout of your house that the driveway is only visible from the master bedroom and bathroom. Your husband witnessed you drive away in his car from the bedroom window. He then went downstairs to the living room to supervise his children. He saw you put the grey suit on the back seat. Mr. Bremer did not give up this information willingly."

Marlee flushed. "Well, he should have. He should have told the investigators this when they asked him to hand over the clothes he was wearing that night. He never said a word."

"But he did. He told the truth as much as he knew the truth to be, that you had taken his suit to the drycleaners. You had a system of running the household. Ran a tight ship, was the reference your husband made. Furthermore, you *said* you had taken his suit to be cleaned. What else could *monsieur* think but that his grey suit was at the drycleaners? It wasn't until CSU found remains of a suit at the crime scene that M. Bremer realized what you had done."

"And what had I done?"

"It was not possible that you would take the suit in to be cleaned and forget that you had done so. It was not possible that you would lose the claim slip. This is not your temperament, Madame Bremer. You took your husband's suit to the fire pit at the trailer on Saturday morning and burned it."

Fournier cleared her face of all expression.

"Do you really believe I would go to such lengths to protect my husband?"

"*Mais non.* You were not protecting M. Bremer. You had to destroy his suit because there was no blood on it. You were implicating M. Bremer."

Marlee sank back in her chair, breathing heavily. "Ridiculous. Why would I want Trey to go to prison for rape and murder? If you knew how much suffering his crime has caused this family, you would know how offensive this conversation is to me."

"I do not deny you have paid a penalty for taking your revenge. You sent your husband to prison for the murder of Teresa Musgrave because you discovered he had been sleeping with Teresa Musgrave. Your five-year-old daughter was your unwitting informant."

The change in Marlee Bremer was very subtle.

"Trey raped Teresa and then he killed her, detective. My husband has been tried by a jury of his peers who examined the evidence and convicted him. I had nothing to do with that."

Rompré's voice was as calm and uninflected as before, and yet Fournier's heart pounded. Marlee

Bremer wouldn't break. She was going to slip away.

"You are lying, *madame*. You are too astute to have been fooled. Your husband told us you had started going through his cellular phone. You were suspicious. It is impossible for a woman of your faculties to be otherwise. Mr. Bremer's methods were not subtle. You might have been merely annoyed by his absences at first. But then you noticed a pattern. On the nights he drove Teresa home, he would disappear for three or four hours claiming to be at work or running errands or visiting a friend. His phone would be turned off. You could not reach him at the dealership. He always had an excuse.

"The truth is your husband was deeply in love with the girl, wasn't he? It must have been very painful to observe his attraction to her growing day by day. You could not help but see what was happening between them. Perhaps Mr. Bremer was in love with her from the beginning. Perhaps that is why he insisted on hiring her."

Marlee Bremer raised her hand. "Stop it! Stop. That's enough. You've said enough." She eyed them both. Her mouth trembled. "Trey wasn't in love with her. That wasn't love."

Fournier risked a glance at Rompré.

Marlee's face glowed pink. "They think we don't see. We see everything."

Silence ticked through the house.

"The trouble with jealousy," Rompré said quietly, "is there is no way to rationalize it away. There is no freedom once it takes hold. It consumes the mind. We don't choose jealousy; it chooses us. How did you learn of your husband's affair?"

"From my five-year-old daughter, as you have guessed," she said stiffly. "Violet told me Teresa had taken them to the place with the silver palm tree. I was alarmed. Where had Teresa taken my children? Violet became frustrated the way children do when they're trying to be understood and shouted 'Oasis! It's called Oasis!' And it all came together—or I should say it fell apart. It was a coming together and a falling apart at the same time."

Marlee blinked and looked away. "Up until then I only suspected Trey of being unfaithful. He was very careful with his phone and credit cards. I didn't know who the other woman was until Violet said Daddy was at the trailer with Teresa. And then, of course, it was obvious. When I asked him about it, he claimed Teresa was leaving Del and he was showing her the trailer. He was lying. I knew he was lying. If it happened today, I might not have gone off the deep end. I was still in love with him back then."

"How long was this before Teresa's murder?"

"The week before."

Marlee straightened her shoulders and picked up her cup of coffee. "Living with a philanderer is a little like having a revolver pressed to one's head as he whispers 'trust me.' Trust him to pull the trigger. Dave Gomer probably knew more about my husband's sex life than I ever would."

"Why didn't you leave him?" asked Fournier, on impulse.

"It's not that easy to leave a person. You'll learn that one day."

Rompré's brown eyes had softened to liquid chocolate. "Monsieur Bremer had no alibi for the night of the murder but then neither did you. You had motive and opportunity to kill Teresa and then you implicated your husband by burning his suit."

"No! It wasn't me. You can't possibly know what I went through that night. Trey had left hours before, supposedly driving Teresa home. He wouldn't answer his cell phone and with two small children I might as well have been chained in the attic for all the freedom I had. I didn't go to the trailer until the next morning. What would you have done in my place? I had to see it for myself. When I got there, Teresa was inside. She was already dead."

ALVINA KEPT her head down, watching her black Converse sneakers as she walked toward the office. The sidewalk was rounded up, cracked and worn away in places just like the sidewalks in the small Ontario towns her parents had lived in. The towns were different but the sidewalks were the same. It was a green-gold afternoon. The sun was hot but the air was cooling. The sky had deepened to sapphire as the earth tilted toward autumn. The river was the colour of asphalt, grey speckled black.

She wouldn't have access to the van much longer. It would be put up for sale soon, she thought as she climbed in. Alvina turned the ignition and drove through the village and then up the highway toward Martingale. For all of her determination, she almost missed the turn-off to the river. The trailer was still there. Marlee had not made good yet on her threat to have it towed away. A squat pink canned ham. She turned into the parking spot and shut off the van.

The river pulled along across the road, shiny and

black as a snake.

She reached for her camera. Violet will have gone to the police by now or at least to her mother and told her everything. Del will be brought in for questioning. They'll find him at the Camp if they go there first.

She thought back to this morning that had arrived grey and cool outside Del's cabin window. From the bed, Alvina had watched him move about, silently getting ready for work so as not to disturb her. A dry light wind had risen with the dawn and driven off the humidity. The front door was open, screened by a door he'd salvaged from the dump off the highway. Cool air drifted in. He'd kissed her and asked her if she was coming back later.

"If I say yes, will you regret it?"

Del had laughed but Alvina could tell he was already regretting it. Through the long night, she'd watched the fireflies and listened to the night birds, and by morning she understood that she and Del couldn't be together. Dave's murder was between them, and Teresa's, and Del's abusive father. The three of them were intertwined and off-limits. He could never be honest with her about that part of his life. She'd never really know him, know his dark side. It would be like making a pet of a python.

*He tried to warn you.*

Alvina opened the trailer door. Photograph everything, she thought; the bed, the blood stain, the dinette table, and outside, the palm tree and the name Oasis. She reasoned that she didn't have a choice; she needed a job. But as she swung her camera over the crime scene, Alvina was surprised and oddly proud that she'd found this self buried in her core. It was like discovering a beast caged up in her basement. A hurt, wounded beast, without a conscience.

*I didn't think you had it in you, Moon.*

She didn't either.

Alvina put the camera in the van. The article would take a couple of days to write but when the news broke about his arrest, she'd have it ready to sell. She opened her satchel and pulled out the charcoal sketch of Teresa. It was beautiful, signed by the artist. A nude sketch too, which escalated its value as Teresa was the victim of sexual assault. Brutally murdered and now her husband was about to be arrested for killing the man he held responsible. She stole it after Del left for work. She'd become another person, a person who'd go through celebrity garbage for dirt. It was a shitty thing to do. She was ashamed of herself. Maybe the article would help him when it came time for sentencing. Maybe the judge would be lenient. Someone was going to write his story —why not her? She'd write it with more compassion than anyone else would. He might even thank her one day.

Sure, he would, during one of their cosy chats behind a glass partition. If she did this to him, sold his story, he'd never want to see her again. So this really was the end. No second chances.

Alvina carried the sketch to the river's edge. Her teeth chattered, rattling hollowly in her skull but the sun burned. The wind fluttered the sketch, as if reminding her of her purpose.

*It's either him or you.*

With a scream of rage, she tore it down the centre and then again and again until it was in tiny squares. She balled them in her fist. Her heart pounded. She couldn't go back and there was no way forward. They will have arrested him by now.

Funny that she should see Del as the wronged one. He murdered her boss, a man who took an actual interest in Alvina's life. A guy told her once that she'd only fallen in love with him because he couldn't be caught. She was flattered he imagined her to be so independent she could only love a man who was unavailable. It wasn't true but it was a nice thought at the time.

*Now you have nothing.*

She opened her hand. The bits of torn sketch paper were caught by the wind, lifted up, and flung swirling over the river like confetti. She watched them as they drifted down, scattered white specks on the river's dark surface. Alvina sat down on the swimming rock, removed her sneakers and waded into the river. The current grabbed her ankles, pulling her off balance. Her arms flailed out.

A raven perched on a white pine, peered at her.

Across the river, as if in a dream, she saw Del standing on the opposite bank. His back was ramrod straight and his shoulders were pulled back like a soldier's. He couldn't see her—in fact he wasn't even looking her way. He was damp and glistening in the sun, wearing clothing she didn't recognize, the way it is in a dream when the one you love appears to you in a different body. Alvina had fallen in love with that stance when she first met him. In love with his long arms, the curving grace of his fingers, like a ballet master's. She had fallen painfully in love with all the parts of him he didn't seem to be aware of: the droop of his eyelid, the fullness of his mouth.

Her calves were numb with cold. She was such a

coward. When she had set out to write the story, she had the balls to face everyone's contempt. Not so much now. Dagmar would find out she slept with Del when she should've gone to the police. Missy would too. They all would. Falling in love with a known killer, shielding him, sleeping with him—it was a pathetic identity that would dog her forever online. She knew how these things worked. She was in the media.

Alvina submerged herself in the water. She was grateful for the cold, glad that her heart had better things to do than crack inside her chest. It was mercifully too cold even to cry. The frigid river seeped into her body's core like an anaesthetic, shutting down all sensation. Ice baths in insane asylums made complete sense. She stopped fighting and let the current tug her from shore. The rapids would probably finish her off if she got that far. They were rougher than they looked from the road, plenty of boulders and gullies to catch one's foot, to pin her under the rush of water and suffocate her. She didn't know how much longer she'd remain conscious.

Each moment was tiny and slow, not at all how she imagined the end would be.

In the light and the dark and the sensation of falling she saw Del slipping away through the forest, through the mist that rose off the dew when the morning sun hit it. He won't survive prison, she heard herself think. It'll be a death sentence. Separated from his art, friendless and alone, even Gerry Dunn will abandon him. He'll have no one, no one.

Alvina's body shot to the surface. Her hand flung out blindly grabbing hold of an aspen growing out from the bank. She clung to it, struggling against the river's force.

Gushing water seared her nose and throat. She gagged and coughed, and then there came the horrible intake of breath.

Hand over hand, clutching at shrubs along the bank it took some effort to resist the river's pull. Then the current eddied, slowing her trajectory. The edge of the riverbank had filed down into a beachhead of sorts, fine dirt, silt that had compacted into a hard black verge. She caught hold of a thicket that was blistering with tiny barbs. Pain shot through her hand but she pulled herself out of the river and up the embankment.

Alvina lay flat on her back, gasping for breath. She wiped her eyes with the back of her hand, the one burning with tiny thorns. Black dirt stuck to her clothes, branches and thorns had scratched her arms and legs. But she was still alive. When she'd slipped under the water, the decision had felt permanent. It had been a relief to have it over with. And now this.

The raven laughed and wheeled over her head in a slow winding arc.

In that moment, the sun flared over the horizon catching a white pine tree in its rays. August sunshine gilded the branches of blue green needles and mottled grey trunk, transforming it to gold. A golden tree set against a sapphire sky. As she watched, a flash of her future entered her mind, a gift of foresight that she wouldn't recognize until much later; a future in which she belonged to a life greater than the one she could imagine for herself. The vision danced and shimmered like the heat off the highway, seen, but not realized.

Alvina pulled herself up and hiked back to the trailer in her bare feet. She grabbed her sneakers from the swimming rock, climbed into the van and turned the ignition. The Oasis, the pines and the old broken highway disappeared in her rear view mirror as she drove away. Not fully understanding what she was going to do or why, Alvina turned in the direction of Del's cabin.

A decision had been reached that she could only obey. It would take her out of Stollerton and away from the river forever.

# EIGHTEEN

"PLEASE SPEAK clearly for the microphone, Mrs. Bremer."

Marlee blinked at Fournier and then Rompré. It was like coming out of a terrible fog. "Yes, of course. What do you want to know?"

"The morning you discovered Teresa Musgrave dead inside the trailer, describe what happened from the beginning please."

They had adjourned to the kitchen where the police could spread out and set up their recording machine. Marlee lifted her gaze to the river beyond the beautiful walls of her house, steadying herself. She hadn't thought about the day she found Teresa in seven years. It had been easy to turn it out of her mind.

"I showered and dressed, gathered the drycleaning and grocery bags from the laundry room. Harry was playing in Violet's room with their toys. I didn't want to disturb them so I left them with Trey who was upstairs sleeping. He had blocked me in but that wasn't the reason I took his car instead of my own. My car had the child seats in it and if there were an emergency Trey would have to take the kids. It was only sensible to leave him my car. I didn't plan any of this, you see. It just unfolded. I wasn't thinking clearly enough to plan. When I put the drycleaning in his car ... pregnant

277

women have a heightened sense of smell. I could smell lavender on his suit. Teresa always used a lavender soap. *Always.* That confirmed it for me. I drove to the trailer. It took me a few tries but eventually I found the entrance to the campsite."

"*Oui, madame.*"

"Well, I went inside. Teresa was on the bed. She was ... she had been murdered."

Marlee remembered experiencing awe that such a powerful creature could be disposed of so rapidly. The laughing confidence Teresa had had from the moment she stepped over the threshold—it was like inviting a vampire into the house. People think a man sleeping with his children's babysitter is no different from any other affair. It is a very different betrayal. Marlee's children had hugged Teresa, trusted her, sat on her lap while she read stories to them—even as she was killing their mother and destroying their lives.

"Were you frightened?"

"No. To be honest, I didn't give much thought to how she came to be killed. She was gone and I was glad that she was gone. I didn't care how." She lifted her eyes to Rompré and smiled. "And I thought at least Trey couldn't lie to me anymore. The police would find his semen and his DNA would be identified. He couldn't deny screwing her when there was *forensic* evidence to the contrary. I can't tell you how happy that made me after being told so often that *I* was the one with the problem." She laughed.

Teresa dead presented an opportunity. An idea crept into Marlee's thoughts the way these things can, shocking her like a private lust. As the minutes in the trailer ticked past, she began to think it wouldn't be hard to do, certainly not as hard as living with his lies had been. The answers fell into place as if they had existed all along. Marlee discovered she could be quite analytical under pressure. Trey was the last person to see Teresa alive. His fingerprints, semen and clothing fibers would be found in the trailer. The fact that she'd taken Trey's car was a lucky break. The flashlight was a problem. She wiped the handle and set it on the table. Trey's suit was still in the car. That was a problem because the suit had no blood spatter and there was no solution to getting blood on the suit that didn't revolt her.

"I decided to burn it."

Constable Fournier glanced up. Marlee Bremer met her gaze.

"There was a tin of campfire fuel in the storage compartment of the Blazer. I poured it on the suit, and then set it on fire in the stone fire pit. I didn't think I had it in me until I struck the match."

Marlee had warmed her hands at the fire, the orange heat flaring over her face and reflecting in her green eyes. She was far away by then, in another country, miles and miles from where she had started out when she fell in love with Trey. She had crossed a personal Rubicon. All she wanted now was to see him destroyed.

"I wiped down the trailer's door handle, the sides of the door, and anywhere else that I had touched. Then I got in the car and drove home. Please don't think this was *sang-froid* on my part. Believe me, I often wish I'd done as Judy Finney did and just turned a blind eye. I know I'm an accessory after the fact or whatever the charge is called. You can think what you like of what I did. The choice Trey left me with was no choice at all."

Rompré sat back in his chair, one leg crossed over the other. "You went to a great deal of trouble to protect Teresa Musgrave's real killer."

"I have done nothing except burn a suit."

"You have lied under oath and obstructed justice. You aided and abetted in a capital crime. You deliberately and maliciously ensured an innocent man went to prison."

"Innocent?" Marlee's eyes widened. "Trey wasn't innocent. Trey was the cause of the whole tragedy. He dropped his affair at my feet and expected me to live with it. If he didn't go to prison, Detective Rompré, I would've had to find a way to rise above the humiliation and keep the marriage going. I certainly couldn't afford to divorce him. I had three small children—where would we live? Not here. I couldn't afford to buy him out of this house on a dental hygienist's salary. Do you think Trey would take time off work to care for his children when they were sick—or when there was a Professional Development day at school—or when the weather kept the school buses from running? It would fall to *me*. Through I had done *nothing* wrong, I would be single-handedly caring for three children while trying to earn a living. Trey would enjoy all the benefits of fatherhood without having *earned* those benefits. Consider that before you judge me, Detective."

It was quiet. Not a car to be heard. Not even a bird.

"I have one final question, *madame*." Rompré leaned forward, his elbows resting on his knees and his hands clasped. "Whose flashlight was it?"

Marlee shook her head. "To be blunt—this entire discussion is irrelevant. Not one bit of what I've said into that recording device of yours changes anything for Trey. He could have been naked when he killed Teresa. She certainly was. He could have washed the blood off in the river, dressed and come home." She looked hard at Rompré. "But it's clear I'm not telling you anything you haven't already thought of."

"Yes, if it were not for an anonymous note written in green ink. 'Where did he get the flashlight?'" Rompré quoted softly.

"Ask Trey's lawyers. I'll bet they're the ones behind the poison pen," Marlee hissed. Letting her rage show when she'd been managing so well to keep it contained. "They would resort to any number of tricks to keep this case alive. The Bremer family has deep pockets."

"It is fortunate then that you have discharged them from the case." Rompré's eyes revealed nothing. "But your husband's release is not in your best interest is it?"

"Trey went to her funeral," she said flatly. "He said he had to go out of respect. I couldn't go, of course. Someone had to stay home with the children. He left the house without even saying goodbye. His mind was on her, on being with her even if it was in a group of mourners. Looking at her photo, talking about her, *crying*, oh, what a relief it must have been for him to grieve his lover openly!"

The flesh of her face was warm. The only sound in the room was the ticking of the wall clock. Marlee pushed away from the table. She couldn't breathe.

"My husband had sex with a nineteen-year-old. I'm not a fool. If he did it once, he would do it again. To this day, he's never told me the truth. He's keeping his options open, you see, just in case he ever gets out of prison. To answer your question, I married a liar and a cheat. To use Violet's religious terminology, Trey has not repented. So no, his release is not in my best interest."

The day was dragging into late afternoon. Harry and Stanley were upstairs, bathed and hiding out in their room playing with Lego. Violet was wandering the garden like a wraith, staring anxiously at the house. Marlee made a pot of Earl Grey tea and poured Constable Martine Fournier a glass of Pepsi. She set out a platter of cheese and crackers with slices of cucumber and summer tomatoes, alternating rows of green and red. The constable said it wasn't necessary but Marlee seemed to understand that it was. Fournier made a show of flipping through her notes earlier but they had nothing. They had her admission of destroying evidence but that was all. Rompré, however, appeared in no mood to leave. Setting out the food quieted Marlee's nerves and restored her to herself. She smoothed her hair and resumed her seat.

"Help yourself, Constable Fournier. The tomatoes are fresh from the market in the village. A little sea salt and pepper and they are delicious."

"Motherhood still meant something to some men." Rompré tapped his pencil on his black notebook and frowned. *"Les responsabilités incombant à une mère de famille.* M. Gomer took your responsibilities as a mother seriously. He was concerned about your daughter Violet."

There was a flicker inside her being, revealed in the fluster with which she handled her napkin. Marlee held her breath without appearing to be doing anything of the sort. "Who told you that?"

"Alvina Moon perceived a change in his mood when you announced that your daughter had turned to religion. In anyone else the change would not have been remarkable but Dave Gomer was a larger-than-life personality. He appeared to be affected by the news."

"Oh yes." Marlee nodded. "You see it was Dave who persuaded me to hire Teresa in the first place. I suppose he felt responsible for Violet's emotional challenges."

Rompré leaned back against the dining chair. "Until the day he died you could say."

"I'm not sure I understand you."

"You are a very clever woman, Mrs. Bremer. Yet it did not cross your mind that Dave Gomer could have murdered Teresa Musgrave?"

Marlee laughed. "No, it most certainly did not. What a world you must live in! I told you. I didn't give her murderer a second thought. I'm sorry but that is the truth. Selfish, low, base—but the truth. Besides, Dave Gomer was a godsend. Was I going to question the man who was standing up for me in this community? Absolutely not."

"You would not, but your daughter Violet would. The sins of Dave Gomer were a blessing she would question very deeply, especially if one of them had resulted in the imprisonment of her father. The recent visit to the trailer rekindled a dormant memory. Violet was suddenly aware her father was not in possession of the flashlight that killed Teresa. But Dave Gomer could have been. He was involved. Violet is the author of the anonymous note."

Marlee's hand jumped, knocking her tea cup to the floor. A delicate porcelain cup painted with pale pink roses and sage green leaves and stems. Marlee scooped it up and examined it. The handle was broken off. Her favourite tea cup. Ruined. She carried it to the kitchen sink and half-flung it, harder than she meant to. It connected with the granite edge of the counter and exploded into a thousand tiny shards.

"Is everything all right, Mrs. Bremer?" Constable Fournier was speaking in the distance. "Do you need help?"

*No. Yes. Please leave now.*

Marlee reached under the sink for the dustpan and whisk broom. "I'll manage, thank you." She forced her hands to move slowly to sweep up the glass. "Violet remembered going to the trailer when she was five. She told you so herself. I don't see how that makes her a writer of poison pen messages she knows would only hurt me. Furthermore, there was no opportunity for her to do such a thing. I drive my daughter everywhere and I did not pay a visit to the *Record*." She banged the dustpan against the garbage can to empty it.

"We will ask her how she managed to deliver the message, but in the summer months children roam the village unnoticed. The raft provided distraction and an influx of young people. Violet could have slipped to the office, delivered her note and rejoined the other children unnoticed."

"Well, she didn't. I don't allow Violet to *roam* about in the summer or at any other time. Twelve-year-olds are susceptible to peer pressure. Supervision is crucial at this age."

"But not at Harry or Stanley's age, perhaps. Your sons have more freedom. Violet could have enlisted her brothers to deliver the note." Rompré rested his elbows on the polished surface of the table and linked his hands together. "After Dave Gomer's body was discovered, Violet provided us with a handwritten statement. We were able to match that sample to the anonymous note. She has a green pen in her room and the paper itself is also a match."

Marlee swivelled to face Rompré. "All right, you win. She wrote the note. I didn't know she had. She must have been very confused and angry not to have talked to me first. It's a difficult age."

"She has powerful feelings, your daughter. A difficult age for an average child, torment for a child of intelligence and sensitivity. Violet is tall for her age and athletic. She has the strong-will, the temperament, the religious fire to combat evil. She sent the note to alert Dave Gomer that he had not gotten away with murder. He had taken her father's place for seven years but he would no more. Where did he get the flashlight? Violet knew the flashlight was Dave's."

Marlee didn't have to summon courage, it appeared as cold rage. She approached the table where Rompré sat sphinx-like and set her face for battle. "I don't like the direction this conversation is going. Violet is a little girl who played a mean prank on some grown-ups. That is all. Or do I need to call my lawyer to make that clear to you."

"Seeking legal counsel would be a wise course of action, *madame*. In a moment, I am going to ask Constable Fournier to call your daughter into the room. I am arresting Violet Bremer for the murder of David Gomer."

Marlee made a half-choking sound and willed herself not to cough. She sank to the chair. Her eyes swerved over their faces. "This is madness. Violet didn't murder Dave. She—she was sitting on the dock under my yellow umbrella. I saw her there. Dave waved at her.

She told you."

"All you could see at the end of the dock from your office window was a large yellow umbrella. You assumed your daughter was there. She knew Dave would be fishing as he did every morning. When he motored into view, she waved him over. Dave was naturally responsive. He was concerned about the girl. Perhaps he saw this meeting as an opportunity to make amends for the harm he had done when he was drinking. Violet though was in no mood to forgive. Dave Gomer knew her father was not a rapist. Why did he not say so in court? He knew her father did not have a flashlight with him in the trailer. His silence was the same as lying. Perhaps Dave confessed more to her than he should have. Or perhaps he refused to help Trey. Regardless, Violet waved him over and got into the boat that morning with one intention. She lifted the mallet and swung, killing Monsieur Gomer instantly."

Marlee kept her eyes fixed on Rompré's face. "He had a bottle of vodka you said. He was drinking."

"Monsieur Gomer did not drink vodka. He drank scotch. You daughter did not know this. She stole the first bottle that came to hand. If you check your liquor cabinet will find there is a bottle of vodka missing."

"She's a child ... she's just a little girl!"

Rompré sat back, his expression solemn. "She is a child but a clever one. The young lady thought it out very carefully. Violet removed Dave's coat and hat, slipped them on and then dumped his body into the river. She motored downriver to her dock but was wise enough to continue around the bend to where the shore is wilder and she could remove the coat and hat unseen and wipe off her prints. The boat was set adrift.

Violet hiked through the bush to the dock where she resumed her place under the umbrella. The vodka bottle indicates the murder was premeditated. That is a first degree sentence. Your daughter will be in her forties before she is released."

Marlee threw back her head and screamed.

Fournier leapt up, reaching for her gun. And then her hands dangled at her sides like a fool when she saw Marlee Bremer twisted in a paroxysm of grief. The constable stepped quickly to the sink and ran cold water over a tea towel. The cold compress was held to Marlee's neck and face. Strangely, it did help.

"The worst of it is over, *madame*," said Rompré. He refilled his cup with tea and selected a cracker topped with cheese. A good cheese from a region in Québec famous for its cheeses.

Marlee met his brown eyes. Years later, she would remember this moment as the one in which they both came to the same realization at the same time. But of course this wasn't the case. Rompré had known all along what she would do. She was only discovering it now.

THE FLAT hard light of afternoon showed a shrivelled meadow and faded trees parched by the dry, hot summer.

Alvina slung her satchel over her shoulder and approached the cabin with more caution than she'd ever had in the past. Her feet crackled over the grass. The screen door squealed open.

Del was not inside. The bed was neatly made. The dishes washed and set on the shelf. His paintings were stowed above the bed as usual. She looked harder. Del's paints and brushes were missing. She searched the cabin for a note. There was none.

They couldn't have arrested him yet. They would have called her if they'd made an arrest. Or he would have told them to call her. Cold dread ran through her as she moved from the bathroom, to the bed, to the tiny kitchen and back again. His clothes and toothbrush were still there. The art books were piled on the stool. With shaking hands, Alvina pawed through his meager belongings. Maybe Del decided to run. He came home from work just long enough to pack up his paints and brushes and left without a word.

She lurched outside, her tongue and throat swallowing dust. He was gone. There was no point in crying. She was only going to tell him to run away. He didn't wait to be told. Good for him.

A noise floated across the meadow. Alvina looked up. It was Del coming out the forest carrying the birch bark canoe over his head. His tee-shirt dangled from the waistband of his shorts. His muscles bunched and his skin gleamed. Alvina's breath caught.

"You're here."

He dropped the canoe beside the burn barrel and came toward her. "I just got home. What the hell happened to you? You look like you've been dragged through a hedge backwards."

"I fell in the river." There was a wad of dirt clotted in her hair.

His face darkened. "You fell in the river? What's wrong, Alvina."

"You have to leave. You have to get out of here. Violet's probably gone to the police by now. That's all I came to tell you. I don't want you to go to prison but I can't forgive you. Dave made mistakes but he was doing his best to make up for them. Alcoholism is a disease. He needed your compassion, not your hate. He wasn't a bad guy."

"I'm sure he wasn't. Alvina—I didn't kill Dave."

Her face flared and her body shook. "You did! You did! Don't lie to me! Lie to everyone else if you have to but don't lie to me. I can't take it. Sleeping with you last night was a mistake. It's making this really hard to do ... making you leave is hard enough, don't make it harder by lying to me!"

"How did you fall in the river?"

"I fell. I don't remember how." Her sinuses were still sore from inhaling water. "I'm not a very good swimmer. I didn't think the current was strong."

He lifted one of her arms and rolled it over, seeing the bruises. "You weren't going for a swim; you're in your street clothes. Alvina, I'm taking you to a doctor. You're hurt pretty bad."

"No!" She gasped a little, trying to pull away from him. "It was a stupid mistake, that's all."

"It looks like you were trying to grab on to something, to push yourself up. That's instinctual in someone who's drowning. You probably didn't even know you were doing it."

Her head felt like a vague appendage. A person in her mental state probably ought to be under a doctor's care, she thought, but she was too depressed to take what happened in the river seriously. "I must have got those during the swim."

"You weren't swimming, you were sinking." Del pushed her hair off her face. "Why did you do it?"

"Look, stop. It wasn't that. It wasn't serious." She

was shaking and exhausted and felt a crying jag coming on.

"I'll believe whatever you want me to believe. I'll believe you lost your footing and the current was too strong for you if that's what you want me to think. But you can't do this again. If I take you to the hospital, they'll put you on a suicide watch but at least I know you'll be safe. What's it going to be?"

Her body shook with chattering teeth, nearing hysteria. "Don't you get it? You killed Dave. I can't turn you in and I can't get on with my life because now I have no life. I never did, but now it feels worse, a million times worse because of last night. Look, I don't want to talk about it anymore. Just pack your bags and get out of here before the police come."

He pushed her away from him. "So that's the only reason you're here now? You didn't go through with it because you had to come back to *warn* me. You were going to let me hear about your drowning on the six-o'clock news? I don't fucking believe this—Alvina, I did not kill Dave!"

"Violet saw you!"

"I don't know who Violet saw. It wasn't me! Why would I kill Dave? I hardly knew the guy."

"Don't," she implored, "don't make me be the one to say it. Dave helped Trey seduce your wife. Dave knew they met in the trailer. He knew all about it. He probably gave Trey the flashlight that killed Teresa. Don't tell me you didn't know Dave was involved! You hated the *Record*! You pretended you didn't know what the Oasis was. I'm sick of people faking it with me. You read the newspaper articles he wrote about the trial and you held him responsible for Teresa's murder, for hurting your marriage, for everything that happened."

He put his arms around her. "Shhh, shhh, take it easy. I didn't know anything about the case. I didn't read the transcripts or the newspaper articles. I've told you that already."

She resisted his embrace, crossing her arms over her middle, setting her face. "You have amnesia. That's what you said. But when you read the article about Marlee, you saw the name of the trailer—Oasis—you knew the truth then. Yes, I could see it in your face! You realized Teresa had been cheating on you—not raped—an *affair*. You confronted Dave and he told you everything. It was the wrong thing to do but that's Dave—he has to do the Steps. Make amends. Maybe you didn't mean to kill him—maybe you lost control. I wish ... I wish...."

Alvina stopped talking. It was too hard. Her nerves had collapsed out from under her.

"What do you wish?" Del watched her closely.

She sighed wetly and sagged against him. "I wish it was just you and me again. We'd eat sandwiches and drink beer and what happened in the past wouldn't be the end of the world. We'd canoe the river and camp out in your painting spot. Everything bad disappears in the wilderness."

Del hung on to her. He wanted that too. More than anything, Del wanted to have a beer and talk to Alvina until he assumed the shape she needed him to be. He took her hand and pulled her toward the stack of logs, dragging her behind him like a little caboose. "Come here, come. Summer will be over before you know it. The snow'll fly and none of this will matter anymore."

She sat down beside him. "It will. I'm sorry, but

eventually, it will. I shouldn't have fallen in the river. I won't do it again, I promise. But I can't stay with you, Del."

"It makes you that unhappy."

"Yes."

The smell of earth drying in the heat rose to his nose. There had to be more to life than mere survival, Del thought. He could survive by keeping his mouth shut and she would leave him. Like she said, that would be a hell of a lot easier to face if they hadn't slept together. But telling her.... Del could barely coax his body to stay upright at the thought of telling her.

Within him warred a pitched battle for supremacy between a heroic eight-year-old boy and an abusive adult male.

"When I was quite young," he began, "I discovered if I was going to get to school at all I'd have to get there on my own. In the beginning, my mom would buy my school supplies, pack my lunches and check my homework the night before, but after a few months of this she'd withdraw into a world of her own and I'd have to fend for myself."

He could tell she was listening. She was sitting very still, her chin resting on her fists, her elbows on her knees. Alvina's hair screened her face but she was listening to every word.

"I did my best but I was always missing my gym clothes or homework assignments or money for the school trips. In the fifth grade, my art teacher tried to talk to my parents about the problems I was having but that only led to a beating for goofing off in school. I learned to hide report cards and forge signatures. My teachers would always pass me through, sending me to the next remedial class. I never learned a thing in those classes except how to cut them. My dad noticed. He'd say 'Are you stupid? What's the matter with you? Dummy—can't you read, dummy? What's this say? *Gas-o-line.*' Because everyone can read, can't they? What are you, stupid? You can read can't you?"

She turned. Del met her eyes.

"You can't read."

"No." He looked away. He couldn't stand to see her reaction. "I didn't read the article you wrote about Marlee Bremer or the trailer; I didn't know it was called Oasis. I didn't know anything about the crime. A cop told me I should read the transcripts if I wanted information because I was asking for details and she couldn't talk about the case. She said if I wanted to talk to someone—a therapist, there was no shame in it. I wasn't ashamed. I just didn't know how to go about it. I can't do phone books, newspapers or catalogues. I'm good with numbers. My art books are mostly paintings —photographs. These logs we're sitting on for my studio. I couldn't build it after Teresa died because I needed someone to read the plans and the instructions for the cement and so forth. At the Arts and Letters Festival when Graham was pissed off about not getting my biography, I thought being a writer you'd figure it out. There are no books or magazines in the cabin."

"Your vocabulary is excellent. You're very articulate." Alvina protested weakly. "You can talk about anything."

"I listen to the radio, the CBC has programs. And I learn from listening to people at the Camp. I like learning. I can get by if the words are simple and I'm given plenty of time. Pictures help. Gerry's always bugging me to take a promotion at the Camp but I can't read all the contracts, advertising and government paper work. I had the phone disconnected after Teresa died because I couldn't read the directions for payment. Gerry handles my banking. He's never asked. Maybe he's guessed by now. I can drive but I can't get a license so I can't get a car. I quit school at fifteen. Whatever life holds that requires reading, I can't do it."

"You could have told me."

"No. I couldn't have. Don't expect me, or any guy who can't read, to spill his guts to a girl. It's humiliating. I've never told anyone I can't read. I got really good at faking it."

Alvina clutched her arms about her chest. He was a good-looking guy. A hundred times over watching him sleep last night, she had to pinch herself. He was so beautiful, so perfect. She didn't know a thing about him except that his dad beat him. She never asked how parents trapped in violence could get a little boy to school. Did she even care? "You've been as alone with me as you've ever been with anyone in your life," she said. He didn't have to answer. They both knew that it was true. The cedar logs were warm and sweet smelling. She rested her head on her knees. "So that wasn't you Violet saw in the boat."

"No, I was on my way to the Camp by then, heading in the opposite direction."

Alvina gazed at the tops of the yellowing trees and closed her eyes with relief. The wind rustled the leaves high above them. "God, I'm sorry, Del. I am so sorry."

"I would've told you last night if I'd known you were going to throw yourself in the river over it."

"That's not funny."

"It's not meant to be. I'm really pissed with you for doing that."

Her reasons for choosing death seemed flimsy now compared to the solid life all around her. "One thing went wrong and then another and another until the river seemed my only option."

"It's not."

They were quiet then, grateful for the second chance they'd been given.

"I wonder who it was," Del murmured, pressing his face to her hair. "If it wasn't me, who did Violet see in Dave's boat?"

# NINETEEN

"**T**HESE MEN and their games."

Marlee's voice was wet, resigned and clogged with mucus. God only knew how she looked. At least the children were not here to witness this. "I wasn't going to kill Dave. I was going to get him drinking again. Let him kill himself."

"Constable Fournier would you fetch Madame Bremer another cup of tea, *s'il vous plait*." Rompré filled a small plate with cheese, crackers and cucumber slices. "Eat a little. It will help."

But Marlee was filled with a strange calm. There was so much tension in concealing a crime. She had no idea how criminals managed it on a regular basis. The terror of being found out and then when one was—there was relief. "Thank you but I'm all right now. I'm ready to make my statement. Constable, if you want to begin recording?"

The constable shot the DS a look, the second one Marlee had intercepted since Rompré announced he was going to arrest Violet. The officer was obviously out of her depth.

"Whenever you are ready, *madame*."

Marlee leaned back in her chair. "Dave came to my house on Sunday night with a wild story about seeing Teresa in his office. He said he had to talk to me about

Violet immediately. An anonymous note had rattled him. Teresa was very fond of the children he said, despite the rest of it. I asked him what rest of it? I was not supposed to know anything about the affair, remember. But I was curious how much Dave knew. So I played the role of the wronged wife and asked Dave what he meant, never thinking ... never imagining...."

Marlee faltered for a moment. She knew if it ever came down to it, this would be the hardest part to recall.

"You were a valuable client," said Rompré. "He was reluctant to tell you the truth because the deal with MetMedia would fall through without your business."

"Oh no, apparently none of that mattered to him anymore. He was only concerned about Violet and her religious mania. He thought writing poison pen letters to the newspaper was a cry for help. The kid should get therapy were his exact words. I asked why my child would question the flashlight. How would she know anything about it? That man sat across from me and told me that while my children were under his drunken supervision my husband was inside the trailer with their babysitter playing a sex game. Those strawberries Violet remembered were not for a picnic. They were props." Marlee focused on Rompré's face which helped in an odd way to make her feel grounded. "I asked Dave to please explain. He said my husband had a sex fantasy of assaulting young women and Teresa was in the trailer, cooperating or enabling—whatever you want to call it. Dave described it as an addiction. Maybe he imagined that after all these years it wouldn't matter to me. I asked him if he knew Trey had this 'addiction' when he encouraged me to hire Teresa. He said he did."

"And then he went a step further and told you

Teresa had the same fantasy."

Marlee flung her head back, clutching her arms over her breasts. The light in the dining room was changing as the sun moved to the west. "Oh no, that was the best part about his confession. What Dave Gomer did to my family was far worse than that. He *coached* Teresa to tell my husband she had a rape fantasy. She would not have told Trey this of her own accord. I'm not even sure it was true but Dave encouraged her to seduce Trey with it. She was used as David's bait to land a lucrative ad contract, and in exchange, Teresa landed a rich man. It turned out Trey's wild child wanted a house, babies and a two car garage. The last laugh was on Trey with that one."

Her teeth began to chatter despite the sultry warmth of the room. The constable—what's her name— made her eat a cracker and swallow some tea.

"I'm all right if I have a plan," she said. "I'm very good in a crisis. Dave put temptation in Trey's path— justice would be served if I put temptation in Dave's path. He had no idea how furious, sick and betrayed I felt. To him, I was the wronged but forgiving wife and now I would be the wronged but forgiving friend. We parted on good terms; I believe I even thanked him for letting me know about Violet.

"Early the next morning, I went down to the dock. I had slipped a bottle of vodka into the pocket of my raincoat. My two boys were engrossed in cartoons in the family room. Violet was still upstairs asleep and likely would be until nine. My office door was closed to let my children know I was in there working and could not be disturbed. The rain was a mixed blessing. I worried it might keep Dave from fishing and this was the psychological moment to start him drinking again. Judy Finney had told me that if an alcoholic relapsed after years of sobriety, the decline was swift, undignified and painful."

"If you didn't plan to kill him," said Constable Fournier, "how did his skull come to be crushed in two places?"

"Dave remembered the smoke was on the wrong day," said Marlee, bemused that such a small detail could cause such damage. "Apparently Trey had called him the night Teresa was murdered. Dave had been drinking all day; he had no memory of the call. Instead of going to the trailer, he passed out on his dock and when he came to on Saturday morning, he smelled smoke. Dave Gomer should have been a forest firefighter. The SOPFEU was his first love. There was a burn restriction on that week; he checked the archives to confirm. Yet someone was burning on Saturday morning."

It was a clumsy and impulsive reason to kill a man. Dave Gomer could have smelled smoke from any number of places but she could see the wheels turning in his mind. Dave Gomer was a career newspaperman. He asked questions even when he wasn't working. "You see how it was. I couldn't take the chance he wouldn't talk it over with Alvina or Ray. He'd tell one of them about waking up on his dock on Saturday morning to the smell of smoke in the air. Alvina had already questioned me about the flashlight. I had to do something. Dave turned his back on me for a split second. I lifted the mallet and hit him."

That blow was easy. The second one took all of her willpower to execute. His blue eyes turned on her, full of dismay and pity. This man, this friend had exposed her children to Trey and Teresa's filthy minds and their filthy addictions. Remembering that made it easy again. "I brought the club down on Dave's skull one final time."

His pulse was checked. His hat and windbreaker were removed. This took some effort. Dave was a big man and the wet windbreaker stuck to his arms. Then his body was pushed over the side, out of the boat. She watched as it sank to the bottom of the Gatineau River.

Put on the windbreaker. Now the hat. Now start the motor.

Clean the fingerprints from all the surfaces that had been touched. There were not many. The rain would take care of the rest. Dave's windbreaker and hat were shucked off quickly and left in the bottom of the craft. The bottle of vodka had been emptied on the trip down. She confessed to taking a swallow or two before wiping it clean and dropping in Dave's tackle box. The Princecraft was abandoned, left to float where the current took it.

It happened just as Rompré had described, only it wasn't Violet in the boat. Violet was on the dock under Marlee's yellow umbrella. Seeing her daughter had frightened Marlee badly. She raised her hand, forcing herself to wave as Dave would wave, and to keep the same steady speed.

She asked Rompré. "I don't understand though. How did you know?"

"The morning of Dave's disappearance, you said you saw your daughter on the dock from your office window. Yet your daughter did not see you. We confirmed that this was possible. The only difficulty with your story, Madame Bremer, is that your nature would not permit such an event. If you had seen Violet sitting in the rain you would have called her into the house."

"That's ridiculous."

Rompré shrugged and helped himself to a second slice of delicately flavoured cheese.

DEL MUSGRAVE was six when he became aware his family wasn't the same as other families. He got his first hint of this from watching TV. On television, men raised their voices but there was a difference and he couldn't understand what it was. Then it became clear on the rare occasions he was invited to a friend's house that their fathers didn't shout. Or slam their fists into the walls. Or smash the dishes.

He was a quiet boy. He had few friends although he was friendly enough. He liked the other boys in his class. But without realizing it, Del had erected a barrier between him and them. He couldn't bring kids to his house so he unconsciously deflected their attempts at friendship. The solitariness of his boyhood was self-inflicted but he wasn't aware of this. He came to believe that there was something wrong with him. Grade school gave way to middle school and Del became increasingly solitary in his games on the playground and was overlooked in his class.

There were all kinds of programs on TV that encouraged kids to *Stand Up to a Bully. Talk it Out. Use Your Words.* Del was eight years old when he tried to stop his dad from hitting his mom. It began when he heard a crash in the kitchen. His father's dinner plate had been flung against the wall. The storm had been brewing for hours. He jumped to his feet, eyes wide and ran as fast as his thin legs would carry him to the kitchen. His mother was on her hands and knees trying to clean up the mess. Owen Musgrave swung his leg and kicked her in the ribs. Del heard the soft humph as the boot connected with his mother's stomach. He'd never witnessed his father hit his mother before; the violence always happened in the kitchen or in the bedroom out of sight. Up until this moment a small part of him was able to pretend that it wasn't really happening at all, it was a play they were rehearsing, or a game or a story like on TV.

His father's black boot. Spit polished for his job as a security guard.

Del rushed into the kitchen. His father turned and swung a hard sinewy fist that connected with the boy's midsection and knocked the wind out of him so severely that he lay flat unable to speak or even cry.

His mother whimpered. "Don't hit him. Don't hit him."

Del laid still, closed his eyes. Violence crashed over him. Dishes breaking. A war zone. If they had lived in town the neighbours would have heard the battle and called for help. But their house was at the end of a dead-end street, the only house in a proposed subdivision that never got off the ground. Swamp and bush and raccoons and chipmunks surrounded their house.

He tried to make his parents happy but nothing worked for long. After awhile, Del stopped trying. He would come home after school, disappear into his room and draw. He lost interest in family life and then he lost interest in everything else. From ages ten to fourteen, his childhood was a blank. Violence dominated. Which he could have borne were not for the occasional glimpses of happiness: his mother bringing home a poinsettia from work at Christmas; his father laughing with a friend who'd stopped by. Confusing, hurtful glimpses into a life his parents had outside their home. Del had only the home, the violence, and the neglect.

"THE DAY he died, I was the only one in the house. I heard an explosion and then a scream. I ran to the back yard and saw my dad's clothes were on fire. He screamed at me get the fire extinguisher from the shed but I couldn't figure out how to operate it. I'd never seen it done. The instructions were on the side of the canister. He was screaming and screaming and I stood in the yard, useless, holding the damn thing. And finally the screaming stopped."

"You said before that he let the fire take him."

"The paramedics said that. They thought that's what must have happened." Del rubbed his eyes. "He wanted to be saved. The fire extinguisher was still in my hands when the responding officer got there. He thought it must've malfunctioned and then he guessed the truth. He told my mother he was making a note in his file that I didn't let my father die on purpose. He recommended academic counselling but nothing came of it. I left home soon after."

The air in the cabin was fresh and clean. Alvina lay on top of him with her ear pressed to his chest while he talked about himself, a smooth ribbon of talk that softened her bones to jelly. About working all over the country at odd jobs, his earnings rarely topping the poverty line, and about the day he realized he loved to paint. He was proudest of the birch bark canoe he'd built because it was tricky and he was working from memory. He talked without stopping. He liked to talk and she liked to listen. It had been a long time since she didn't have to do anything but listen.

"Were you always good-looking?" she asked.

He laughed. "I don't know. I never thought about it. Someone was always looking at me though, talking to me, asking me questions. Not the kids. Kids knew when to back off. The adults, though. God, the adults never left me alone. They weren't going to go to my house and make my father stop beating my mom. They weren't going to change anything. So why keep asking me how things were at home? Why try to get me to talk?"

Del rose naked from the bed to pull a couple of beers from the fridge.

"Maybe they knew you were falling behind. If you were homely, they wouldn't have cared," said Alvina, speaking from experience.

Del turned and caught her staring at him.

"Sorry," she said, blushing furiously.

He handed her a bottle. She sat up, tucking the sheet over her breasts. The beer was cool and sharp in her mouth. Aided by her empty stomach and the heat, the alcohol blasted over her central nervous system.

"Why do you do that?" He nodded to the sheet wrapped over her body.

"It was the way I was raised. I'm shy."

Del wasn't shy. He enjoyed being naked. He was broader and stronger than she remembered him being before she slept with him. Del Musgrave became a bigger presence close up. Alvina always imagined it would be the other way around. That if she were with him in real life, he'd lose his magic and shrink down to human size. Being with him was the most meaningful life Alvina had lived so far and because of that she knew it couldn't last. She was trying not to make more of this time with him than it was fated to be.

He climbed under the sheet beside her, balancing his beer in one hand.

"Did Teresa know?" she asked.

"That I couldn't read?" Del's mouth set. "No. Teresa didn't know. Nobody did. She thought I was a good-looking guy with no ambition who had a talent with paint. Artists are neglectful when times are good and hell when times are bad. I only wanted to paint. I wanted it like a drug. She was disappointed. She didn't get the life she wanted or even deserved. She could have done better."

His eyes were haunted and red-rimmed, staring as if Teresa was standing right in front of him. It didn't matter if she was in his mind or in the cabin, his dead wife was back and whatever she'd brought with her was draining the life out of him.

Alvina huddled under the sheet. "Is that why she was leaving?"

He turned to her. His face was fixed. "You don't know that. You heard a rumour. Don't make what happened to Teresa more complicated than it already is."

But it was complicated. Del couldn't get a divorce. He couldn't get a mortgage or a driver's license or take the job as supervisor at the Lodge. Del couldn't read. The way Alvina saw it, Teresa leaving him complicated everything. In her mind, she saw Teresa's laughing mouth followed by a terrible loneliness. This was it. The material point. This is what he was trying to tell her that day in the rain. The ground he had fought to secure.

Slants of light and the spires of trees. His life. His art. He had trusted and put the whole of it at the mercy of a girl who didn't want what he offered but was going to take everything he had.

The wind flapped the laundry hanging outside on the line. The leaves on the trees were curling in the heat. The wind was too sultry to be a relief.

"Alvina, where did the sketch of Teresa go?" Del nodded to the space above their heads.

Her throat closed. "I took it to do a story on you. It went in the river when I did." The words fell out of her mouth in a rush. "It's gone."

The whole of his being seemed to go still. "A cop or a counsellor back then told me that we forget much more than we remember. We had to or we'd go insane. I can't remember what she looks like without that sketch." Del squinted at the bright world beyond the window. "I have to go back to the Camp for a few hours and prep the cabins for the Labour Day long weekend. Gerry has a big group booked. You can stay here if you want."

"Del, you don't owe me anything just because we slept together. I knew what I was doing when I took the sketch and I don't expect you to forgive me. In fact, it's probably better if you don't. I should get going. Before Missy decides I've already moved out and she puts my stuff up for sale on Kijiji."

"You should tell your roommate to go to hell."

"One of these days, I will."

Del didn't move. They sat shoulder-to-shoulder in silence. Alvina took a long swallow of beer and listened to the whine of the cicadas outside the cabin.

"Tell her now. You could always move in here if you have nowhere else to go."

Breathing took effort. "I *have* nowhere else to go," she said, her voice tight. "I've already told you that so don't make the offer it if you don't mean it."

"I mean it. I'm not sorry the sketch is gone. I'm in love with you, Moon."

Her heart stopped.

"I just wanted you to know that."

Alvina nodded. Her eyes were on the window and the sun-kissed trees. It was hard to be coolly noncommittal when out of nowhere and for no reason, there was joy.

"I'm in love with you too, Del."


DEL STEERED the Harber Craft upriver to the Camp as the sun slouched behind the hills. Alvina had gone home to pack. She said she'd be back in the morning.

There's no trick to love, Del thought. It's either there or it isn't. He didn't love Teresa enough to tell her he couldn't read. He didn't even love her enough to forgive her. It was like he'd been a ghost all his life walking the earth in Del Musgrave's skin, possessed by thoughts that roamed everywhere and never landed. Programs on the radio, discussions of one thing or another would quicken his interest and then frustrate him, hobbled by a brain that froze up at the first dark corner. There were days he was afraid of seizing up altogether, of closing his mind even to the radio because he couldn't see the whole picture.

If he hadn't met Alvina, none of that would matter to him. He wouldn't even be thinking about it. For seven years, he had forged an uneasy alliance with his illiteracy, a detente that allowed him to live with the frustration as long as he stuck to the four walls of the cabin, his art and the river. And now they were at war. When she wasn't with him, life was a dead thing in which he feigned interest. And when she was with him, at the hot pinnacle of his joy, he had to feign coolness so it wouldn't matter when she left.

If she didn't show up at the cabin tomorrow, he wouldn't call her, or ask after her, or even mention her name.

One day she would leave him. It was inevitable. And when it happened, he prayed a merciful guide would take over and lead him out of this hell.

# TWENTY

THE RIVER glinted. The sun was sinking with the exquisite slow progress of mid-summer. Marlee reached in the fridge for the bottle of organic Pinot Grigio. She allowed herself one glass of good wine every afternoon. As she was in perfect health, she refused to discuss the habit anymore. She had learned the hard way it was a waste of energy arguing with people who were projecting their own addictions onto her. Not everyone had her self-control.

Constable Martine Fournier suggested she wait until the interview was over.

"The interview is over, constable," she said, filling her glass. "I've told you everything I know. I've confessed and I'm only waiting for my lawyer to call back to tell me what to do next. We might as well relax. This early evening light is quite beautiful, don't you think? We could sit outside for awhile if you think there is time."

"There is one final question, *madame*."

Marlee laughed. "You asked your final question five or six questions ago."

"*Oui.* I am still waiting for an answer. Where did he get the flashlight?"

The front door closed. Marlee stood up, alert. Violet had come in. She held up her hand, a silent request of the police that they hold their questions for a moment. "Did you remove your shoes?" she called.

"Yes."

Violet snuffled into the kitchen, her eyes were red with crying. Marlee squeezed her daughter's shoulder. "Take your bath now. Tell Harry and Stanley I've ordered a pizza for dinner. Everything is going to be fine. Judy Finney is coming over with Annabel to watch a movie with you and the boys."

"Why?" Violet whispered. "Where are you going?"

"I'm going to the station with Detective Sergeant Rompré and Constable Fournier to make a statement. And then I might have to go to court. But I won't be alone, so don't worry about me. My lawyer will be there to help. I don't think I'll be gone for more than one night. Judy is going to stay until I get back. I've told Harry and Stanley I'm going on a business trip. Now, go upstairs and have your bath before Judy arrives."

Violet nodded, speechless, and ran from the room.

Marlee turned to Rompré. "When Teresa died it was supposed to be over, but it will never be over, will it?"

"*Non, madame*, not until you tell the whole truth. Where did he get the flashlight?

"What makes you think I know?"

"Because you left it behind."

The detective had removed his suit jacket and hung it over the back of his chair. The jacket was made of a light material but Marlee's house was not air-conditioned. He appeared to be more comfortable without it. By contrast Constable Fournier remained swaddled in her bullet-proof vest and a weighty belt of police issue hardware.

Rompré troubled Marlee. In fact the entire interview

had troubled her. She felt that she had been trapped into confessing to Dave's murder, but how could Rompré have known? She didn't do or say anything in their brief meetings that could have led him to suspect her. "You'll have to explain, detective. I'm not following you." She put a wedge of cheese on a cracker. "I admit I left the flashlight behind in the trailer. What else could I do with it?"

"What else could you have done with the weapon that you took the trouble to wipe clean of fingerprints? You could have thrown it in the river. You could have destroyed it in the fire you started to burn the suit. You could have taken it with you and tossed it into the wilderness where it would never have been found. But you did none of these things. You left it in the trailer." Rompré turned to a page in his black notebook. 'To be honest,'" he quoted, reading aloud, "'I didn't give much thought to how she came to be killed.'" He looked up. "Why did you not give it much thought?"

"I don't know. I guess I was only glad she was dead and out of my life."

"When your husband found the body, he said he was afraid her killer might be nearby. His first thought was for his personal safety. Self-preservation is instinctive; only an innocent man would react so. We'll let his response stand for a moment and compare it to yours. You were on the scene much earlier than your husband. You were six months pregnant, vulnerable and in a highly emotional state and yet you 'did not give much thought to how she came to be killed.'" The murder weapon, smeared with the victim's blood, scalp and hair, was on the floor. You picked it up. It did not occur to you that the killer could be nearby, lurking in the thicket. You set about cleaning the weapon of prints and left it on the table where the investigators could not miss seeing it."

"I did, yes."

"The logical explanation is that you recognized the flashlight. You had seen it before; therefore you were not concerned the killer was lurking nearby because you knew who the killer was. And this person did not frighten you."

Marlee took a sip of wine. "I wasn't frightened, Detective Rompré because as you have said yourself, I am not of the temperament. I don't imagine bogeymen around every corner. Besides, if I recognized the flashlight wouldn't it make more sense to dispose of it?"

Rompré frowned, deep in thought. "You wanted your husband in prison. Your intention was to remove him from your home without the financial sacrifice of divorce. Constable Fournier, how did it benefit Madame Bremer to have the flashlight taken in evidence?"

"CSU was able to quickly identify and trace the make and model of the flashlight to a manufacturer in Germany. The flashlights were sold in Canada to security firms, municipal police and fire departments, military engineers and automotive mechanics. We were able to establish the murder weapon had in all probability come from the service bay at the dealership. Trey Bremer became the prime suspect."

"*C'est juste*. Investigators concentrated their resources on making the case against M. Bremer. Swift arrests are the delight of the public." Rompré leaned back. "Yet you caused a delay when you lied about taking the suit to the drycleaner. This puzzled me. Why risk your husband slipping though the net?

How did you benefit from this diversion? *Voilá.* With one lie, you convinced your husband he could trust you. The investigation was closing around him; your sudden confirmation of his story, that his clothes had no blood on them, earned his gratitude. It was a role well played. Your loyalty, comfort and support were rewarded with your husband's position in the company. He made arrangements to give you managing control of the family business should he be unable to perform his duties, which came into effect when you retracted your statement. The suit was found and M. Bremer was arrested."

"I admit I tampered with the scene of the crime and evidence. You have it on record. The flashlight makes no difference to anything now," Marlee said with finality.

Rompré twisted in his chair so his body faced Marlee. He rested his elbows on his knees and his hands linked together. His eyes hardened. "It makes a difference to your children, *madame.* The Crown may resist dropping the charge against your husband on your testimony alone. It could take a year or more before he is released from prison. If a grandparent will not assume responsibility for the children, they will be separated and placed in foster care. Of course, once your husband is released, your children will be restored to their home. However, Bremer will not be declared innocent. The public will continue to think him guilty. I am sorry, but this is a fact of human nature. If Teresa Musgrave's real murderer is not captured, your husband will be regarded as a rapist and murderer released from prison on a technicality."

Marlee set her wine glass down. "Good. Let him suffer as I have suffered. People thought I knew how perverted he was and helped him to do what he did. He started the fire. Let him be the one to burn in it."

"Your children will burn with him. Harry, Stanley and Violet will be isolated socially. Mothers will not allow their children to play in the home of a convicted killer of a teenaged girl. And your children will be plagued by doubt as well. They will suffer long into adulthood. You know that what I say is true. What is more, you know it will be far worse than I have described. Your husband will not shield them as you did. He will not humble himself in the community for their sakes as you did."

"What do you want me to say?" Tears blurred her vision.

In a voice so low, Marlee had to strain to hear, Rompré asked: "Whose flashlight was it, *madame*?"

Marlee sagged. The battle was over. There was nothing to do now but surrender all if there was to be peace. "It was in his boat when he dropped Teresa off for work that morning. A heavy, black metal flashlight. It belonged to Del Musgrave."

Her hand shook as she lifted the glass of wine to her lips. She was resolved to enjoy the taste of it in spite of everything. This could be her last glass of wine for some time.


FOURNIER TOSSED her notepad to the desk. Marlee Bremer's statement had been recorded and would be transcribed in due course. The woman was presently sequestered with her lawyer.

"You watch," the constable fumed. "The charge will be reduced to second degree, though it should be first because of the vodka bottle. Her lawyer will argue

Dave Gomer injured Marlee's family. All she needs is a sympathetic judge and a shrink who'll diagnose her as suffering from temporary insanity and Marlee Bremer could be a free woman in seven years."

"You do not think justice will be served."

"No, sir, I don't. But I can tell you admire her because she was clever enough to get her husband wrongly imprisoned. You like it when the criminal is smarter than the system."

Rompré smiled. "I admire her, Fournier, because she is clever, yes, but primarily because she has the moral sense. She tried to protect Del Musgrave."

"You believed her story?"

"About the flashlight, certainly. That it belonged to Del Musgrave. That she called him at the Camp that night to inform him of his wife's infidelity and encouraged him to confront the lovers at the trailer. Of this account, yes, I believe *madame*."

"I didn't believe her. Not a word of it." Constable Fournier removed her vest and hung it over the chair. "If Trey didn't kill Teresa, then Marlee must have done it. She had means, motive and opportunity. If the flashlight belonged to Del Musgrave, Teresa might have left it at the house or Marlee could have stolen it out of Musgrave's boat. She knew about the affair a week before the murder giving her plenty of time to plan. It is too convenient that suddenly she remembers calling Del Musgrave that night."

"There was no blood on her clothing. It is unavoidable, the blood. With no other tire treads found at the scene, the killer either came on foot or by boat. The family did not own a boat at the time of the murder." Rompré leaned back in his chair. "Marlee

Bremer went to great lengths to protect Musgrave until it was clear her children would suffer. Sensibly, she tells us the truth about the flashlight. She saw it lying on the floor. She recognized it. There is no doubt in her mind of who is the killer. When she found the *au pair* brutally murdered, she understood that she had set the tragedy in motion by calling young Musgrave the night before. We must accept that Mrs. Bremer is not Teresa's killer and move on."

"With all due respect, sir, I was afraid this would happen. We've cast doubt on Trey Bremer's conviction and we don't have a viable suspect in his place. Del Musgrave's alibi for the night of the murder is rock solid. Five guests testified he was at the Camp with them. Gerry Dunn said the men were playing cards inside the main lodge and Del was in the kitchen. They could hear him moving around, washing up. Gerry was on the porch when Del came out and went down to the dock to ready the fishing gear for the trip the next day. Then Musgrave said good-night and turned in. Gerry remained on the porch until the guests went to bed at approximately one o'clock in the morning. If Del had started up a motor boat in that time, Gerry would have heard it."

"And a canoe?"

Fournier read over the statement. "There's no mention of a canoe. Paddling downriver wouldn't be a problem but how did he make it back?"

"I have seen his paintings in a gallery in Québec City. They are quite remarkable."

The constable nodded. "So I've heard, sir. I haven't seen his work myself."

"He documents the wilderness. An accomplished

guide and canoeist, I imagine he has the strength and skill to paddle upriver, though admittedly it would be difficult. The question is was it possible in the time given?"

"Marlee said she called at around nine p.m. Del must have been in the kitchen and that's why he answered and not Gerry. Gerry couldn't hear the phone ring from where he was on the porch. At least, he didn't mention a phone call when the police took his statement. Teresa was killed between ten and midnight. I just have to say, sir, that if Del Musgrave is guilty of this crime, Marlee Bremer is the one who loaded the gun."

"Feet that hurry to run to evil," quoted Rompré.

"What is that?"

"A proverb. It instructs us not to escalate trouble."

"Amen to that. If Mrs. Bremer had kept her mouth shut, the affair would've petered out on its own. Lovers get sick of each other faster than married people do. Trey Bremer wasn't going anywhere."

Rompré frowned. "Marlee Bremer said it isn't easy to leave a person."

"*Oui, c'est ça. Qu'en penses-tu?*"

"What was Monsieur Musgrave's motive for killing his young bride? The fear of divorce? Divorce is not a compelling motive for murder. Jealousy? It was jealousy that led Madame Bremer to call him that night." Rompré tilted his head back and closed his eyes. "Del learns his wife is sleeping with another man. Though the journey is long and he can be observed by his boss, in a jealous rage, he canoes to the trailer and kills his wife."

"What's wrong with it?"

"I do not know. But it is wrong. What do we know about Del Musgrave?"

Fournier referred to the file. "Full name is Delmar Musgrave. His father was Owen, now deceased. His mother, Diana Musgrave is still living in New Brunswick. Del moved to the area when he was nineteen or twenty. No known previous address. Paid cash for the place he lives in now. Works for minimum wage so money would be tight if they divorced. Twenty-one when he married. Wife killed six months later and he's been a widower ever since."

She sat at the desk and typed DEL MUSGRAVE into the search engine. "He's a name in the art community but he keeps to himself. Described as enigmatic—whatever that means. He doesn't give interviews...," Fournier scanned the articles onscreen, "...or attend the *vernissages* of his work, which is unusual but probably adds to his mystique. He's attractive to women."

"Handsome and talented. Not passionate about the woman but the art, I would think. Is losing one's art reason enough to kill? In an older man, perhaps, but Musgrave was only twenty-one. He was not so far along in his career that he risked losing much should he have to sell the property and start again."

"A jealous rage then, sir. She was with another man. What young guy can stand that?"

Rompré reached for the photos of Teresa Musgrave's battered body and examined them dispassionately. "It was not jealousy that did this damage. This was panic; a drowning man who stands on his rescuer and drowns them both." He hesitated, thinking. "What did his father do for a living?"

Fournier swivelled to the file and glanced at it. "Security guard."

"Quite possibly the provenance of the flashlight."

She met Rompré's eyes. "Should we pick him up, sir?"

"Not yet. Go back to Gerry Dunn. We need a precise account of Del Musgrave's movements that night. If Mr. Dunn is not able to provide you with one, establish how long it would take to get to the trailer and back either on foot or by canoe. Take Constable Lemen with you. Call me as soon as you have a result."

THE VISIT to Martingale Hunt and Fish Camp proved inconclusive. Or rather, Fournier's test hadn't delivered the definitive conclusion Rompré would have liked going into tomorrow's interview with Musgrave. Gerry Dunn was unshakeable. Musgrave was at the fishing boats at nine thirty p.m. after which he turned in. However, he was bunking in one of the cabins at the south end of the property, away from the main lodge and out of sight. The path Musgrave took continued south but eventually led to a locked gated fence. Gerry was the only person with a key. The canoes were beached downriver of the motor boats. One had to follow a path in view of the main lodge to reach them. Del would have been spotted by Gerry if this was his mode of transport. Gerry Dunn swears he did not doze off at any point. Fournier described him as a tough little man with miles of energy.

The best theory Fournier could come up with was that Musgrave had climbed the fence and followed the boardwalk that ran past a decrepit swimming pool and tennis court, but more importantly, led to the old highway. This route shaved off ten kilometres to the trailer as the crow flies. However, it was akin to bushwhacking; a difficult undertaking especially at night but it had the advantage of concealment.

The station was too cold for Rompré's enjoyment. He expected heat in the summer and could see little reason to avoid it. At least it was quiet. The public was at its peaceable best in the early evening. Trouble usually arrived at nightfall and wore on into early morning. He gathered together the papers and files on his desk and slipped them into his briefcase, determined to get away before the next shift arrived. It had been a long day, and a difficult one.

He knew with cold certainty that Musgrave had battered his wife to death. There was very little proof. A security guard's flashlight and the testimony of a confessed killer. As Fournier pointed out, Madame Bremer had a vested interest in placing blame elsewhere. That did not concern him. He needed to know *why* did Del Musgrave murder his wife? What caused this young man to lash out? Answer that and everything else will fall into place.

Rompré shrugged into his suit jacket and adjusted the cuffs of his shirt so they presented neatly at his wrists. Any pleasure he might have derived from securing Marlee Bremer's confession today was marred by his dissatisfaction with his method. He had not liked using the child. His daughter, Sophie, was close in age.

Would have been, he corrected himself.

The hand Rompré passed over his face trembled slightly. And so it goes, he thought. One's child would be this age and this height. One's marriage would be this far along, this anniversary, a second child, a home. And so it goes. This is where I would be *if*.

If Fournier were here she would blame the shaking fingers on too much caffeine. Hester Warnock would know better. He glanced at his watch. She will be at home now. He could call from the car and invite himself to dinner. His friend might appreciate the company and he would appreciate the distraction.

But there was another call he would make first. He was not a man given to impulses; he thought it through carefully before lifting the receiver. Informing Alvina Moon of the progress made in the case seemed reasonable in light of her help with the investigation. She was leaving town soon and this could be his last opportunity. He found the girl's phone number in his notes and picked up the landline to make the call.

There were few actions in his career that he came to regret more.

# TWENTY-ONE

**A**LVINA'S BEDROOM window was open. The rickety old screen barely kept the bugs out and let the cool, moist night air in. The sky was brilliant with stars. A shining nail of moon was holding its own over the trees. Missy had gone to bed early in a temper.

Her cell phone rang somewhere under the pile of clothing that she'd heaped on the bed and Alvina debated answering it. Writing up Gerry's story and getting the final issue out took more time than she'd planned. Del was expecting her at the cabin first thing in the morning and she still wasn't packed. It was probably her parents calling her back. She'd left them a message saying she was moving out of the apartment and in with the artist, Del Musgrave. That must've got their attention. Coral and Oliver Moon were always interested in famous artists. Alvina groped for her satchel and pulled out the phone.

It was Detective Sergeant Rompré of the MRC des Collines Police. They had a suspect in custody and a formal charge was pending in the murder of Dave Gomer. "At which time, I will release the individual's name," the detective said.

"Oh my god." Alvina sank to the edge of the bed. "I don't believe it. I know you said he was murdered but I was really hoping you were wrong. Oh god, the paper comes out on Monday. It'll be too late to make an announcement. I'll see if I can get MetMedia to run something. Please if you could—I won't print it—who is it you have in custody? It's really important I know."

Dave's death had been covered on the editorial page of the *Record*. Ray had contributed the In Memoriam. The Paugan Falls took the centre pages and the history of Martingale Hunt and Fish Camp was near the back. Alvina had placed a large photo of Dave on the front page above the fold with the caption: RIP. The paper would probably sell out.

"I cannot identify the suspect but I can tell you this individual provided us with information in another case. With regard to the question asked in the anonymous note, we have an answer."

"Oh?" Alvina cradled the phone to her ear and stuffed clothes into a duffle bag.

"The flashlight belonged to Del Musgrave. He has become a person of interest in the murder of Teresa Fillion."

The shirt Alvina was holding slid to the floor. "I think I misheard you. You mean Teresa brought her husband's flashlight with her to the trailer? Because Dave told me that Del Musgrave had an alibi for the night of the murder." Her heart was pounding between her ears although she couldn't understand why she would be alarmed. It was as if her heart knew before her brain what was about to happen.

Rompré's voice was calm and uninflected. "The alibi is not as sound as once believed. He was seen at ten p.m. walking to the cabins south of the main lodge to retire for the night. There is a path that joins to the old highway; Musgrave could have taken this route to the trailer."

"Yes, I'm familiar with it." Alvina had developed the knack of keeping her voice and expression perfectly neutral even in a crisis—a talent handed down from years of hanging around actors. "I was there recently to do a story."

"The individual we have in custody for Dave Gomer's murder informed Mr. Musgrave that his wife was meeting Trey Bremer in the trailer. Teresa was murdered shortly after this call. I am sorry but that is all I can say at this time. We will be bringing in Monsieur Musgrave for questioning in the morning." There was a pause. "I apologize if this news comes as a shock. The two murders were connected but only indirectly. At the time Mr. Gomer was killed, he was trying to make amends. Ill-advised perhaps, but he was doing his best to set matters right. It might comfort you to know that your boss was not responsible for Teresa Fillion's death."

"That is good to hear." Alvina felt like she was choking. She was thinking of Dot saying *oh that wasn't rape—Dave was well in on it* and the phone call Trey made and that somehow in all of this, Dave *was* responsible. They all were. Teresa, Dave, Trey, Marlee— they all did this to him.

"Did you know Mr. Musgrave?"

"I met him once or twice. No, I didn't know him."

"*Quelle bonne nouvelle. À bientôt,* Mademoiselle Moon."

Her reply in French was brief, as was the call. In a matter of minutes it was over.

DAWN PEELED back a rosy sky, cool air and a cacophony of bird song. Alvina huddled in the armchair, unable to move. She felt like a character out of a Chekov play, full of stifled emotion and questions that couldn't be asked. The way it happened. The way things changed so fast. She'll be dancing on the head of this pin for the rest of her life. It never once occurred to her in all the long night that Del might not be guilty. It was his guilt that made him finally make sense. The acute isolation he lived in. His longing for his dead wife.

I have to do something. I have to do something.

*Move!*

She leapt up, yanked on a pair of shorts and pulled a fresh tee-shirt on over her head. The keys to the van were still in her satchel. It'll be twenty-four hours before MetMedia reports the van missing, by then she'll have ditched it and they'll have escaped into the Québec wilderness. The duffle bag was half-stuffed with clothes. She shoved the remaining pile that was on the bed into the bag. Easy for the others to jeer at her for falling in love with him—easy for Marlee and Missy and her parents—they had jobs and friends and homes. Del had himself and she had no one but Del. Her time with him had meaning. No one would ever know how much. And she would do it all again, from beginning to end. She would have him back, even now. Even after discovering what he'd done.

She scooped up her satchel and camera bag, breathing heavily, her body heaving with silent tears that wouldn't stop. The relief she felt yesterday seemed cruel now. Hope snatched away. No, it was worse than losing hope. It was losing a life. She was going to teach him to read at night after dinner. She was confident he would be proficient by winter. He was the right man for her. He was exactly the right man. The violence in Del's life was what he'd been born into. It wasn't inside him. Del wasn't violent.

Her sneakers were under the bed. Alvina dropped to her knees but she couldn't reach them. She stretched her arm as far as it would go her fingers splayed, reaching, straining, straining—

*Hurry!*

Alvina collapsed. Sagging over the floor like someone had let the air out of her. Her face pressed against the dusty hardwood. When Del said he loved her, she saw herself for the first time as a girl standing at the altar of something big and wide and deep. Those words were all she had now. They would have to sustain her through the journey home and the tight smile in her parents' eyes. Through Coral and Oliver's half-hearted questions, the nights of loneliness and the days when she was afraid of not being anything at all.

Morning crept into the room, grey and pensive. The camera case was in her line of sight, resting against the foot of her bed where she'd dropped it. She remembered the photos she'd taken of the trailer. They were still on the image card. Alvina thought about Teresa Fillion and tried to pray for her, but instead felt the pain of the first blow, and the sound her skull gave when the flashlight connected to the bone.

HER NERVES stretched raw and she was exhausted from lack of sleep. The screen door swung open, squealing on its hinges. Del emerged from the cabin. He looked worse than she did. He smiled when he saw her but his smile faded when he read the expression on her face. Alvina slung the long strap of her satchel across her body and walked toward the cabin, bent over and slow-moving.

He kissed her on the mouth. "I was beginning to think you changed your mind. Where are your bags?"

"In the van," she lied. "It took longer to pack than I thought."

A fire was smouldering in the barrel. Del moved past her to the birch bark canoe that lay upside down near edge of the meadow. Its white-silvery bottom was streaked with pitch. Del picked up an axe and swung.

"No!"

If he heard her he gave no sign. He split the canoe at the main seam, chopped the long strips of bark into pieces and shoved them in the barrel. Alvina saw the can of gasoline in the same moment Del doused the bark and the barrel went up in flames.

"What are you doing? You love that canoe!"

"It wasn't sealed properly. I took it out for a run this morning and the seams were seeping. The seams open if it isn't done right. There's no way to tell until you've put it in water a few times. It's a hazard like this. It could've fallen to pieces under us one day."

He fed the fire with the scraps of his beautiful, pulverized canoe. Alvina stepped back from the inferno. She wished he would turn around and look at her properly. "Something happened yesterday. They caught Dave's killer."

He twisted to look at her but didn't meet her eyes. "That's good news."

Alvina stood in a patch of shadow thrown by a cloud in an otherwise cloudless sky. The heat of the day was already coming on. It was going to be a scorcher. "Something came to light during their investigation that isn't so good. The person they arrested has identified the flashlight that was used to murder Teresa as yours."

His face didn't change. Del pulled his tee-shirt from his waistband and tossed it to her. "Here. Wrap yourself in that. It's got to be thirty degrees Celsius and your teeth are chattering." She pulled it on over her camisole top and huddled in its warmth. Del flung a strip of the canoe's rib into the fire. "When did you hear all this?"

"Last night. Detective Rompré called to update me about Dave's case. He doesn't know we're friends. The police are coming to question you."

"Alvina, we're more than friends. Friends don't sleep together, remember?" His jaw twitched. "When are they coming?"

She swallowed. "Today. This morning"

Del turned away, rubbing his hair. "Jesus."

His skin darkened. His shoulders became broader, thicker. Alvina watched, entranced by his transmogrification. It was as if by the grace of discovery Del could become himself again. "When did the memory come back?" she asked. "Or did it never leave. Tell me the truth."

Del met her gaze. "It's been coming on in flashes since we met, but the day you came to the Camp, I remembered. The flashlight was the only thing of my dad's I kept after he died."

Love costs more than anyone thinks it rightfully should. It asks more and it takes more. But Alvina had to follow it through to the end or nothing would ever change for her or for Del. From this moment on, they had to be different. This is what Alvina thought as she looked at Del and considered what she was going to do.

"Tell me everything."

He hesitated, and then said in a voice that expected nothing, "If I could undo it, I would."

ABOUT HALF a dozen times that night Del told himself Teresa was bluffing. She wasn't going to leave him. Then the telephone rang and he almost didn't answer it because he was up to his elbows in soapy water.

Marlee Bremer was on the line saying don't shoot the messenger. She was only passing along some information she thought he had a right to know. He had a boat—he could check it out for himself if he didn't believe her. They were in a little oasis on the river. Did he know it? Teresa must have mentioned it—the evil bitch had taken Marlee's kids there once. There was a palm tree on the back, but it wasn't in a desert, oh no! Trey and Teresa's little oasis was in an abandoned campsite on the river. They are having sex in a filthy old trailer. Trey wasn't home yet; there was a very good chance Del could catch them in the act if he left now.

"I told her I didn't want to catch them in the act. I was at work, I couldn't go anywhere. I hung up."

Gerry caught up with him going down to the boats. Rigging them up for tomorrow so we can get an early start, Del told him, and then he'd turn in for the night if that was all right. Gerry, clapping him on the shoulder: Sure, sure. Get a good night's sleep. I can take it from here.

Del didn't intend to go to the trailer. A vague cloud was forming in his mind; he had to be alone to think things through. "I cut through the woods so Gerry wouldn't see me, to where the canoes were beached downriver."

His voice reached across the silence and she wanted to stop him from trusting her with this story. "Don't tell me anymore." Alvina sank to her knees. "I don't want them to get any answers or confessions out of me."

"It's not going to come to that."

He watched her out of the corner of his eye, crouched in a tight ball with his tee-shirt pulled down over her body, arms and all, covering her knees.

It didn't take long paddling downriver to reach the trailer. A Manitoba maple was slung out over the water. Del used it as cover to spy on the trailer. It was beginning to get dark. He heard voices arguing. The guy was telling her to get dressed and Teresa refused. It was one thing to suspect she had a lover, it was another thing—a whole other thing—to see her come out of the trailer with him. She was naked. Bremer had his eyes on her.

"Don't ruin this. Don't be a fucking child. I have to get home."

"Call her! Tell her you're not coming home. You said it was over so why go back to her? I told Del it was over. Do you think that was fucking easy? What's holding you back?"

"You two don't have a pot to piss in. It's not as simple as that for me. I have to talk to a lawyer before I do anything. There's a lot at stake. I can't argue with you about this now. She's waiting. Get in the fucking car and we'll talk about it on Monday."

Teresa turned and marched back into the trailer. "Fuck you. Let her wait. I'm not leaving. You know where to find me when you change your mind."

Trey Bremer got in his car, slammed the door and roared away. Del tied the canoe to a branch. The flashlight was clipped to his belt same as always. His maintenance work at the Camp always called for poking into half-lit places. Del walked up to the trailer.

"Teresa looked happy to see me until she realized it was me. She didn't hold anything back. I told her to go if she wanted to, but she wasn't going to get anything out of me. She said she was entitled to half the property and she'd take me to court. Trey would pay for a lawyer."

Del described shoving her to the bed and the thud her head made when it slammed against the wall. Teresa put her hand to the bump, stunned. Now you've done it, she whimpered. That's assault. I'm going to call the cops.

Click, click. He unclipped the flashlight from his belt in one swift motion, an action he'd seen his father do. The shove, the metallic click, click, the black lamp thudding into Teresa's hip. She pushed up as if to lunge at him. He hit her again, this time in the ribcage. She fell back to the bed. Del closed his eyes and swung the flashlight over and over and over again—he didn't know how many times or for how long.

Teresa's face had been left untouched. Who told him that? A grief counsellor had come to the cabin at Gerry's request to talk to Del. Del had wanted to know what she looked like when they found her and did she suffer. The counsellor was honest with the first part of his question and lied through his teeth on the second.

Owen Musgrave never hit a woman in the face. Owen had scruples. A swaggering, handsome braggart who couldn't hold a job and broke Del's mother's arm twice was proud of the fact that he had never hit a woman in the face.

When it was over Del sat in the bloody mess and listened for the death rattle. The wind moved the pines against the trailer. Her eyes were open. Death was excruciatingly slow. But at last it came.

"I looked at the flashlight which still in my hand and saw a piece of her scalp was stuck in it. I flung it away from me. I think it rolled under the table."

Del lurched from the trailer, his gut cramping and staggered to the river. He submerged himself, feeling the intoxicating pull of the current and the almost religious longing to let go. The river rinsed the blood from his clothes, hair and skin. He swam to the canoe and hauled himself in. Paddling upstream was hard but he caught a tail wind from the southwest and made good time.

"My cabin was out of sight of the lodge. No one saw me return. I beached the canoe and made my way through the woods in the dark. I got out of my wet clothes, crawled into bed and fell asleep. For the next two days I expected the police to arrive and arrest me. When it didn't happen, I thought I must have dreamt the whole thing. But I couldn't find my flashlight anywhere. I got home on Monday morning and sat on the edge of the bed, waiting for Teresa to come home. When the police showed up, it was to take me to identify her body. By then, I couldn't remember a thing. I didn't just forget—it was like she never existed. Marlee Bremer bought two of my paintings after Trey was convicted of Teresa's murder. She hung them in plain view on the sales floor of the dealership."

"Is that why you did it? To win Marlee Bremer's patronage so you could paint?" Her voice splintered between them.

"Don't...," he said softly. "You can't hate me." He sat on the ground behind her and pulled her into the V of his legs, stroked her arms and her shoulders between the blades where she held her tension.

"I don't hate you. I hate Marlee Bremer." She tucked her chin in her arms. *Bloody thoughts and violent pace.* Marlee Bremer quoting *Othello* in Café Trémolos happened a million years ago. A lifetime had passed since Dave told her to shred the note and Del took her to the raft and Ray cried into the phone. It had been a lifetime since her last conversation with her mother.

Her eyes blurred. "After seven years, no one is going to believe you had a psychotic episode."

"Do you think that's what it was?"

Alvina twisted her neck to peer up at him. The meadow was floating in soft shades of grey. The wind, the birds and the drone of insects smothered out the world. The loud, demanding, critical world. "I don't know. Have you told me everything?"

A look crossed of wary earnestness passed over his handsome face. "Is it important to you to know everything?"

The ring of her cell phone cut the silence. She met Del's eyes, astonished, as if waking from a dream. Like Big Brother, the cell tower in Low made sure the outside world was never far away. She dug the phone out of the satchel and squinted at the screen. "It's the police."

Del jumped to his feet and walked briskly toward the forest. He was heading for the path that led to the river. Alvina scrambled after him. If he made it to the boat, he could reach the Camp before the police arrived and from there, escape to the highway. "Don't," Alvina begged, panting to keep up.

"I never lied to you." His back and shoulders were straight as a ruler; lean muscle showing in smooth curves under the thin white scars.

"I know that—God, I know! We'll tell them what happened. We'll get a lawyer. Please listen, there's a way through this. *Please!* Because it's too late!" she screamed. "Del! It's too late to run."

He stopped and turned, his chest heaving. Sweat rolled down his cheeks. No, not sweat Alvina realized. She could see the brown streaks where his tears had mingled with the dust on his face. Suffering and useless, Alvina stood at the edge of profound loss.

"He's already here."

# TWENTY-TWO

DETECTIVE ROMPRÉ pulled in front of Del's cabin in an unmarked black sedan, unhurried as though he were a client arriving to buy one of Del's paintings. Alvina held her breath when he climbed out, his hand on the open door. Rompré stopped when he saw them.

She turned to Del, pleading. "He'll help us. It'll be okay. I know he'll help us."

Del grabbed her by the shoulders and pushed her down to the hot dusky meadow grass. The vivid sky swarmed above and the blinding sun. He kissed her fiercely. Then he released her, panting like a wolf, and raced toward the burn barrel. She lifted herself up, staring in shock at his back and the thin white scars. Then understanding what he meant to do, Alvina screamed. "No!"

Alerted, Rompré charged across the meadow. Del reached the barrel first and spun around. For an instant Alvina met his eyes, the fire between them, shivering heat and smoke. And then he lifted a booted foot and kicked the barrel over. Fiery coals of wood scraps and flaming pieces of bark tumbled out over the dry leaf litter at the edge of the forest. The ground ignited and spread rapidly, staggeringly fast. Whatever hope DS Rompré had of stamping out the flames was torched by the fireball that ignited when the gas can exploded.

Rompré whirled back to the sedan, a strange thing to see a suited man running. Frozen to the ground in shock, Alvina watched as he jumped in the vehicle and backed down the laneway at a frightening speed. One hand was on the steering wheel, the other on the radio. She knew that in a matter of minutes the police would have the river blocked off with police boats and a team would be searching the woods for Del.

When the detective reappeared, he ran straight to the van and drove it from the area. Alvina turned round to face the forest and saw the reason why. The blaze had jumped the forest boundary, released like a voracious, searing genie. Flames were bearing down upon the meadow and the logs for the studio that Del would never build.

Alvina darted out of its path, her legs scorched by the heat. In a matter of seconds, the bone dry logs caught and crackled into flame. She held her arms up to shield her face. Del was gone, escaped into the woods. She looked wildly at the place where he had been and saw no sign of him. She screamed his name over and over. Even if he made it to the river, there was no hope of escape. The MRC boats were ten minutes away.

Alvina skirted the flames and ran to the path, covering her face against the smoke. The sacrifice of Del's precious trees had bought him some time. Rompré's back-up team was already arriving at the scene, running up the drive, but they were held back from entering the forest by the inferno. The cops were kept busy stamping out embers in an effort to keep the fire from spreading. They wouldn't give up holding it back, not even for an escaped murder suspect. The deadly seriousness of a fire out of control in a forest as dry as this one would take precedence. They would have to capture Del on the river.

Shimmering between Alvina and the police were clear wavering lines of heat and thin smoke that would soon become black clouds. The fire department and SOPFEU had been alerted and were on their way. Sirens could be heard wailing over the hills. Alvina plunged into the forest, running along the path. Her eyes stung. It wasn't too late. It wasn't too late.

"Del! Del!"

She choked on the smoke. Deep in the forest to her left, a ball of orange suddenly erupted, terrifying her as there was no warning. The fire had entered the root system, popping up out of the ground, consuming vulnerable trees and bushes. A dead ash was caught in a funnel of blasting orange flame. The ground cover was on fire and moving through the forest at a merciless speed. Alvina howled. The path stretched into a black tunnel of smoke. Where was the river? She tried to estimate how far she'd come.

The texture and quality of the smoke had changed. The thin white acrid stuff had given way to noxious black soot. The ash had become fine particle dust impossible to avoid inhaling and the path disappeared in the cloud. The air above her head suddenly incinerated in a shower of sparks.

Alvina looked up and screamed.

DEL CROUCHED in the scrub near the river. His boat was still at the dock. He'd never be able to outrun police boats in the Harber Craft so he stuck to the shoreline, travelling north. He stood a better chance in the deep bush where it was hard enough for a dog to travel never mind a man. The fire was behind him and still clear of the cabin he estimated, but not for much longer. The wind was shifting and wily. The crown was going up. Emergency personnel would have their hands full bringing it under control. Del lingered, worried about Alvina. Would she have tried to follow him? God, he hoped not—if there was a God and He concerned Himself with the prayers of killers.

Alvina said there was still hope. If he turned back now and turned himself in like Alvina wanted, maybe there was a chance. He would have to tell them all of it. About the sounds he heard Teresa making inside the trailer, whimpering, begging Trey to stop, how they were so real, pitch perfect. Making a game of rape and bondage. It wasn't a game to Del's mother. No, he couldn't tell them. It was too close to his flesh.

He would tell them about the illiteracy. There was hope in that, and an explanation. He'd never used it before to excuse anything he did or didn't do. *Make a decision.* Commit to running forever and give up painting with the same degree of agony as giving up sight or hearing or smell. Give up ever seeing Alvina again. Give up the salvation he'd found with her. There was no point in wondering where he would be right now if he'd never sought her out. He'd be far away from here. That much Del knew.

He had wanted Teresa back and she obliged him with a vengeance. Fair enough. Should he be running if that was the case? He asked for her and he got her. Did he have the right to escape what was his due?

Did his father?

Filled with a deep fatigue, Del turned around and

cut across the bush toward home. The forest, the fire he had started and the waiting police—he was running straight toward it. The wind was still with him. He could make it back if he hurried. He would see Alvina at least and if there was a chance. Well. There was a chance.

THE REDDISH dirt of the forest was at eye level. An ant toiled nearby. She had a dull, wobbly memory of Del leaving but she couldn't recall why. It was the strangest feeling to be alive and not alive at the same time. How long had she been lying here? The air was too thick with smoke to see a foot in front of her. Her ankle throbbed and her back felt bruised. She must have tripped over something running from the flames. Where was she? She thought she was running in the direction of the river. Water must be nearby because she couldn't feel the fire here. No flame or heat or noise. Only smoke.

Alvina lay on the cool dirt, resting, her thoughts moving in a cocoon of muffled dark. She had caused this, brought this down on both their heads. The anonymous note led to Violet, Violet led to Marlee and Marlee gave up Del to the police. But the chain started with Alvina Moon. Her good deed for the day. Good citizenship. Such a good girl. If she had shredded the note ... so easy to do ... Del would be free, painting in his forest, canoeing the river. She didn't even get a story out of it. She had destroyed his life for nothing.

*He'd be the first to tell you that wasn't true. The very first.*

A vision of Del shifted and dissolved into the thickening haze. He was running through the forest with a light, loping gait, ducking branches that only he could see. She took his being there as a sign that he was already dead. Del stopped and lifted his eyes to the sky as if he'd just noticed the smoke. His face was gilded by the morning sun, his shoulders pulled back. Then Alvina remembered she didn't believe in the afterlife and almost laughed, thinking how unimportant it was now what she believed. She was disconnected from herself, from what she was made of and desired to be. There was no self left. There was only the dirt of the forest floor, the smoke and the vision of Del before he plunged into the burning forest—that last look back, his lips forming the words *I love you.*

Then she heard his voice coming from the bowels of the smouldering forest. "Alvina!"

Alvina cried out and a face appeared over her blocking the sun. A glow was cast around his head like an angel and she would have laughed at the irony if she could stop crying long enough.

The angel, definitely a male and not an angel at all, said: "What the hell are you doing here?"

Alvina crooked her arm over her eyes. Tears rolled down her face wetting her ears. A riot of anguish under that arm. Grit spiked her sunburnt shoulders. "I'm sorry, I'm so sorry."

"Oh my god, Alvina, oh my god, what have you done? You came after me, didn't you, you stupid woman. Everyone knows you don't run into a burning building or a burning forest."

Panic edged his voice. Dead men don't feel panic. Alvina propped up on one elbow and peered at him. It was pitch black. The sun she thought she saw wasn't the sun at all. She coughed mightily and took a burning, sooty breath. "Del, you're here."

"Jesus, Alvina. I was coming back to turn myself in. The fire has cut off the route to the path. I detoured through the forest. I almost fell over you. Can you walk?"

"I was trying to get to the river. Is it near here? We should go to the river, to your boat."

Del hoisted her up. Her ankle dangled painfully. Alvina bit her lip, feeling like she was going to pass out from the pain. They hobbled a few steps and then the smoke closed in around them. It was impossible to see. He turned to her. His eyes were so beautiful. Like river rock or bottle glass. Not quite brown, not quite green, something in between, like the hills and the river. He was so handsome, a beautiful man, and frightened. She could see it clearly, etched in the sharp planes of muscle in his jaw and the corners of his mouth pulled tight.

"We can't get to the river. Okay. Del, put me down. Run and get help. I'll be fine. Go."

Del lowered her to the ground and trotted to the perimeter of the woods, his eyes on the way ahead, like a wolf seeking escape, trotting back and forth, back and forth.

And then she realized her mistake. Alvina's body experienced first the horror, then despair and finally, understanding. "You won't make back it in time. There isn't enough time to get to the cabin and get back with the firefighters, is there."

"It's the smoke. It'll be hard to breathe in a few minutes."

"Okay, but you can make it, right? You go and I'll just ... hold my breath until help arrives. Someone will find me. Go. Please. You have to go."

"Listen, dig down." He squatted and dug at the

earth, hands moving rapidly, forming a hollow in the ground. "The water bombers will be here soon. If you can hold on—stay low, as low to the ground as you can get. The smoke is above you." He dug deeper, clawing at the earth.

Alvina touched his arm, stopping him. "I'll be fine. Everything is going to be fine." She settled in the hollow he had created and pressed her cheek to the earth. It was cool and smelled of rain. "I'll see you soon. I'm sorry I dragged you into this."

He shook his head. Tears were running from his eyes.

"The water bombers will be here any minute. Please, Del. Leave."

He shook his head again and wiped his face. "No, we have a better chance if we stay together. If I didn't make it out, they wouldn't know where to find you."

Del stretched out beside her. The heat was sharper now, pressing down on the air above them. Consuming oxygen. The crown must be going up. He tried not to show his fear.

"I think we're going to die here," she said simply.

"Don't talk. The water bombers will be here any minute. Don't talk."

"You could still make it, Del."

"If I'm not with you, I'm dead anyway so I'll take my chances here. Stop talking. You're using up all the oxygen."

He stroked the planes of her face, her eyes watchful and so like his. He traced the slope of her hips. He was in love with Alvina Moon's every bone and hollow.

"Do you forgive me?" she whispered.

"Yes," he whispered back. "Do you forgive me?"

"Yes."

The heat seemed to leave them in that moment. The air shone with light, fresh clarity. The water bombers were coming. They could hear the drone in the distance. Alvina laughed, gazing into his face, full of surprise. Del looked up through the canopy to the glittering blue and the golden tree above and smiled. It had all been said. There was nothing more to explain or forgive.

They didn't talk after that but waited for the water to fall out of the sky.

THE POLICE resumed their search for Del Musgrave, fanning out along the shoreline where they believed he would have tried to escape. The SOPFEU had dragged thick hoses to the water, pumps rumbled, dousing strategic sections of bush to contain the fire and keep the flames from jumping to the crown of the forest. Healthy trees could withstand some scorching. But if it got in the crown of compromised trees—the bug infested or drought-weakened conifers, the fire could travel for miles destroying everything in its path. The water truck was already at work hosing the meadow in front of Del Musgrave's cabin to create a firebreak.

Then the wind turned again, twisting away from them, sparking the coals to ferocious life and the fire chief hollered for everyone to clear the area. One minute firefighters were following the flames and the next they were surrounded. The fire had gone underground and was travelling through the parched root system. A fireman not much older than Constable Fournier caught her by the arm to lead her out.

"I have to get inside the cabin," she shouted at him in French. "There's evidence I have to collect in an ongoing investigation!"

The firefighter signalled to the team hosing down the meadow to turn the water blast on the cabin. Fournier darted inside followed by two police officers. Between them, they hauled Del Musgrave's paintings to the cruisers parked on the road, away from the fire. Fournier stacked the canvases on the backseat. Saving the art was an impulse. She had a dim idea the DS would approve; he had said he liked the guy's work. Constable Fournier straightened and looked down the road. She couldn't see Rompré's black sedan anywhere.

Fournier turned back to the rough laneway that led to Musgrave's property and almost slammed into a heavily equipped fireman in the smoke. He covered her head with his arm. The fire was on the move he yelled in hot, hurried French. The danger of the surrounding fields catching was ever present. The likelihood of a full-scale evacuation had become a reality. The crown of the forest was going up, raining hot leafy embers down below. The smoke and heat were too thick to catch their man. The emergency workers, volunteer firefighters and MRC des Collines police had been beaten back by the flames. The law would have to wait. Del Musgrave was less danger to the public safety than the fire. Constable Martine Fournier was ordered out of the area.

NIGHT HAD fallen. Muffled shouts came to Rompré from behind the bullet-proof glass of the sedan. The firefighters had managed to save the cabin. He gazed at his hands and arms. They were covered in soot. The smoke was in his hair, his lungs. It clogged the pores of his skin. Local citizens had gathered to see if they could help but were shooed away by the police and fire captain who didn't want any more fatalities. Rompré's head lifted when he heard this.

Constable Fournier approached the sedan and tapped on the glass of the passenger side window. Rompré nodded and she opened the door and sat down.

"Sir, Del Musgrave was found about thirty metres from the path midway between the river and the meadow. He was either trying to get to the water or trying to come back. He would have made it if he'd kept running."

"Where is he now?"

"He was badly burned. The firefighters are carrying him out. A few minutes more and the water bomber would have extinguished that section of forest."

"*Je ne te comprends pas.* Is he in pain?"

"He did not survive. I am sorry to tell you this, sir. Del Musgrave did not survive."

Rompré let the silence steady him. And then he asked:

"And the girl. What of her."

"*La jeune femme est mort.* I am sorry, sir."

Out of the heat and smoke and charred wood, firefighters emerged with the bodies of Del Musgrave and Alvina Moon.


THE INTERNAL investigation into their deaths concluded that they had become disorientated in the smoke and stumbled away from the path. It was presumed that Alvina Moon had caught up to Del Musgrave. When the wind changed, they were trapped, unable to find their way back to the path which might have led them to safety. Autopsy showed that Del Musgrave's lungs had been seared in his chest. Much as a drowned man's lungs fill with water, Del's had filled with fire. The coroner's report said he was killed instantly. Alvina Moon was found to have a broken ankle. She died from smoke inhalation. Her body was found under Del Musgrave. He had lain on top of her, possibly to shield her from the burning branches that were raining down on them.

The fire burned long into the night and the next day, but at last it was under control and would soon be fully suppressed. The mop up crew would go in after to make sure it was completely extinguished before declaring the area clear. In a few years time, the forest would regenerate.

# EPILOGUE

UNIFORMED POLICE officers flashing identification badges had silenced Missy Cooper and sent her scurrying out of the apartment.

Constable Martine Fournier was left alone with the DS in Alvina Moon's room to examine her belongings. Her parents had been notified. It fell to Rompré to describe their daughter's final minutes of life. Coral and Oliver Moon had demanded to know everything and then regretted being told. There followed a respectful though awkward silence filled unspoken blame for their daughter's death. Coral and Oliver blamed the police and the police naturally refused to accept that blame. They had done everything they could to control the situation. Del had escalated the danger by setting the meadow on fire and Alvina had sealed her fate by chasing after him.

No one could understand what Del was doing in that spot with her. He'd had enough of a lead to escape.

"He was coming back." Rompré lifted Alvina Moon's camera case from the floor and examined it. "He must have come across her in the woods. It was a miracle that they found each other given the thickness of the smoke."

Fournier nodded. It was possible it happened that

way. No one would know for sure. Rompré had overseen the transfer of Musgrave's paintings to Gerry Dunn who was acting as executor of his estate. Diana Musgrave would receive the proceeds from the sale of her son's work which had skyrocketed in value. Gerry Dunn would make enough in commissions alone to finance the restoration of the Martingale Hunt and Fish Camp. As for the flashlight, Diana was able to confirm her husband had owned a standard issue flashlight like the one Del allegedly used to kill Teresa. Del had taken it with him after his father's death.

"What are we looking for, sir?"

The DS's eyes were tired but there was a light behind them. His suit was rumpled. He hadn't been home in days. No wedding ring. Married to the job. Probably just as well this summer when there had been a murder to solve and two accidental deaths.

"After Dave Gomer's body was found," said Rompré, opening the camera case, "Alvina Moon hugged this case to her throughout our interview. I thought she was either in shock, or she was concealing something."

"She took a photo? Something on the image card, sir?"

"*Ah, c'est ici. Voilá.*" Rompré withdrew a cassette tape and held it up.

They had combed Alvina's workplace for evidence to present at the inquest. Fournier remembered seeing the answering machine in a box in the office.

"Dave Gomer tells Marlee Bremer that he received a phone call from her husband on the night of Teresa's murder. But Monsieur Gomer also said he suffered a black-out that night and did not remember this call taking place. So how is this possible, to know a call happened but have no recollection of it happening? M. Gomer had to have proof that it occurred. I believe on this little cassette tape we will hear a recording of that phone call."

"If that's true, sir, then Alvina knew Del Musgrave was guilty all along. She was protecting him."

"We will never know for sure," said Rompré. "But I believe there is more to their story."

Diana Musgrave had told police Del was beaten as a boy. Violence in the family often results in gaps in education and this fact was proved true in Musgrave's case by his school records. Gerry Dunn had provided them with a breakdown of Del's work habits and personal affairs. A pattern had emerged. If Del Musgrave was illiterate, a great deal was explained. If not, then nothing made sense. Teresa leaving him meant selling the property. There would be legal papers. The threat of his illiteracy becoming known could have frightened Del Musgrave to violence. This was motive.

"He was a handsome young man with a strong native intelligence who was fortunate enough to be a genius with paint. With the exception of Mademoiselle Moon, no one probed any deeper into this young man's life."

A CRUSH of media news trucks blocked traffic in the village. The glisten of fame shone on every villager who knew Del and Alvina and could speak coherently on camera. MetMedia was devoting its first issue to their story. The cassette proved to be as DS Rompré predicted —a recording of the conversation between Dave Gomer and Trey Bremer. That, in combination with Marlee's testimony about his suit being blood-free before she burned it, was the break Trey needed. His innocence declared, he was released from Bordeaux in short order and launched into the limelight.

It was true, however, that the staff of Bremer Family Motors were heartbroken when Marlee Bremer was arrested for Dave Gomer's murder. Whereas newspapermen were a dime a dozen, an efficient, considerate CEO was hard to find. They were not thrilled to have Trey Bremer back. Neither was Violet but she wasn't going to tell Constable Martine Fournier that.

"Harry and Stanley aren't used to him. I told Daddy to give them time."

The constable was eating one of the cookies she had brought. Violet didn't understand how a pretty blonde girl could become a cop but she must be good at her job because her mother was in prison. The cookies were a thank you for finding the cassette tape which got her father out of jail, and also for recommending leniency at her mother's sentencing hearing. Marlee would likely qualify for early parole if she responded well to psychiatric treatment.

"How is your father with you?"

Violet picked at her cookie. "Good. He's proud of me for holding down the fort. He's not around much because he's got a lot of catching up to do at work. I thought my grandmother would come to stay but Dad says he can't ask Freesia to make that sacrifice. He spends most of his spare time with Harry and Stanley. They're younger, they need him. But he's happy with me too. He says I'm his good little girl."

"Do me a favour, Violet. Don't be such a good girl. None of this was your fault. Your parents' problems aren't your problems."

Violet nodded but she knew she would to do everything in her power to make it up to Trey and Marlee. At least her father was home and her brothers were safe. Her mother was in prison but they were allowed to visit her. "Mostly, I'm upset about Alvina." She set her cookie down on the plate, her appetite gone. "I wish I knew that she was okay. I liked her."

"I liked her too," agreed Constable Fournier. "She was a likeable girl."

FALL WAS moving over the land. Sweet wood smoke curled from village chimneys. Green leaves paled to rust and lettuce yellows as the chlorophyll shut down. And an astonishing thing happened. Decorating a stretch of the cold, clear river were dozens of perfectly formed spider webs. Shining in the morning mist, the delicate jewelled threads appeared to be made of sunlight suspended between stalks of ragweed, coneflowers and milkweed. Tens of them, hundreds, as though every spider in the hills had decided that today was the day to catch the last of the summer's insects. The collective consciousness of spiders.

Violet Bremer who witnessed the scene from her seat on the school bus took it as a sign.

I am shown beauty, she thought. And I don't have to be smart or talented or perfect to see it. I am shown beauty too.

She knew then that Alvina Moon was home.

**END**

# ACKNOWLEDGEMENT

THIS NOVEL WAS was written between 2012 and 2014. In that time, I lost a publisher, an agent and a brother. I was pulled, tried and tested both personally and professionally like never before. But there were notable bright spots.

I am grateful to literary agents, Diane Banks and Sally Harding for reading the initial manuscript and taking pains to guide me as an author, which I did my best to honour. Friends and fellow artists: Leslie Jones, Janice Moorhead, Nicole Robert, and Wendi Taylor allowed me to lean on them at a difficult time and helped me to hold on. And my grandson, Oliver, during one sleepless night, reminded me that love is the solution to everything.

And lastly, I owe my community a debt of gratitude that I can never repay for their unflagging kindness, affection and interest in my work.

# ABOUT THE AUTHOR

## Nadine Doolittle

 Nadine was born in Comox, British Columbia, the third daughter of an RCAF mechanic and his Scottish wife. A graduate of Vancouver's prestigious Studio 58 Theatre Program, her career detoured from acting to casting for film and television, and finally to writing crime fiction.

Her debut novel, Iced Under was shortlisted for Canada's Arthur Ellis Award for Best First Novel in 2009 (Crime Fiction) and she was hooked. She now spends her days in the Quebec wilderness writing cosy mystery fiction.

Visit www.nadinedoolittlebooks.ca to learn more.

# ALSO BY NADINE DOOLITTLE

## Crime Thrillers

Iced Under
The Grey Lady

## St. Ives Book Club Mystery

Advertisement for Murder
Death Knocks Twice
Dead to the World
The Killing of Honey Gable
The Body in the Ravine
A Deadly Case of Blue
Make Way for Murder
Murder Will Out
The Missing Foot Mystery
The Final Chapter

Manufactured by Amazon.ca
Bolton, ON

34906849R00210